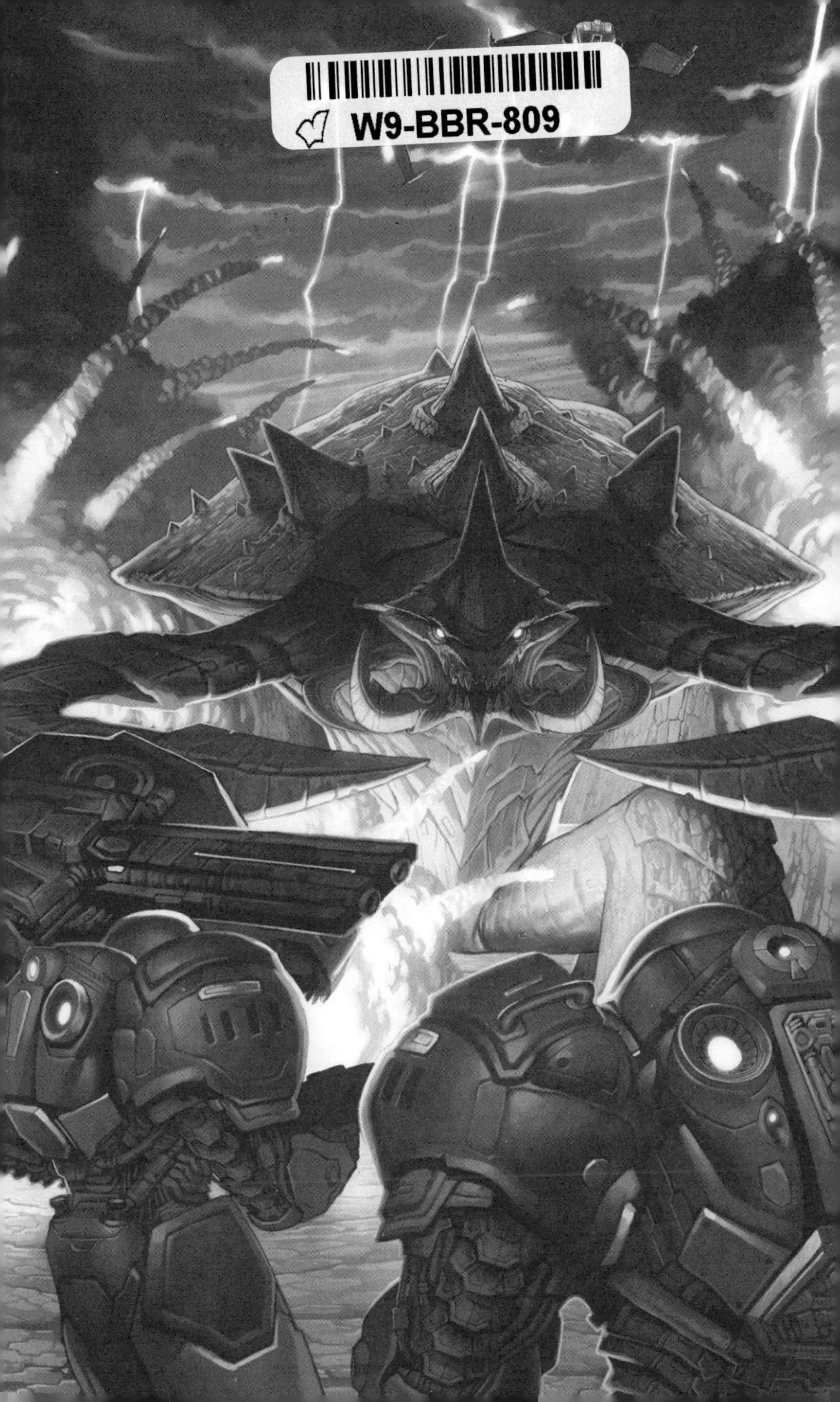

StarCraft: Frontline Vol. 2

Copy Editor - Jessica Chavez
Layout and Lettering - Michael Paolilli and Lucas Rivera
Creative Consultant - Michael Paolilli
Graphic Designer - Louis Csontos
Cover Artist - UDON with Saejin Oh and Joe Vriens

Editor - Paul Morrissey
Digital Imaging Manager - Chris Buford
Pre-Production Supervisor - Vince Rivera
Art Director - Al-Insan Lashley
Managing Editor - Vy Nguyen
Editor-in-Chief - Rob Tokar
Publisher - Mike Kiley
President and C.O.O. - John Parker
C.E.O. and Chief Creative Officer - Stu Levy

BLIZZARD ENTERTAINMENT

Senior Vice President,
Story and Franchise Development - Lydia Bottegoni
Director of Production,
Animation & Creative Development - Phillip Hillenbrand
Lead Editor, Publishing - Robert Simpson
Senior Editor - Cate Gary
Producer - Jeffrey Wong
Story Consultation and Development - Micky Neilson
Art Director - Glenn Rane
Vice President, Global Consumer Products - Matt Beecher
Senior Manager, Global Licensing - Byron Parnell
Additional Development - Ben Brode, Sean Copeland, Samwise Didier,
Justin Parker, Sean Wang

gear.blizzard.com

This book contains material originally published by TOKYOPOP Inc.

First Blizzard Entertainment printing: April 2017

ISBN: 978-1-9456839-0-9

10 9 8 7 6 5 4 3 2 1
Printed in China

StarCraft

Frontline

Volume 2

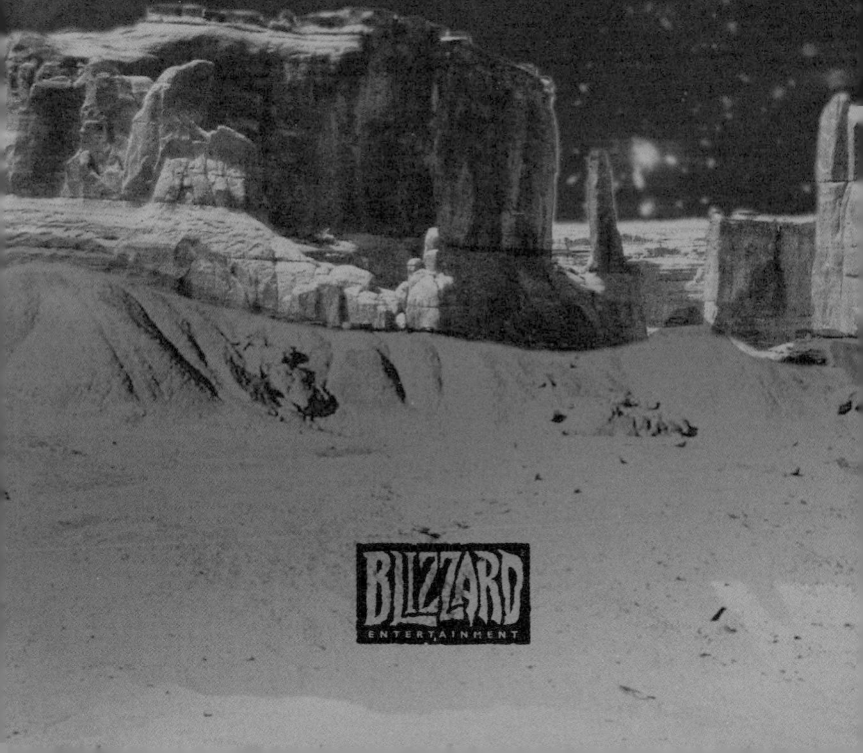
BLIZZARD
ENTERTAINMENT

STARCRAFT

FRONTLINE
VOLUME 2

STARCRAFT

FRONTLINE
VOLUME 2

HEAVY ARMOR - PART 2

Written by Simon Furman

Pencils and Inks by Jesse Elliott

Tones by Chi Wang, Marcus Jones and JC Padilla

Letterer: Michael Paolilli

PREVIOUSLY IN HEAVY ARMOR - PART 1

Viking pilot Wes Carter must protect a colony from his renegade mentor, Captain Jon Dyre—the man who taught him everything about heavy armor. During the military demonstration of a new Viking unit, Dyre went haywire, calling the colony infested and turning his black Viking on civilians! Carter successfully interrupted his mentor's rampage, but now must engage him in a deadly firefight...

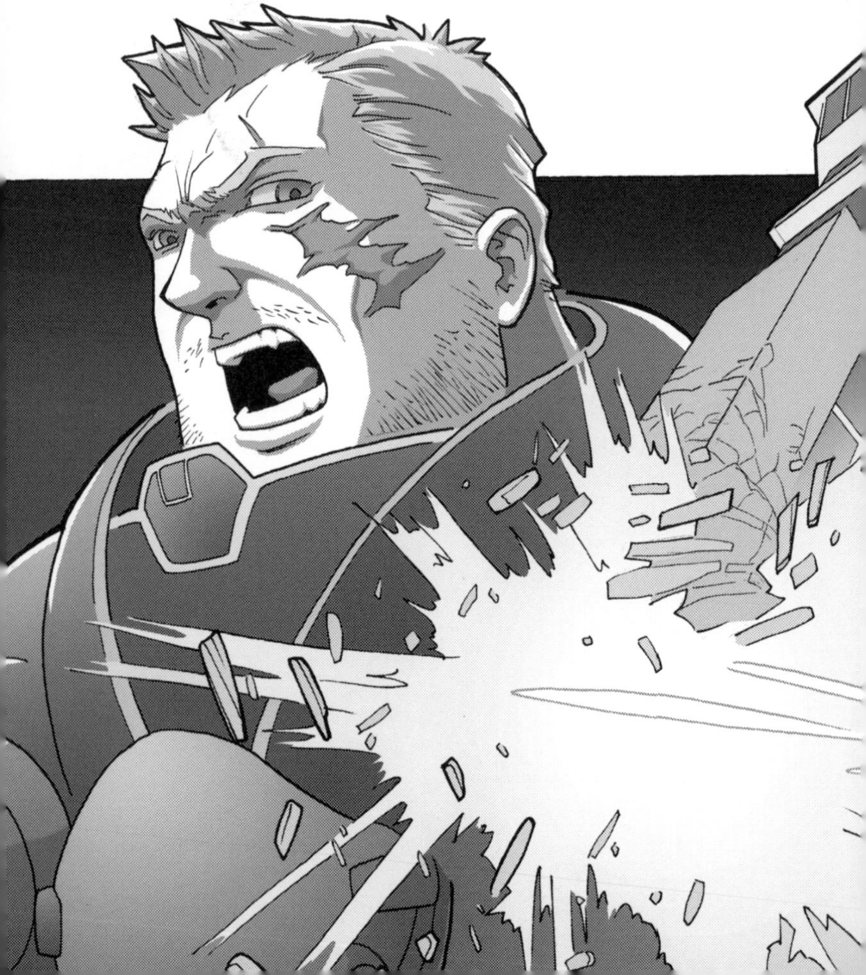

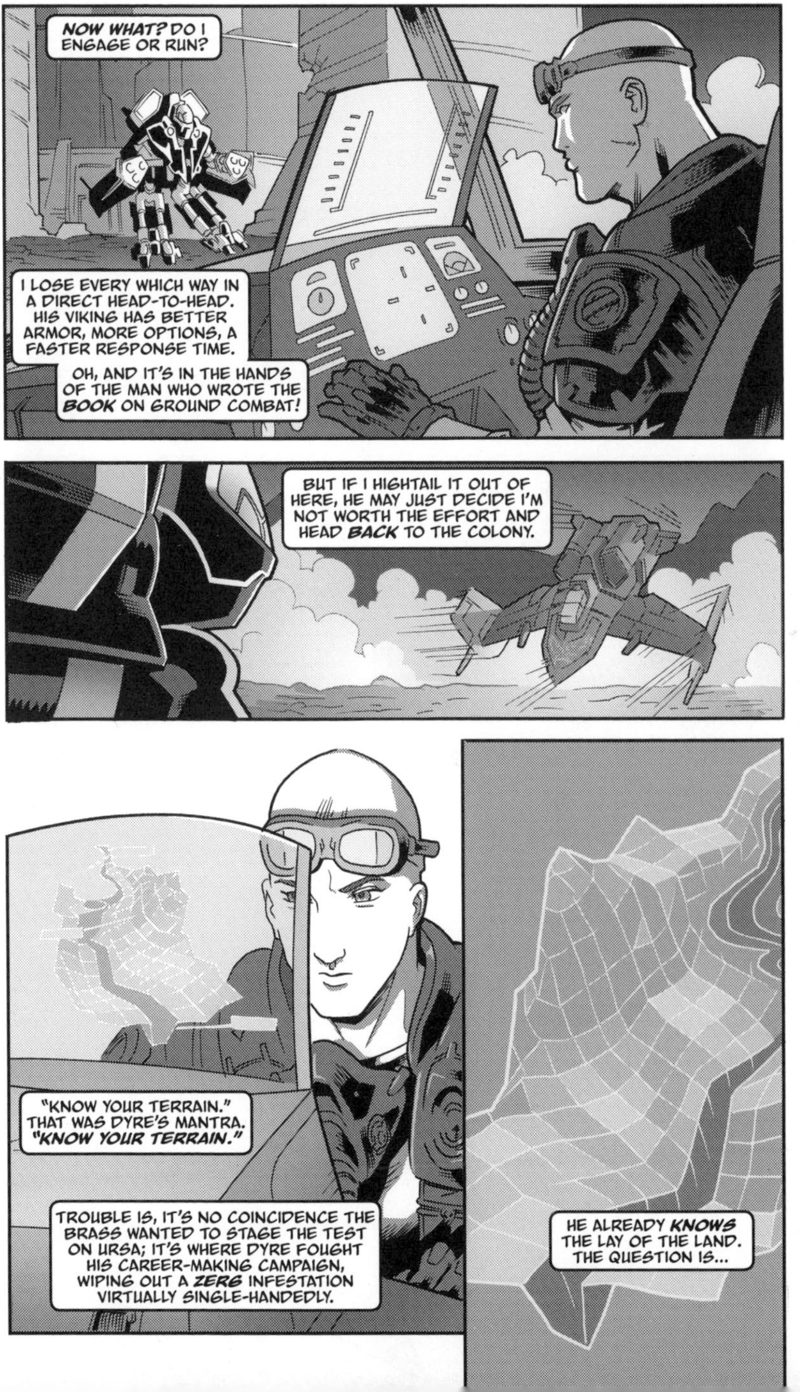
NOW WHAT? DO I ENGAGE OR RUN?
I LOSE EVERY WHICH WAY IN A DIRECT HEAD-TO-HEAD. HIS VIKING HAS BETTER ARMOR, MORE OPTIONS, A FASTER RESPONSE TIME.
OH, AND IT'S IN THE HANDS OF THE MAN WHO WROTE THE BOOK ON GROUND COMBAT!
BUT IF I HIGHTAIL IT OUT OF HERE, HE MAY JUST DECIDE I'M NOT WORTH THE EFFORT AND HEAD BACK TO THE COLONY.
"KNOW YOUR TERRAIN." THAT WAS DYRE'S MANTRA. "KNOW YOUR TERRAIN."
TROUBLE IS, IT'S NO COINCIDENCE THE BRASS WANTED TO STAGE THE TEST ON URSA; IT'S WHERE DYRE FOUGHT HIS CAREER-MAKING CAMPAIGN, WIPING OUT A ZERG INFESTATION VIRTUALLY SINGLE-HANDEDLY.
HE ALREADY KNOWS THE LAY OF THE LAND. THE QUESTION IS...

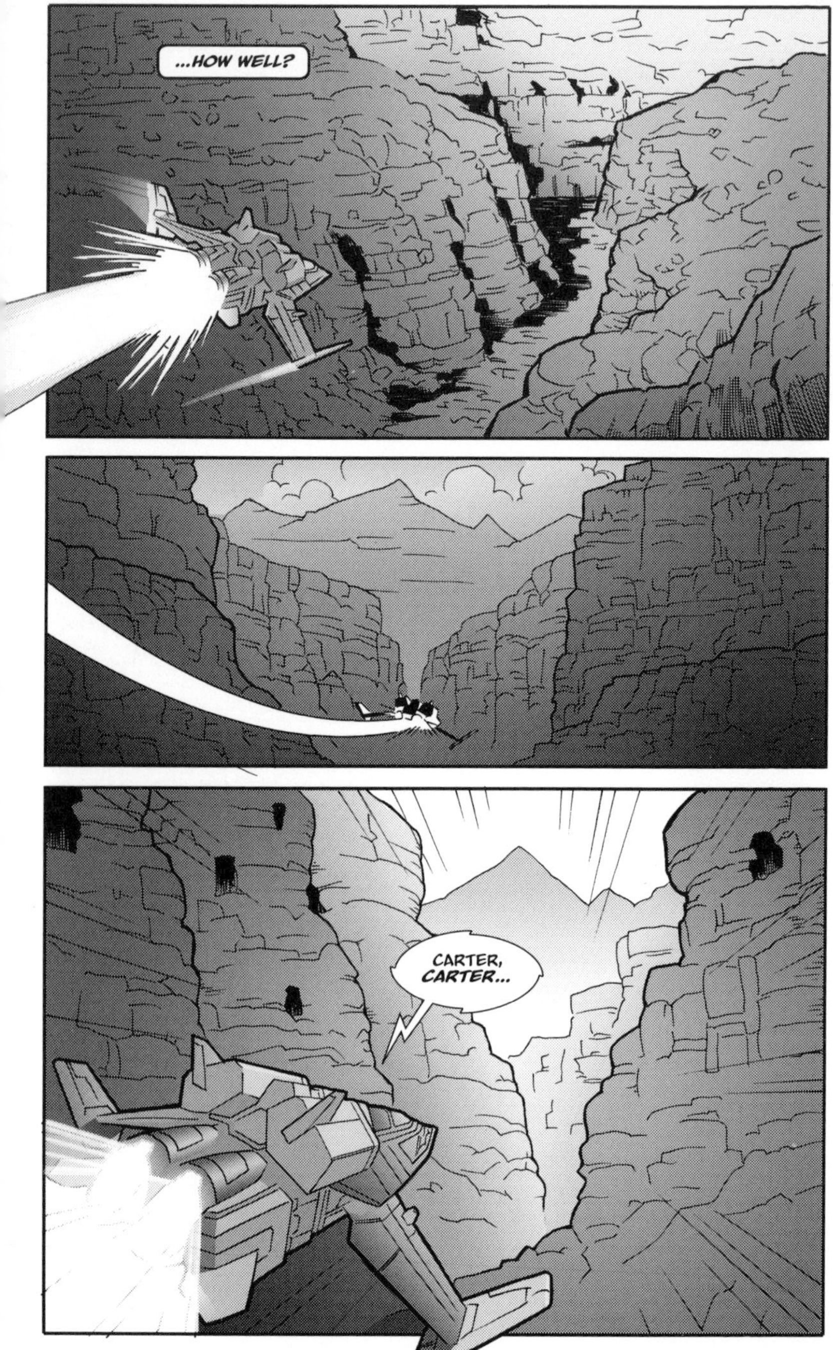
...HOW WELL?
CARTER,
CARTER...

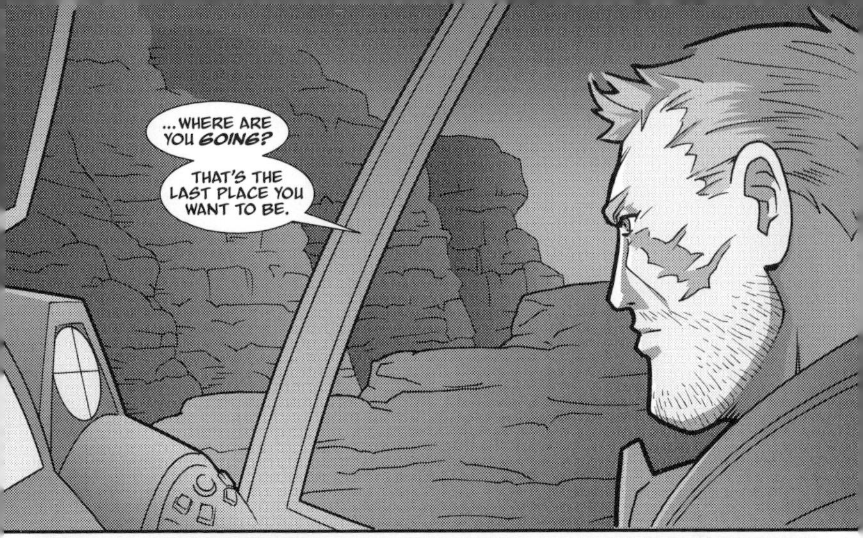
...WHERE ARE YOU GOING?
THAT'S THE LAST PLACE YOU WANT TO BE.

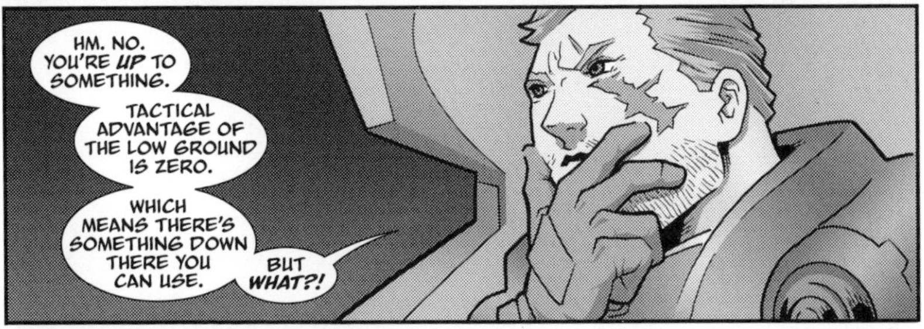
HM. NO. YOU'RE UP TO SOMETHING.
TACTICAL ADVANTAGE OF THE LOW GROUND IS ZERO.
WHICH MEANS THERE'S SOMETHING DOWN THERE YOU CAN USE.
BUT WHAT?!

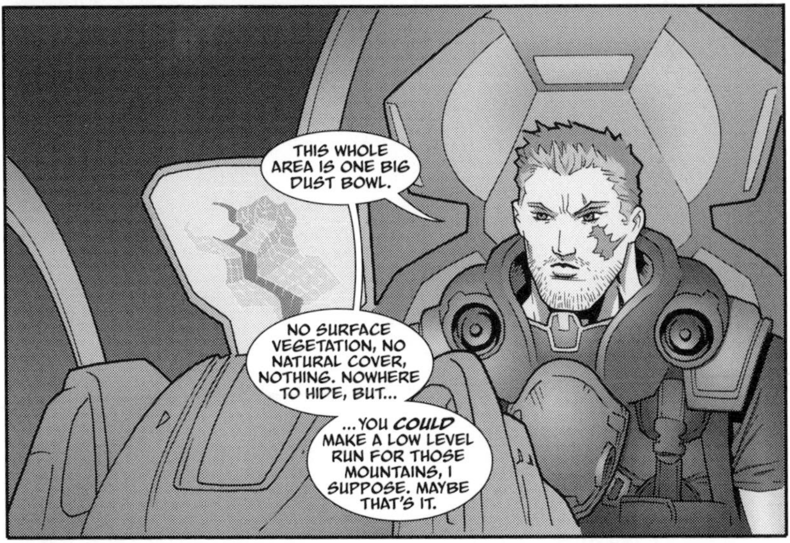
THIS WHOLE AREA IS ONE BIG DUST BOWL.
NO SURFACE VEGETATION, NO NATURAL COVER, NOTHING. NOWHERE TO HIDE, BUT...
...YOU COULD MAKE A LOW LEVEL RUN FOR THOSE MOUNTAINS, I SUPPOSE. MAYBE THAT'S IT.

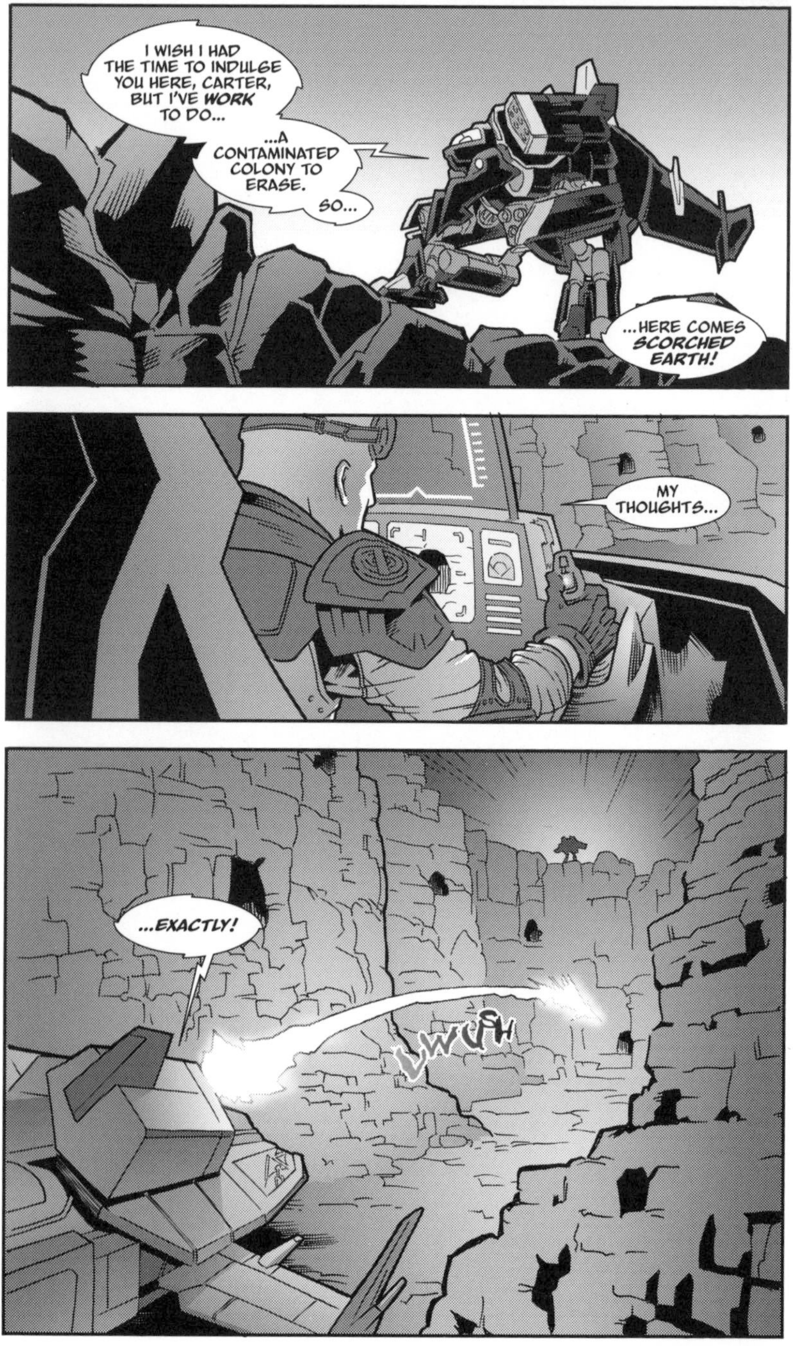
I WISH I HAD THE TIME TO INDULGE YOU HERE, CARTER, BUT I'VE *WORK* TO DO...
...A CONTAMINATED COLONY TO ERASE.
SO...
...HERE COMES *SCORCHED EARTH!*
MY THOUGHTS...
...EXACTLY!
VWUSH

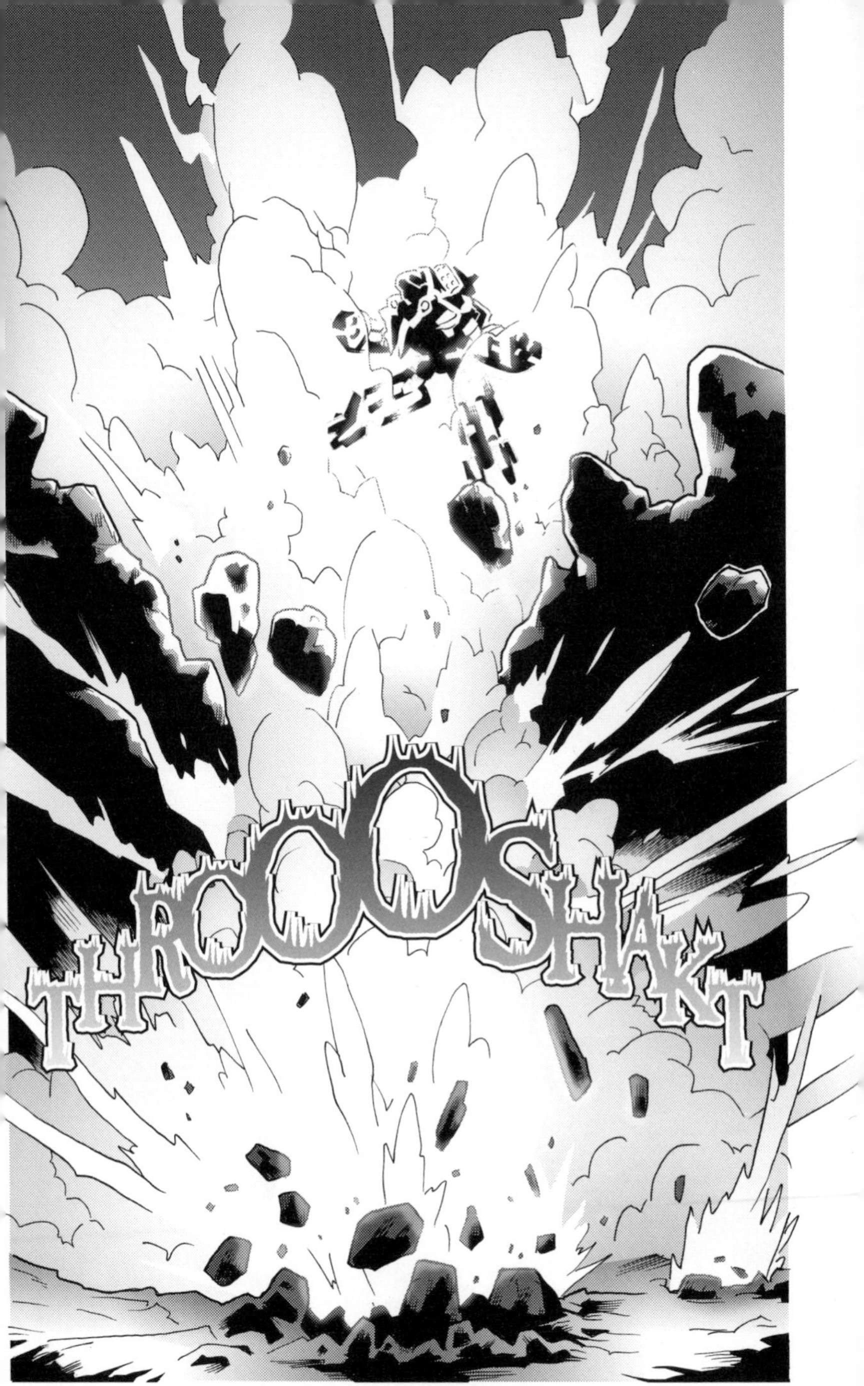
THROOOSHAKT

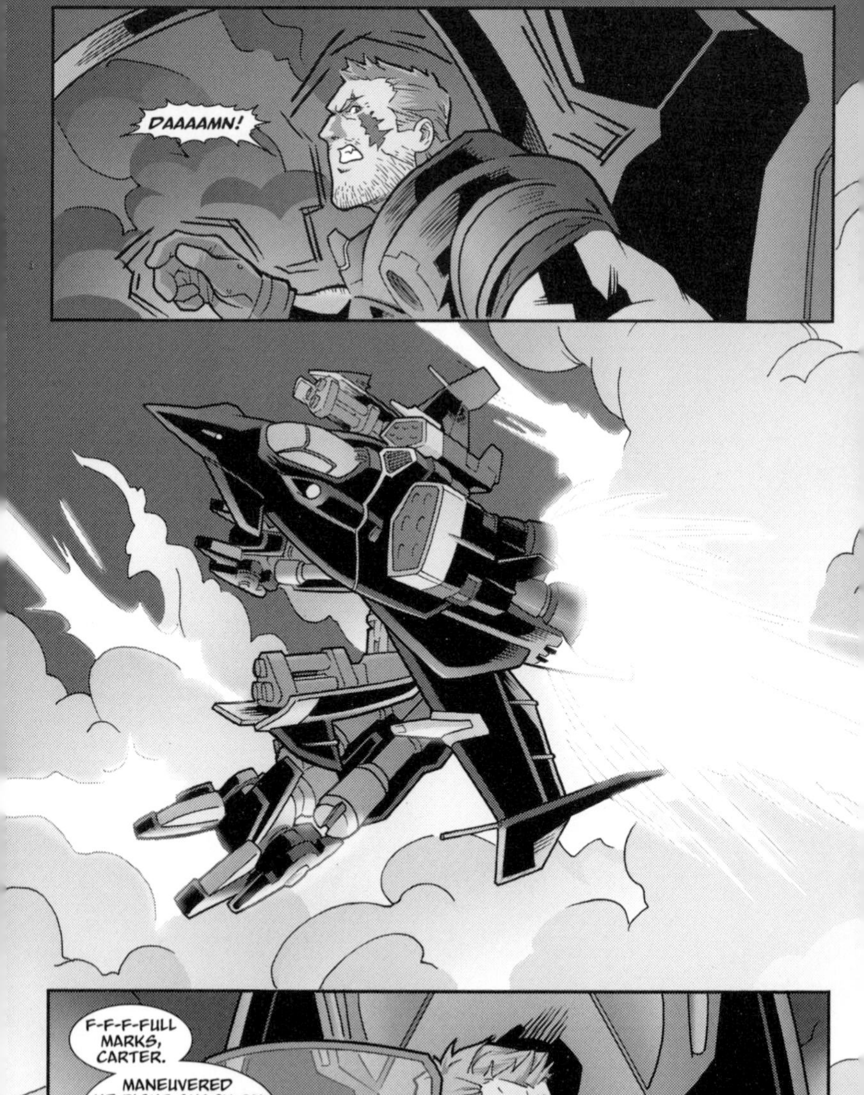
DAAAAMN!
F-F-F-FULL MARKS, CARTER.
MANEUVERED ME RIGHT SMACK ON TOP OF A ***NATURAL GAS*** FIELD AND HIT IGNITION!
BUT I'VE ALREADY ***BEEN*** TO HELL, MORE THAN ONCE...

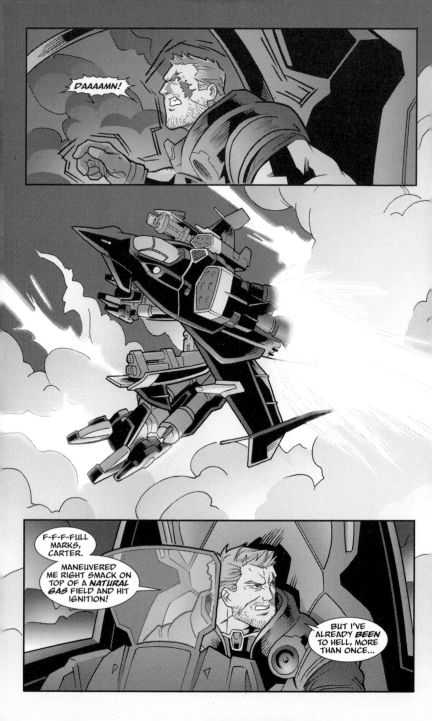

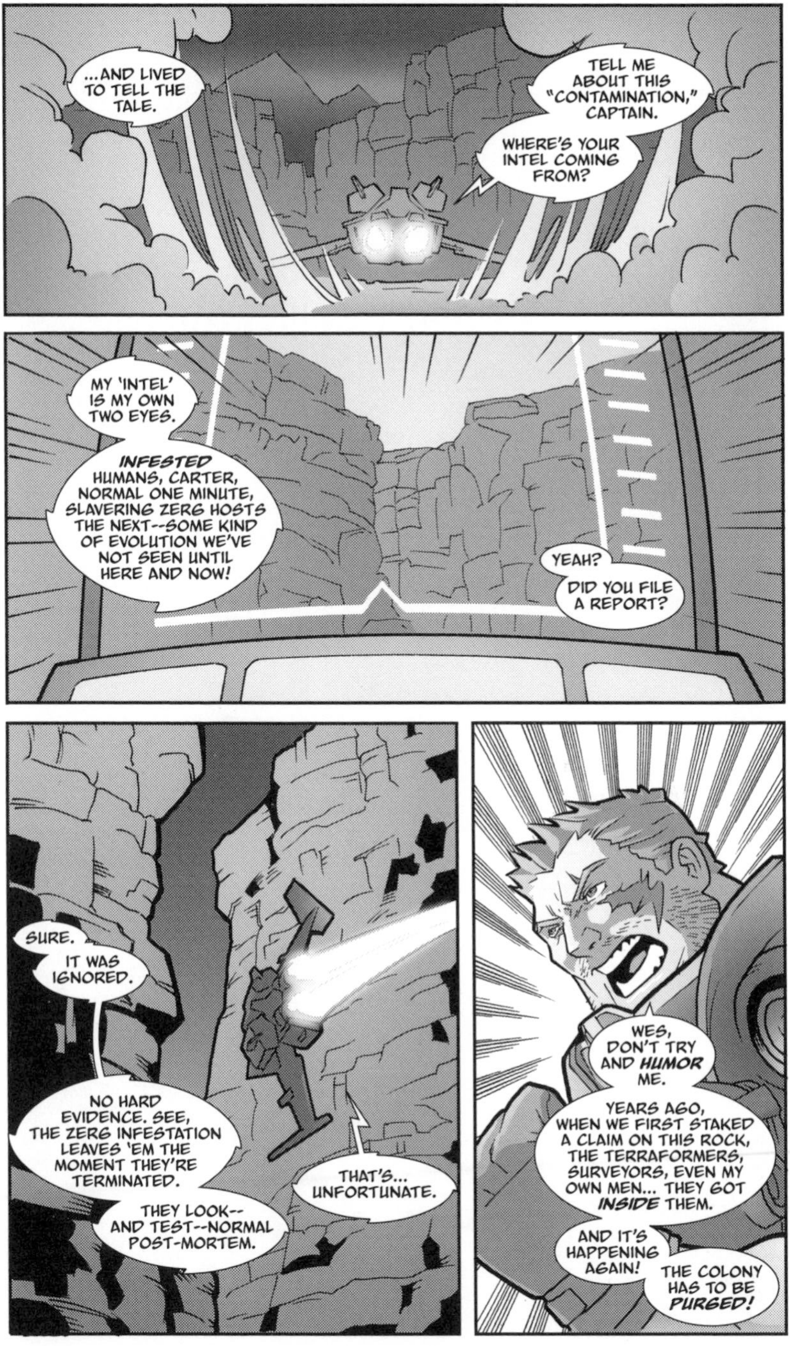

...AND LIVED TO TELL THE TALE.
TELL ME ABOUT THIS "CONTAMINATION," CAPTAIN.
WHERE'S YOUR INTEL COMING FROM?
MY 'INTEL' IS MY OWN TWO EYES.
INFESTED HUMANS, CARTER, NORMAL ONE MINUTE, SLAVERING ZERG HOSTS THE NEXT--SOME KIND OF EVOLUTION WE'VE NOT SEEN UNTIL HERE AND NOW!
YEAH?
DID YOU FILE A REPORT?
SURE.
IT WAS IGNORED.
NO HARD EVIDENCE. SEE, THE ZERG INFESTATION LEAVES 'EM THE MOMENT THEY'RE TERMINATED.
THEY LOOK--AND TEST--NORMAL POST-MORTEM.
THAT'S... UNFORTUNATE.
WES, DON'T TRY AND HUMOR ME.
YEARS AGO, WHEN WE FIRST STAKED A CLAIM ON THIS ROCK, THE TERRAFORMERS, SURVEYORS, EVEN MY OWN MEN... THEY GOT INSIDE THEM.
AND IT'S HAPPENING AGAIN!
THE COLONY HAS TO BE PURGED!

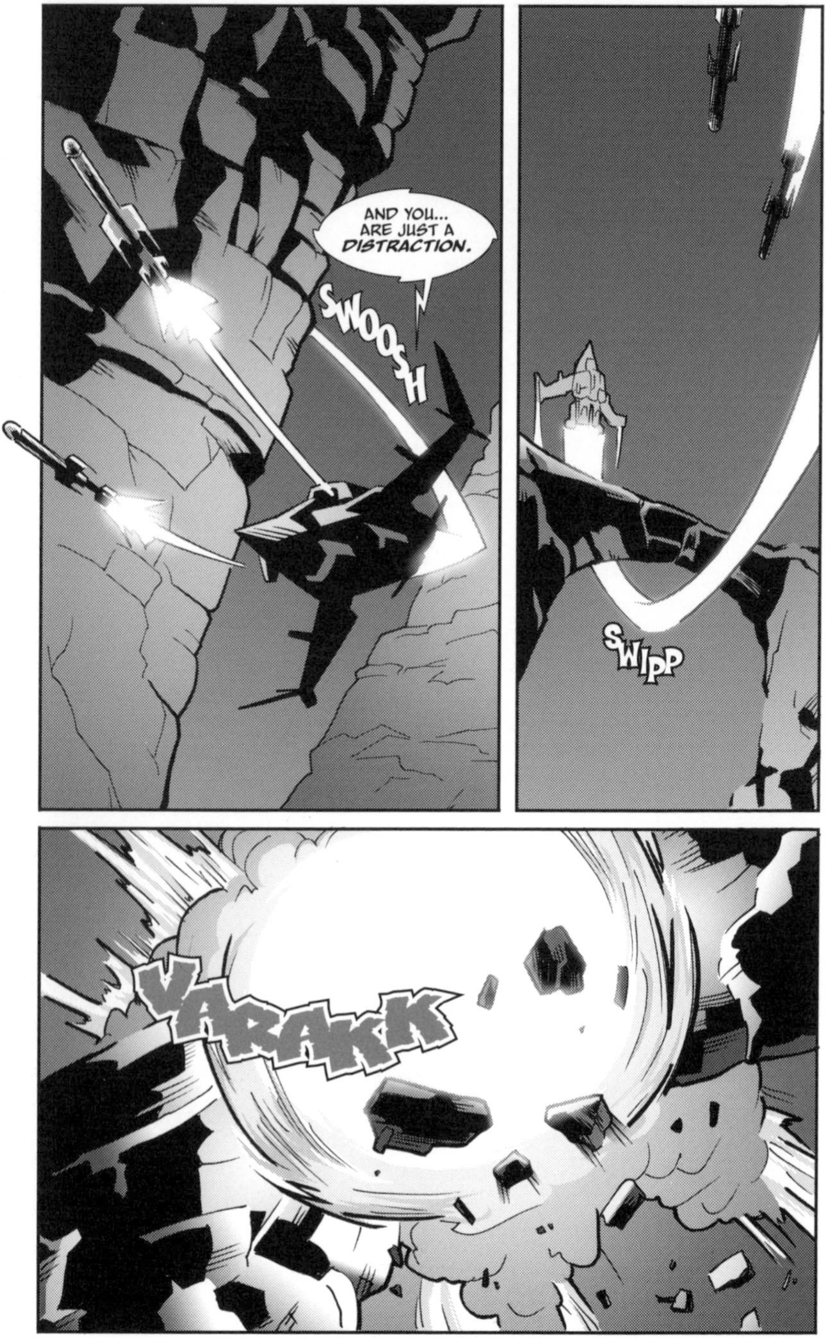
AND YOU... ARE JUST A DISTRACTION.
SWOOSH
SWIPP
VRAKK

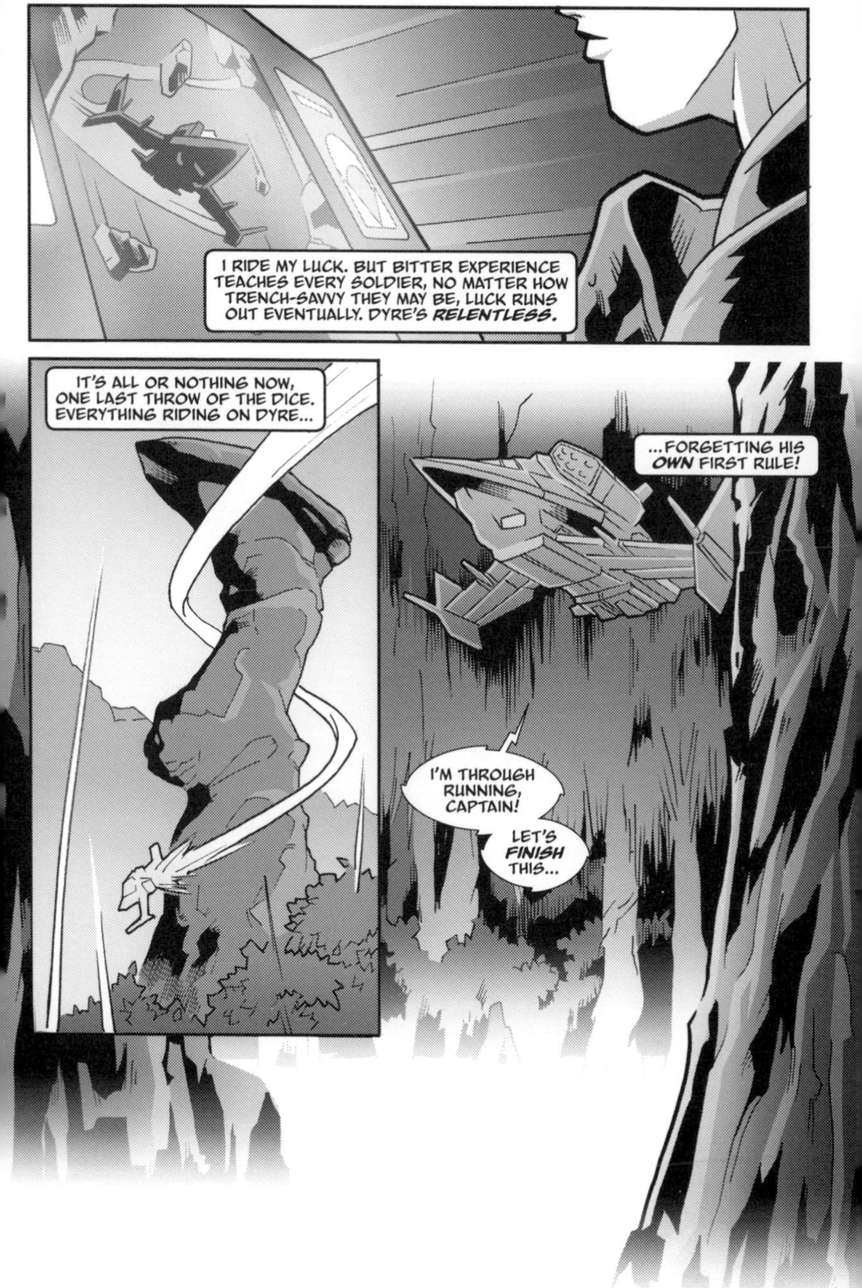
I RIDE MY LUCK. BUT BITTER EXPERIENCE TEACHES EVERY SOLDIER, NO MATTER HOW TRENCH-SAVVY THEY MAY BE, LUCK RUNS OUT EVENTUALLY. DYRE'S ***RELENTLESS.***
IT'S ALL OR NOTHING NOW, ONE LAST THROW OF THE DICE. EVERYTHING RIDING ON DYRE...
...FORGETTING HIS ***OWN*** FIRST RULE!
I'M THROUGH RUNNING, CAPTAIN!
LET'S ***FINISH*** THIS...

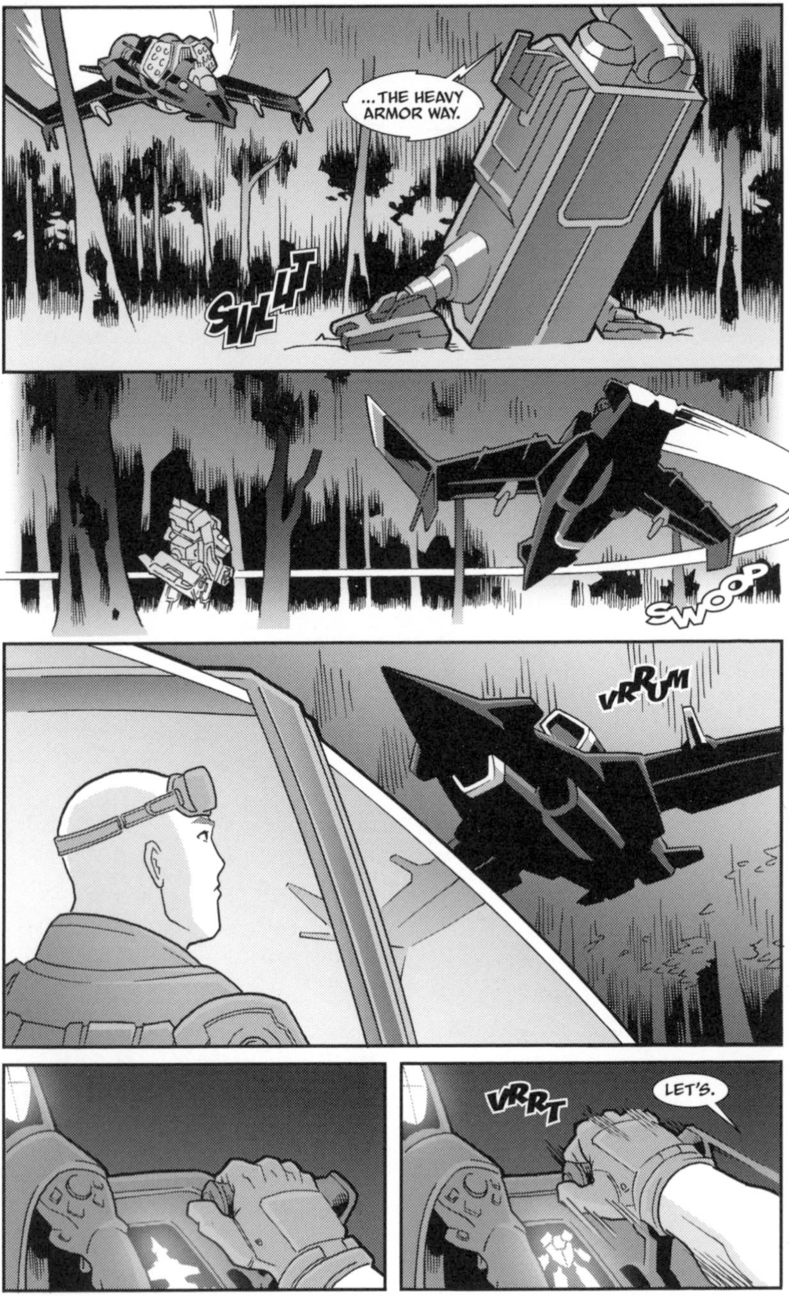
...THE HEAVY ARMOR WAY.
SWLLT
SWOOP
VRRRUM
VRRT
LET'S.

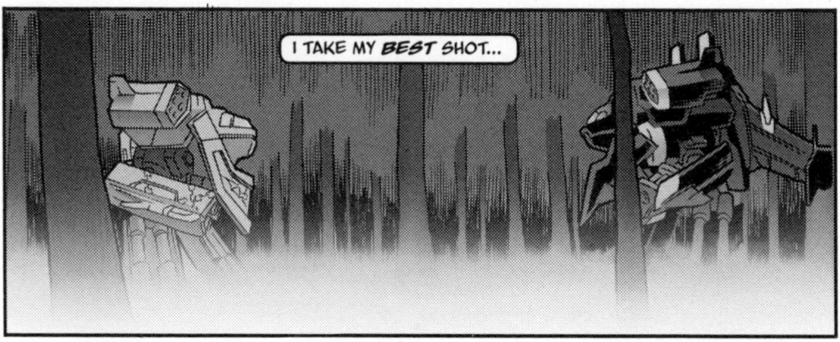
I TAKE MY *BEST* SHOT...

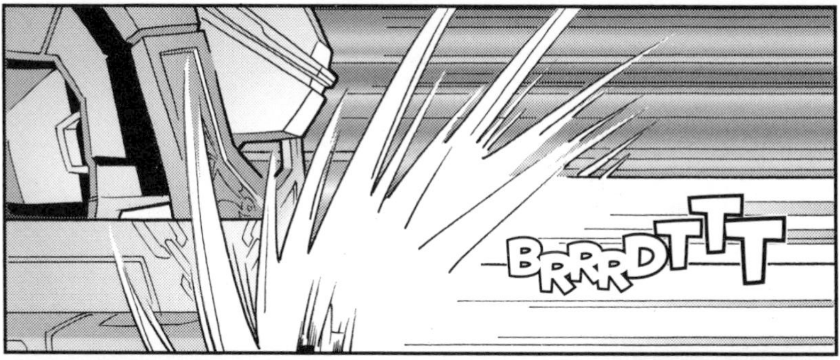
BRRRDTTT

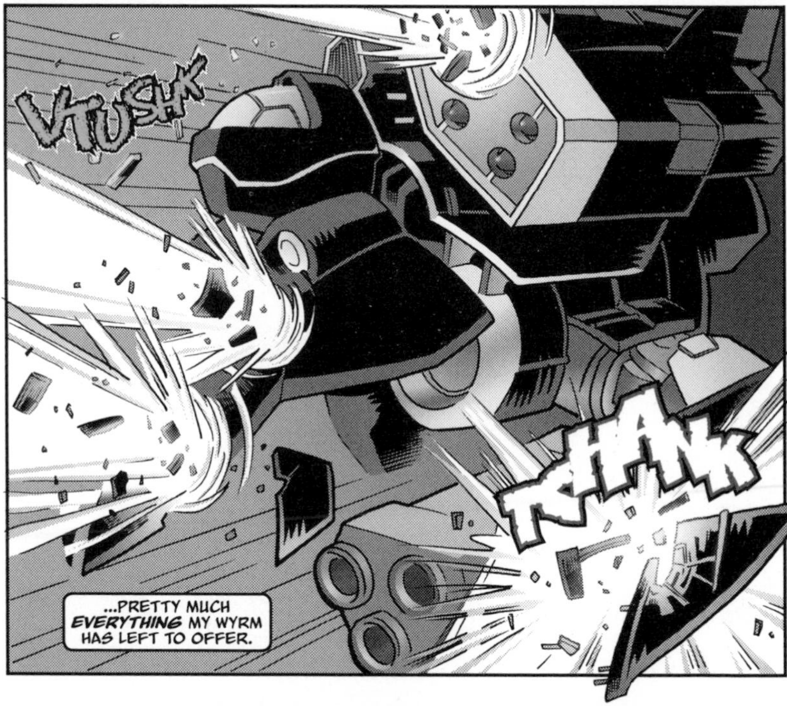
VTUSHK
TCHANK
...PRETTY MUCH *EVERYTHING* MY WYRM HAS LEFT TO OFFER.

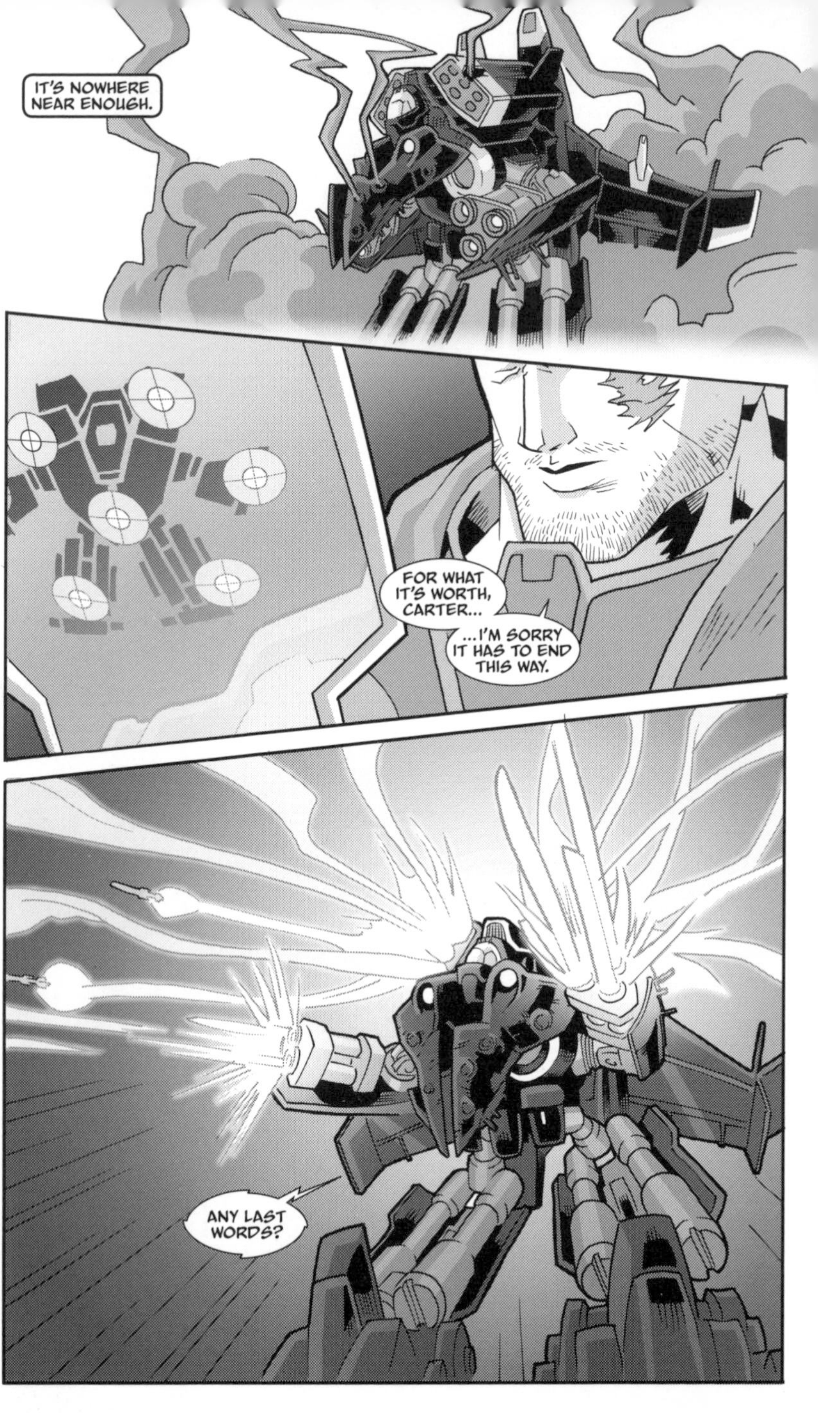
IT'S NOWHERE NEAR ENOUGH.
FOR WHAT IT'S WORTH, CARTER...
...I'M SORRY IT HAS TO END THIS WAY.
ANY LAST WORDS?

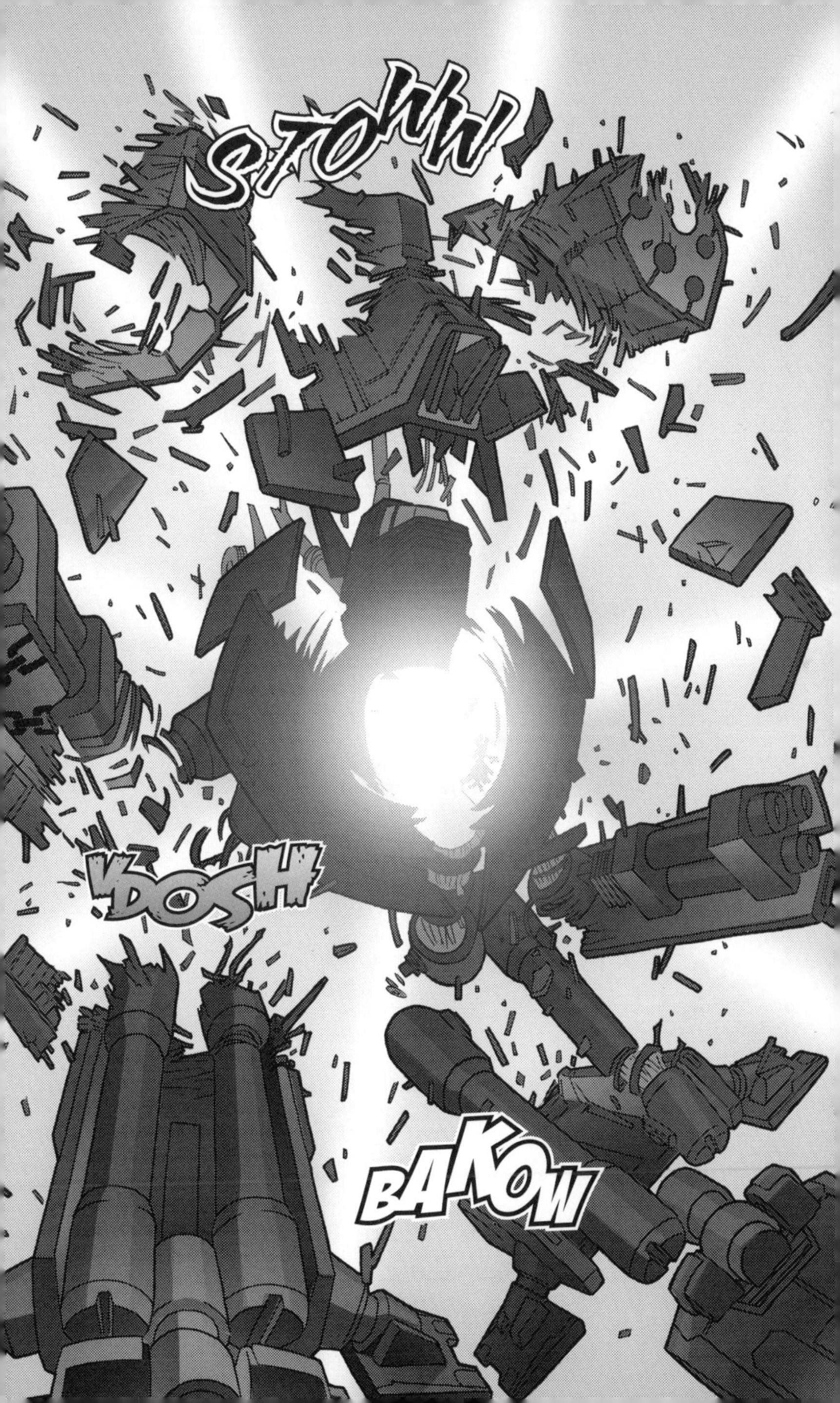
STOMM
VOOSH
BAKOW

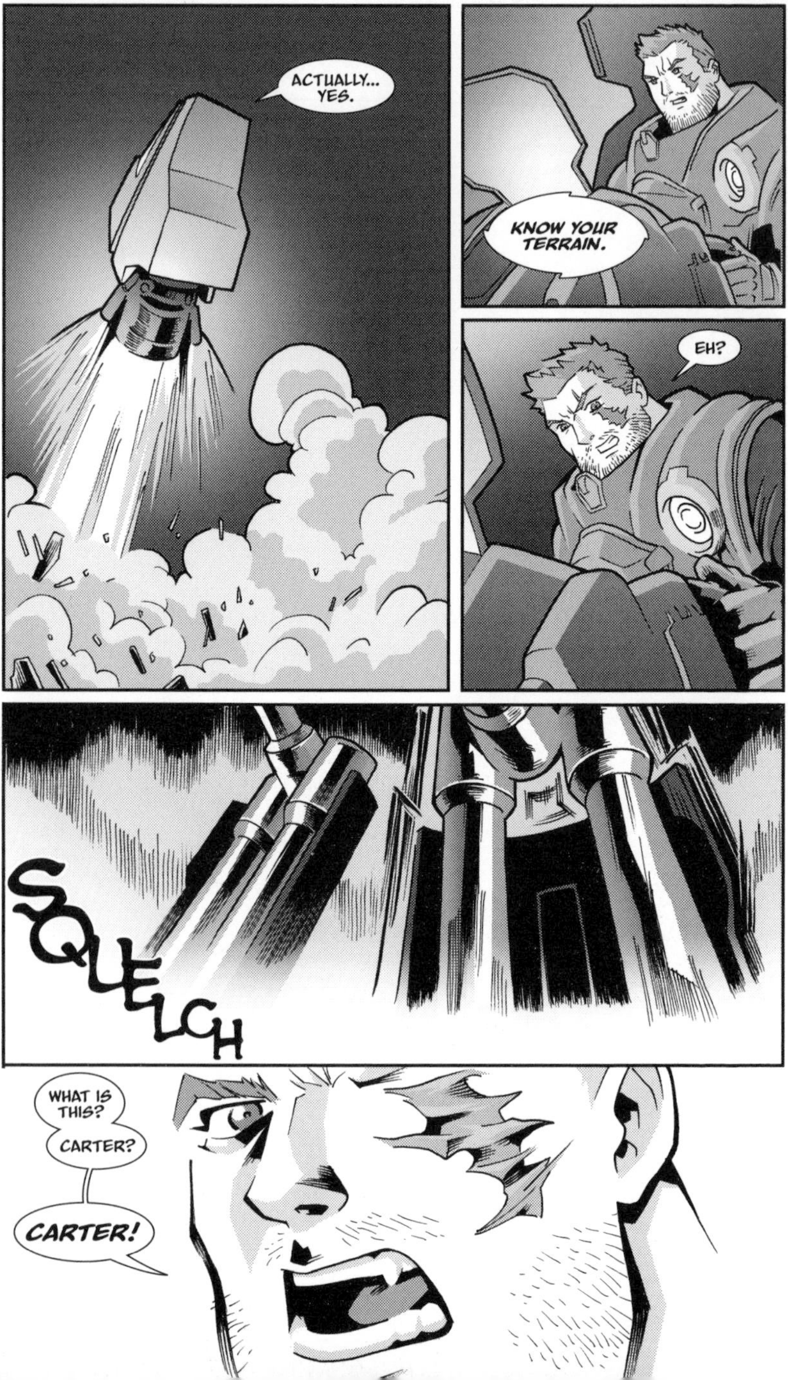
ACTUALLY... YES.
KNOW YOUR TERRAIN.
EH?
SQUELCH
WHAT IS THIS?
CARTER?
CARTER!

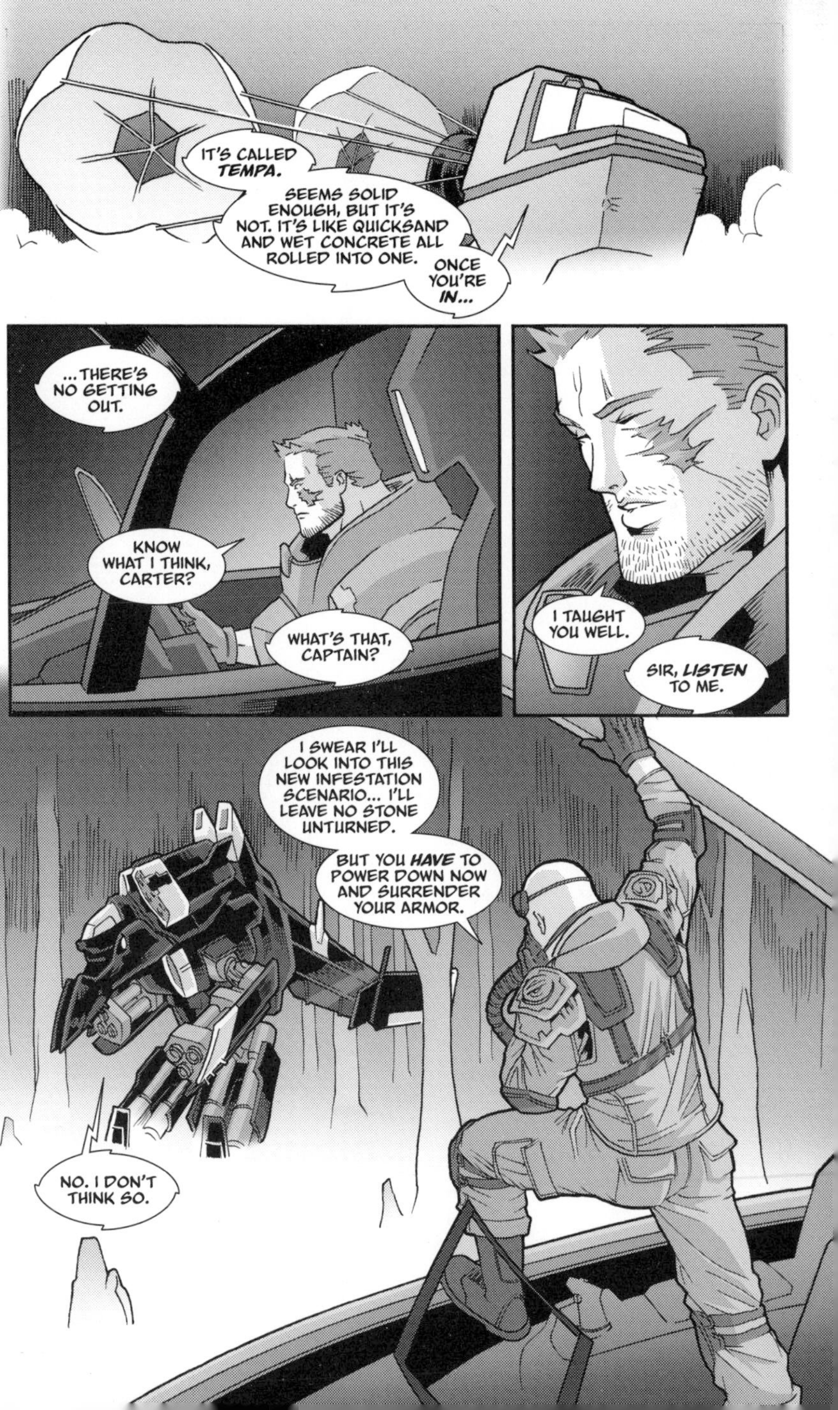
IT'S CALLED *TEMPA.*
SEEMS SOLID ENOUGH, BUT IT'S NOT. IT'S LIKE QUICKSAND AND WET CONCRETE ALL ROLLED INTO ONE.
ONCE YOU'RE *IN*...
...THERE'S NO GETTING OUT.
KNOW WHAT I THINK, CARTER?
WHAT'S THAT, CAPTAIN?
I TAUGHT YOU WELL.
SIR, *LISTEN* TO ME.
I SWEAR I'LL LOOK INTO THIS NEW INFESTATION SCENARIO... I'LL LEAVE NO STONE UNTURNED.
BUT YOU *HAVE* TO POWER DOWN NOW AND SURRENDER YOUR ARMOR.
NO. I DON'T THINK SO.

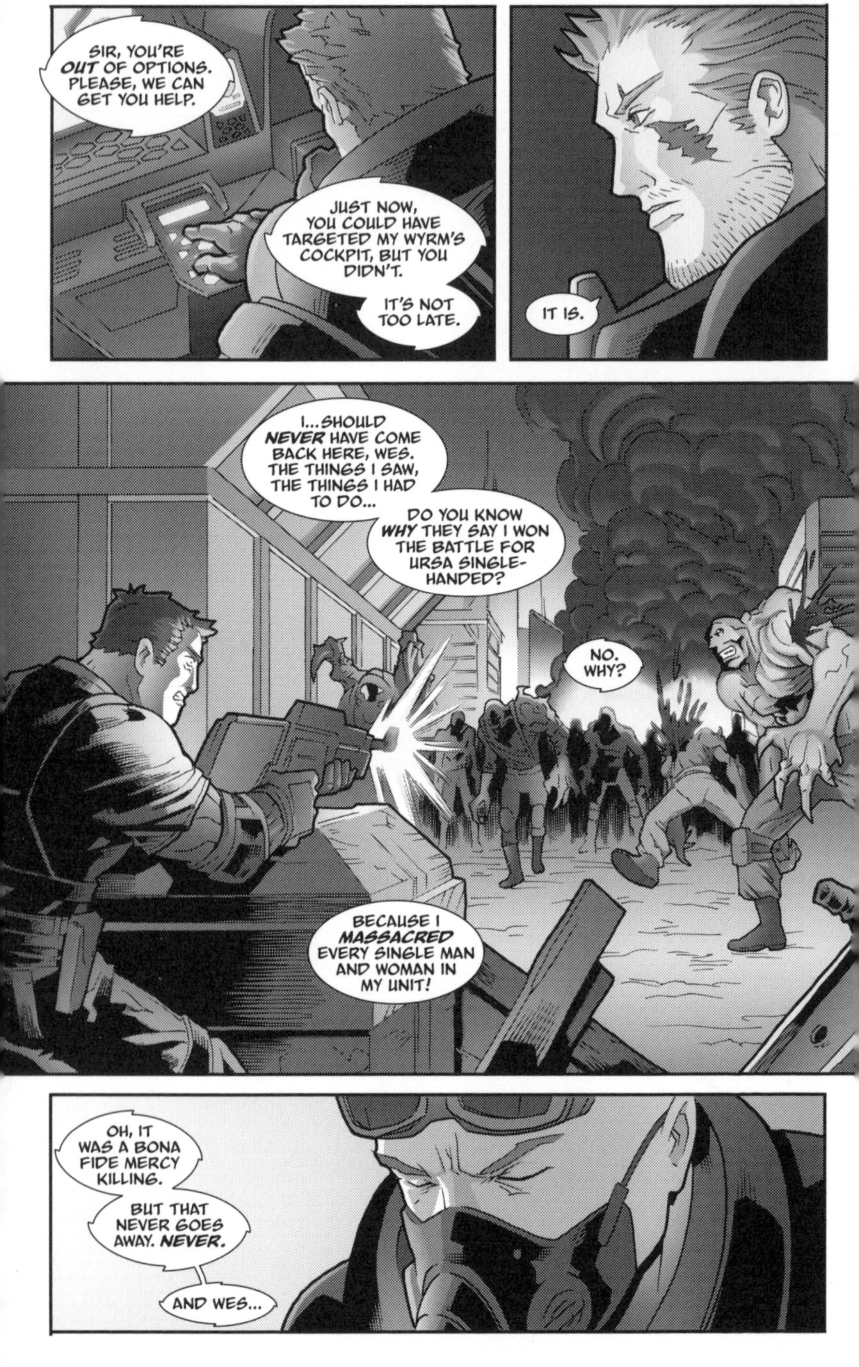

SIR, YOU'RE *OUT* OF OPTIONS. PLEASE, WE CAN GET YOU HELP.
JUST NOW, YOU COULD HAVE TARGETED MY WYRM'S COCKPIT, BUT YOU DIDN'T.
IT'S NOT TOO LATE.
IT IS.
I...SHOULD *NEVER* HAVE COME BACK HERE, WES. THE THINGS I SAW, THE THINGS I HAD TO DO...
DO YOU KNOW *WHY* THEY SAY I WON THE BATTLE FOR URSA SINGLE-HANDED?
NO. WHY?
BECAUSE I *MASSACRED* EVERY SINGLE MAN AND WOMAN IN MY UNIT!
OH, IT WAS A BONA FIDE MERCY KILLING.
BUT THAT NEVER GOES AWAY. *NEVER.*
AND WES...

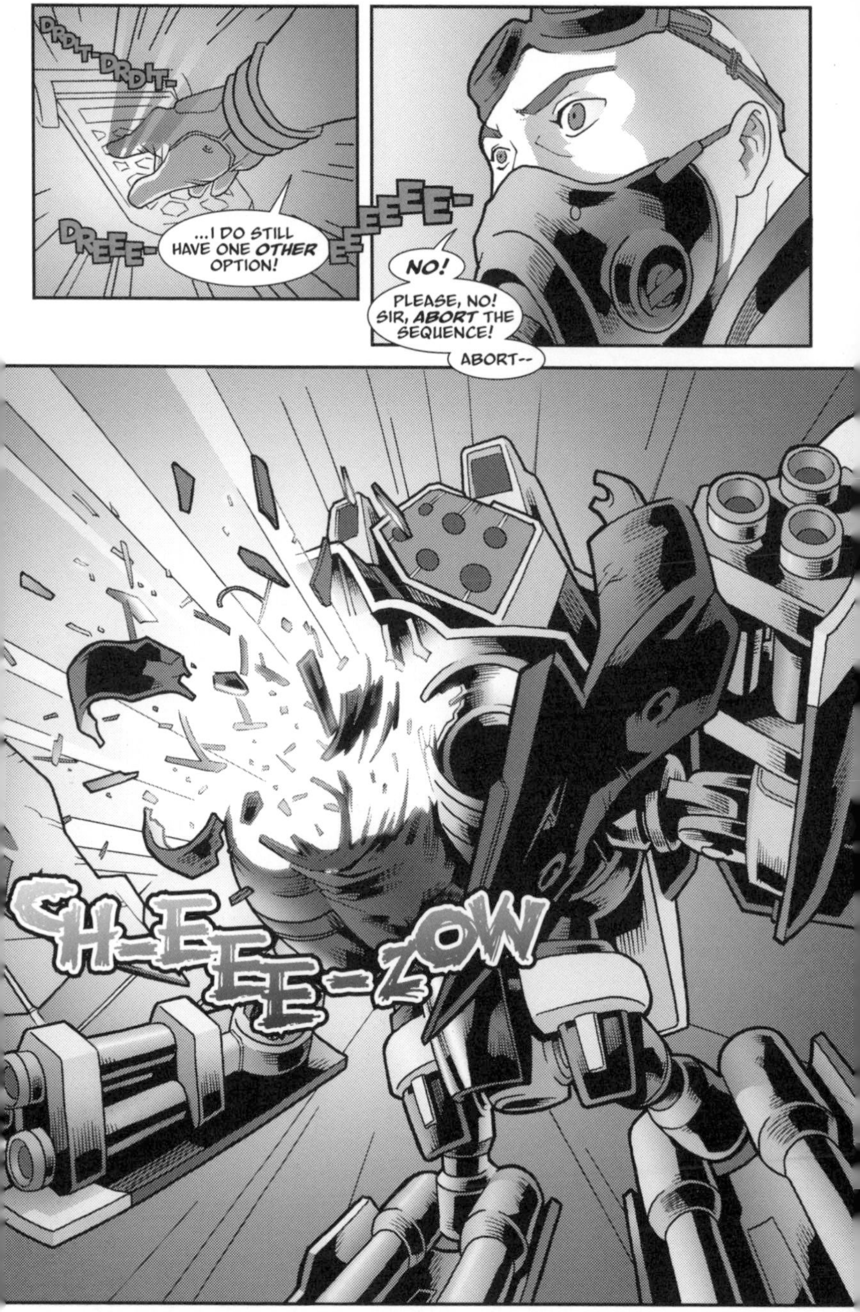
DRDIT-DRDIT-
DREEE-
...I DO STILL HAVE ONE OTHER OPTION!
EEEEEE-
NO!
PLEASE, NO! SIR, ABORT THE SEQUENCE!
ABORT--
CH-EEE-ZOW

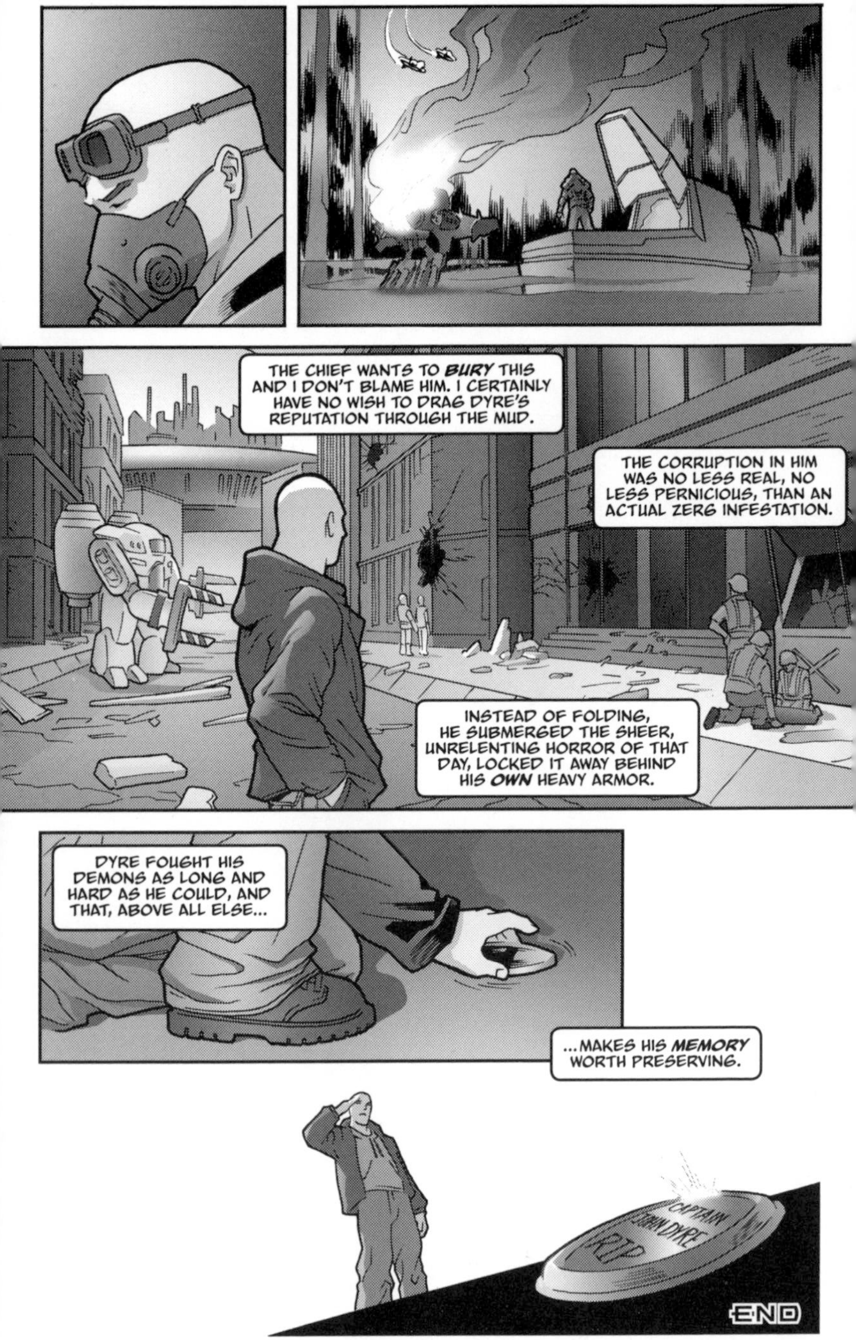
THE CHIEF WANTS TO BURY THIS AND I DON'T BLAME HIM. I CERTAINLY HAVE NO WISH TO DRAG DYRE'S REPUTATION THROUGH THE MUD.
THE CORRUPTION IN HIM WAS NO LESS REAL, NO LESS PERNICIOUS, THAN AN ACTUAL ZERG INFESTATION.
INSTEAD OF FOLDING, HE SUBMERGED THE SHEER, UNRELENTING HORROR OF THAT DAY, LOCKED IT AWAY BEHIND HIS OWN HEAVY ARMOR.
DYRE FOUGHT HIS DEMONS AS LONG AND HARD AS HE COULD, AND THAT, ABOVE ALL ELSE...
...MAKES HIS MEMORY WORTH PRESERVING.
CAPTAIN JOHN DYRE
R.I.P.
END

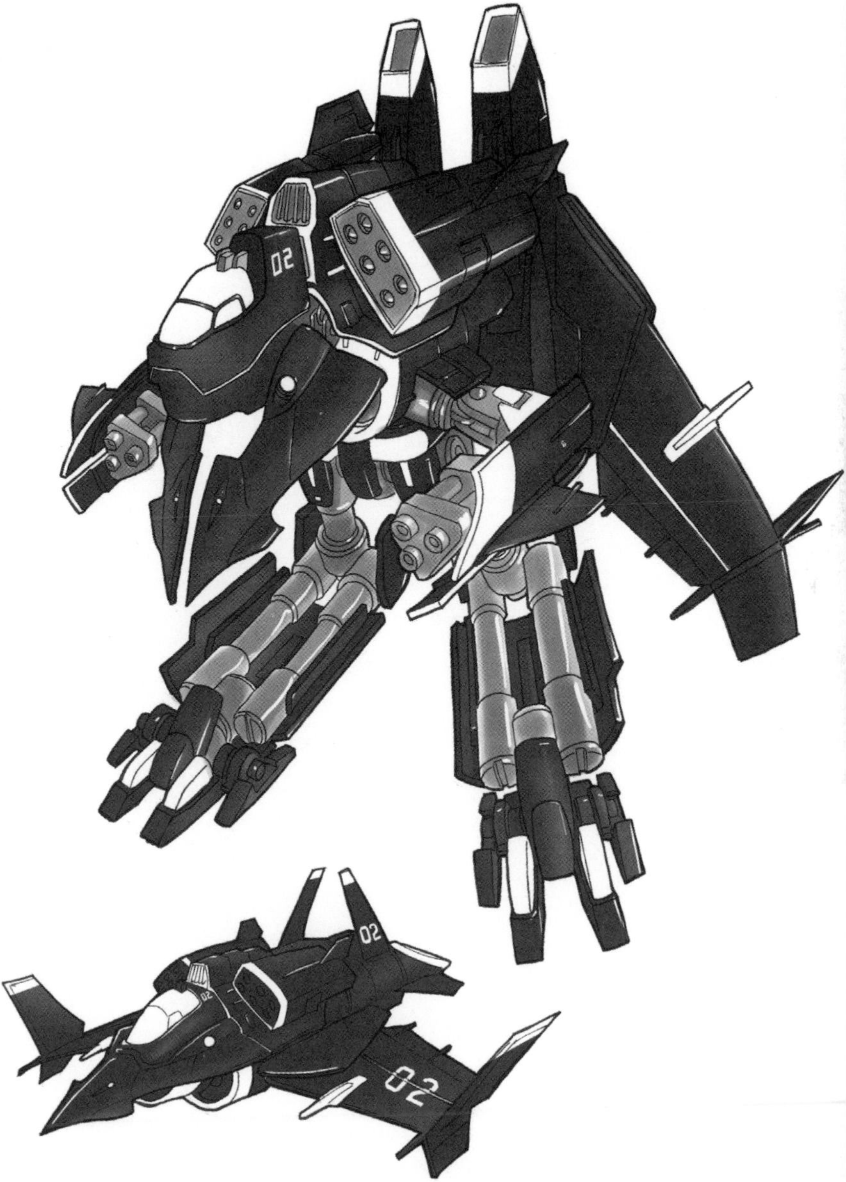

STARCRAFT

FRONTLINE™

VOLUME 2

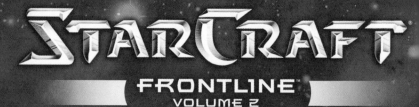

CREEP

Written by Simon Furman

Pencils by Tomás Aira
Inks by Tomás Aira and German Erramouspe
Tones by Tomás Aira, Wally Gomez and Ariel Lacci

Letterer: Michael Paolilli

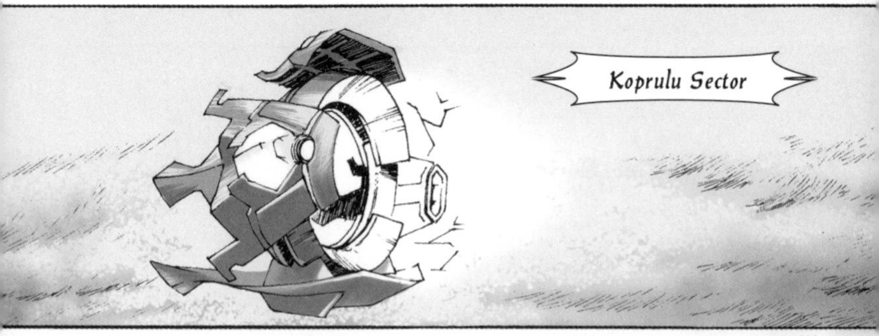
Koprulu Sector

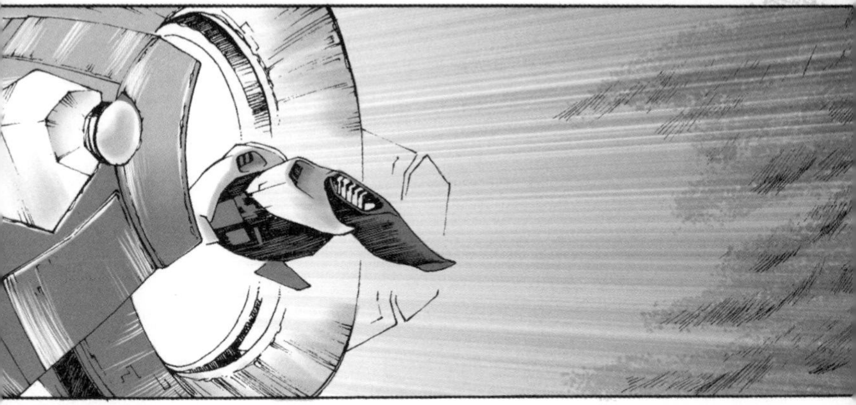

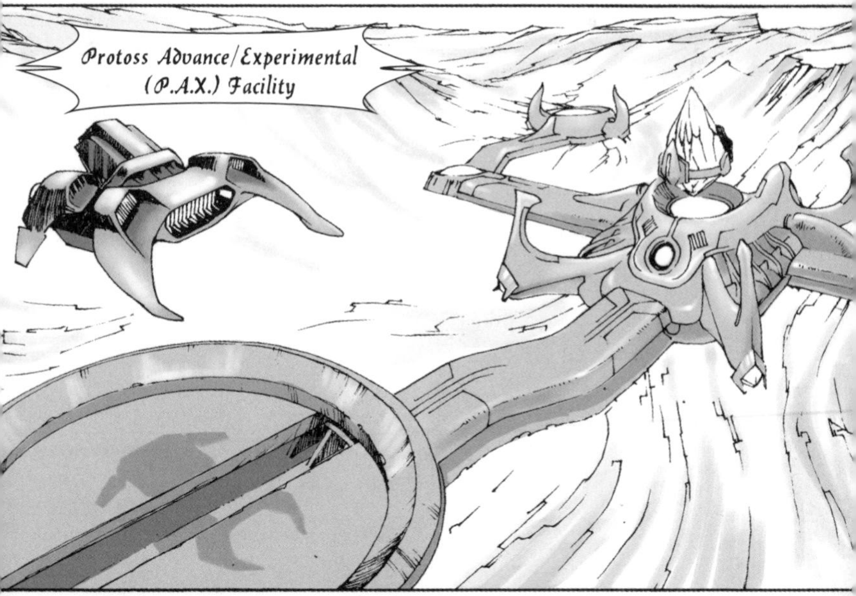
Protoss Advance/Experimental
(P.A.X.) Facility

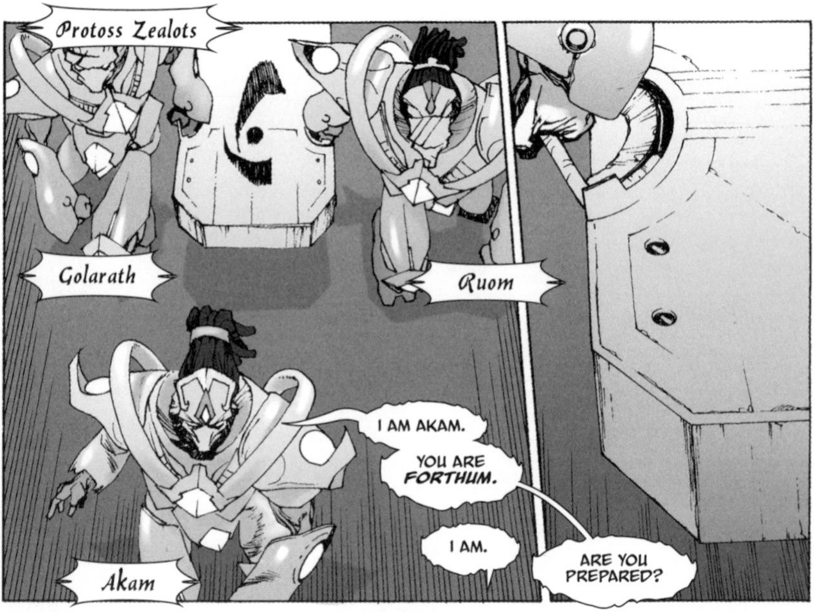
Protoss Zealots
Golarath
Ruom
Akam
I AM AKAM.
YOU ARE FORTHUM.
I AM.
ARE YOU PREPARED?

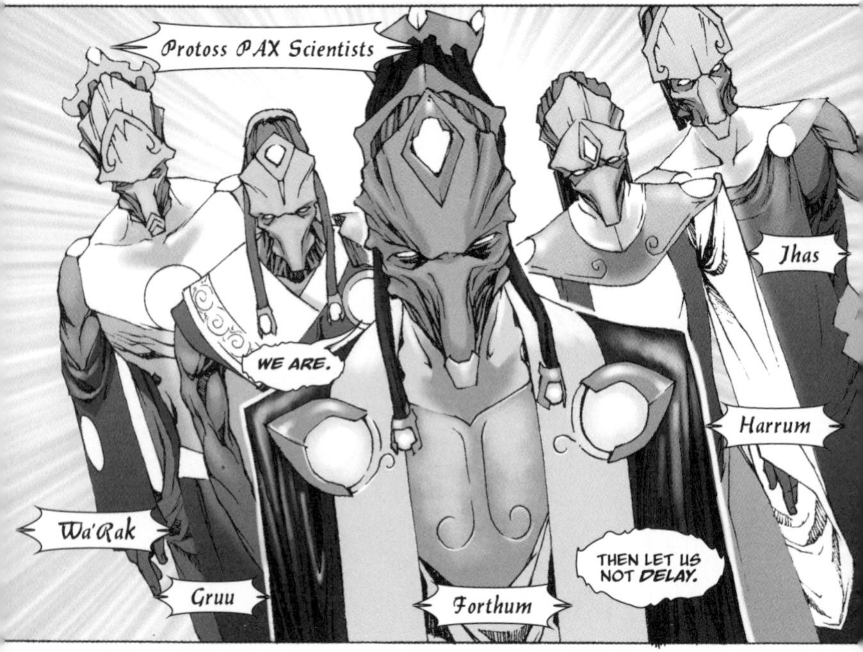
Protoss PAX Scientists
Jhas
WE ARE.
Harrum
Wa'Rak
Gruu
Forthum
THEN LET US NOT DELAY.

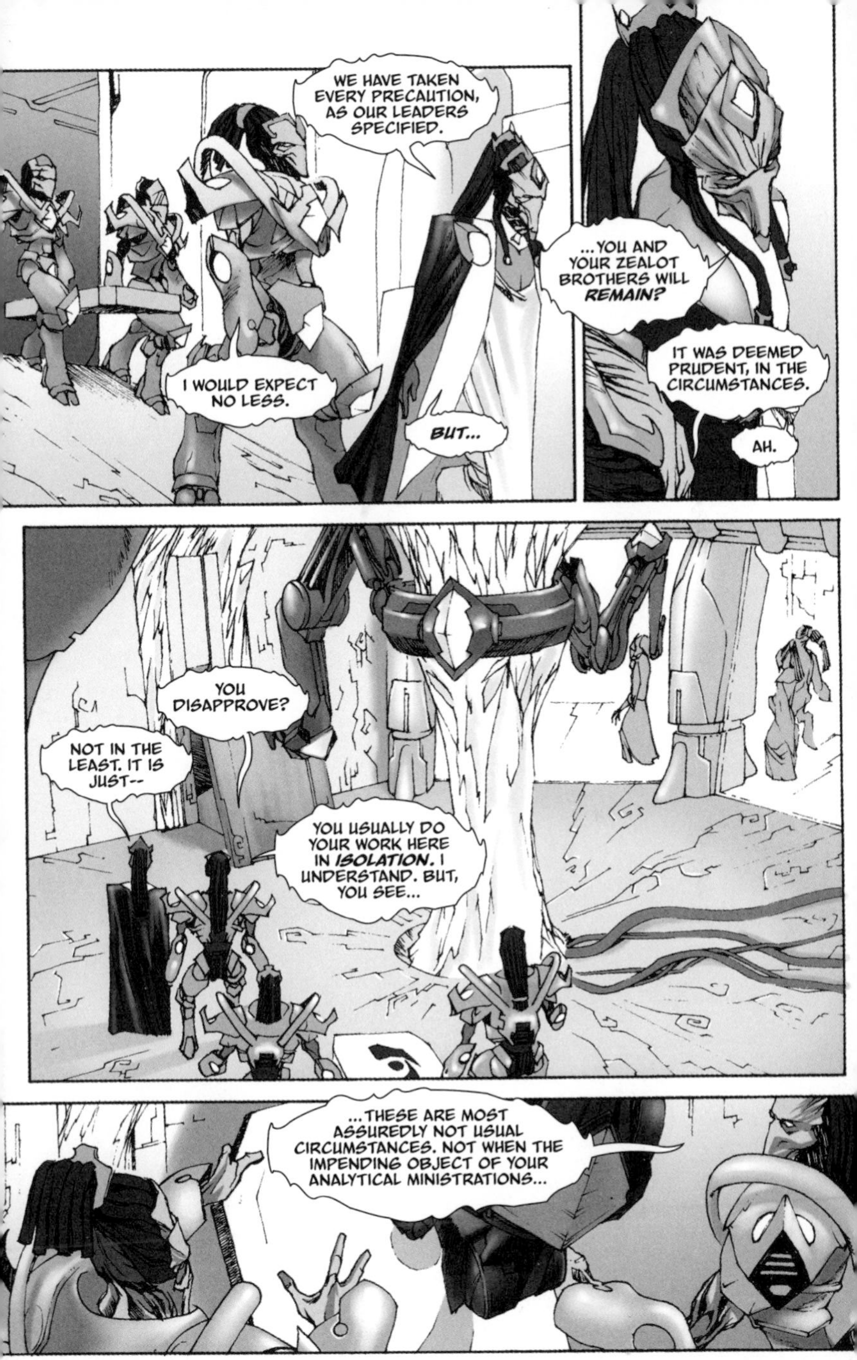

WE HAVE TAKEN EVERY PRECAUTION, AS OUR LEADERS SPECIFIED.
I WOULD EXPECT NO LESS.
BUT...
...YOU AND YOUR ZEALOT BROTHERS WILL REMAIN?
IT WAS DEEMED PRUDENT, IN THE CIRCUMSTANCES.
AH.
YOU DISAPPROVE?
NOT IN THE LEAST. IT IS JUST--
YOU USUALLY DO YOUR WORK HERE IN ISOLATION. I UNDERSTAND. BUT, YOU SEE...
...THESE ARE MOST ASSUREDLY NOT USUAL CIRCUMSTANCES. NOT WHEN THE IMPENDING OBJECT OF YOUR ANALYTICAL MINISTRATIONS...

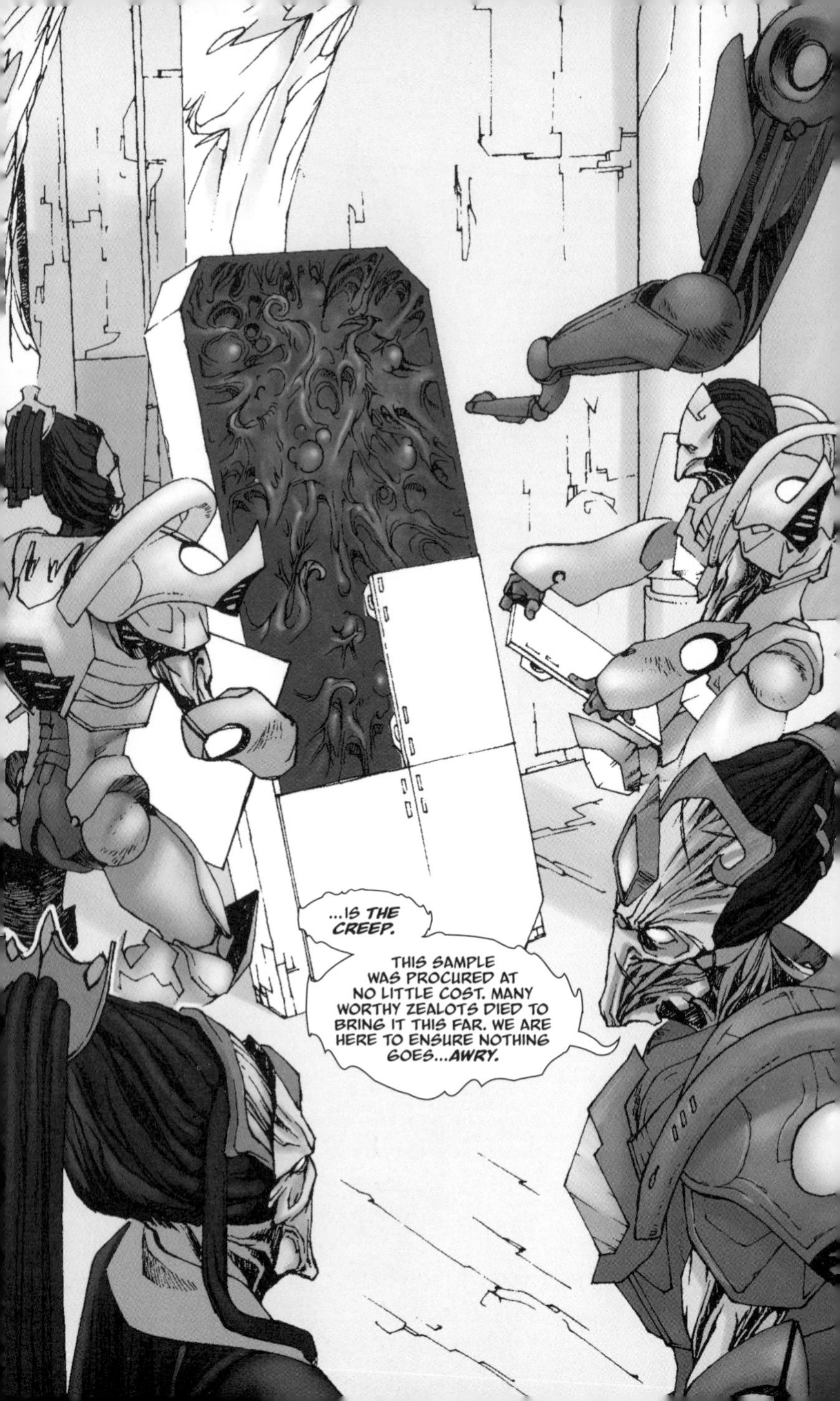
...IS THE CREEP.
THIS SAMPLE WAS PROCURED AT NO LITTLE COST. MANY WORTHY ZEALOTS DIED TO BRING IT THIS FAR. WE ARE HERE TO ENSURE NOTHING GOES...AWRY.

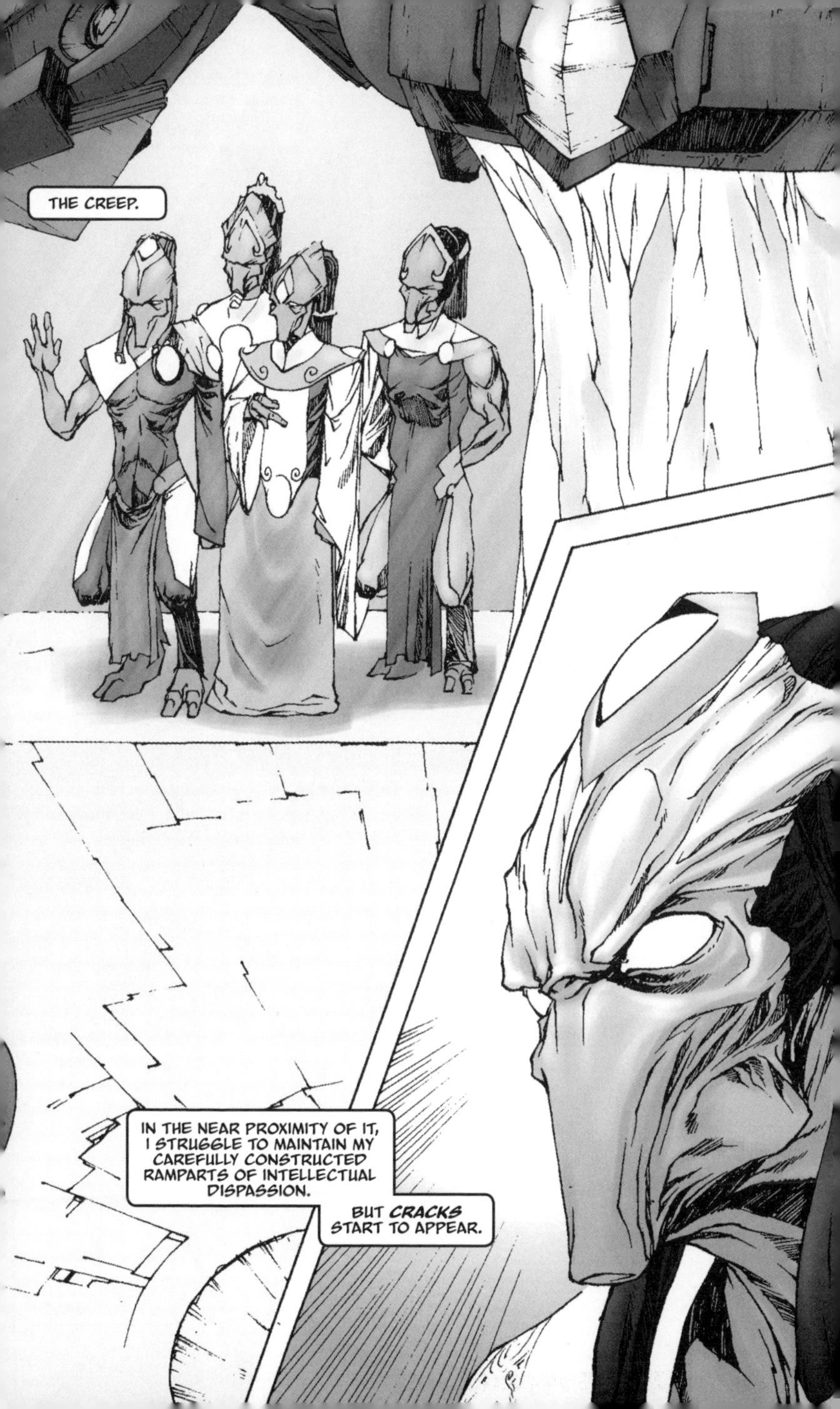
THE CREEP.
IN THE NEAR PROXIMITY OF IT, I STRUGGLE TO MAINTAIN MY CAREFULLY CONSTRUCTED RAMPARTS OF INTELLECTUAL DISPASSION.
BUT *CRACKS* START TO APPEAR.

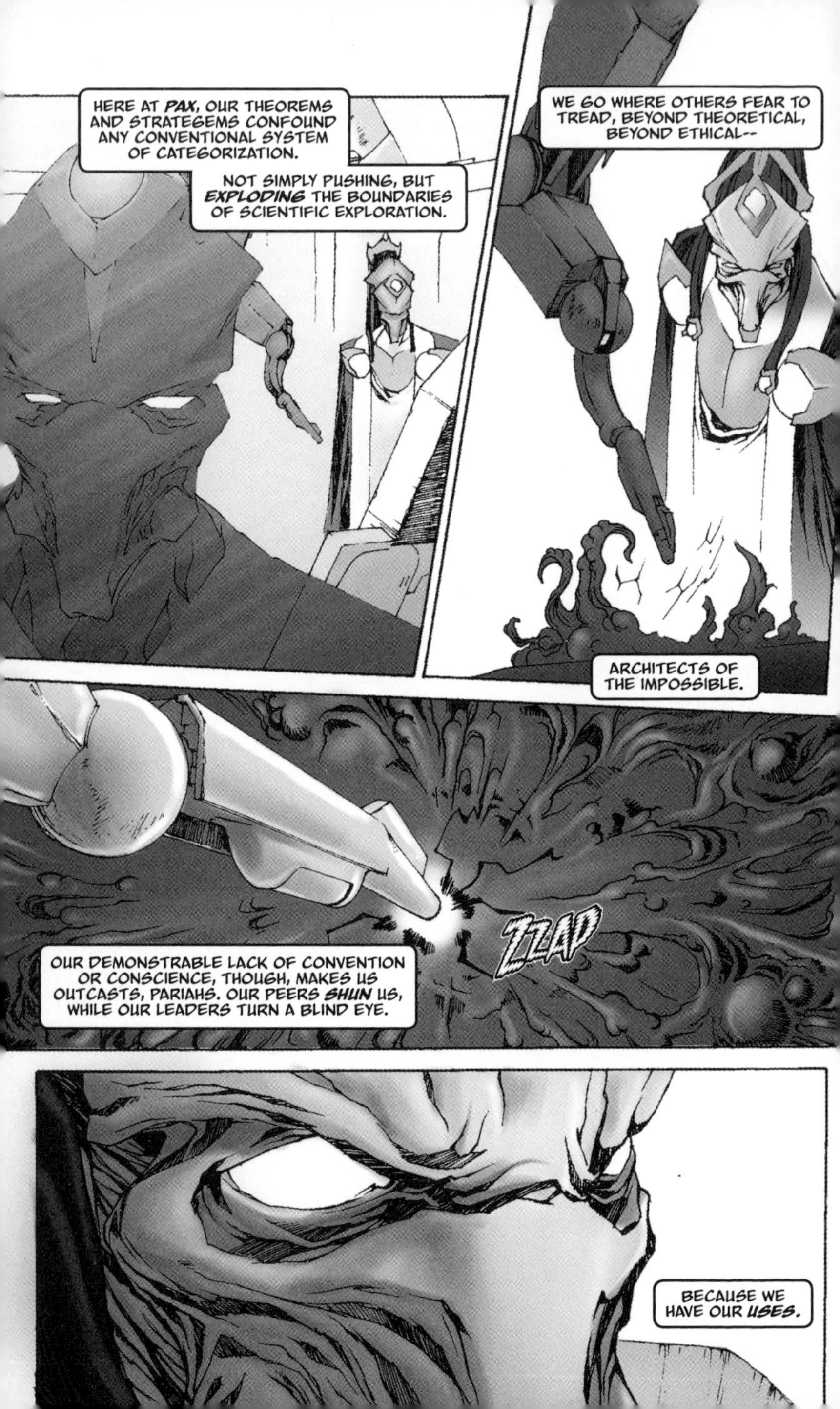
HERE AT PAX, OUR THEOREMS AND STRATEGEMS CONFOUND ANY CONVENTIONAL SYSTEM OF CATEGORIZATION.
NOT SIMPLY PUSHING, BUT EXPLODING THE BOUNDARIES OF SCIENTIFIC EXPLORATION.
WE GO WHERE OTHERS FEAR TO TREAD, BEYOND THEORETICAL, BEYOND ETHICAL--
ARCHITECTS OF THE IMPOSSIBLE.
ZZAP
OUR DEMONSTRABLE LACK OF CONVENTION OR CONSCIENCE, THOUGH, MAKES US OUTCASTS, PARIAHS. OUR PEERS SHUN US, WHILE OUR LEADERS TURN A BLIND EYE.
BECAUSE WE HAVE OUR USES.

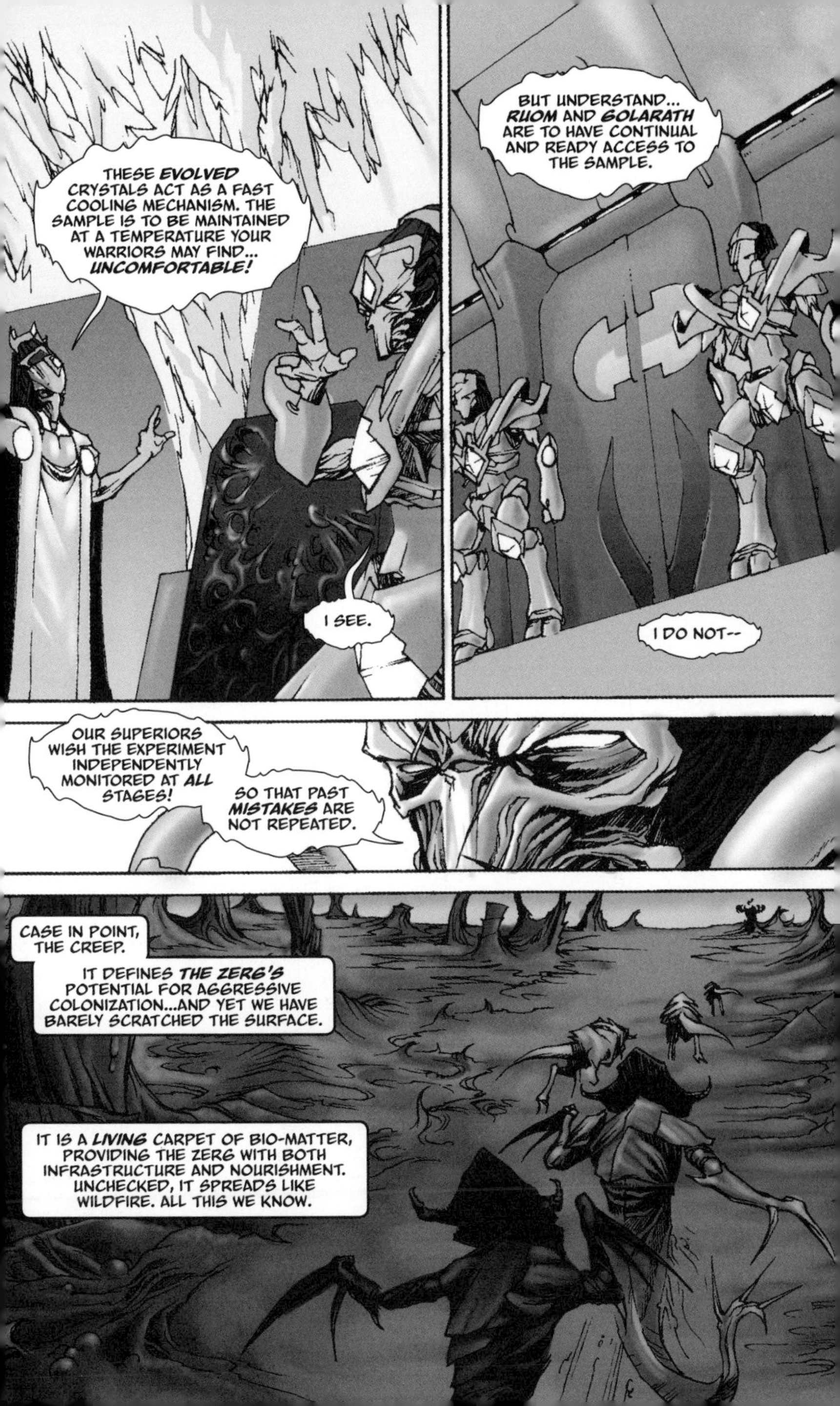

THESE *EVOLVED* CRYSTALS ACT AS A FAST COOLING MECHANISM. THE SAMPLE IS TO BE MAINTAINED AT A TEMPERATURE YOUR WARRIORS MAY FIND... *UNCOMFORTABLE!*
I SEE.
BUT UNDERSTAND... *RUOM* AND *GOLARATH* ARE TO HAVE CONTINUAL AND READY ACCESS TO THE SAMPLE.
I DO NOT--
OUR SUPERIORS WISH THE EXPERIMENT INDEPENDENTLY MONITORED AT *ALL* STAGES!
SO THAT PAST *MISTAKES* ARE NOT REPEATED.
CASE IN POINT, THE CREEP.
IT DEFINES *THE ZERG'S* POTENTIAL FOR AGGRESSIVE COLONIZATION...AND YET WE HAVE BARELY SCRATCHED THE SURFACE.
IT IS A *LIVING* CARPET OF BIO-MATTER, PROVIDING THE ZERG WITH BOTH INFRASTRUCTURE AND NOURISHMENT. UNCHECKED, IT SPREADS LIKE WILDFIRE. ALL THIS WE KNOW.

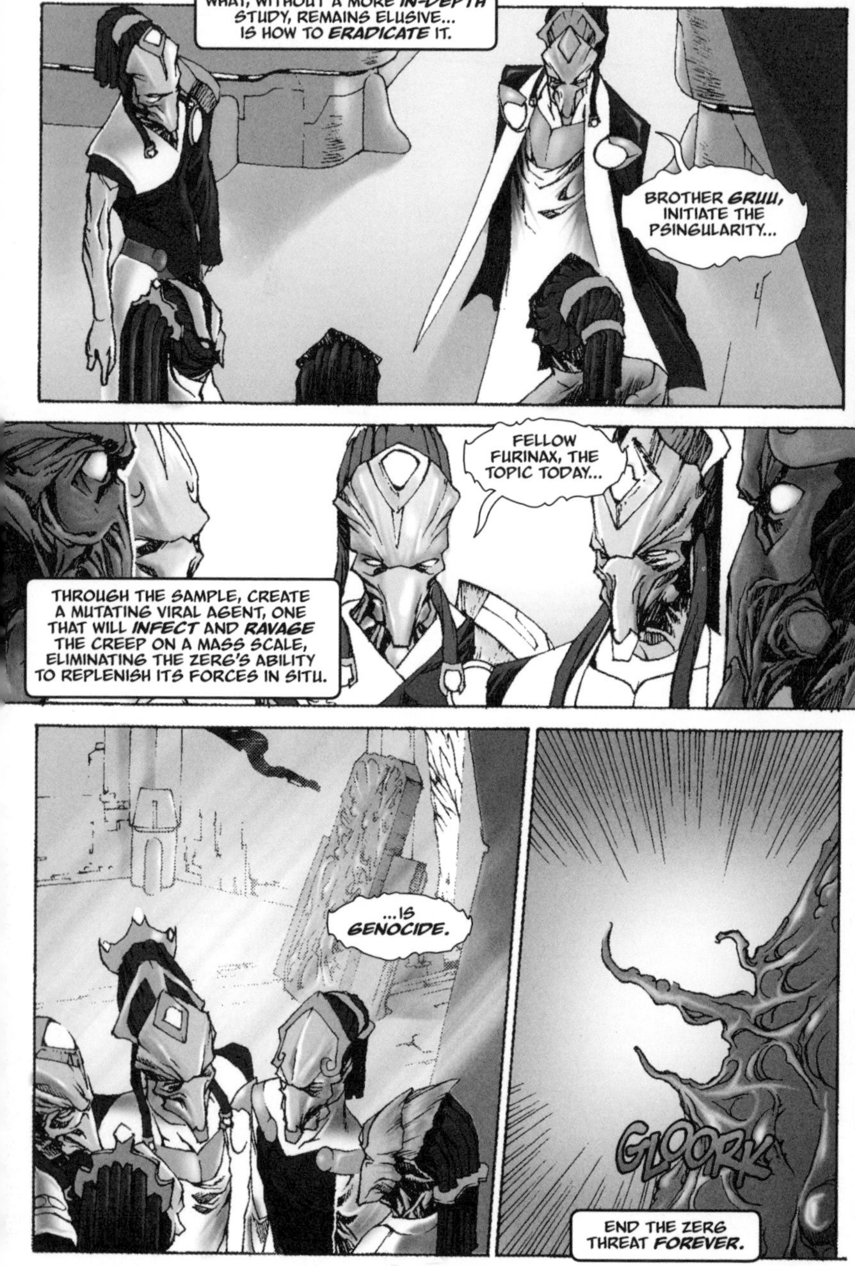
WHAT, WITHOUT A MORE IN-DEPTH STUDY, REMAINS ELUSIVE... IS HOW TO ERADICATE IT.
BROTHER GRUU, INITIATE THE PSINGULARITY...
FELLOW FURINAX, THE TOPIC TODAY...
THROUGH THE SAMPLE, CREATE A MUTATING VIRAL AGENT, ONE THAT WILL INFECT AND RAVAGE THE CREEP ON A MASS SCALE, ELIMINATING THE ZERG'S ABILITY TO REPLENISH ITS FORCES IN SITU.
...IS GENOCIDE.
GLOORK
END THE ZERG THREAT FOREVER.

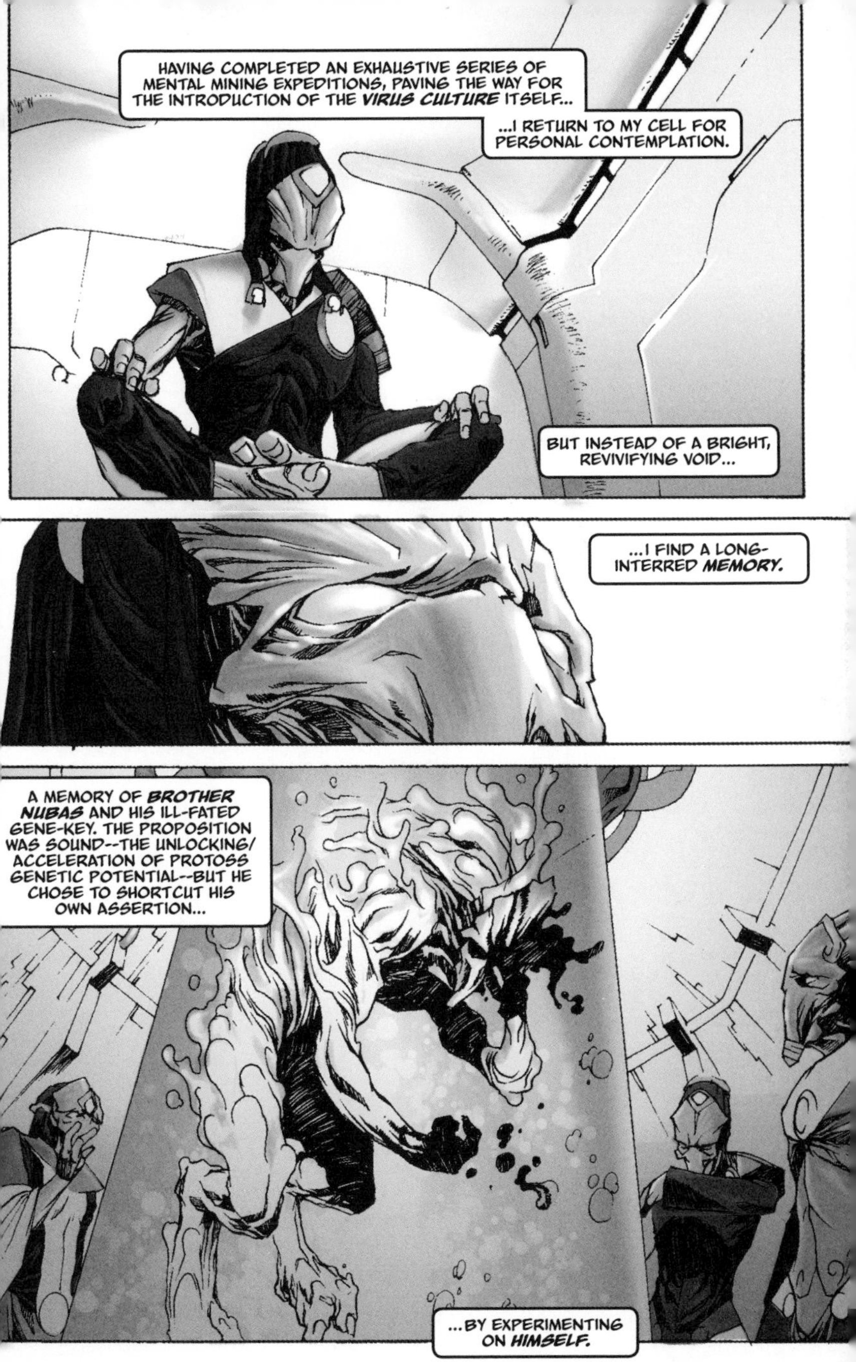
HAVING COMPLETED AN EXHAUSTIVE SERIES OF MENTAL MINING EXPEDITIONS, PAVING THE WAY FOR THE INTRODUCTION OF THE *VIRUS CULTURE* ITSELF...
...I RETURN TO MY CELL FOR PERSONAL CONTEMPLATION.
BUT INSTEAD OF A BRIGHT, REVIVIFYING VOID...
...I FIND A LONG-INTERRED *MEMORY.*
A MEMORY OF *BROTHER NUBAS* AND HIS ILL-FATED GENE-KEY. THE PROPOSITION WAS SOUND--THE UNLOCKING/ ACCELERATION OF PROTOSS GENETIC POTENTIAL--BUT HE CHOSE TO SHORTCUT HIS OWN ASSERTION...
...BY EXPERIMENTING ON *HIMSELF.*

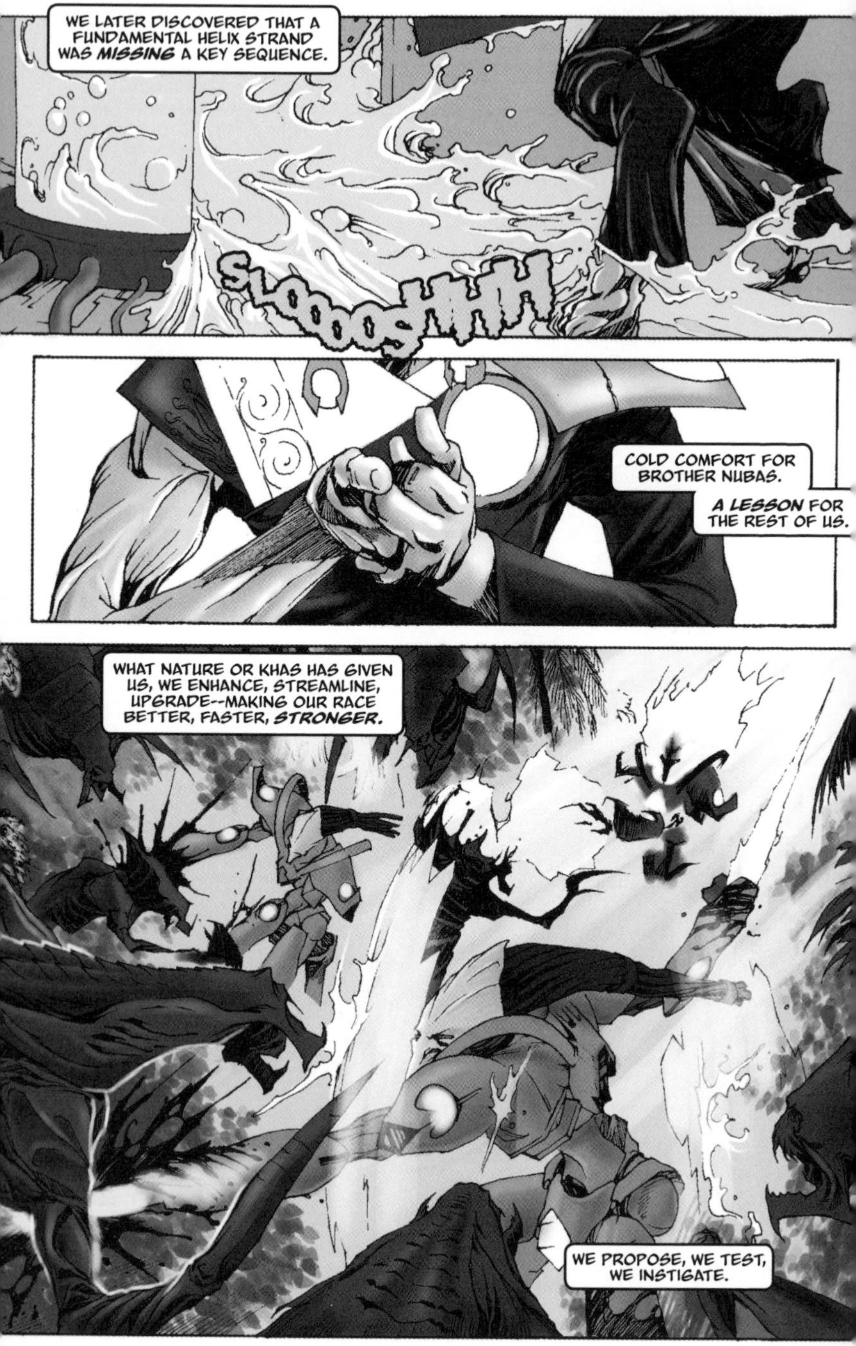

WE LATER DISCOVERED THAT A FUNDAMENTAL HELIX STRAND WAS *MISSING* A KEY SEQUENCE.
SLOOOSHHH
COLD COMFORT FOR BROTHER NUBAS.
A LESSON FOR THE REST OF US.
WHAT NATURE OR KHAS HAS GIVEN US, WE ENHANCE, STREAMLINE, UPGRADE--MAKING OUR RACE BETTER, FASTER, *STRONGER.*
WE PROPOSE, WE TEST, WE INSTIGATE.

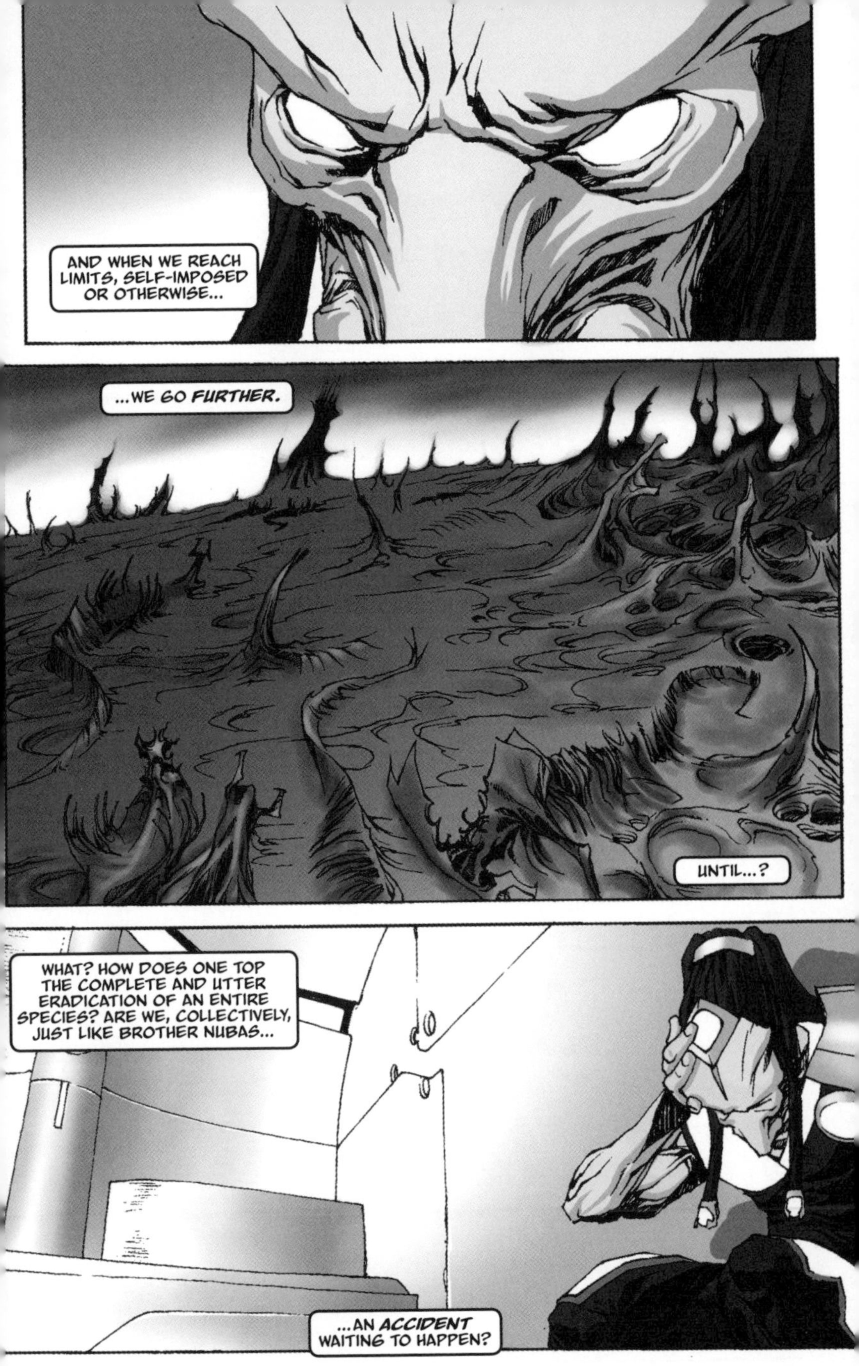
AND WHEN WE REACH LIMITS, SELF-IMPOSED OR OTHERWISE...
...WE GO FURTHER.
UNTIL...?
WHAT? HOW DOES ONE TOP THE COMPLETE AND UTTER ERADICATION OF AN ENTIRE SPECIES? ARE WE, COLLECTIVELY, JUST LIKE BROTHER NUBAS...
...AN ACCIDENT WAITING TO HAPPEN?

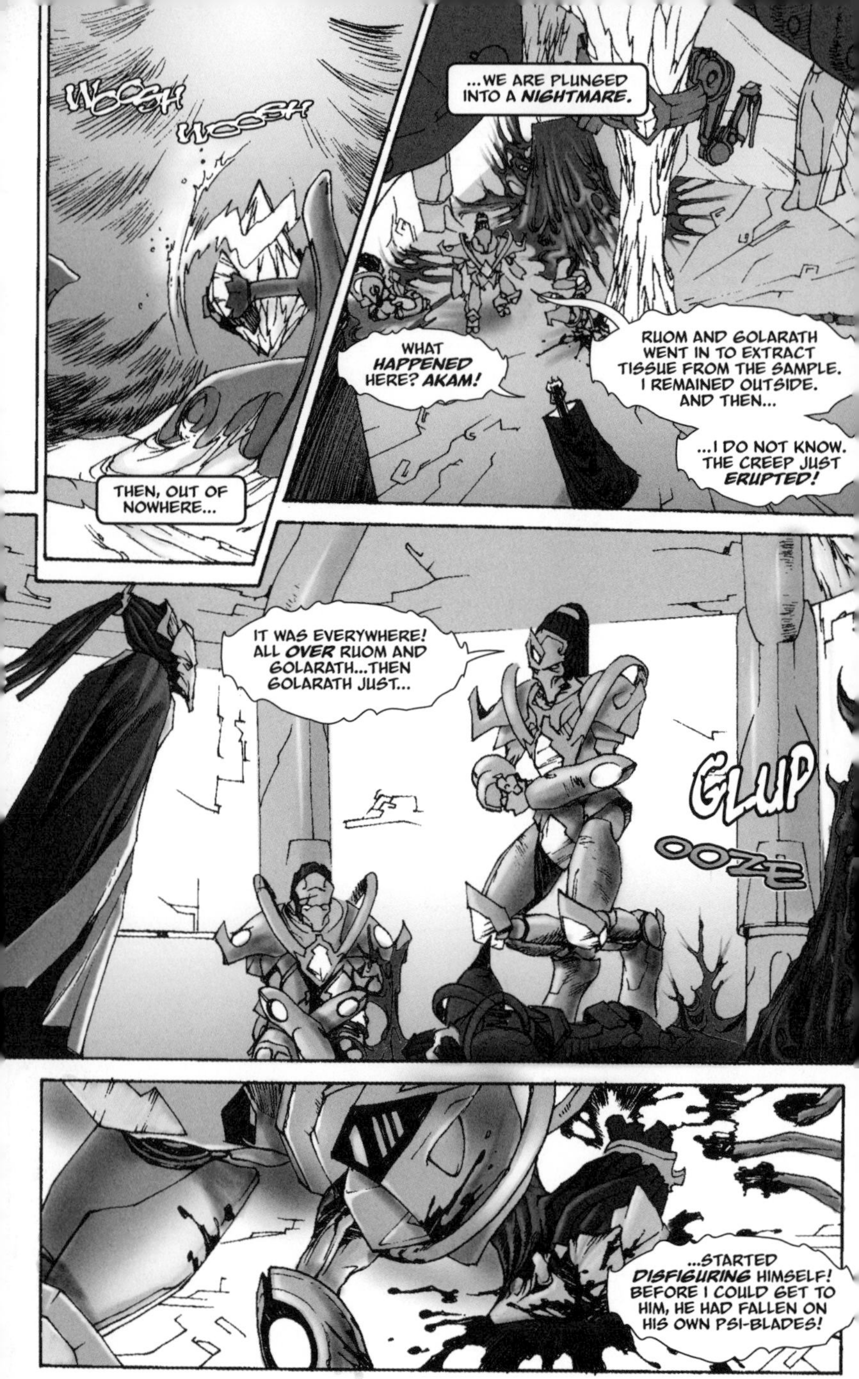
WOOSH
WOOSH
THEN, OUT OF NOWHERE...
...WE ARE PLUNGED INTO A NIGHTMARE.
WHAT HAPPENED HERE? AKAM!
RUOM AND GOLARATH WENT IN TO EXTRACT TISSUE FROM THE SAMPLE. I REMAINED OUTSIDE. AND THEN...
...I DO NOT KNOW. THE CREEP JUST ERUPTED!
IT WAS EVERYWHERE! ALL OVER RUOM AND GOLARATH...THEN GOLARATH JUST...
GLUP
OOZE
...STARTED DISFIGURING HIMSELF! BEFORE I COULD GET TO HIM, HE HAD FALLEN ON HIS OWN PSI-BLADES!

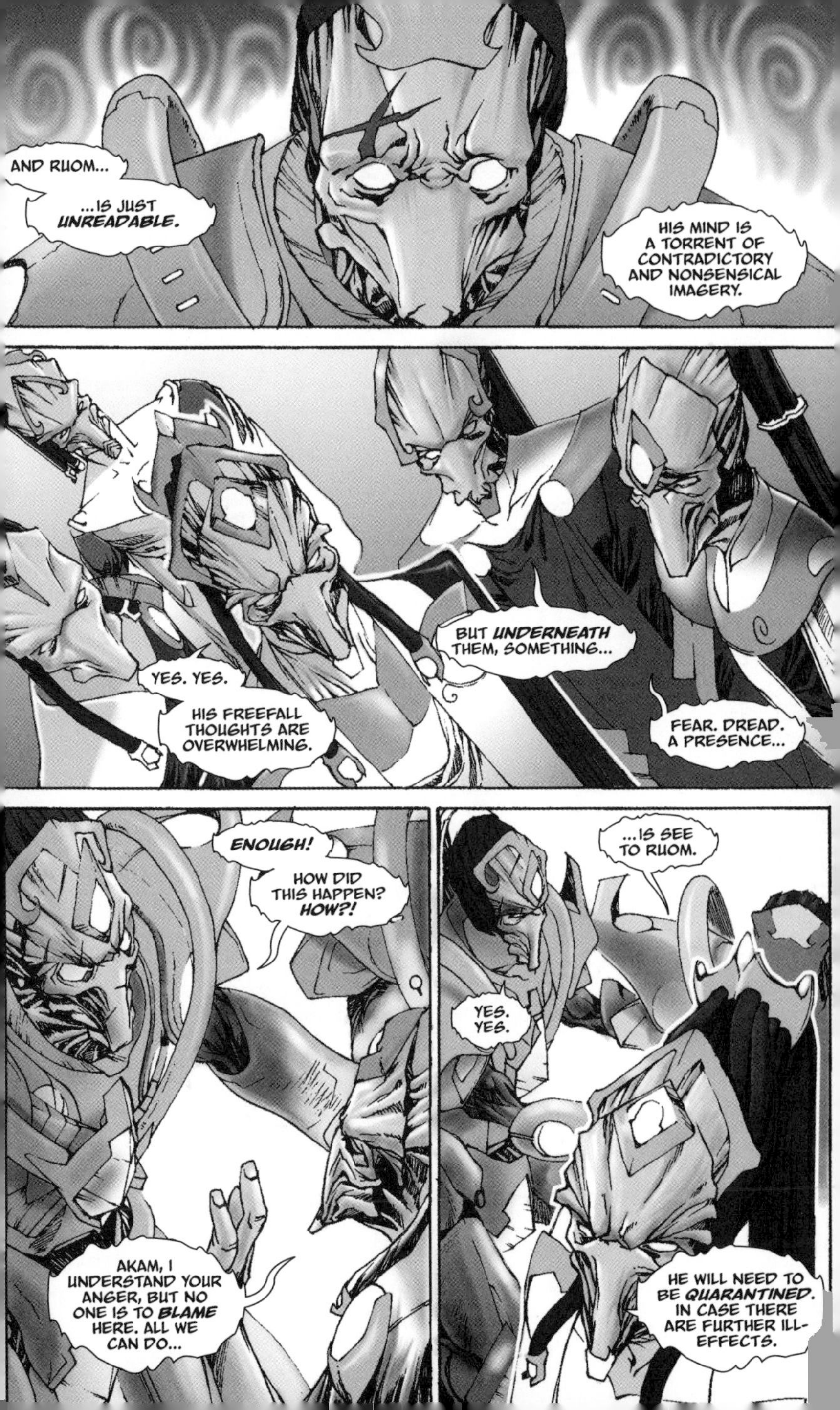
AND RUOM...
...IS JUST UNREADABLE.
HIS MIND IS A TORRENT OF CONTRADICTORY AND NONSENSICAL IMAGERY.
BUT UNDERNEATH THEM, SOMETHING...
YES. YES.
HIS FREEFALL THOUGHTS ARE OVERWHELMING.
FEAR. DREAD. A PRESENCE...
ENOUGH!
HOW DID THIS HAPPEN? HOW?!
AKAM, I UNDERSTAND YOUR ANGER, BUT NO ONE IS TO BLAME HERE. ALL WE CAN DO...
...IS SEE TO RUOM.
YES. YES.
HE WILL NEED TO BE QUARANTINED. IN CASE THERE ARE FURTHER ILL-EFFECTS.

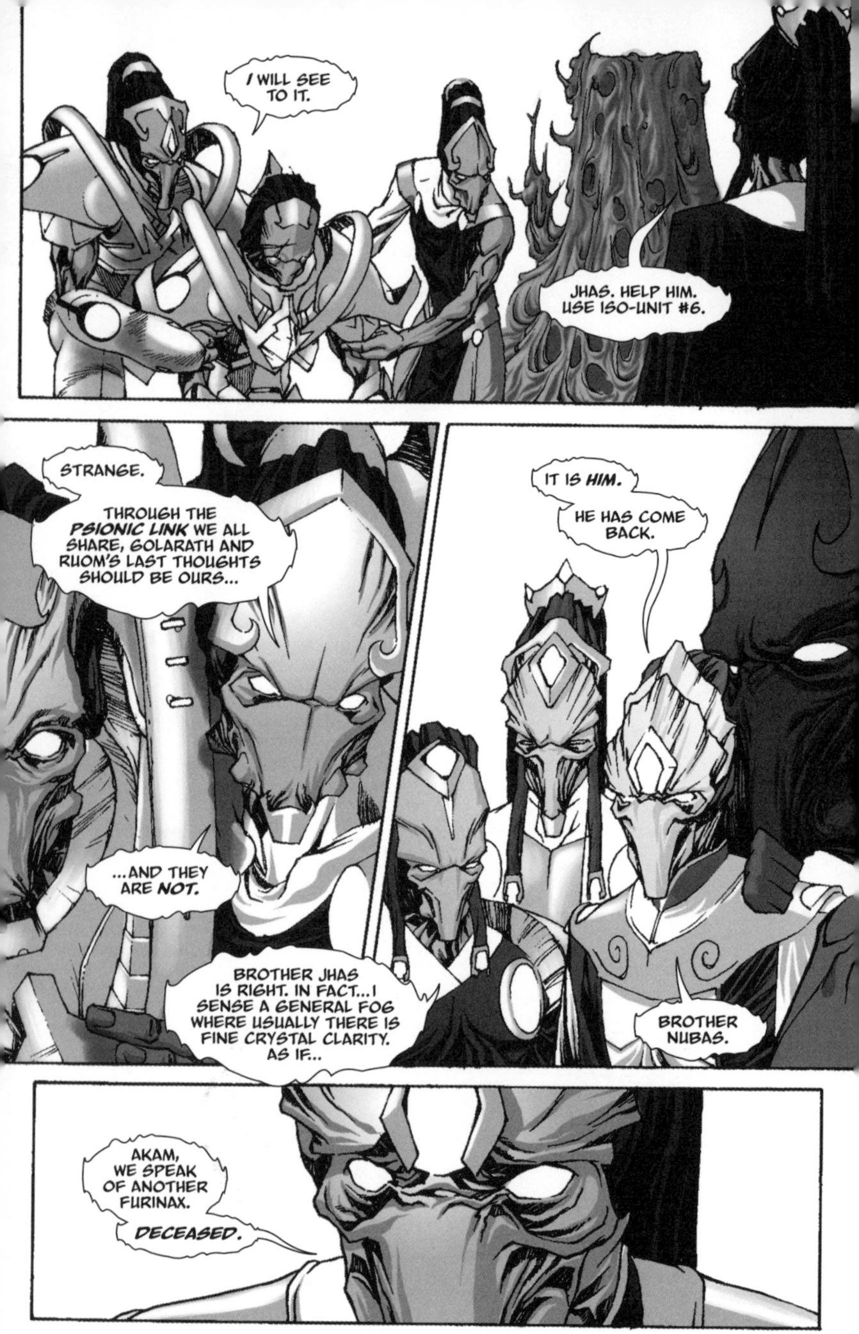
I WILL SEE TO IT.
JHAS. HELP HIM. USE ISO-UNIT #6.
STRANGE.
THROUGH THE PSIONIC LINK WE ALL SHARE, GOLARATH AND RUOM'S LAST THOUGHTS SHOULD BE OURS...
...AND THEY ARE NOT.
BROTHER JHAS IS RIGHT. IN FACT...I SENSE A GENERAL FOG WHERE USUALLY THERE IS FINE CRYSTAL CLARITY. AS IF...
IT IS HIM.
HE HAS COME BACK.
BROTHER NUBAS.
AKAM, WE SPEAK OF ANOTHER FURINAX.
DECEASED.

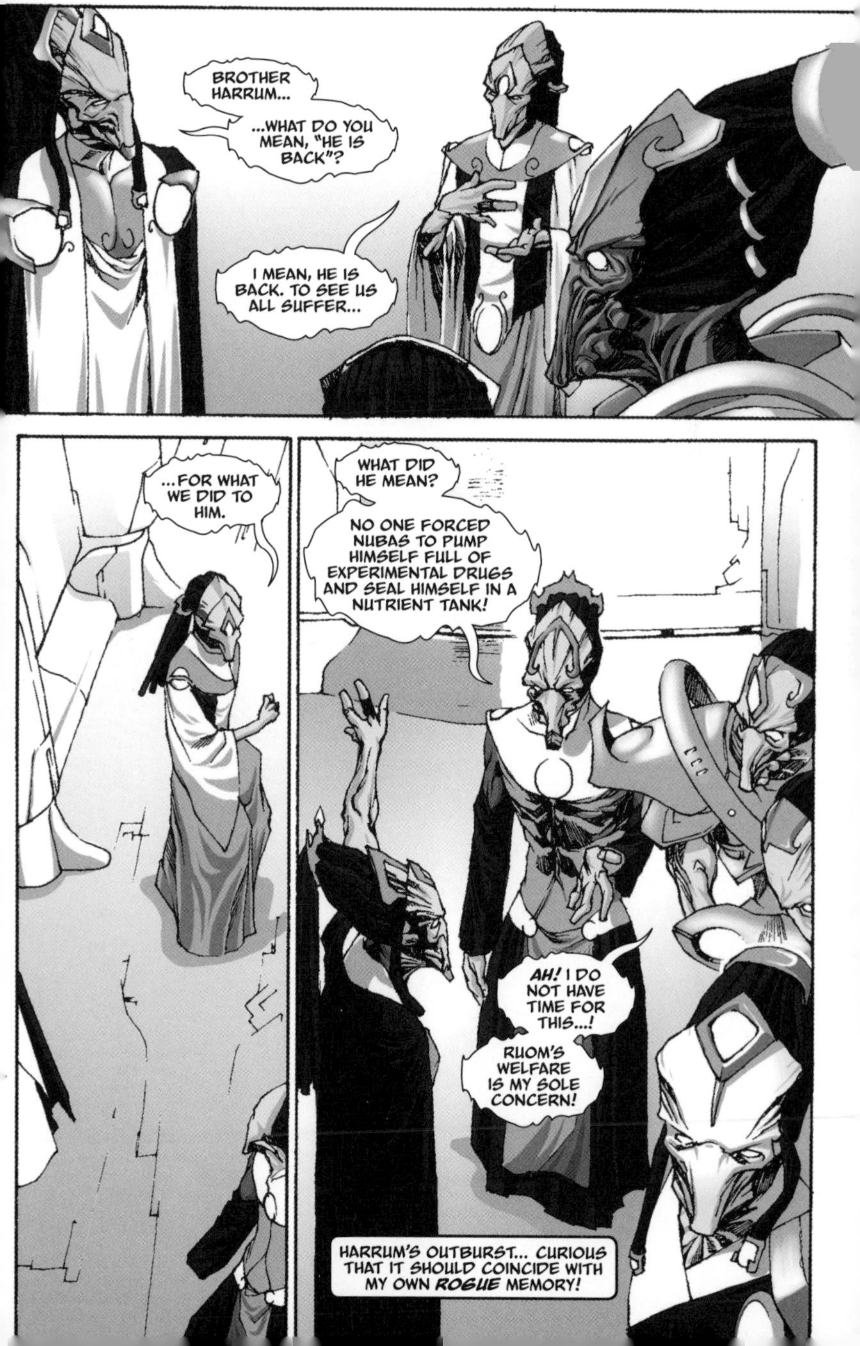
BROTHER HARRUM...
...WHAT DO YOU MEAN, "HE IS BACK"?
I MEAN, HE IS BACK. TO SEE US ALL SUFFER...
...FOR WHAT WE DID TO HIM.
WHAT DID HE MEAN?
NO ONE FORCED NUBAS TO PUMP HIMSELF FULL OF EXPERIMENTAL DRUGS AND SEAL HIMSELF IN A NUTRIENT TANK!
AH! I DO NOT HAVE TIME FOR THIS...!
RUOM'S WELFARE IS MY SOLE CONCERN!
HARRUM'S OUTBURST... CURIOUS THAT IT SHOULD COINCIDE WITH MY OWN ROGUE MEMORY!

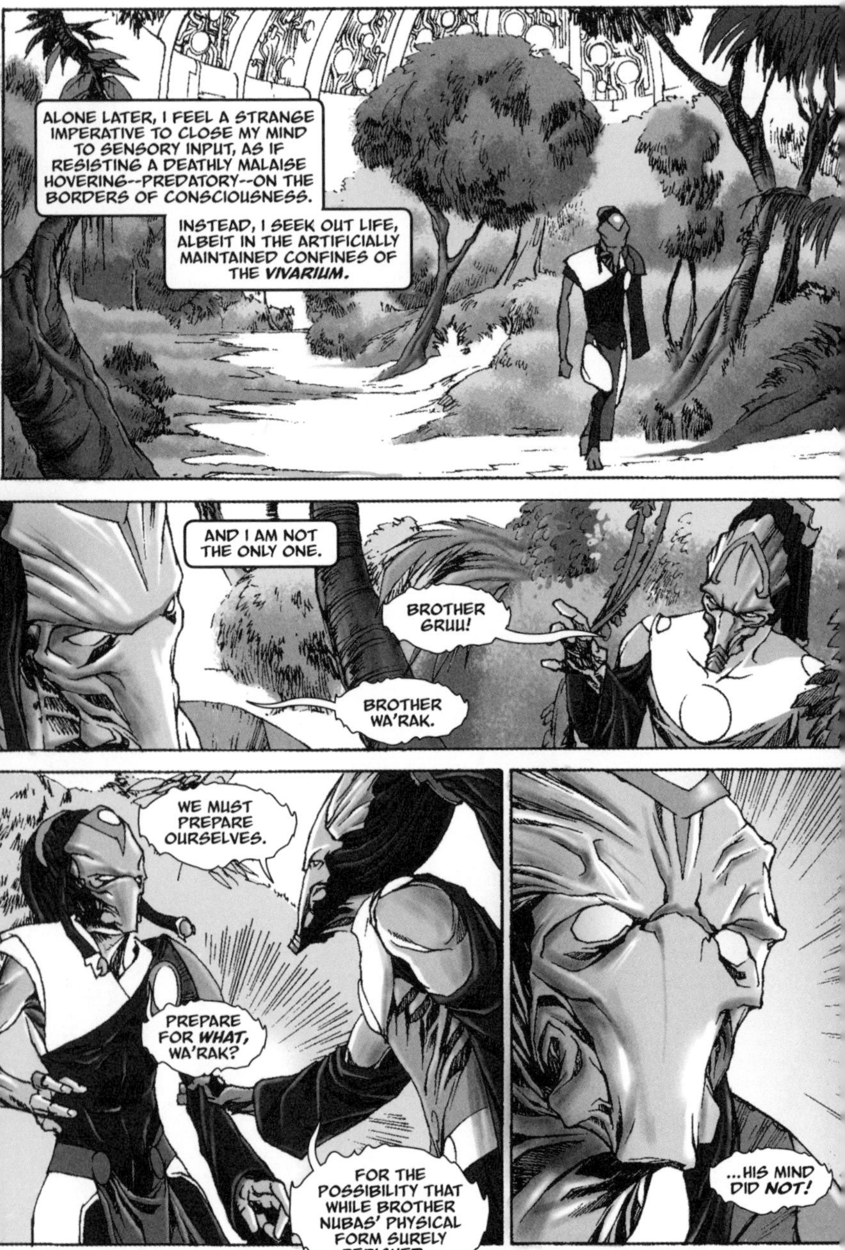
ALONE LATER, I FEEL A STRANGE IMPERATIVE TO CLOSE MY MIND TO SENSORY INPUT, AS IF RESISTING A DEATHLY MALAISE HOVERING--PREDATORY--ON THE BORDERS OF CONSCIOUSNESS.
INSTEAD, I SEEK OUT LIFE, ALBEIT IN THE ARTIFICIALLY MAINTAINED CONFINES OF THE *VIVARIUM.*
AND I AM NOT THE ONLY ONE.
BROTHER GRUU!
BROTHER WA'RAK.
WE MUST PREPARE OURSELVES.
PREPARE FOR *WHAT,* WA'RAK?
FOR THE POSSIBILITY THAT WHILE BROTHER NUBAS' PHYSICAL FORM SURELY PERISHED...
...HIS MIND DID *NOT!*

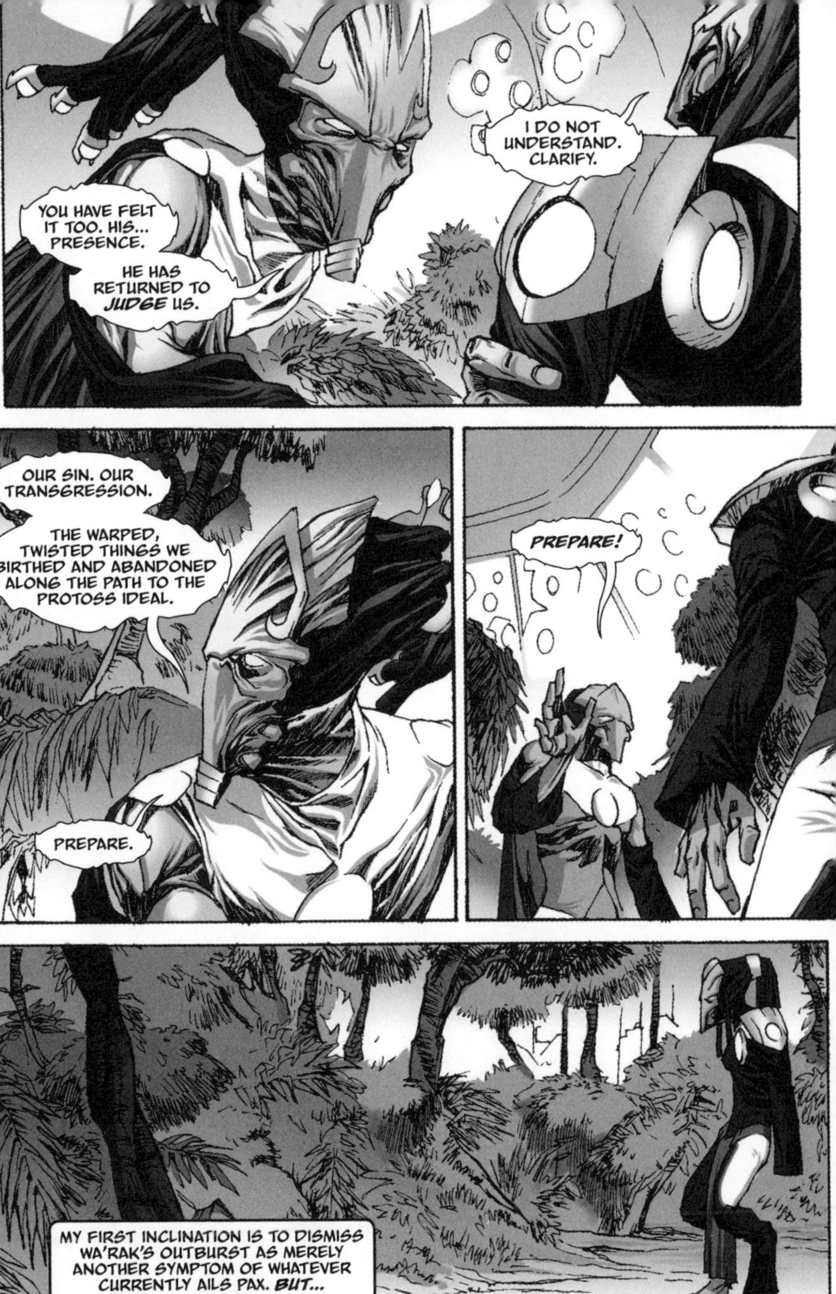
I DO NOT UNDERSTAND. CLARIFY.
YOU HAVE FELT IT TOO. HIS... PRESENCE.
HE HAS RETURNED TO ***JUDGE*** US.
OUR SIN. OUR TRANSGRESSION.
THE WARPED, TWISTED THINGS WE BIRTHED AND ABANDONED ALONG THE PATH TO THE PROTOSS IDEAL.
PREPARE.
PREPARE!
MY FIRST INCLINATION IS TO DISMISS WA'RAK'S OUTBURST AS MERELY ANOTHER SYMPTOM OF WHATEVER CURRENTLY AILS PAX. ***BUT...***

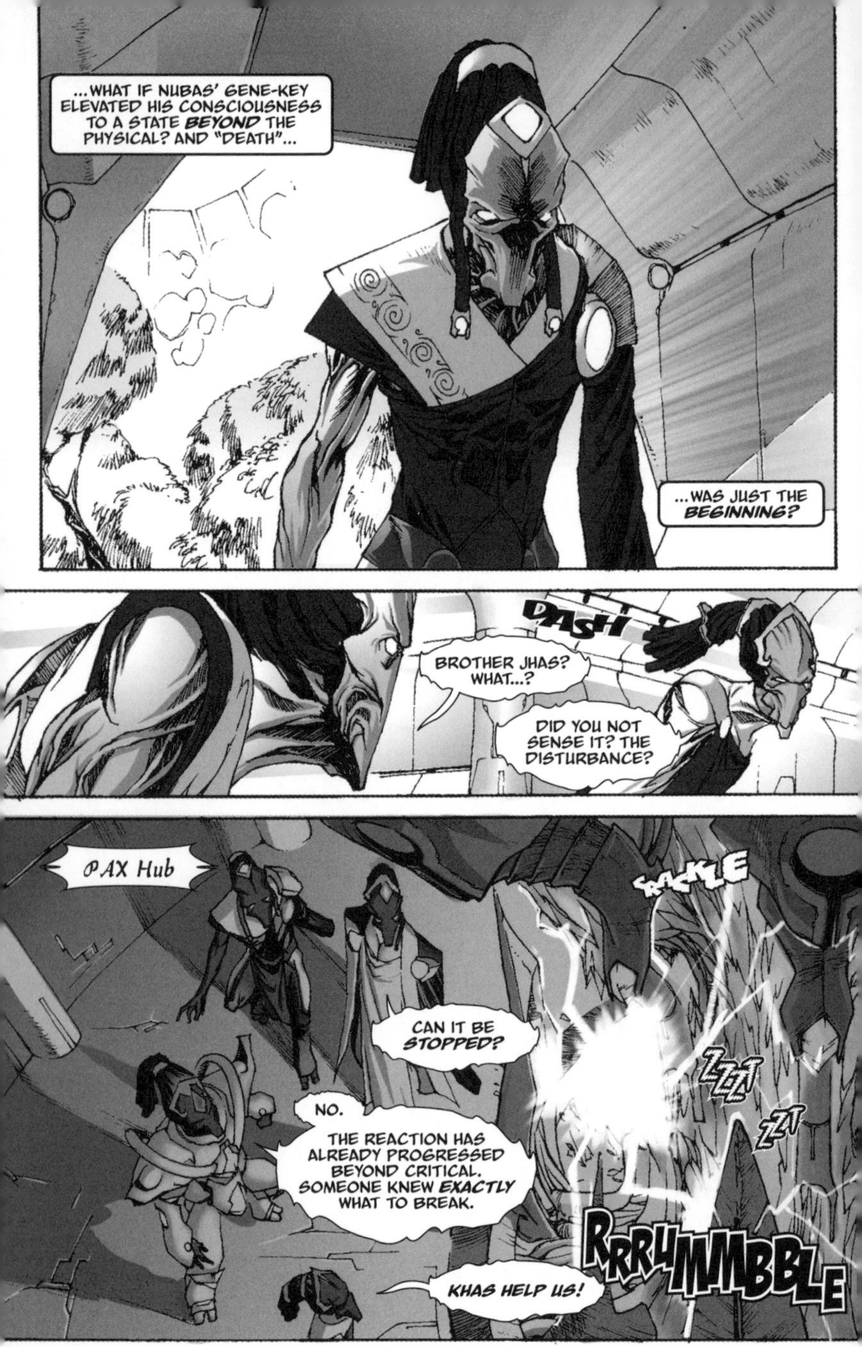
...WHAT IF NUBAS' GENE-KEY ELEVATED HIS CONSCIOUSNESS TO A STATE *BEYOND* THE PHYSICAL? AND "DEATH"...
...WAS JUST THE *BEGINNING?*
DASH
BROTHER JHAS? WHAT...?
DID YOU NOT SENSE IT? THE DISTURBANCE?
PAX Hub
CRACKLE
CAN IT BE *STOPPED?*
NO.
THE REACTION HAS ALREADY PROGRESSED BEYOND CRITICAL. SOMEONE KNEW *EXACTLY* WHAT TO BREAK.
ZZZT
ZZZT
RRRUMMMBBLE
KHAS HELP US!

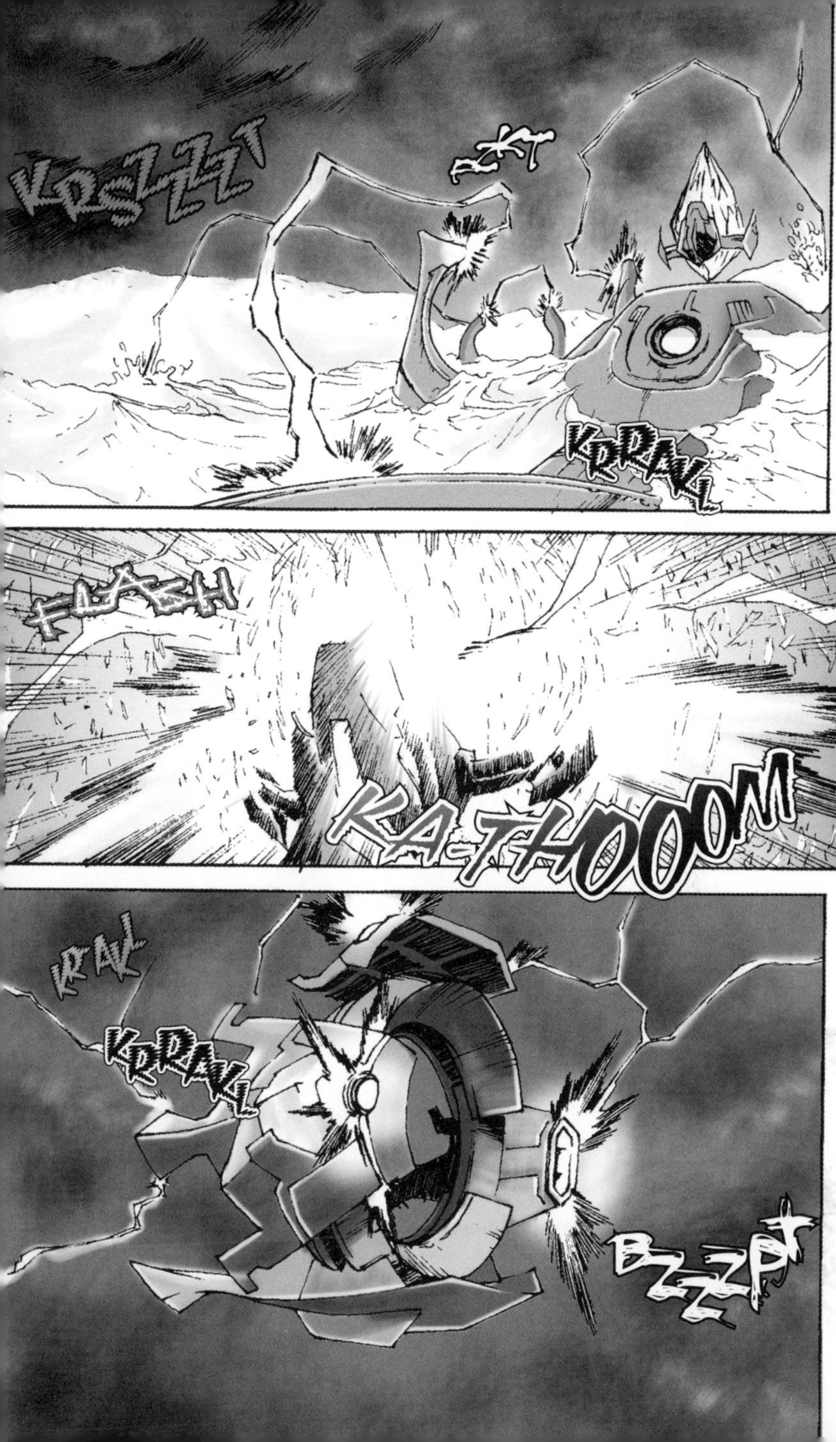
KRSZZZT
KT
KRRAK
FLASH
KA-THOOOM
KRAK
KRRAK
BZZZPT

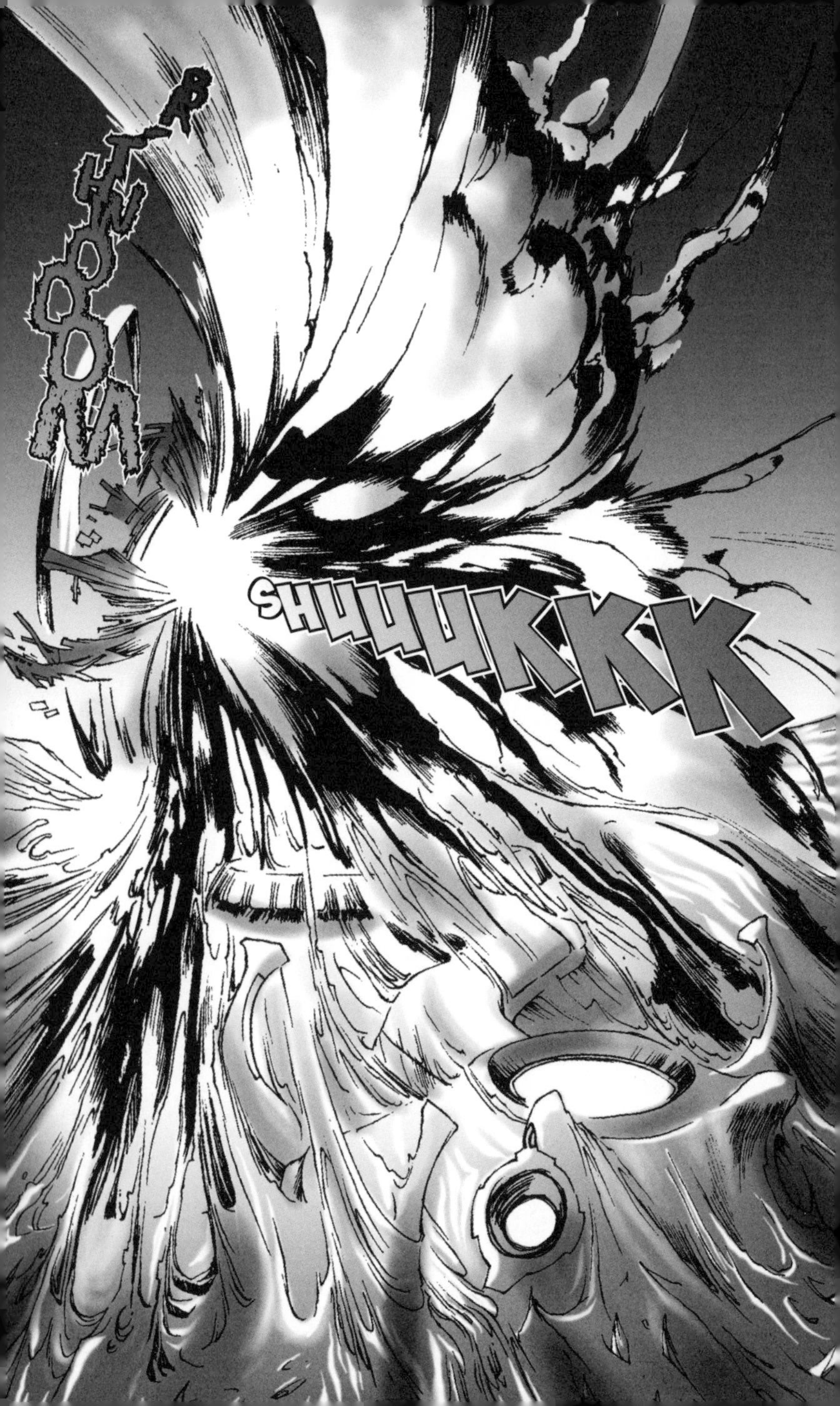
SHUUUKKK

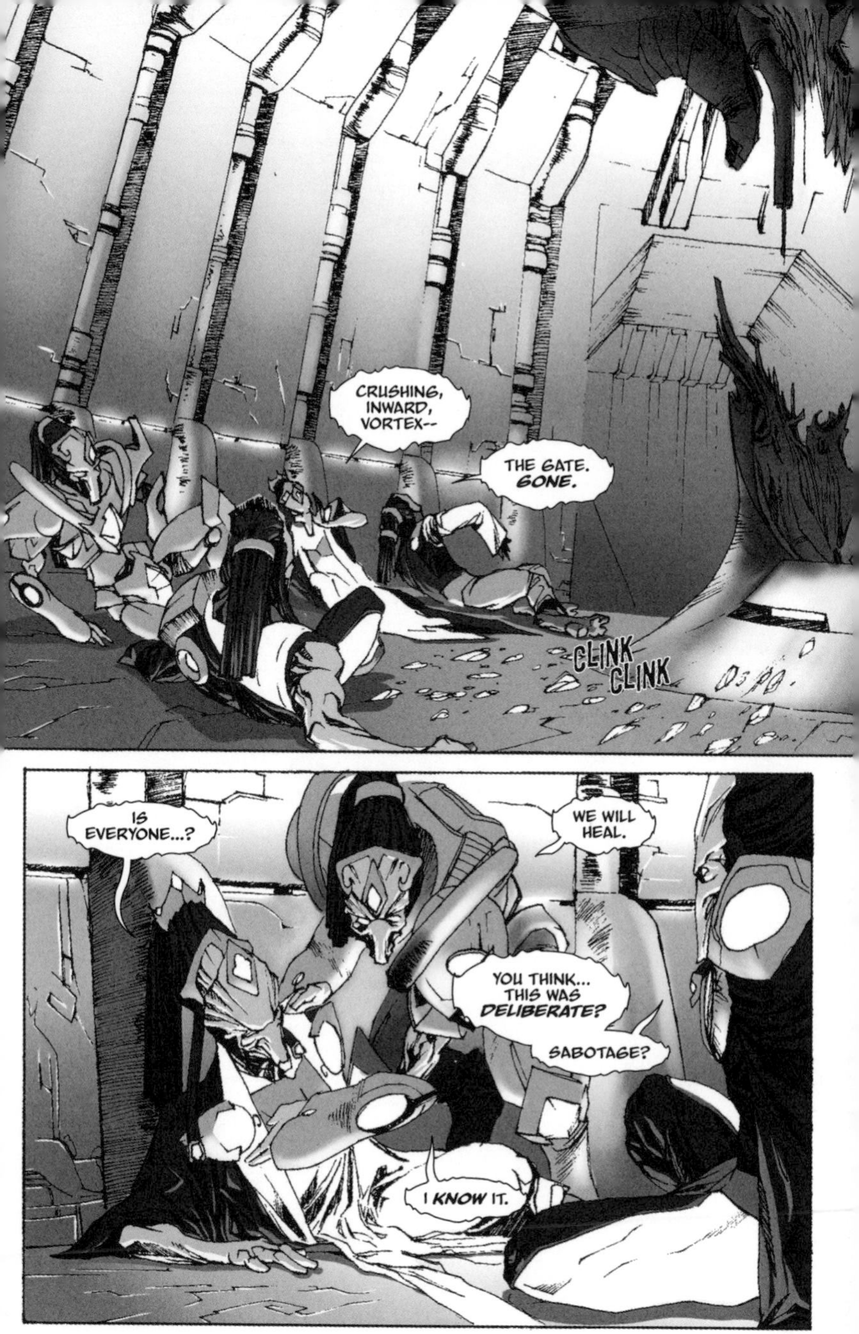

CRUSHING, INWARD, VORTEX--
THE GATE. GONE.
CLINK CLINK
IS EVERYONE...?
WE WILL HEAL.
YOU THINK... THIS WAS DELIBERATE?
SABOTAGE?
I KNOW IT.

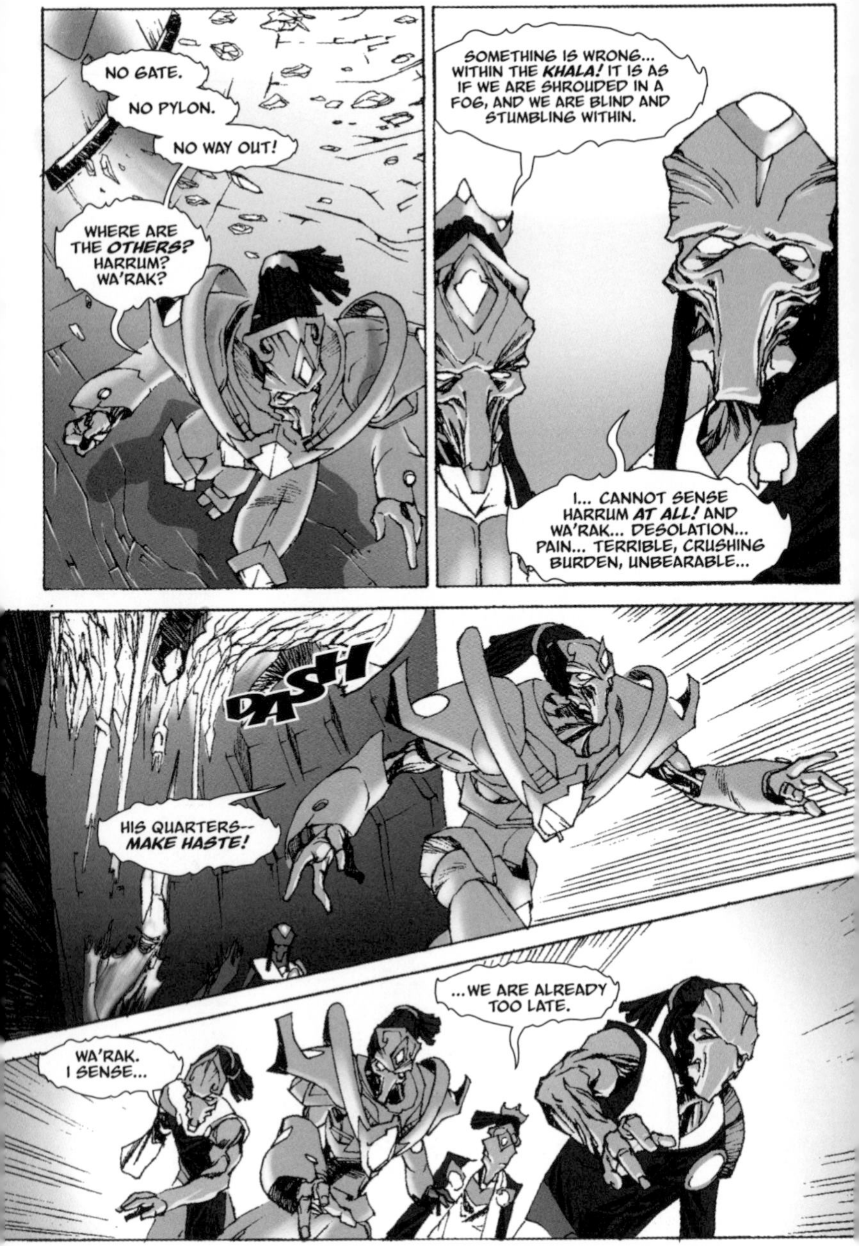
NO GATE.
NO PYLON.
NO WAY OUT!
WHERE ARE THE OTHERS? HARRUM? WA'RAK?
SOMETHING IS WRONG... WITHIN THE KHALA! IT IS AS IF WE ARE SHROUDED IN A FOG, AND WE ARE BLIND AND STUMBLING WITHIN.
I... CANNOT SENSE HARRUM AT ALL! AND WA'RAK... DESOLATION... PAIN... TERRIBLE, CRUSHING BURDEN, UNBEARABLE...
DASH
HIS QUARTERS-- MAKE HASTE!
WA'RAK. I SENSE...
...WE ARE ALREADY TOO LATE.

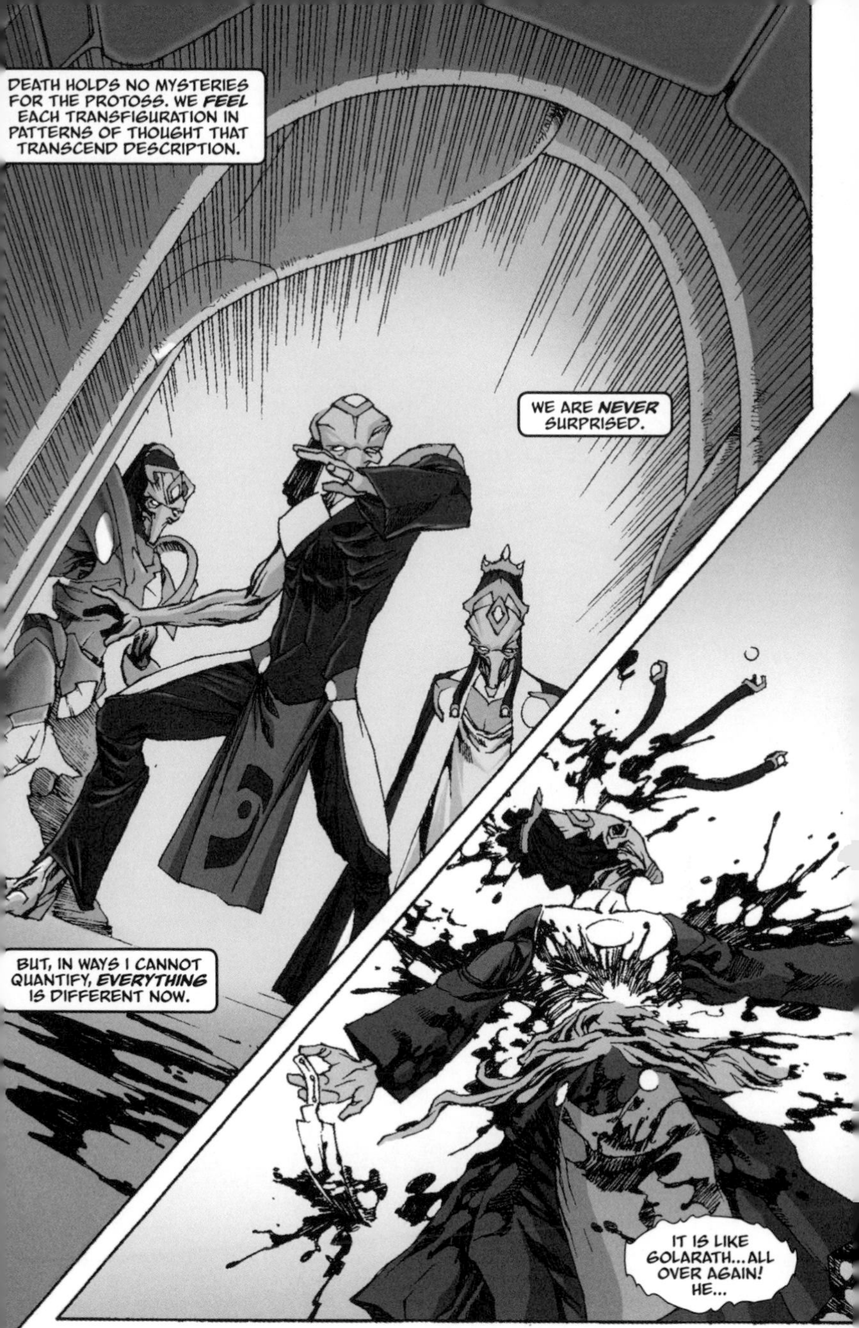
DEATH HOLDS NO MYSTERIES FOR THE PROTOSS. WE *FEEL* EACH TRANSFIGURATION IN PATTERNS OF THOUGHT THAT TRANSCEND DESCRIPTION.
WE ARE *NEVER* SURPRISED.
BUT, IN WAYS I CANNOT QUANTIFY, *EVERYTHING* IS DIFFERENT NOW.
IT IS LIKE GOLARATH...ALL OVER AGAIN! HE...

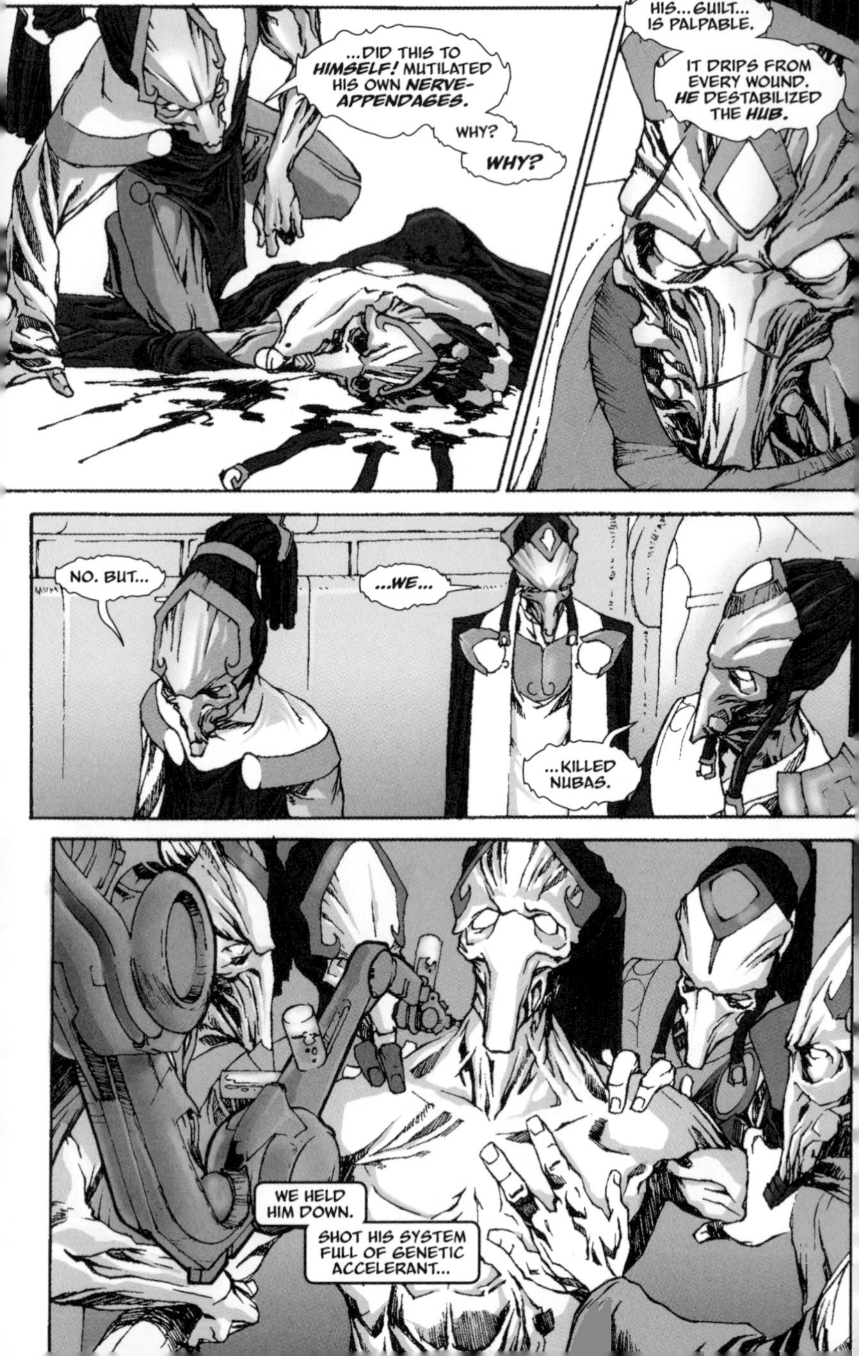
...DID THIS TO HIMSELF! MUTILATED HIS OWN NERVE-APPENDAGES.
WHY?
WHY?
HIS...GUILT... IS PALPABLE.
IT DRIPS FROM EVERY WOUND. HE DESTABILIZED THE HUB.
NO. BUT...
...WE...
...KILLED NUBAS.
WE HELD HIM DOWN.
SHOT HIS SYSTEM FULL OF GENETIC ACCELERANT...

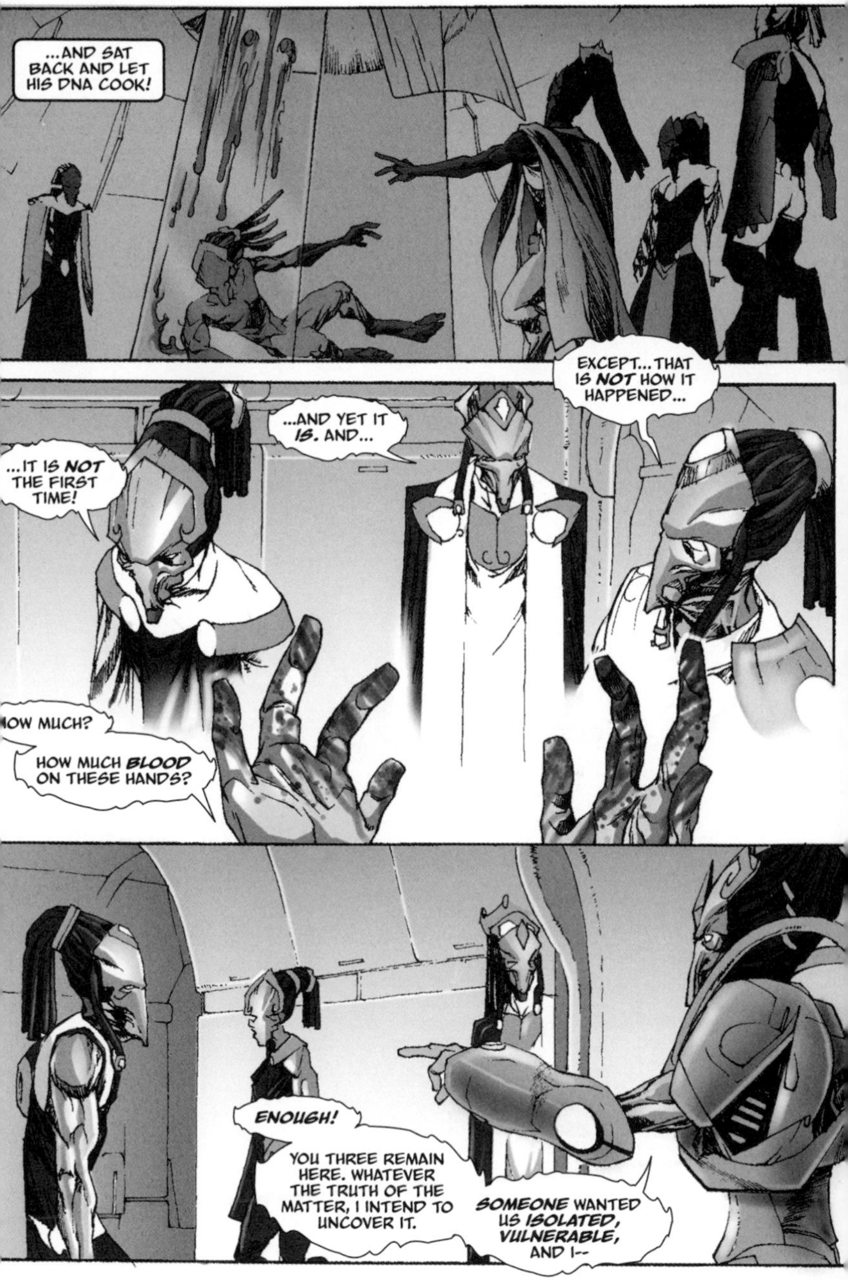
...AND SAT BACK AND LET HIS DNA COOK!
...IT IS NOT THE FIRST TIME!
...AND YET IT IS. AND...
EXCEPT... THAT IS NOT HOW IT HAPPENED...
HOW MUCH?
HOW MUCH BLOOD ON THESE HANDS?
ENOUGH!
YOU THREE REMAIN HERE. WHATEVER THE TRUTH OF THE MATTER, I INTEND TO UNCOVER IT.
SOMEONE WANTED US ISOLATED, VULNERABLE, AND I--

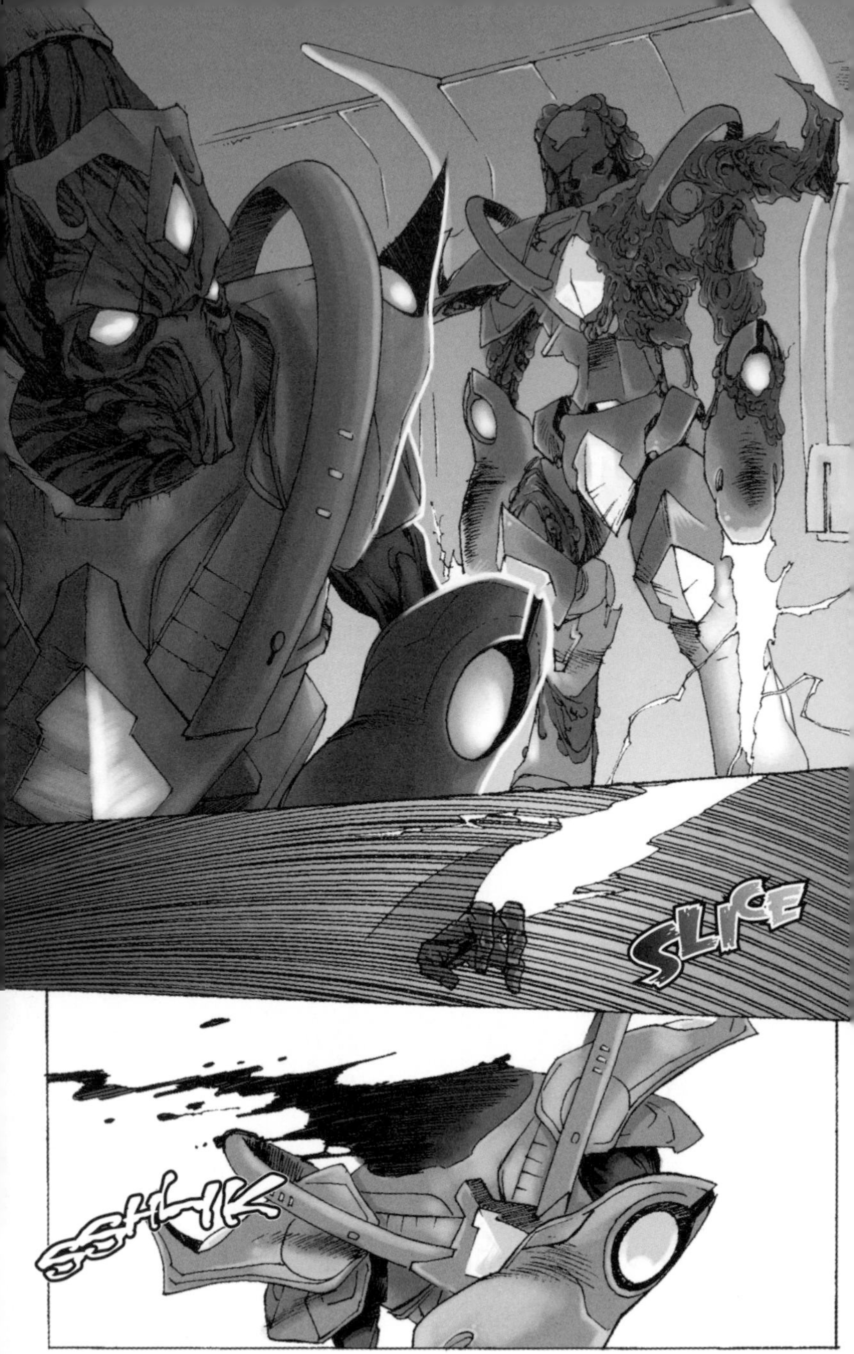
SLICE
SSHLIK

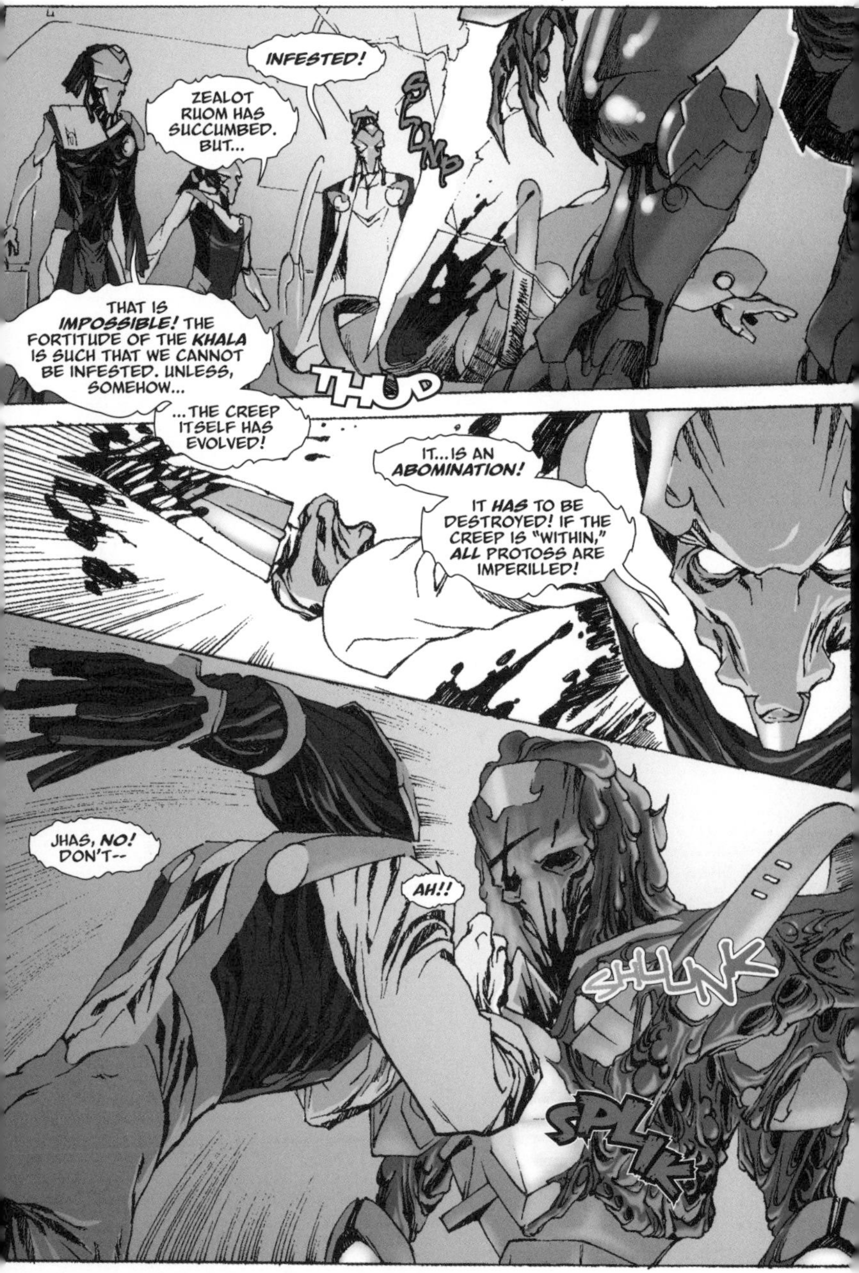
ZEALOT RUOM HAS SUCCUMBED. BUT...
INFESTED!
SLUNP
THAT IS IMPOSSIBLE! THE FORTITUDE OF THE KHALA IS SUCH THAT WE CANNOT BE INFESTED. UNLESS, SOMEHOW...
THUD
...THE CREEP ITSELF HAS EVOLVED!
IT...IS AN ABOMINATION!
IT HAS TO BE DESTROYED! IF THE CREEP IS "WITHIN," ALL PROTOSS ARE IMPERILLED!
JHAS, NO! DON'T--
AH!!
SHLUNK
SPLIK

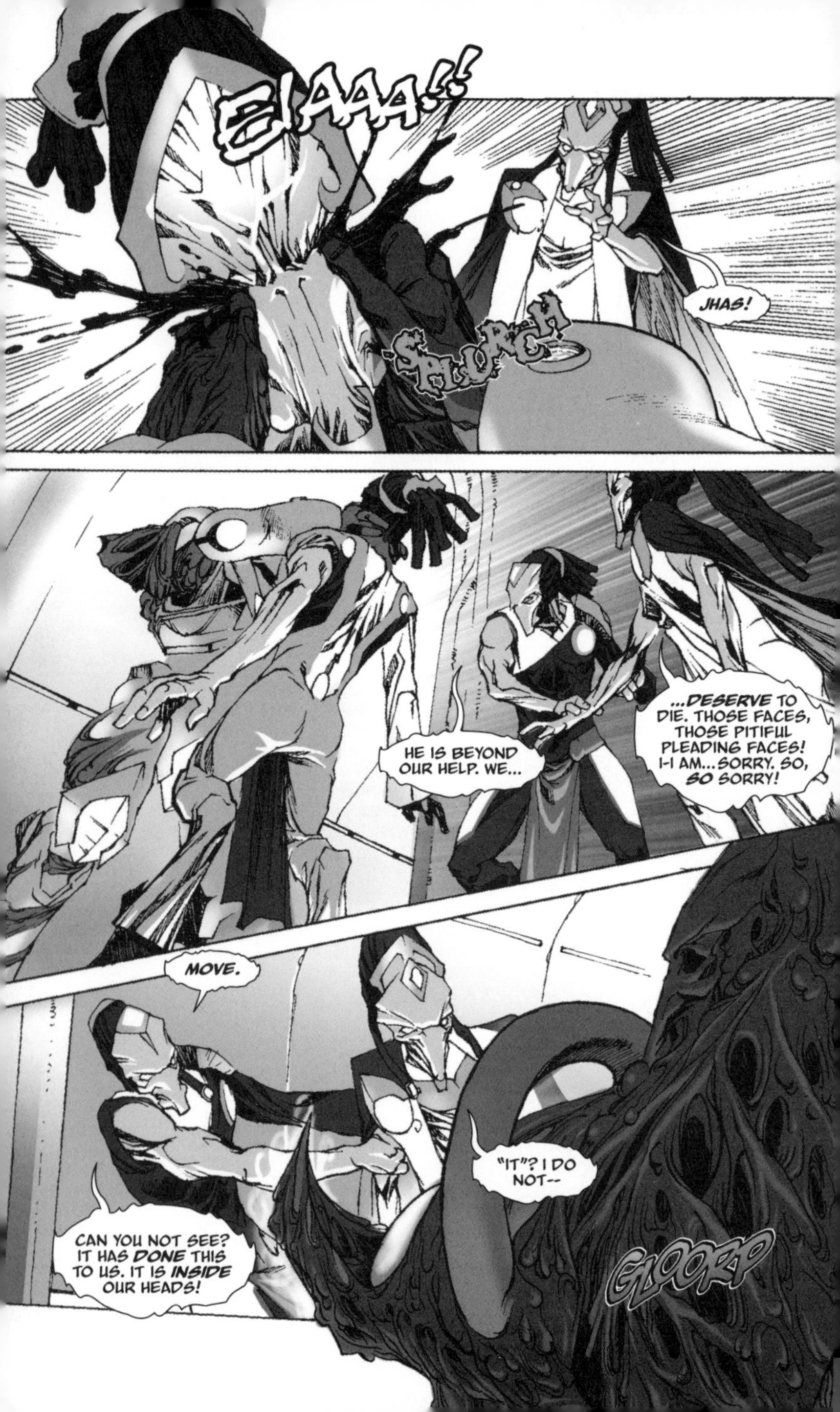
EIAAA!!
SPLURCH
JHAS!
HE IS BEYOND OUR HELP. WE...
...DESERVE TO DIE. THOSE FACES, THOSE PITIFUL PLEADING FACES! I-I AM...SORRY. SO, SO SORRY!
MOVE.
CAN YOU NOT SEE? IT HAS DONE THIS TO US. IT IS INSIDE OUR HEADS!
"IT"? I DO NOT--
GLOORP

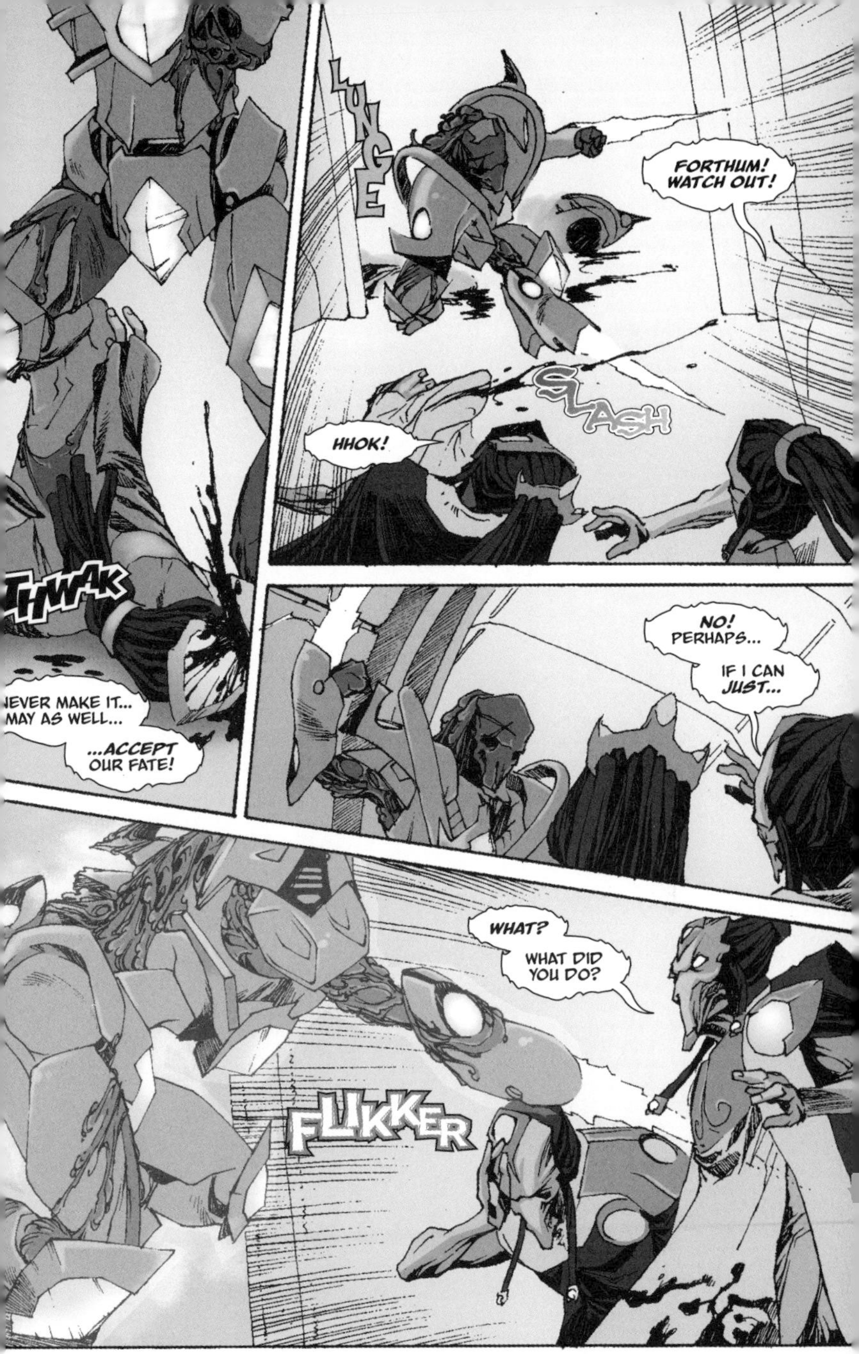
THWAK
NEVER MAKE IT... MAY AS WELL...
...ACCEPT OUR FATE!
LUNGE
FORTHUM! WATCH OUT!
SLASH
HHOK!
NO! PERHAPS...
IF I CAN JUST...
WHAT?
WHAT DID YOU DO?
FLIKKER

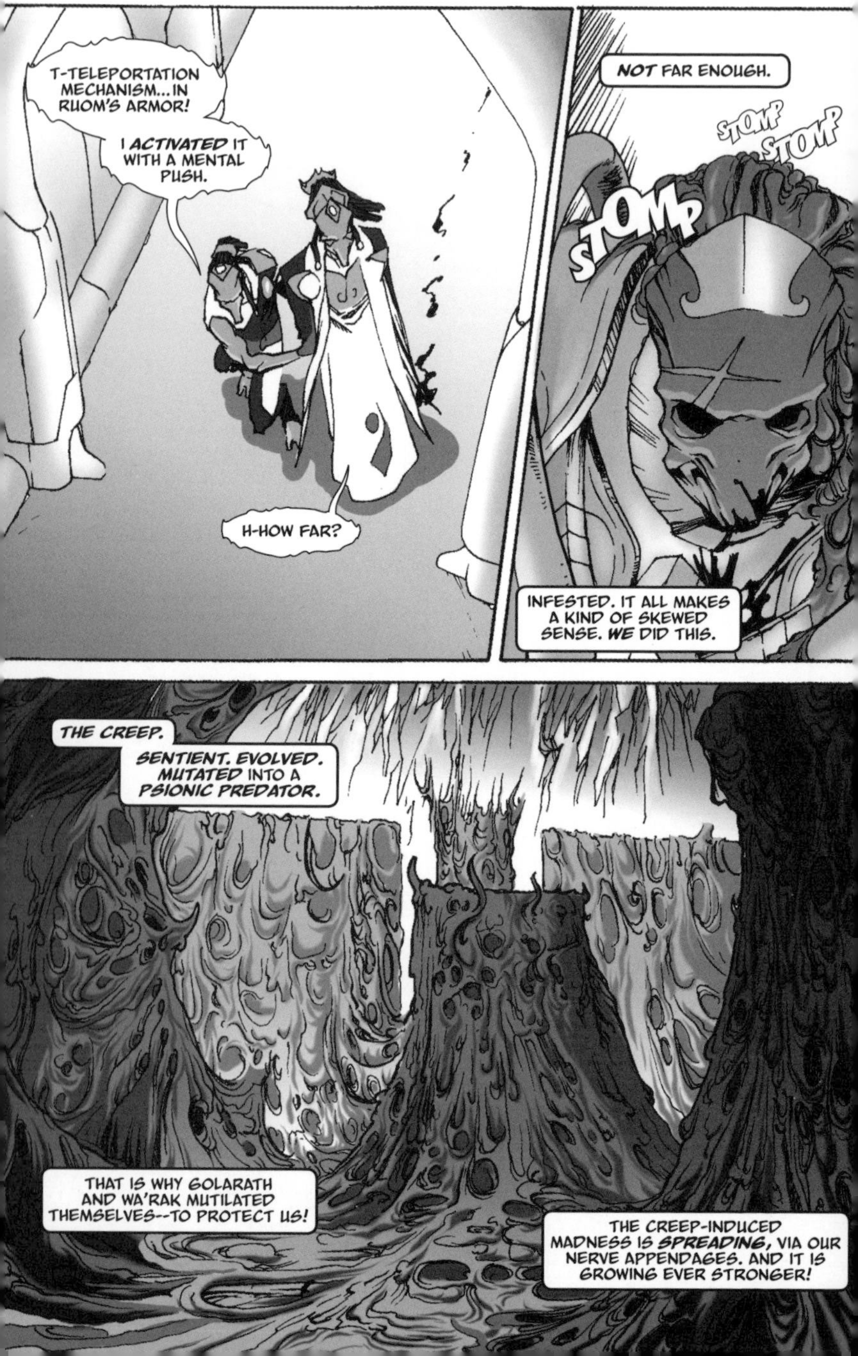
T-TELEPORTATION MECHANISM...IN RUOM'S ARMOR!
I ACTIVATED IT WITH A MENTAL PUSH.
H-HOW FAR?
NOT FAR ENOUGH.
STOMP STOMP
STOMP
INFESTED. IT ALL MAKES A KIND OF SKEWED SENSE. WE DID THIS.
THE CREEP.
SENTIENT. EVOLVED. MUTATED INTO A PSIONIC PREDATOR.
THAT IS WHY GOLARATH AND WA'RAK MUTILATED THEMSELVES--TO PROTECT US!
THE CREEP-INDUCED MADNESS IS SPREADING, VIA OUR NERVE APPENDAGES. AND IT IS GROWING EVER STRONGER!

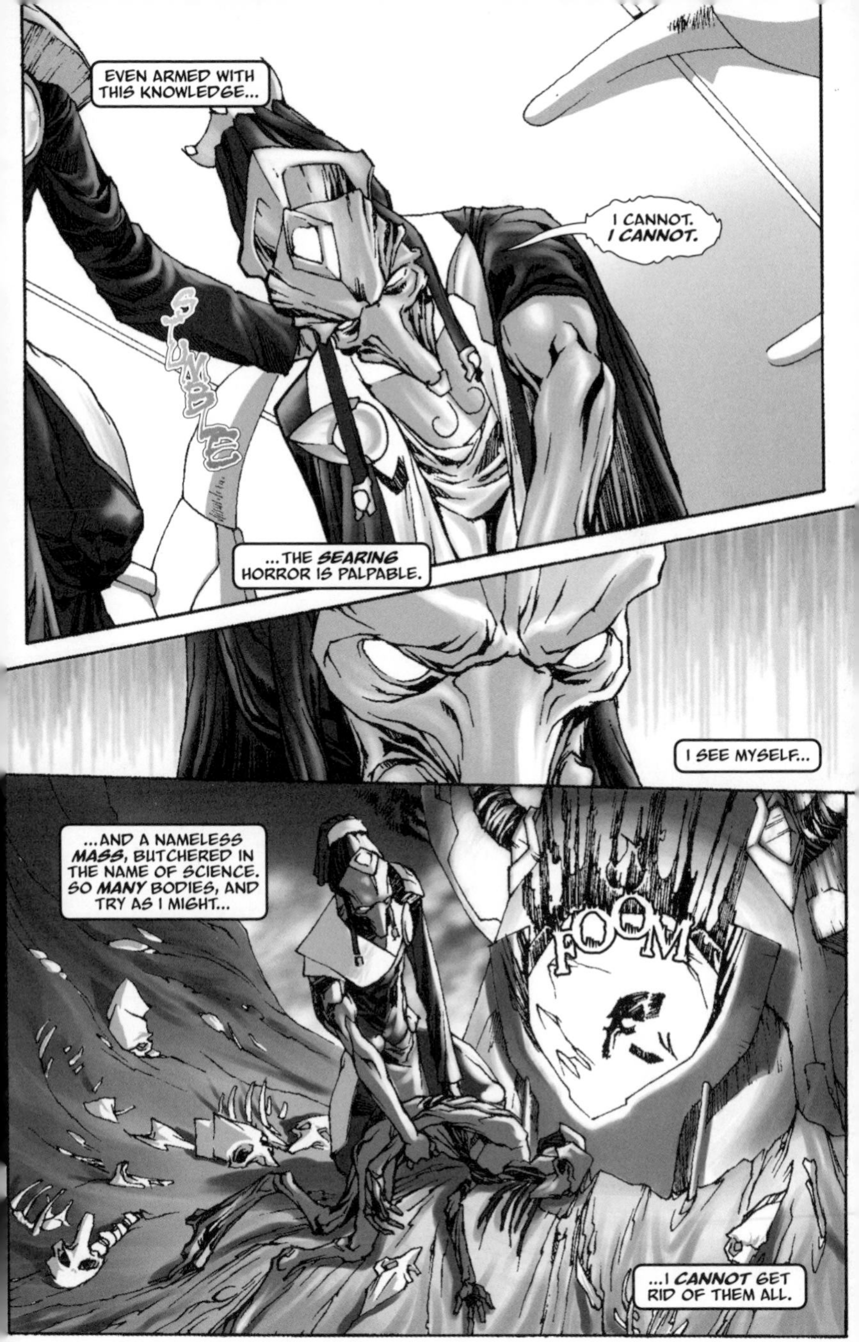
EVEN ARMED WITH THIS KNOWLEDGE...
I CANNOT. I CANNOT.
STUMBLE
...THE SEARING HORROR IS PALPABLE.
I SEE MYSELF...
...AND A NAMELESS MASS, BUTCHERED IN THE NAME OF SCIENCE. SO MANY BODIES, AND TRY AS I MIGHT...
FOOM
...I CANNOT GET RID OF THEM ALL.

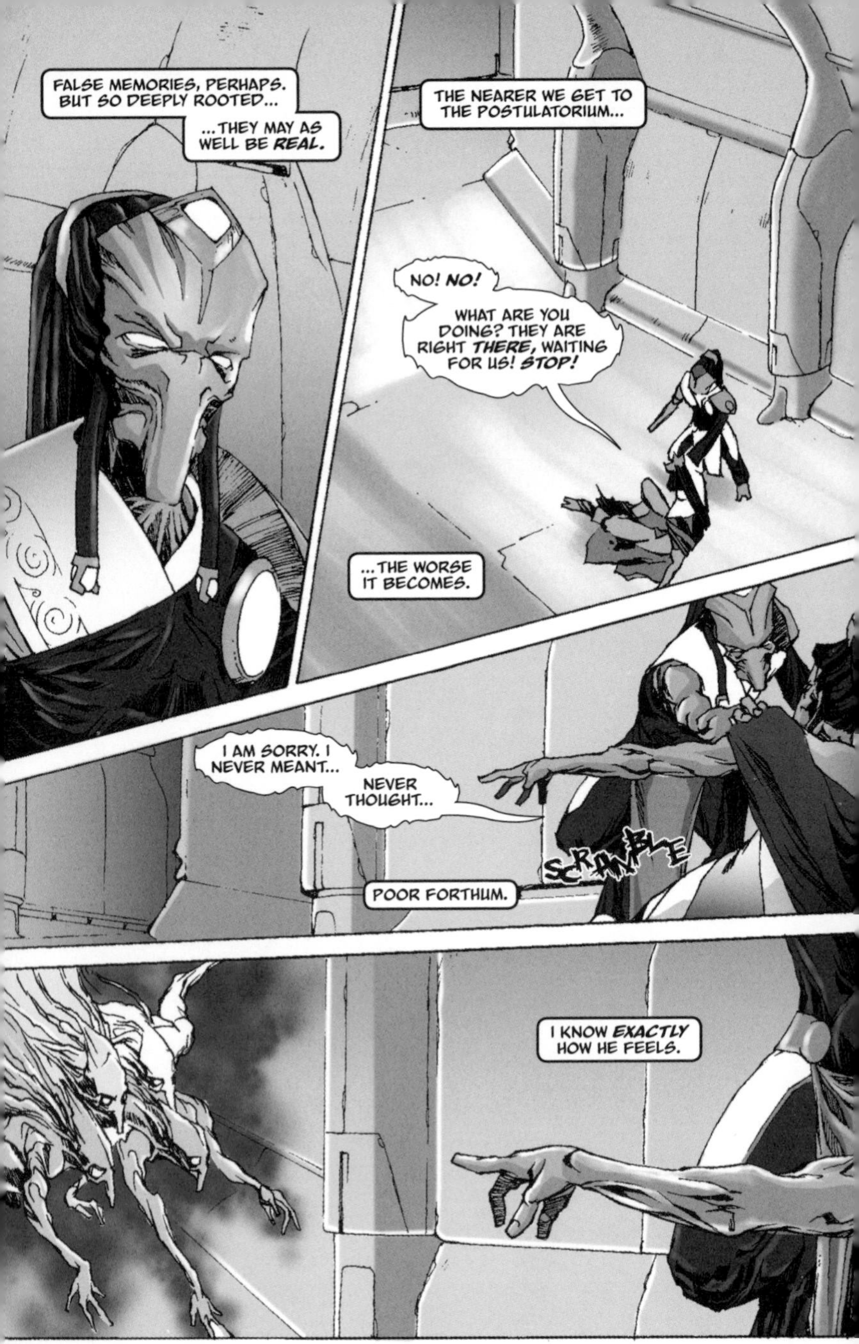
FALSE MEMORIES, PERHAPS. BUT SO DEEPLY ROOTED...
...THEY MAY AS WELL BE REAL.
THE NEARER WE GET TO THE POSTULATORIUM...
NO! NO!
WHAT ARE YOU DOING? THEY ARE RIGHT THERE, WAITING FOR US! STOP!
...THE WORSE IT BECOMES.
I AM SORRY. I NEVER MEANT...
NEVER THOUGHT...
SCRAMBLE
POOR FORTHUM.
I KNOW EXACTLY HOW HE FEELS.

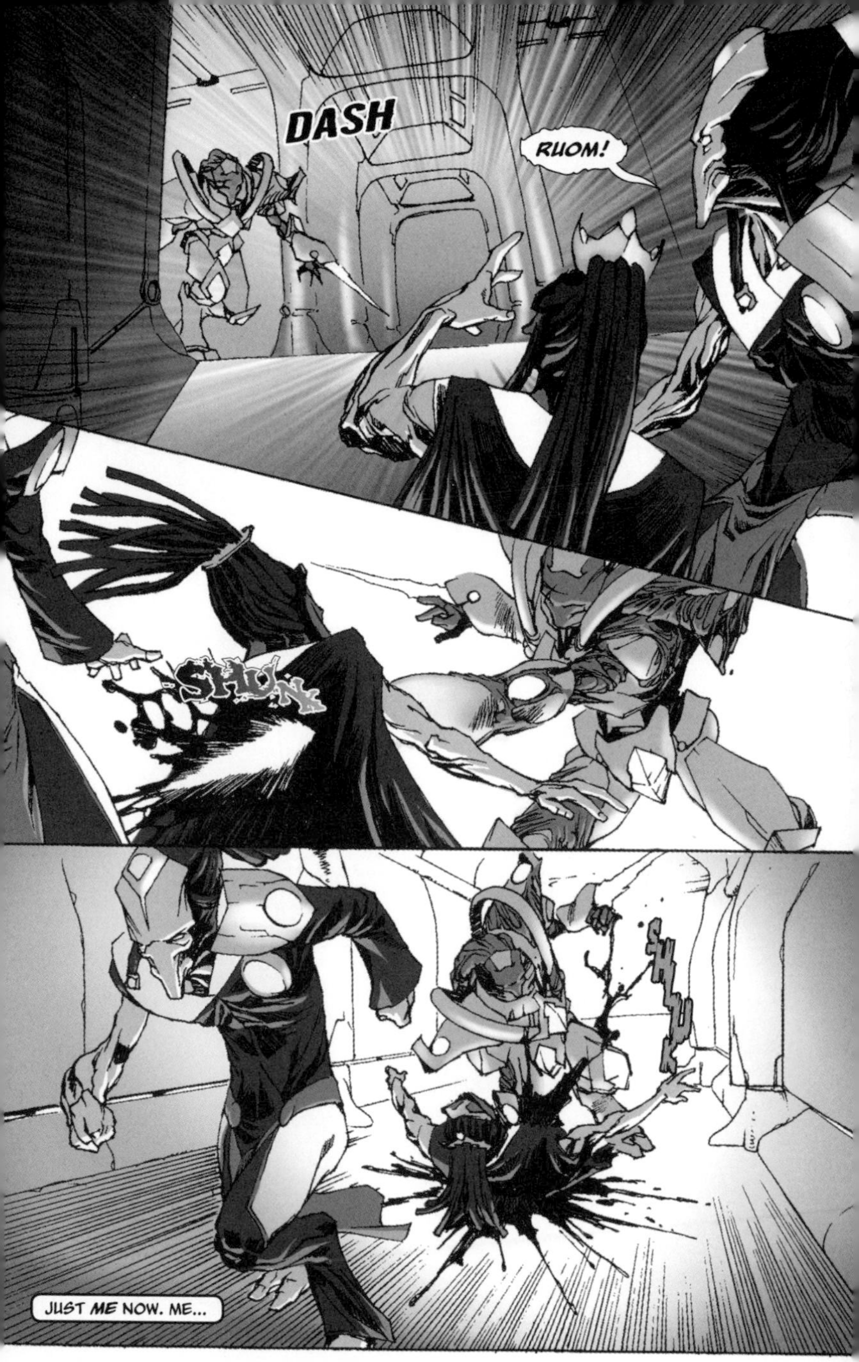
DASH
RUOM!
SHUNK
SHLUK
JUST ME NOW. ME...

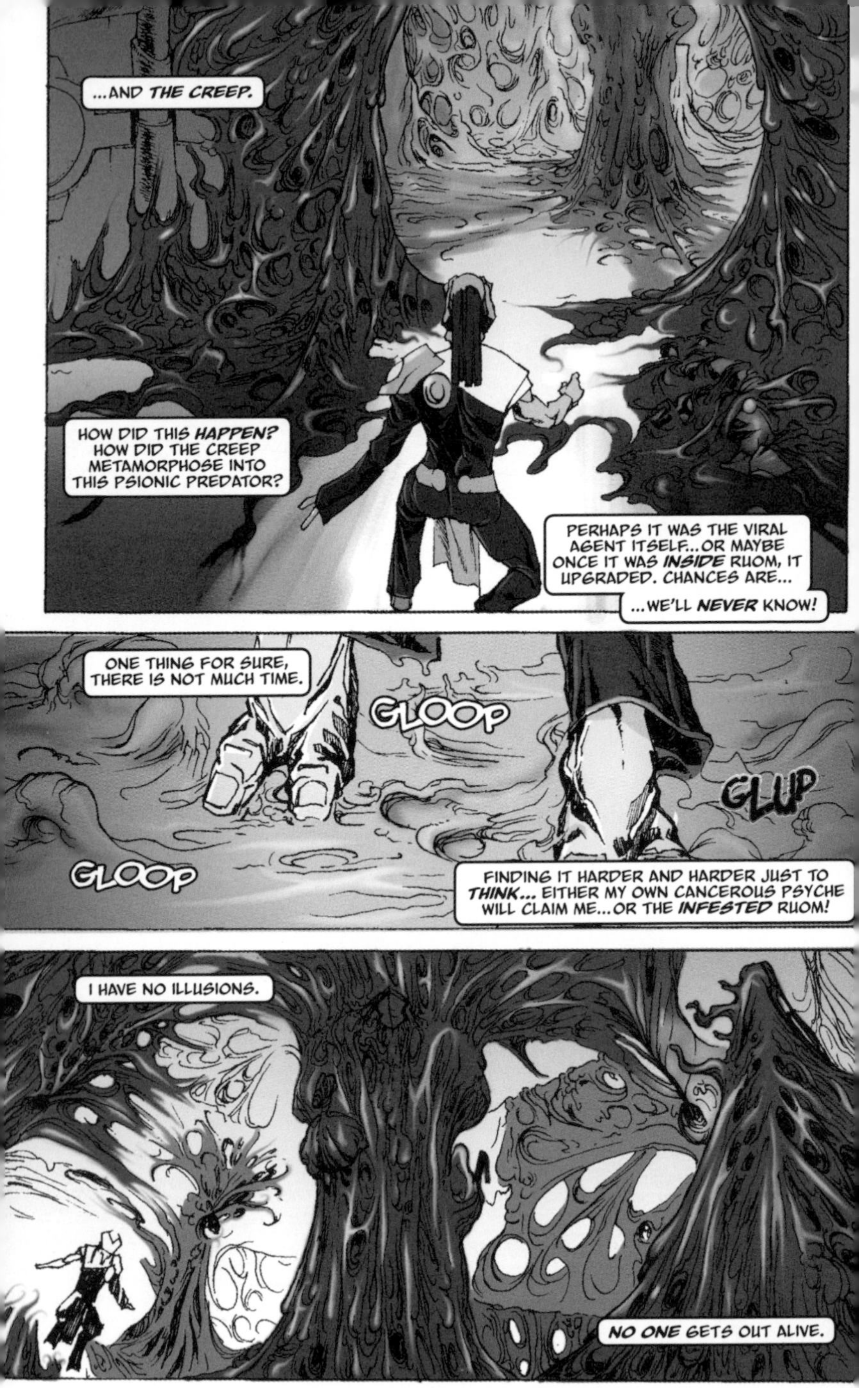
...AND THE CREEP.
HOW DID THIS HAPPEN? HOW DID THE CREEP METAMORPHOSE INTO THIS PSIONIC PREDATOR?
PERHAPS IT WAS THE VIRAL AGENT ITSELF...OR MAYBE ONCE IT WAS INSIDE RUOM, IT UPGRADED. CHANCES ARE...
...WE'LL NEVER KNOW!
ONE THING FOR SURE, THERE IS NOT MUCH TIME.
GLOOP
GLUP
GLOOP
FINDING IT HARDER AND HARDER JUST TO THINK... EITHER MY OWN CANCEROUS PSYCHE WILL CLAIM ME...OR THE INFESTED RUOM!
I HAVE NO ILLUSIONS.
NO ONE GETS OUT ALIVE.

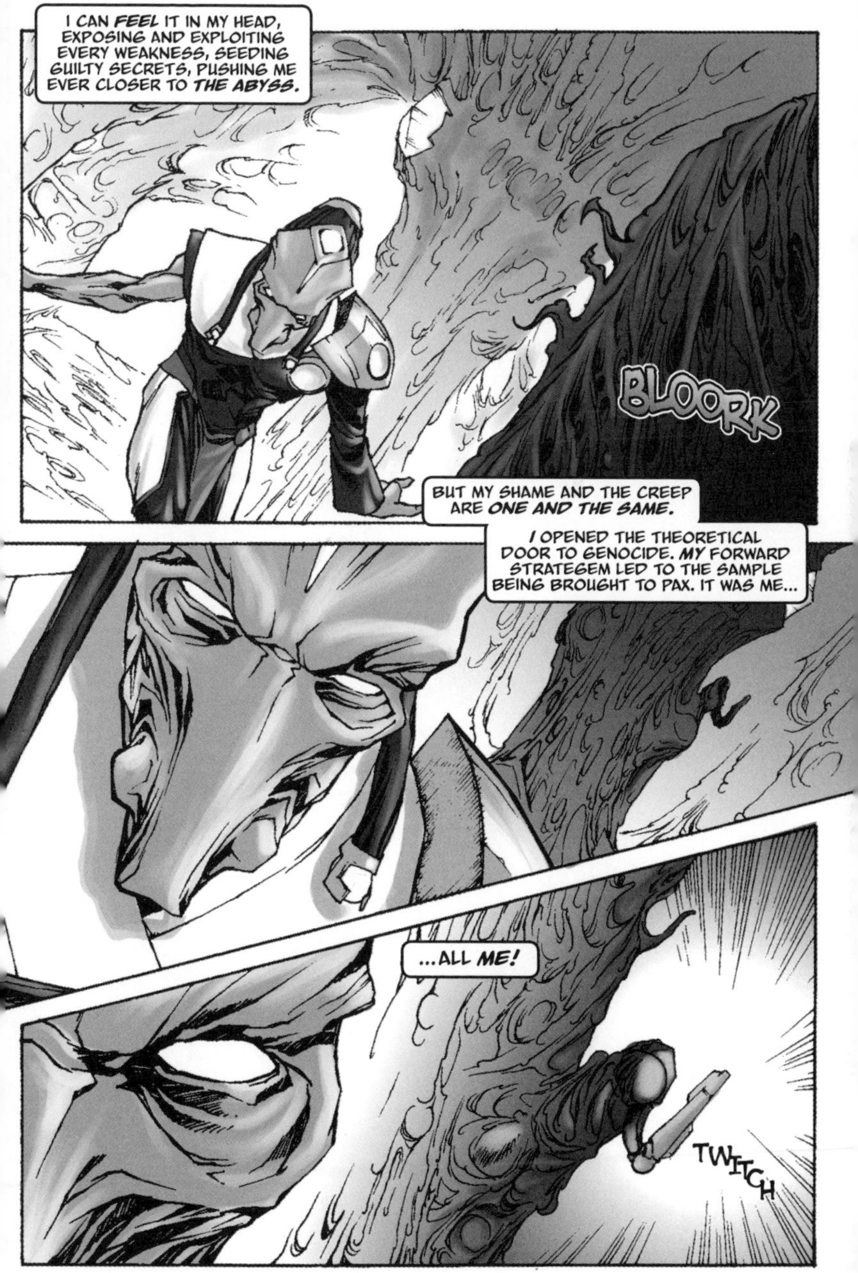

I CAN FEEL IT IN MY HEAD, EXPOSING AND EXPLOITING EVERY WEAKNESS, SEEDING GUILTY SECRETS, PUSHING ME EVER CLOSER TO THE ABYSS.
BLOORK
BUT MY SHAME AND THE CREEP ARE ONE AND THE SAME.
I OPENED THE THEORETICAL DOOR TO GENOCIDE. MY FORWARD STRATEGEM LED TO THE SAMPLE BEING BROUGHT TO PAX. IT WAS ME...
...ALL ME!
TWITCH

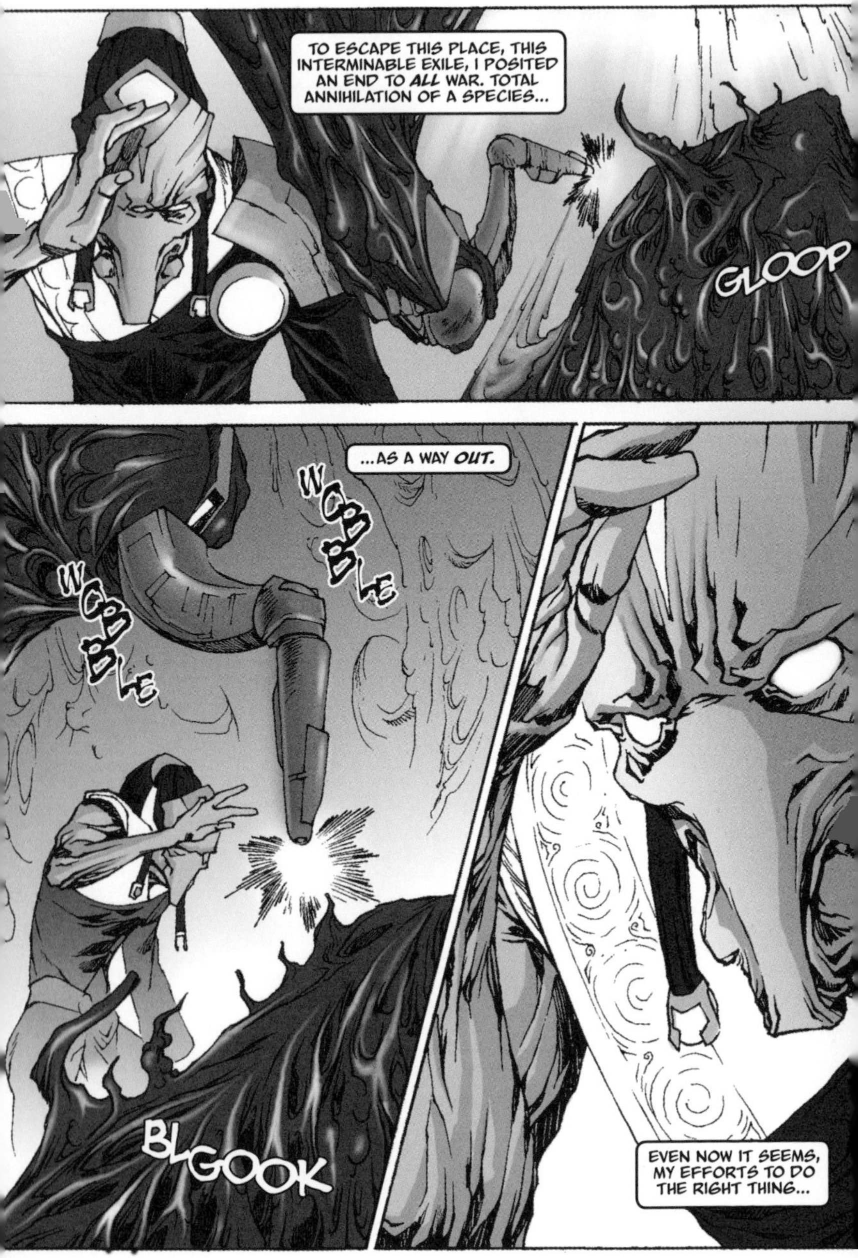
TO ESCAPE THIS PLACE, THIS INTERMINABLE EXILE, I POSITED AN END TO *ALL* WAR. TOTAL ANNIHILATION OF A SPECIES...
GLOOP
...AS A WAY *OUT.*
WOBBLE
WOBBLE
BLGOOK
EVEN NOW IT SEEMS, MY EFFORTS TO DO THE RIGHT THING...

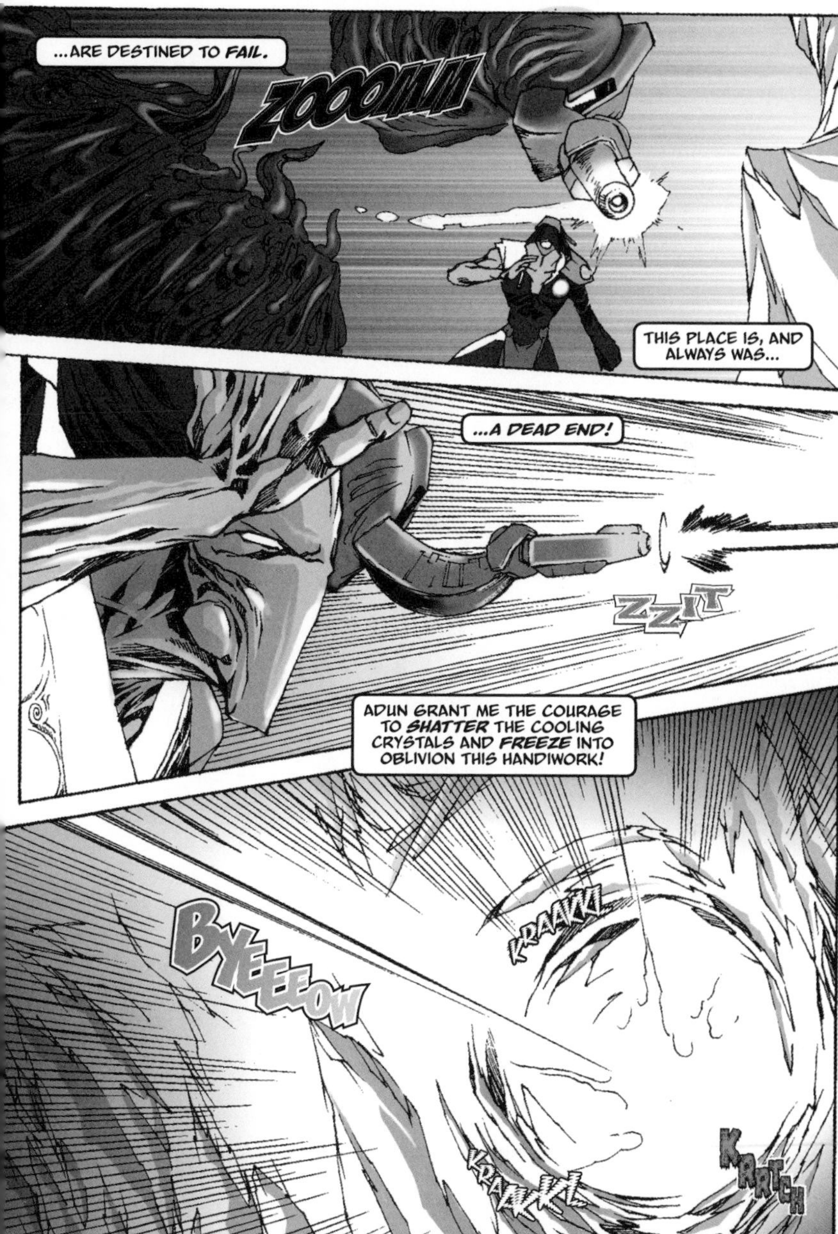
...ARE DESTINED TO FAIL.
ZOOOMM
THIS PLACE IS, AND ALWAYS WAS...
...A DEAD END!
ZZIT
ADUN GRANT ME THE COURAGE TO SHATTER THE COOLING CRYSTALS AND FREEZE INTO OBLIVION THIS HANDIWORK!
BYEEEOW
KRAAKKL
KRAAKKL
KRRTCH

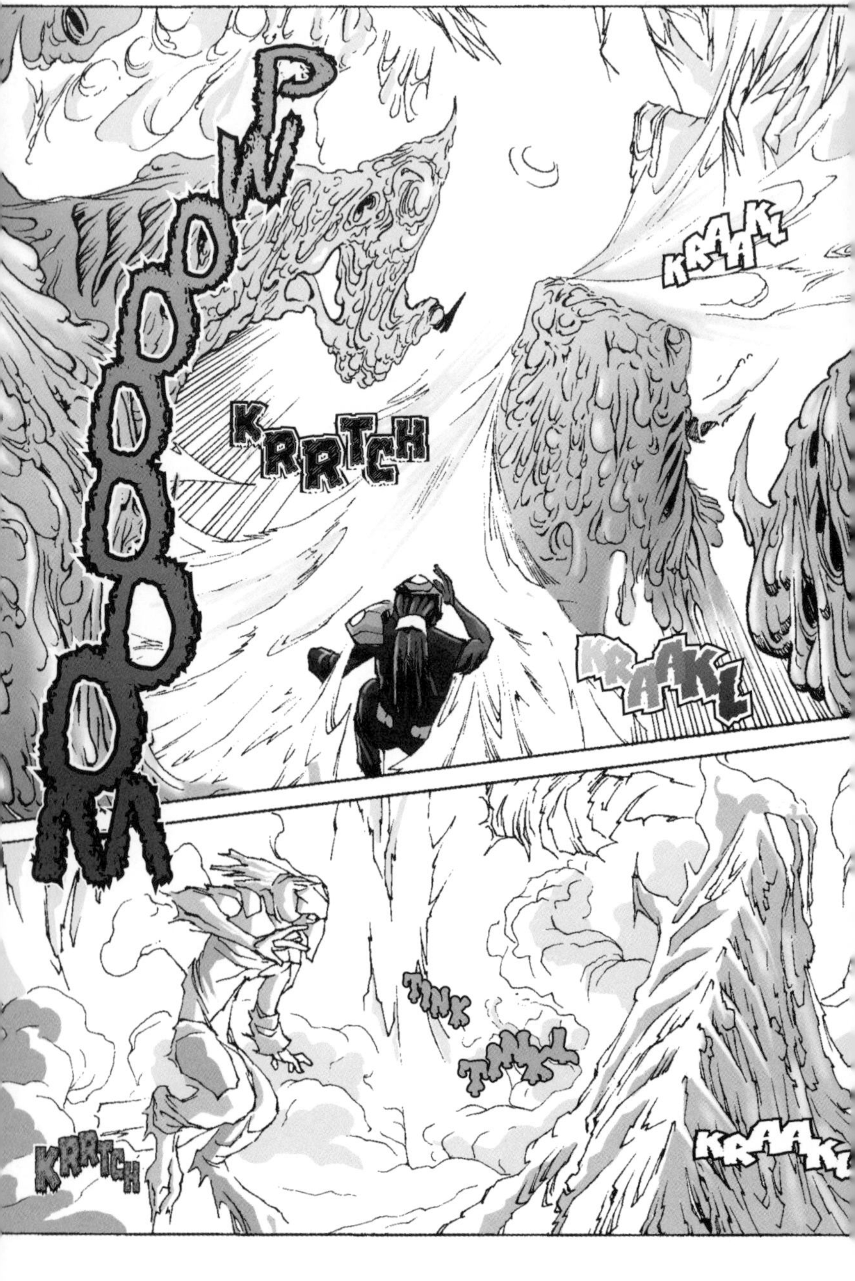
PWOOOOOOM
KRAAAKL
KRRRTCH
KRAAAKL
TINK
TINKL
KRRTCH
KRAAAKL

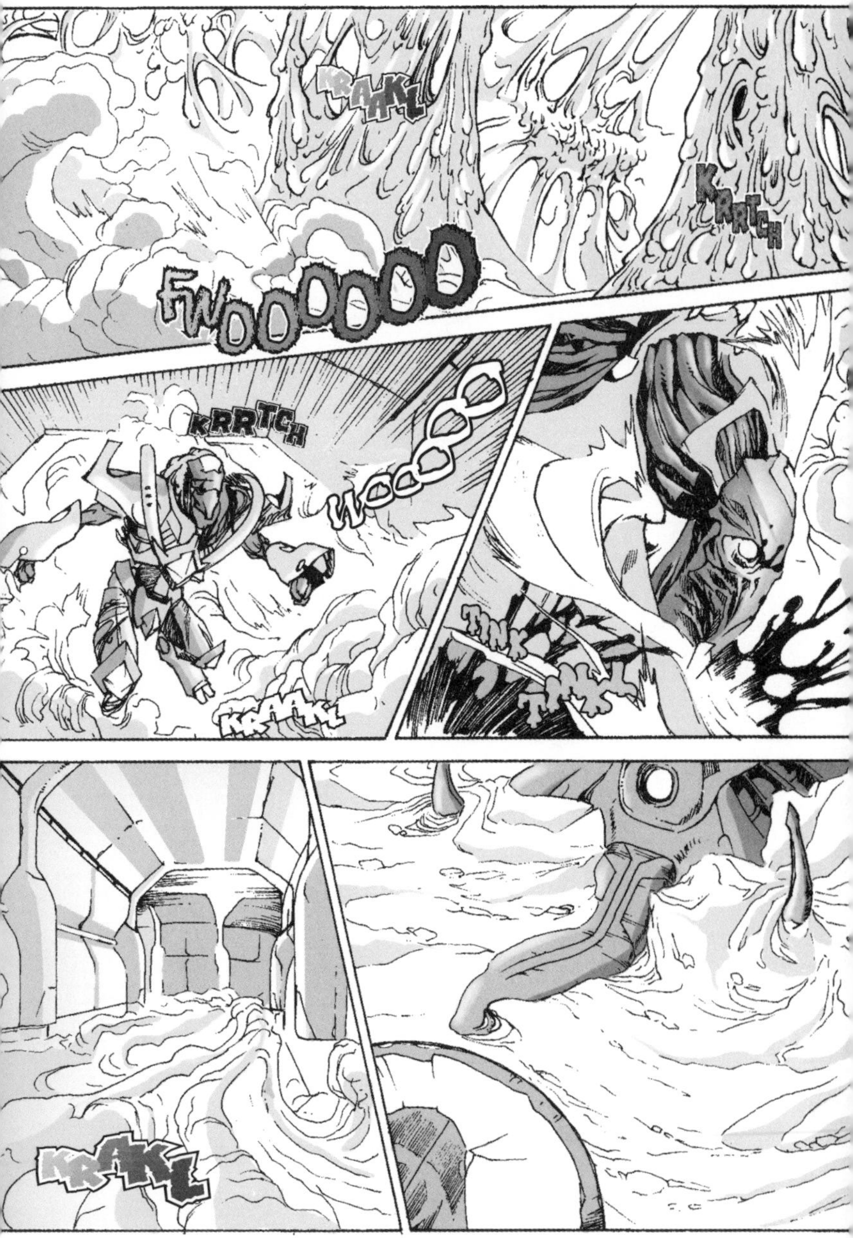
KRAAKL
KRRTCH
FWOOOOOOO
KRRRTCH
WOOOOO
KRAAKL
TINK TINK
KRAKL

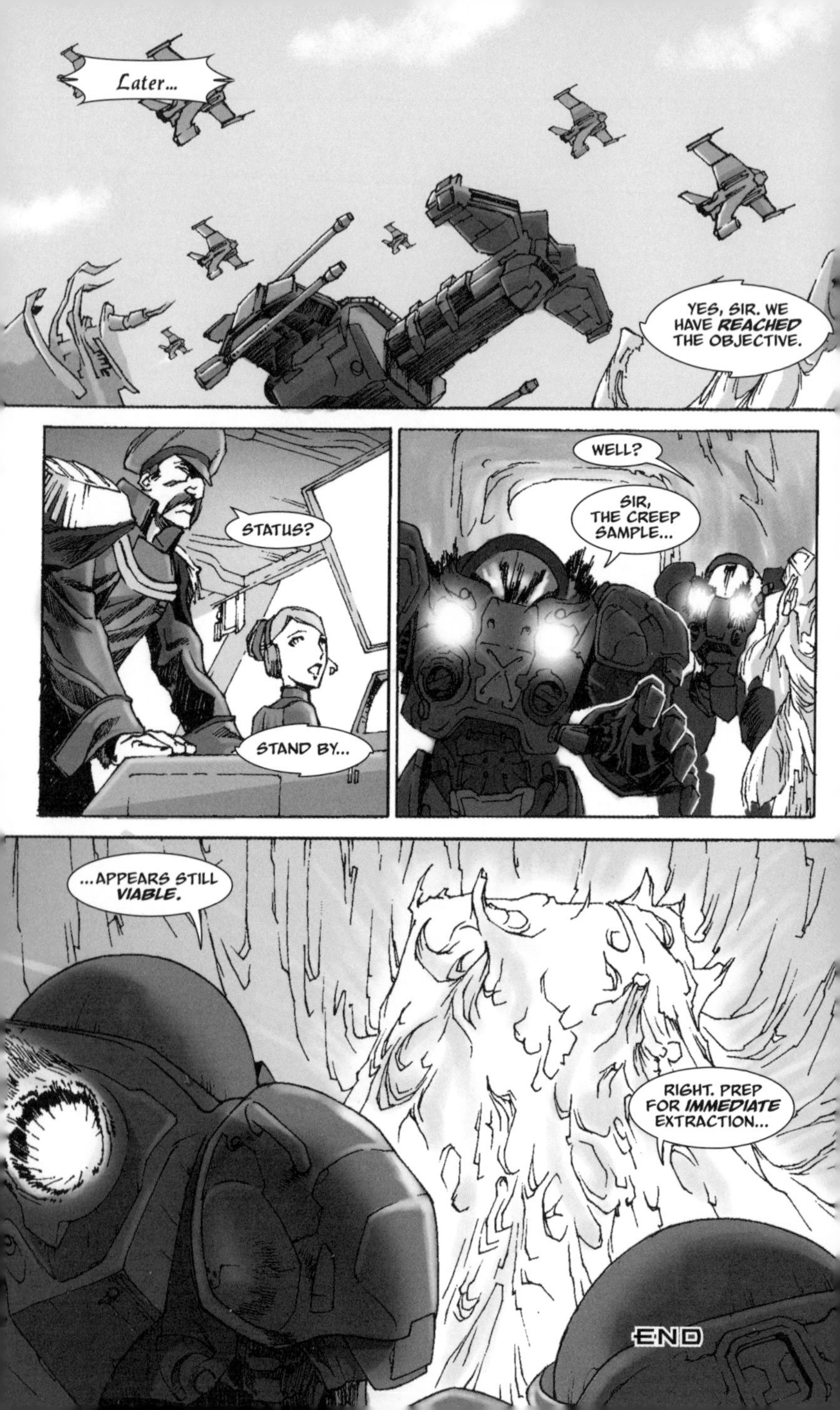
Later...
YES, SIR. WE HAVE REACHED THE OBJECTIVE.
STATUS?
STAND BY...
WELL?
SIR, THE CREEP SAMPLE...
...APPEARS STILL VIABLE.
RIGHT. PREP FOR IMMEDIATE EXTRACTION...
END

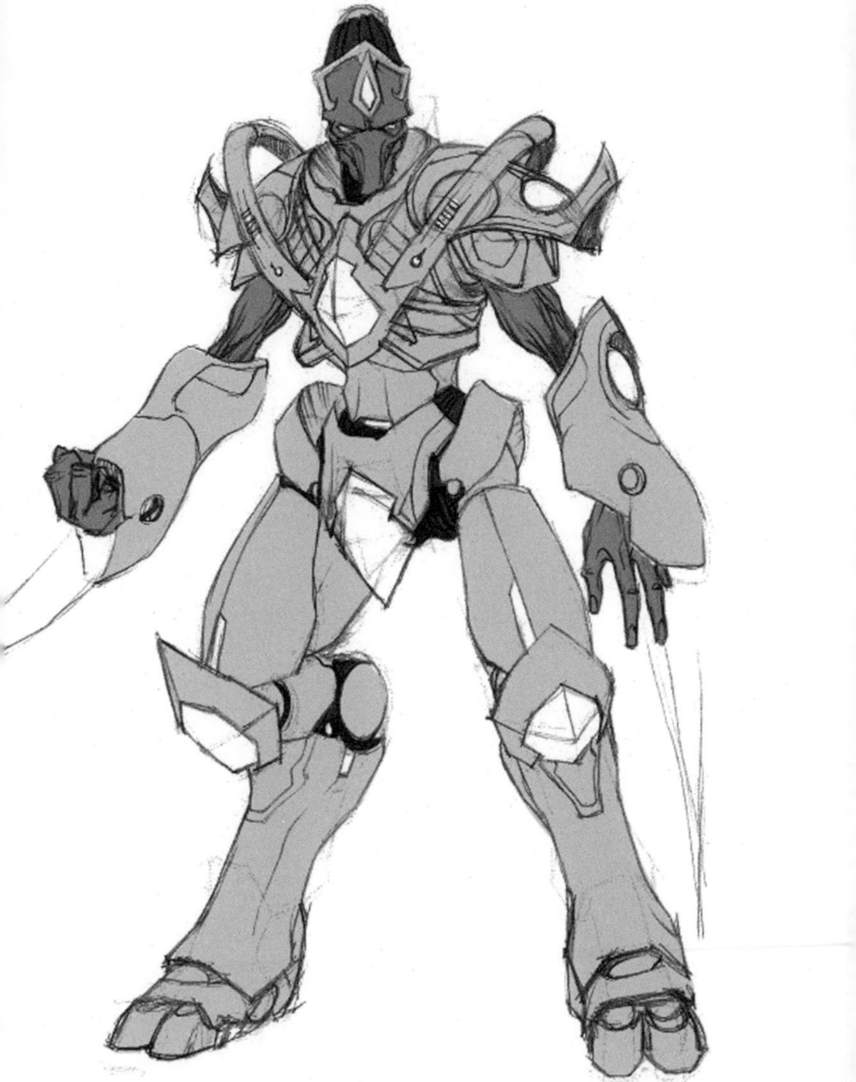

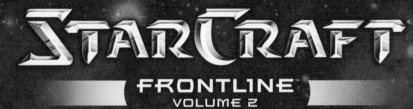

StarCraft

Frontline
Volume 2

Newsworthy

Written by Grace Randolph

Art by Nam Kim
Inks by Matt Dalton
Tones by Studioil
Studioil Staff: AJ Ford 3, Ben Harvey & Shiwah Wong

Letterer: Michael Paolilli

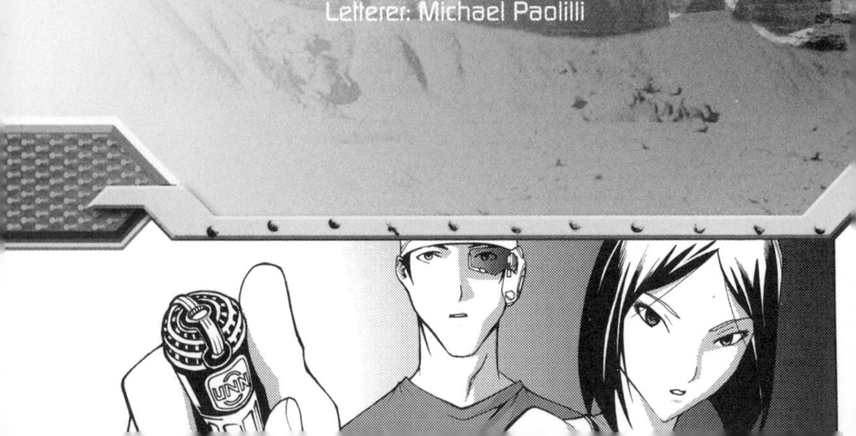

UNN

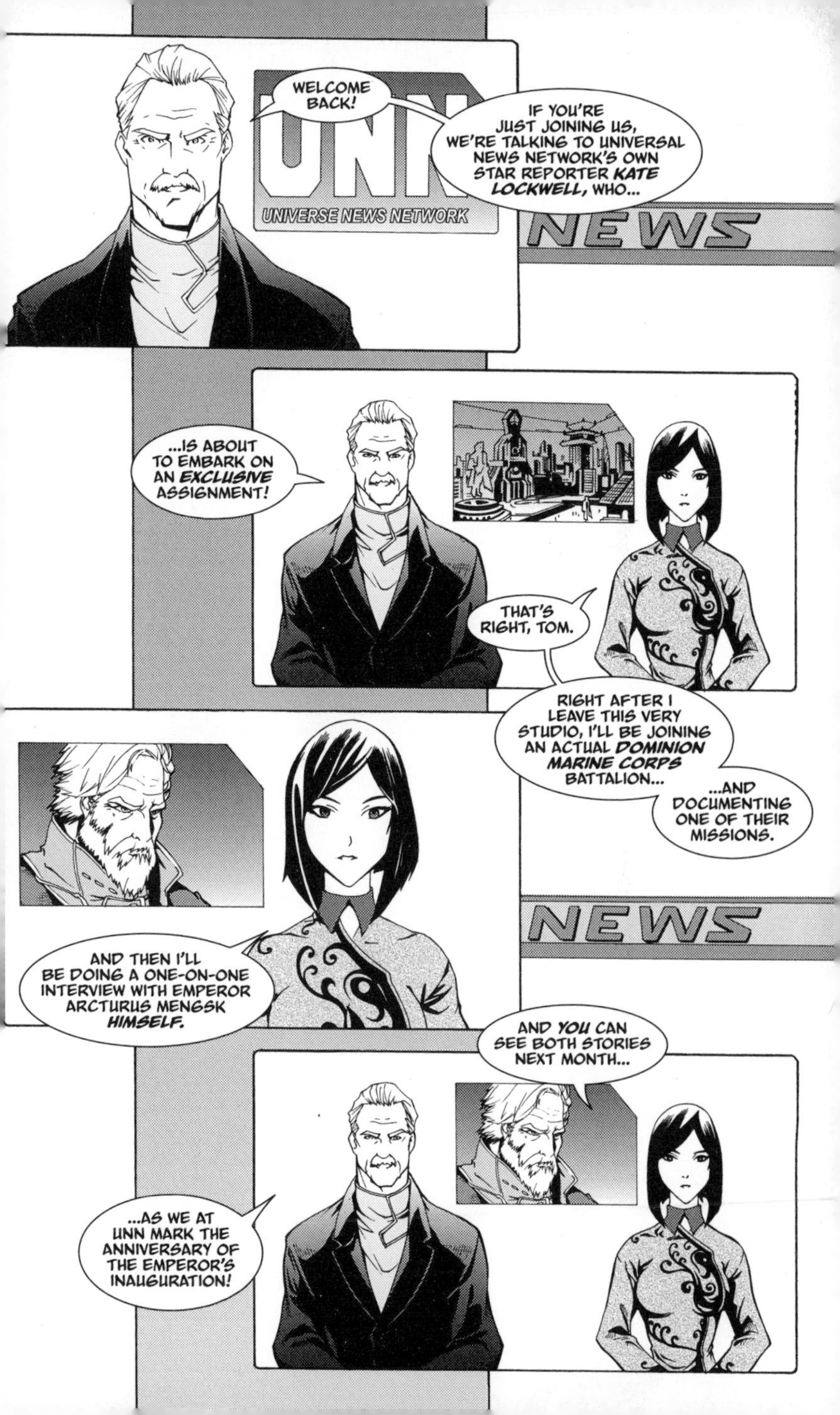

WELCOME BACK!
UNN
UNIVERSE NEWS NETWORK
IF YOU'RE JUST JOINING US, WE'RE TALKING TO UNIVERSAL NEWS NETWORK'S OWN STAR REPORTER KATE LOCKWELL, WHO...
NEWS
...IS ABOUT TO EMBARK ON AN EXCLUSIVE ASSIGNMENT!
THAT'S RIGHT, TOM.
RIGHT AFTER I LEAVE THIS VERY STUDIO, I'LL BE JOINING AN ACTUAL DOMINION MARINE CORPS BATTALION...
...AND DOCUMENTING ONE OF THEIR MISSIONS.
NEWS
AND THEN I'LL BE DOING A ONE-ON-ONE INTERVIEW WITH EMPEROR ARCTURUS MENGSK HIMSELF.
AND YOU CAN SEE BOTH STORIES NEXT MONTH...
...AS WE AT UNN MARK THE ANNIVERSARY OF THE EMPEROR'S INAUGURATION!

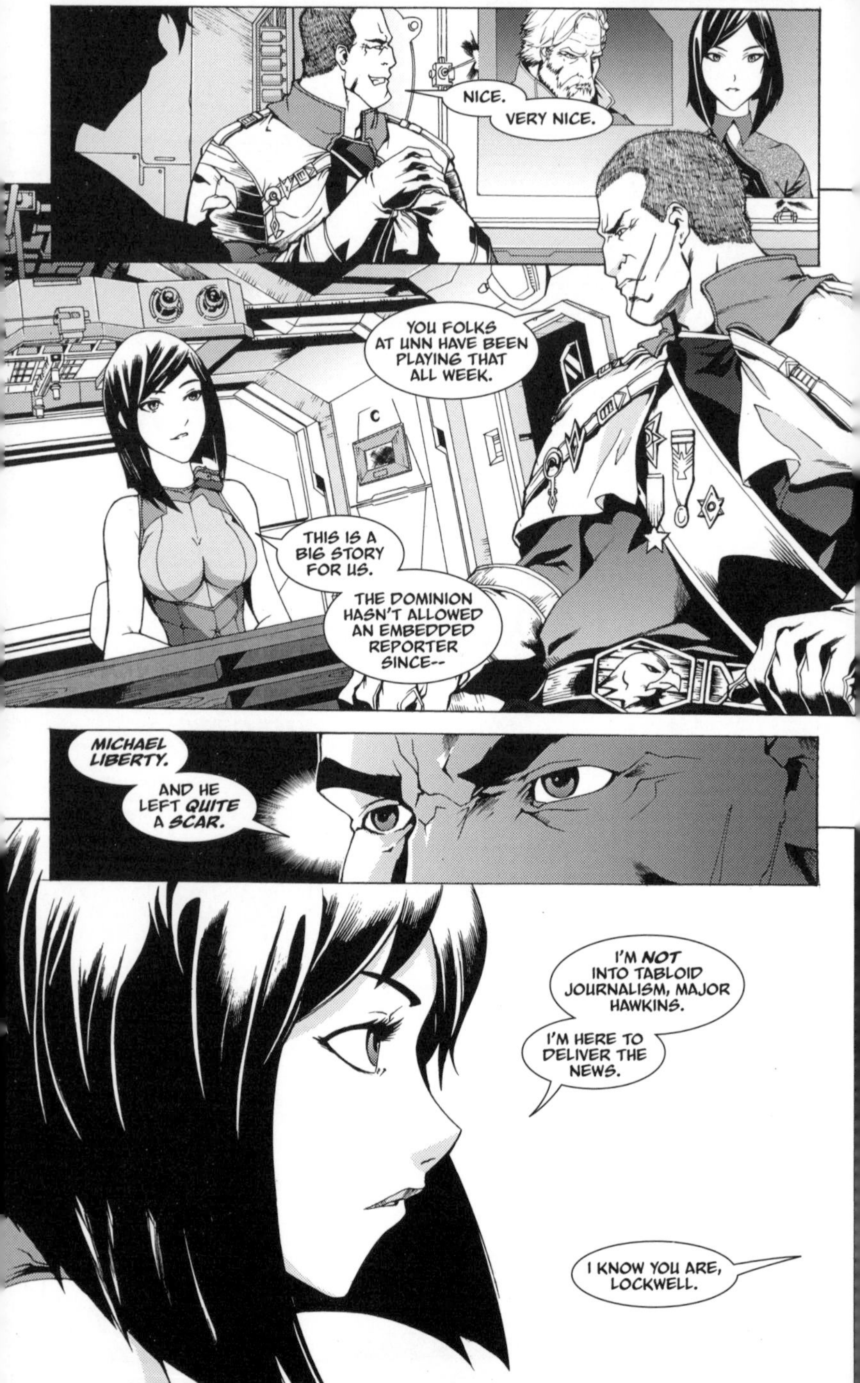

NICE.
VERY NICE.
YOU FOLKS AT UNN HAVE BEEN PLAYING THAT ALL WEEK.
THIS IS A BIG STORY FOR US.
THE DOMINION HASN'T ALLOWED AN EMBEDDED REPORTER SINCE--
MICHAEL LIBERTY.
AND HE LEFT QUITE A SCAR.
I'M NOT INTO TABLOID JOURNALISM, MAJOR HAWKINS.
I'M HERE TO DELIVER THE NEWS.
I KNOW YOU ARE, LOCKWELL.

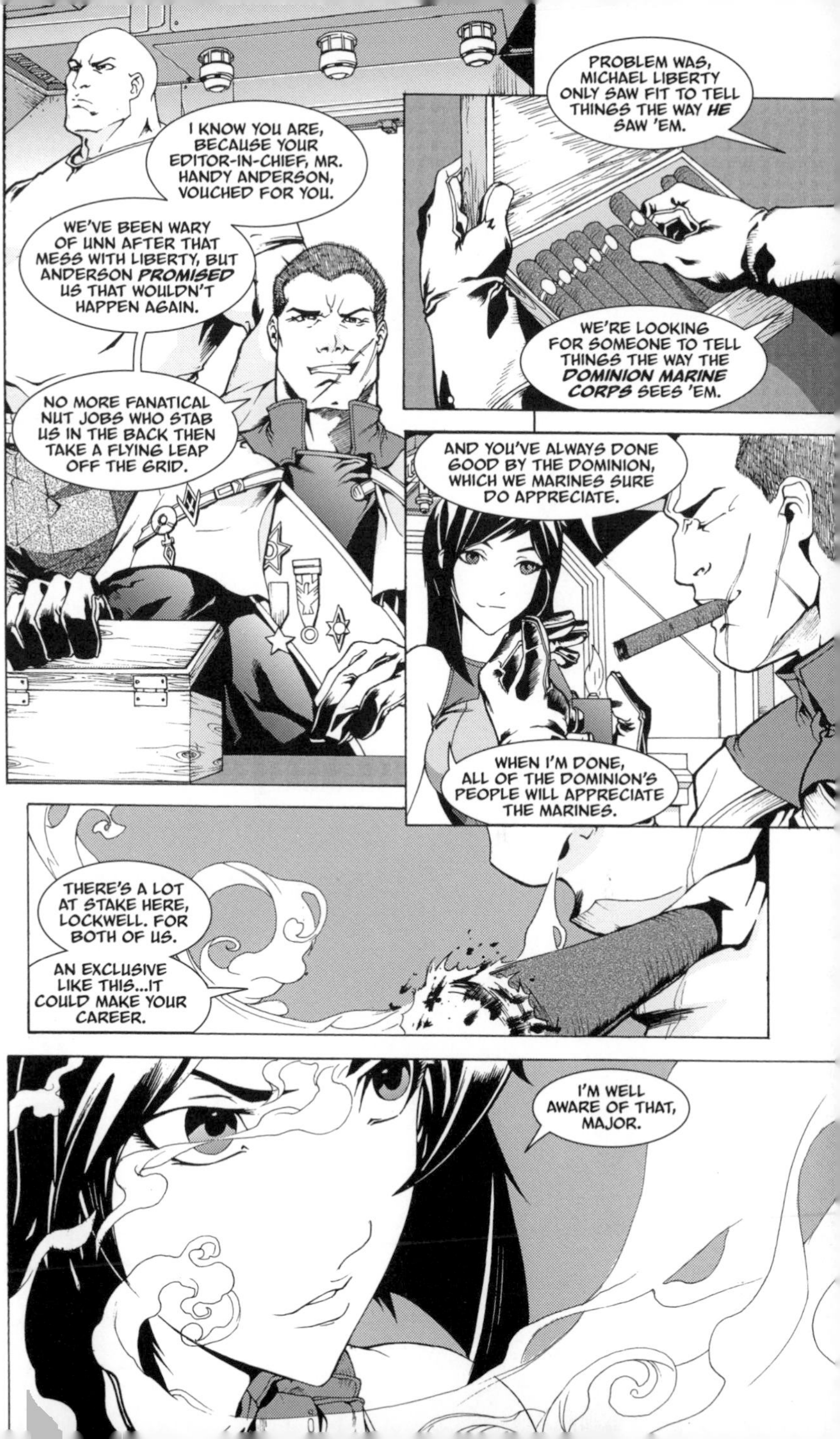
I KNOW YOU ARE, BECAUSE YOUR EDITOR-IN-CHIEF, MR. HANDY ANDERSON, VOUCHED FOR YOU.
WE'VE BEEN WARY OF UNN AFTER THAT MESS WITH LIBERTY, BUT ANDERSON *PROMISED* US THAT WOULDN'T HAPPEN AGAIN.
NO MORE FANATICAL NUT JOBS WHO STAB US IN THE BACK THEN TAKE A FLYING LEAP OFF THE GRID.
PROBLEM WAS, MICHAEL LIBERTY ONLY SAW FIT TO TELL THINGS THE WAY *HE* SAW 'EM.
WE'RE LOOKING FOR SOMEONE TO TELL THINGS THE WAY THE *DOMINION MARINE CORPS* SEES 'EM.
AND YOU'VE ALWAYS DONE GOOD BY THE DOMINION, WHICH WE MARINES SURE DO APPRECIATE.
WHEN I'M DONE, ALL OF THE DOMINION'S PEOPLE WILL APPRECIATE THE MARINES.
THERE'S A LOT AT STAKE HERE, LOCKWELL. FOR BOTH OF US.
AN EXCLUSIVE LIKE THIS...IT COULD MAKE YOUR CAREER.
I'M WELL AWARE OF THAT, MAJOR.

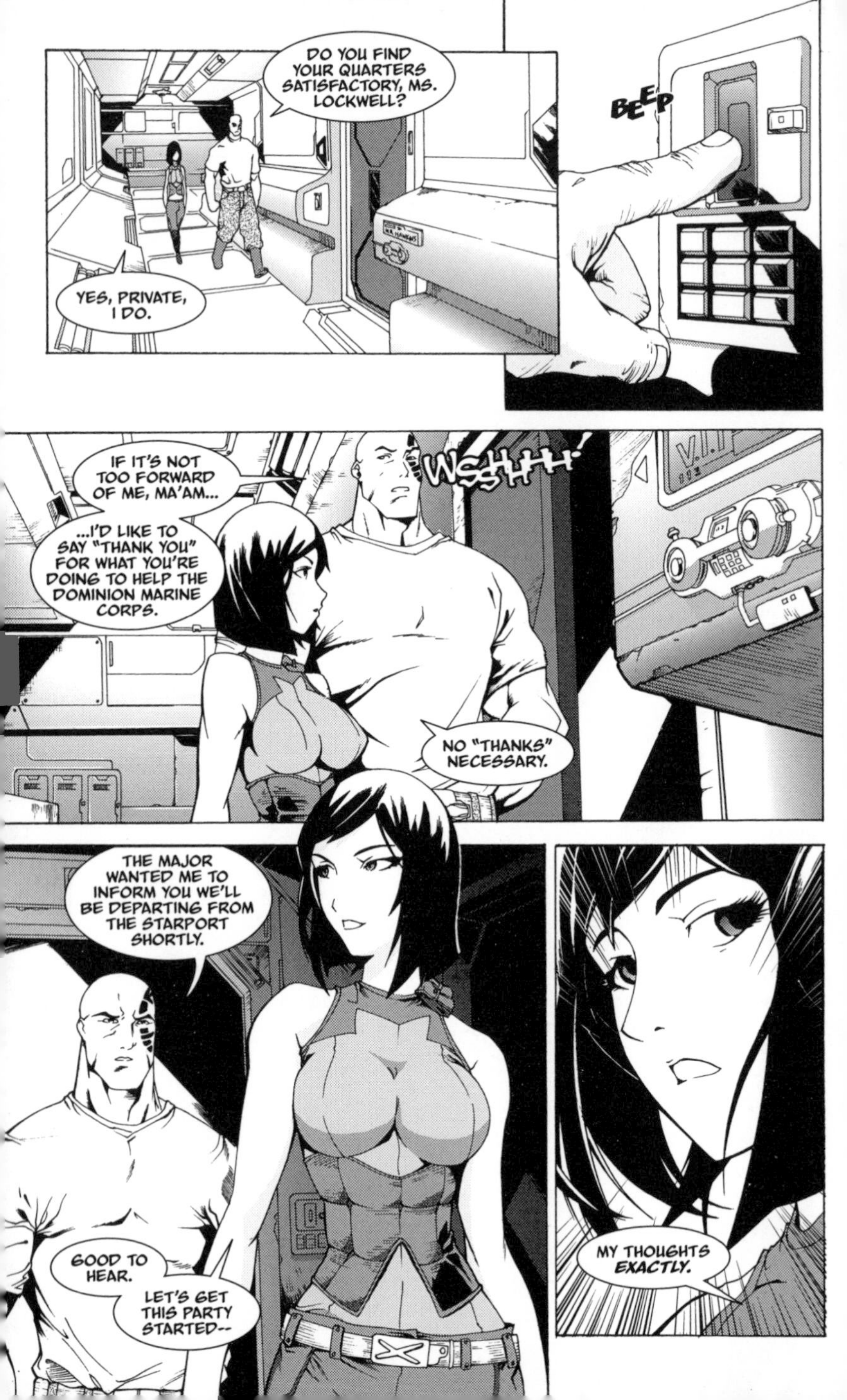
DO YOU FIND YOUR QUARTERS SATISFACTORY, MS. LOCKWELL?
YES, PRIVATE, I DO.
BEEP
IF IT'S NOT TOO FORWARD OF ME, MA'AM...
...I'D LIKE TO SAY "THANK YOU" FOR WHAT YOU'RE DOING TO HELP THE DOMINION MARINE CORPS.
WSSHHH!
NO "THANKS" NECESSARY.
THE MAJOR WANTED ME TO INFORM YOU WE'LL BE DEPARTING FROM THE STARPORT SHORTLY.
GOOD TO HEAR.
LET'S GET THIS PARTY STARTED--
MY THOUGHTS *EXACTLY.*

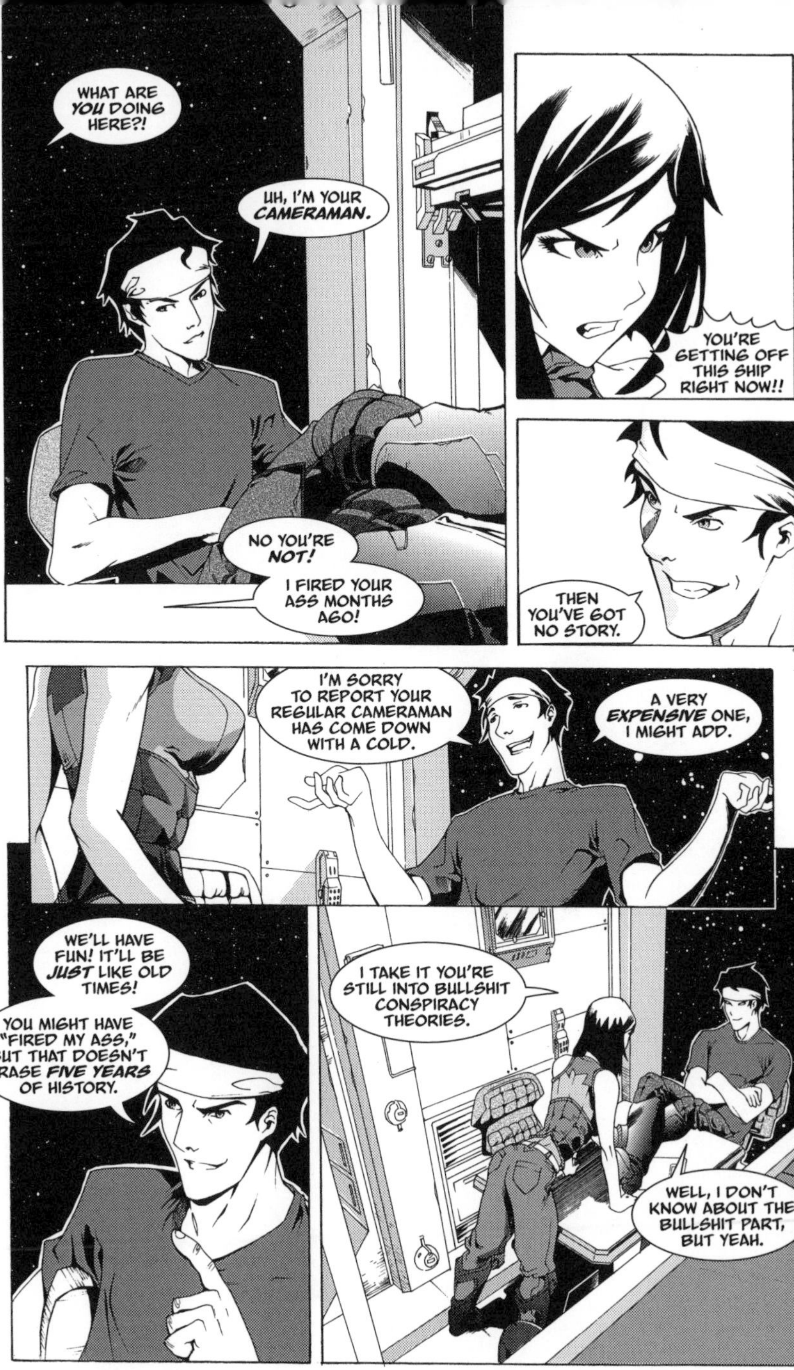

WHAT ARE YOU DOING HERE?!
UH, I'M YOUR CAMERAMAN.
YOU'RE GETTING OFF THIS SHIP RIGHT NOW!!
NO YOU'RE NOT!
I FIRED YOUR ASS MONTHS AGO!
THEN YOU'VE GOT NO STORY.
I'M SORRY TO REPORT YOUR REGULAR CAMERAMAN HAS COME DOWN WITH A COLD.
A VERY EXPENSIVE ONE, I MIGHT ADD.
WE'LL HAVE FUN! IT'LL BE JUST LIKE OLD TIMES!
YOU MIGHT HAVE "FIRED MY ASS," BUT THAT DOESN'T ERASE FIVE YEARS OF HISTORY.
I TAKE IT YOU'RE STILL INTO BULLSHIT CONSPIRACY THEORIES.
WELL, I DON'T KNOW ABOUT THE BULLSHIT PART, BUT YEAH.

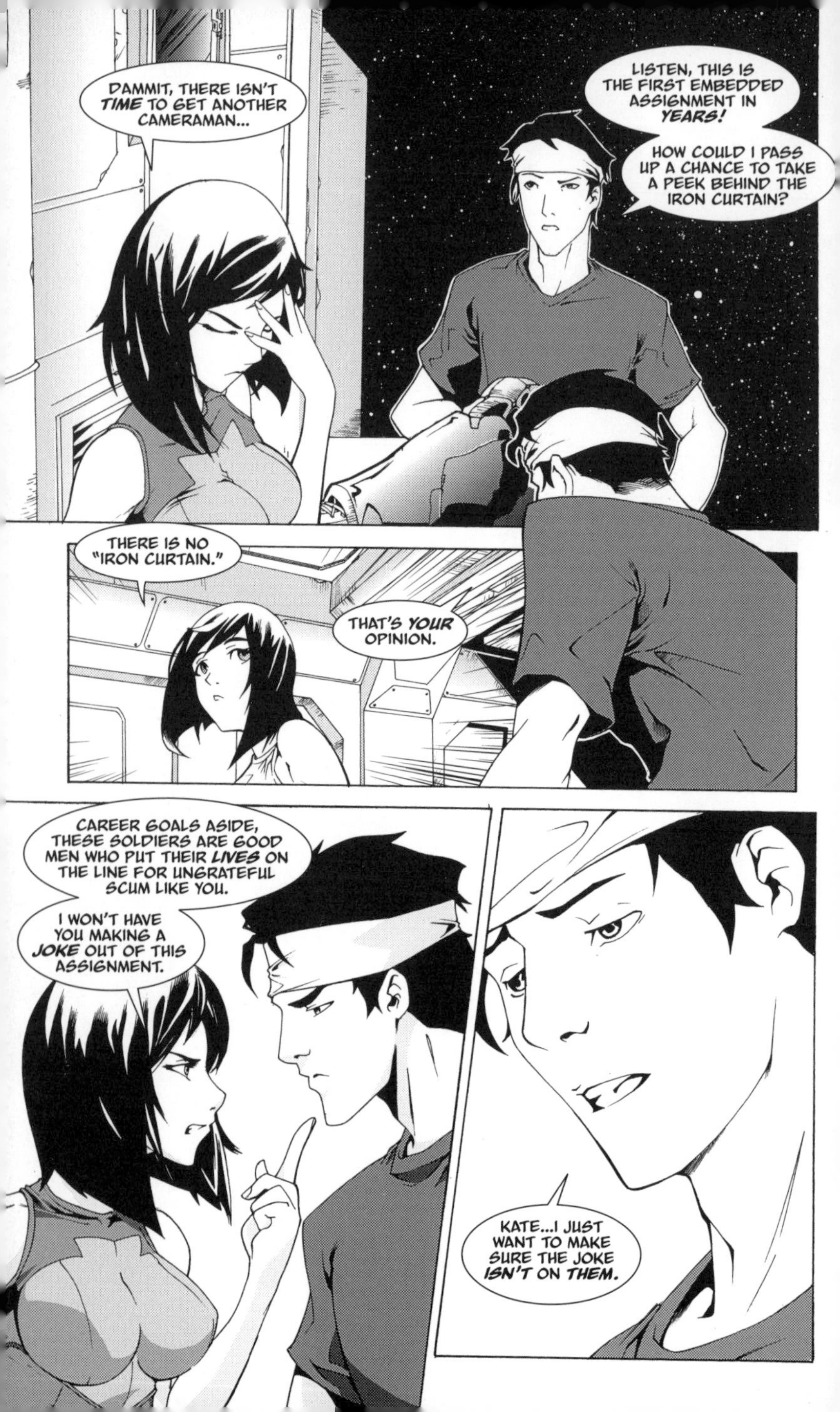
DAMMIT, THERE ISN'T *TIME* TO GET ANOTHER CAMERAMAN...
LISTEN, THIS IS THE FIRST EMBEDDED ASSIGNMENT IN *YEARS!*
HOW COULD I PASS UP A CHANCE TO TAKE A PEEK BEHIND THE IRON CURTAIN?
THERE IS NO "IRON CURTAIN."
THAT'S *YOUR* OPINION.
CAREER GOALS ASIDE, THESE SOLDIERS ARE GOOD MEN WHO PUT THEIR *LIVES* ON THE LINE FOR UNGRATEFUL SCUM LIKE YOU.
I WON'T HAVE YOU MAKING A *JOKE* OUT OF THIS ASSIGNMENT.
KATE...I JUST WANT TO MAKE SURE THE JOKE *ISN'T* ON *THEM*.

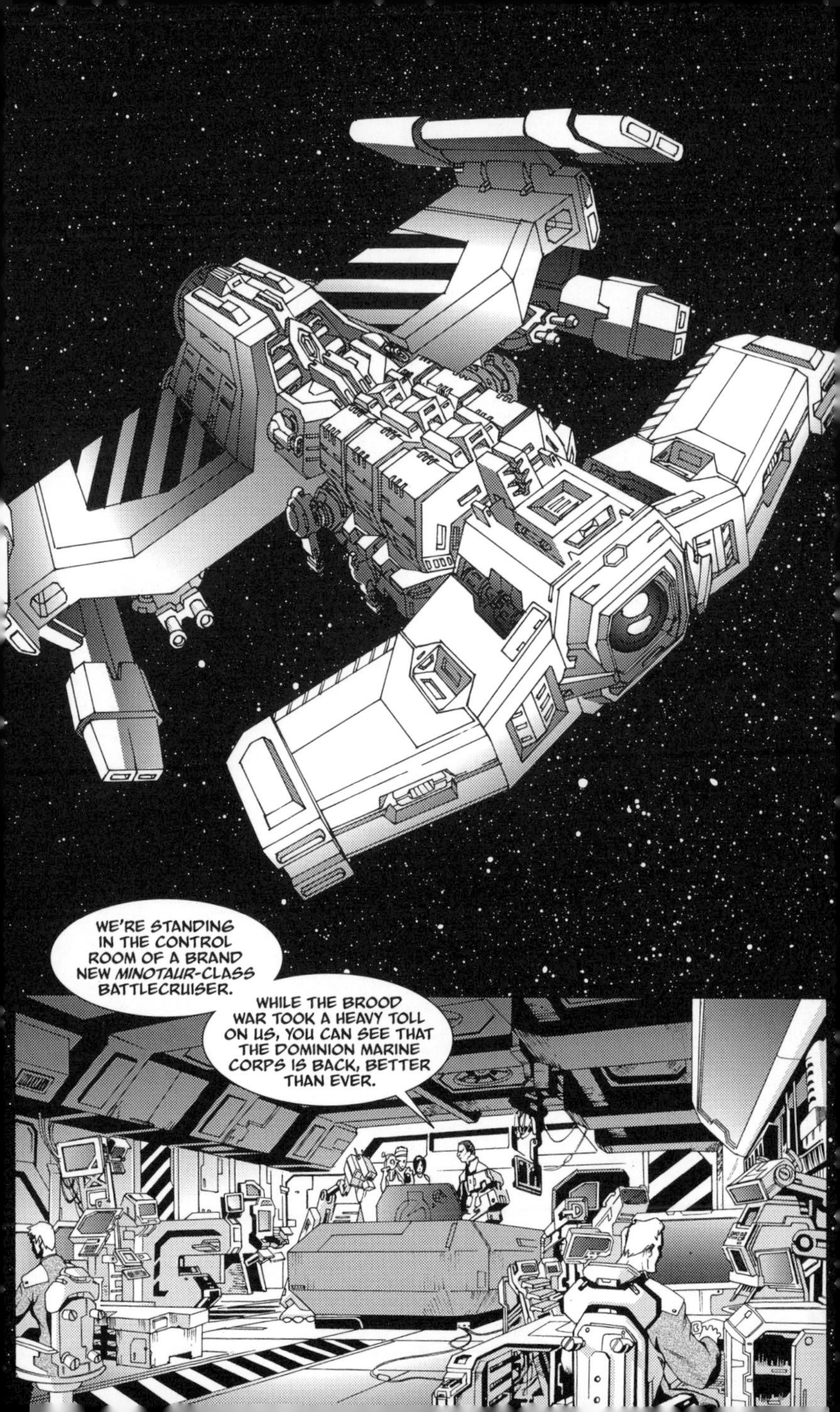
WE'RE STANDING IN THE CONTROL ROOM OF A BRAND NEW *MINOTAUR*-CLASS BATTLECRUISER.
WHILE THE BROOD WAR TOOK A HEAVY TOLL ON US, YOU CAN SEE THAT THE DOMINION MARINE CORPS IS BACK, BETTER THAN EVER.

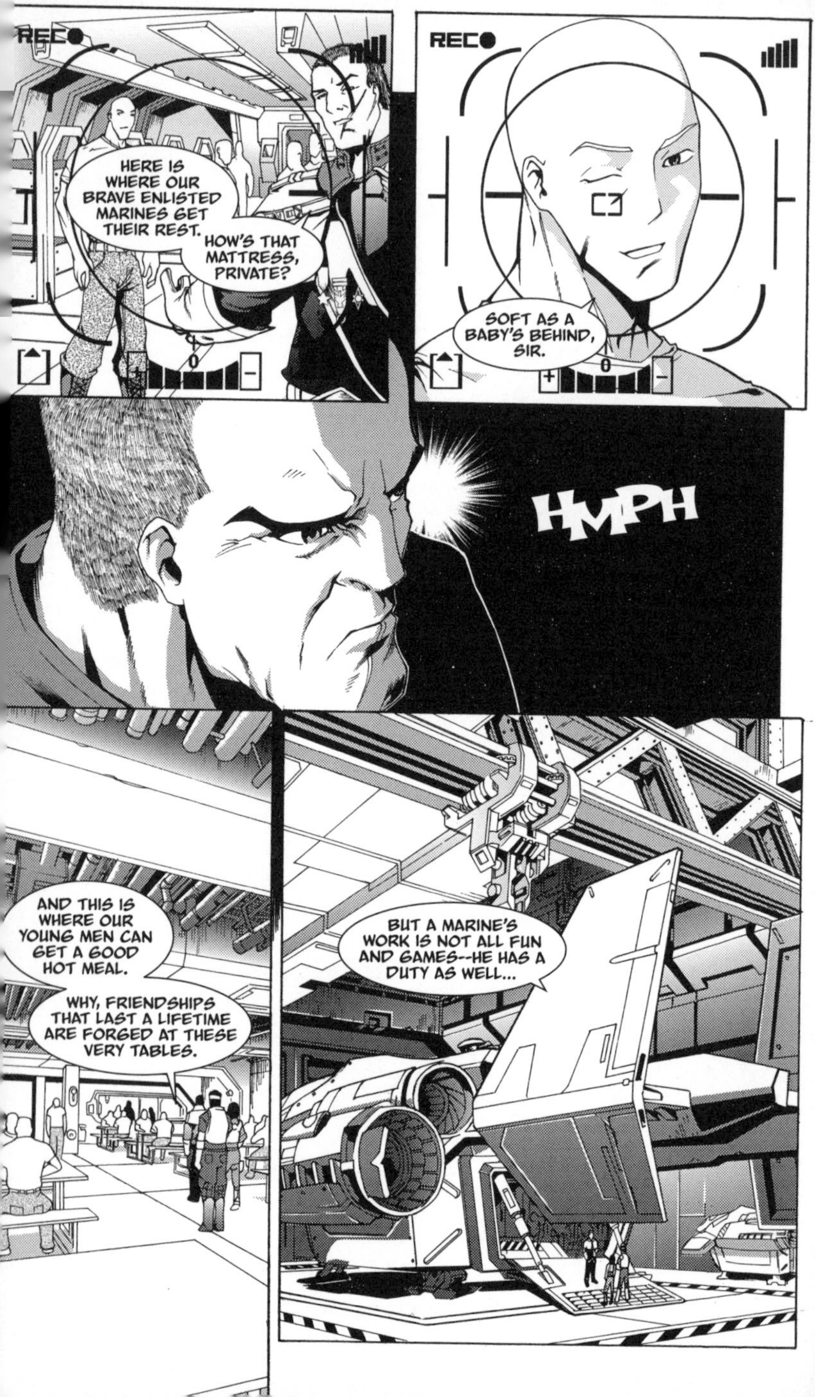

REC
HERE IS WHERE OUR BRAVE ENLISTED MARINES GET THEIR REST.
HOW'S THAT MATTRESS, PRIVATE?
0
REC
SOFT AS A BABY'S BEHIND, SIR.
0
HMPH
AND THIS IS WHERE OUR YOUNG MEN CAN GET A GOOD HOT MEAL.
WHY, FRIENDSHIPS THAT LAST A LIFETIME ARE FORGED AT THESE VERY TABLES.
BUT A MARINE'S WORK IS NOT ALL FUN AND GAMES--HE HAS A DUTY AS WELL...

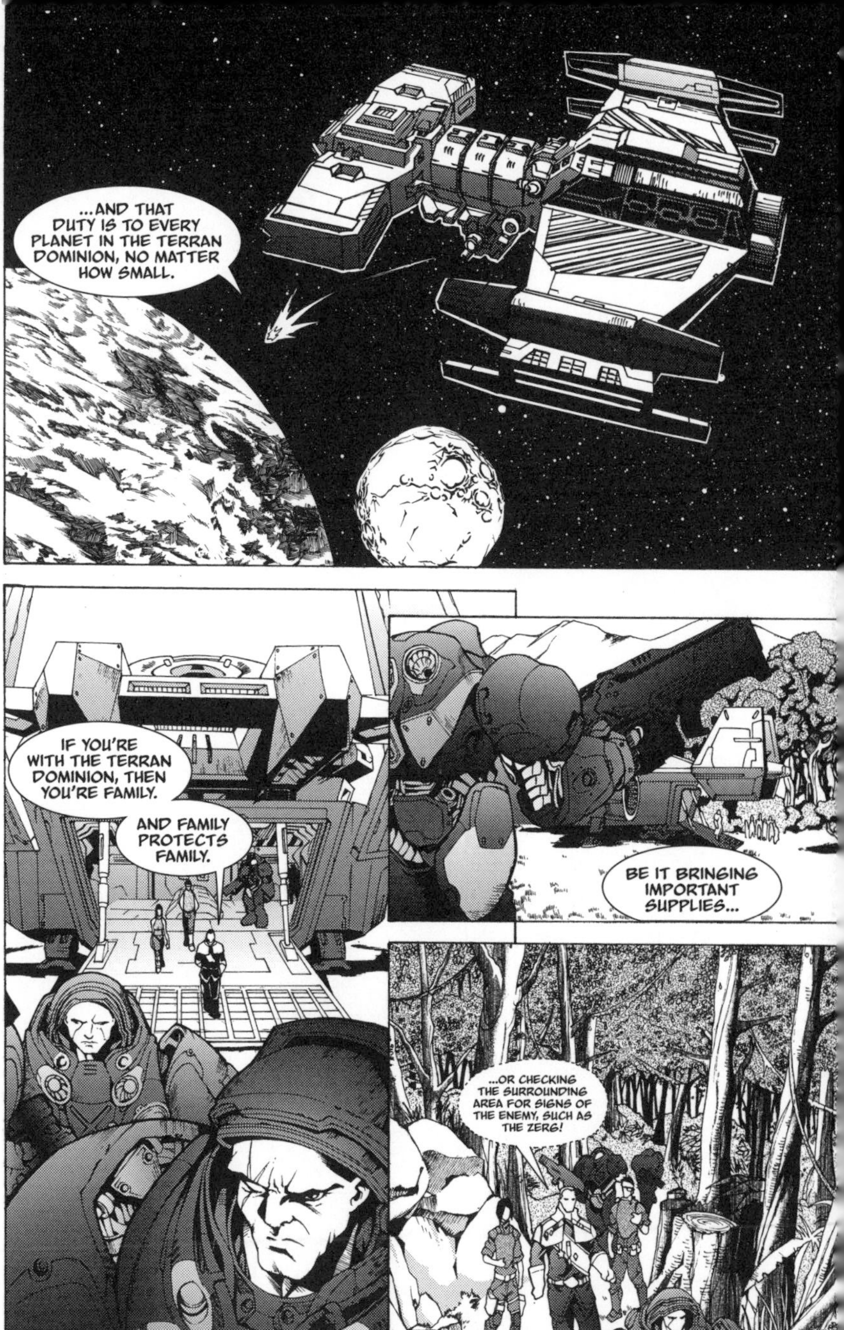
...AND THAT DUTY IS TO EVERY PLANET IN THE TERRAN DOMINION, NO MATTER HOW SMALL.
IF YOU'RE WITH THE TERRAN DOMINION, THEN YOU'RE FAMILY.
AND FAMILY PROTECTS FAMILY.
BE IT BRINGING IMPORTANT SUPPLIES...
...OR CHECKING THE SURROUNDING AREA FOR SIGNS OF THE ENEMY, SUCH AS THE ZERG!

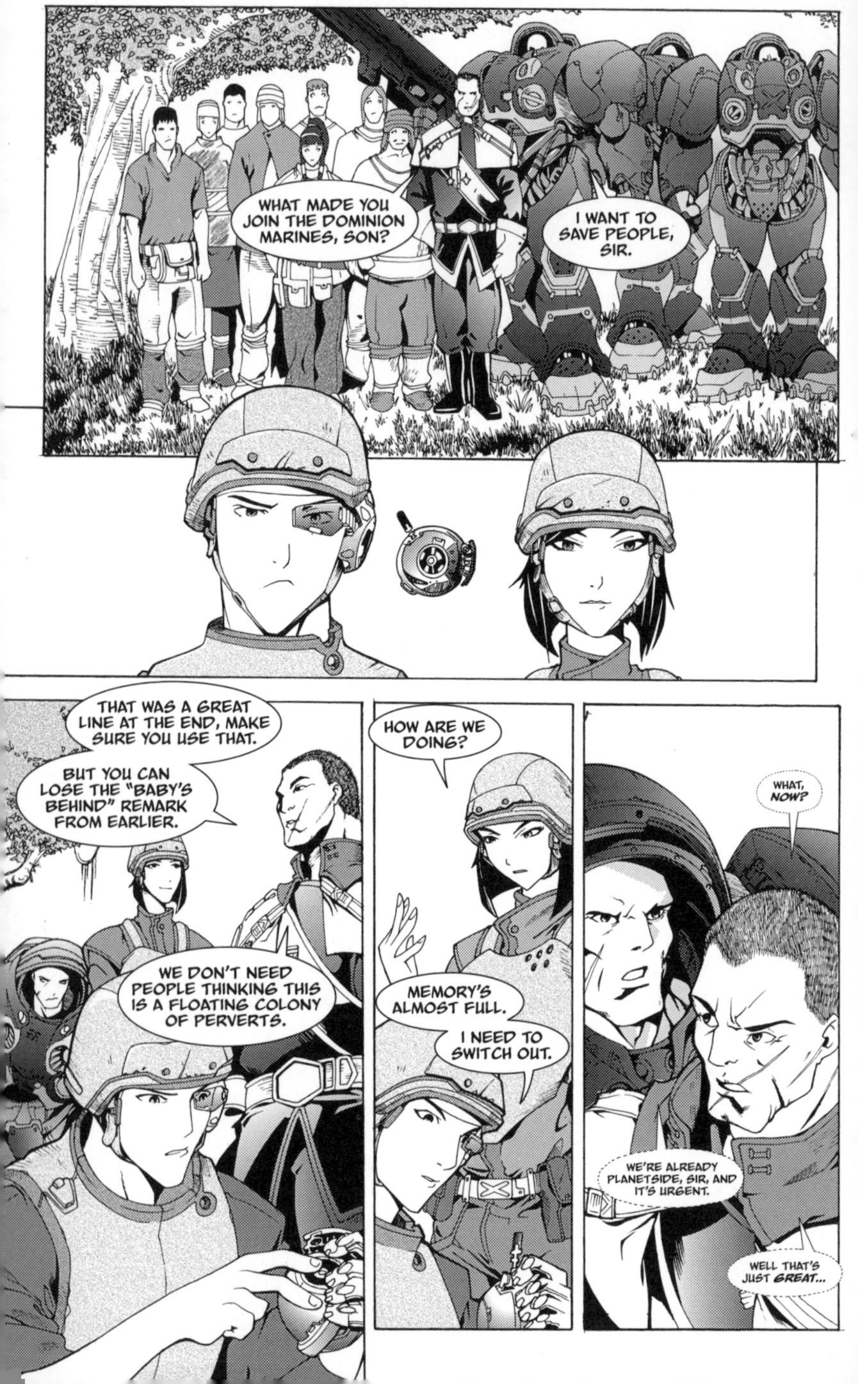
WHAT MADE YOU JOIN THE DOMINION MARINES, SON?
I WANT TO SAVE PEOPLE, SIR.
THAT WAS A GREAT LINE AT THE END, MAKE SURE YOU USE THAT.
BUT YOU CAN LOSE THE "BABY'S BEHIND" REMARK FROM EARLIER.
WE DON'T NEED PEOPLE THINKING THIS IS A FLOATING COLONY OF PERVERTS.
HOW ARE WE DOING?
MEMORY'S ALMOST FULL.
I NEED TO SWITCH OUT.
WHAT, NOW?
WE'RE ALREADY PLANETSIDE, SIR, AND IT'S URGENT.
WELL THAT'S JUST GREAT...

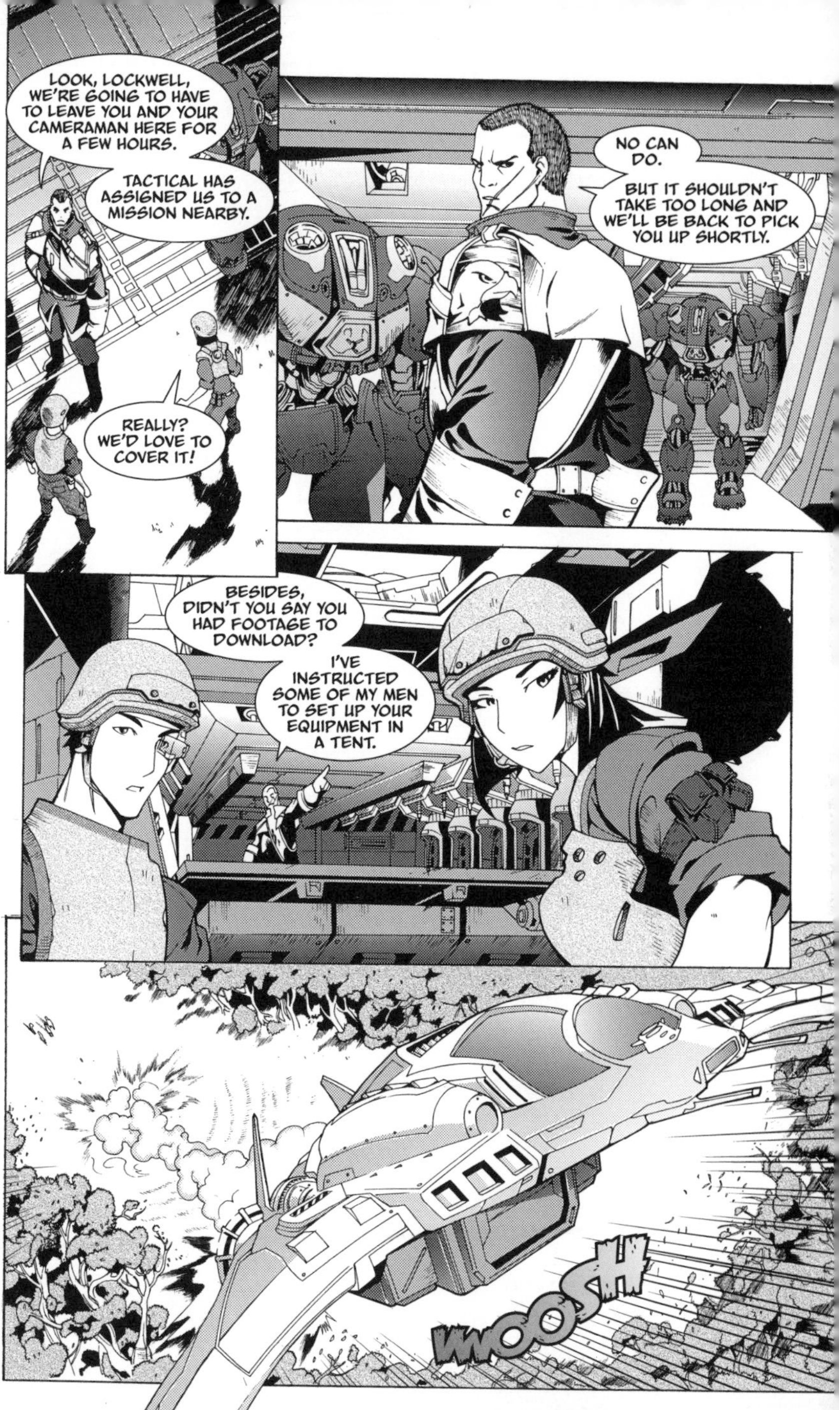

LOOK, LOCKWELL, WE'RE GOING TO HAVE TO LEAVE YOU AND YOUR CAMERAMAN HERE FOR A FEW HOURS.
TACTICAL HAS ASSIGNED US TO A MISSION NEARBY.
REALLY? WE'D LOVE TO COVER IT!
NO CAN DO.
BUT IT SHOULDN'T TAKE TOO LONG AND WE'LL BE BACK TO PICK YOU UP SHORTLY.
BESIDES, DIDN'T YOU SAY YOU HAD FOOTAGE TO DOWNLOAD?
I'VE INSTRUCTED SOME OF MY MEN TO SET UP YOUR EQUIPMENT IN A TENT.
WOOSH

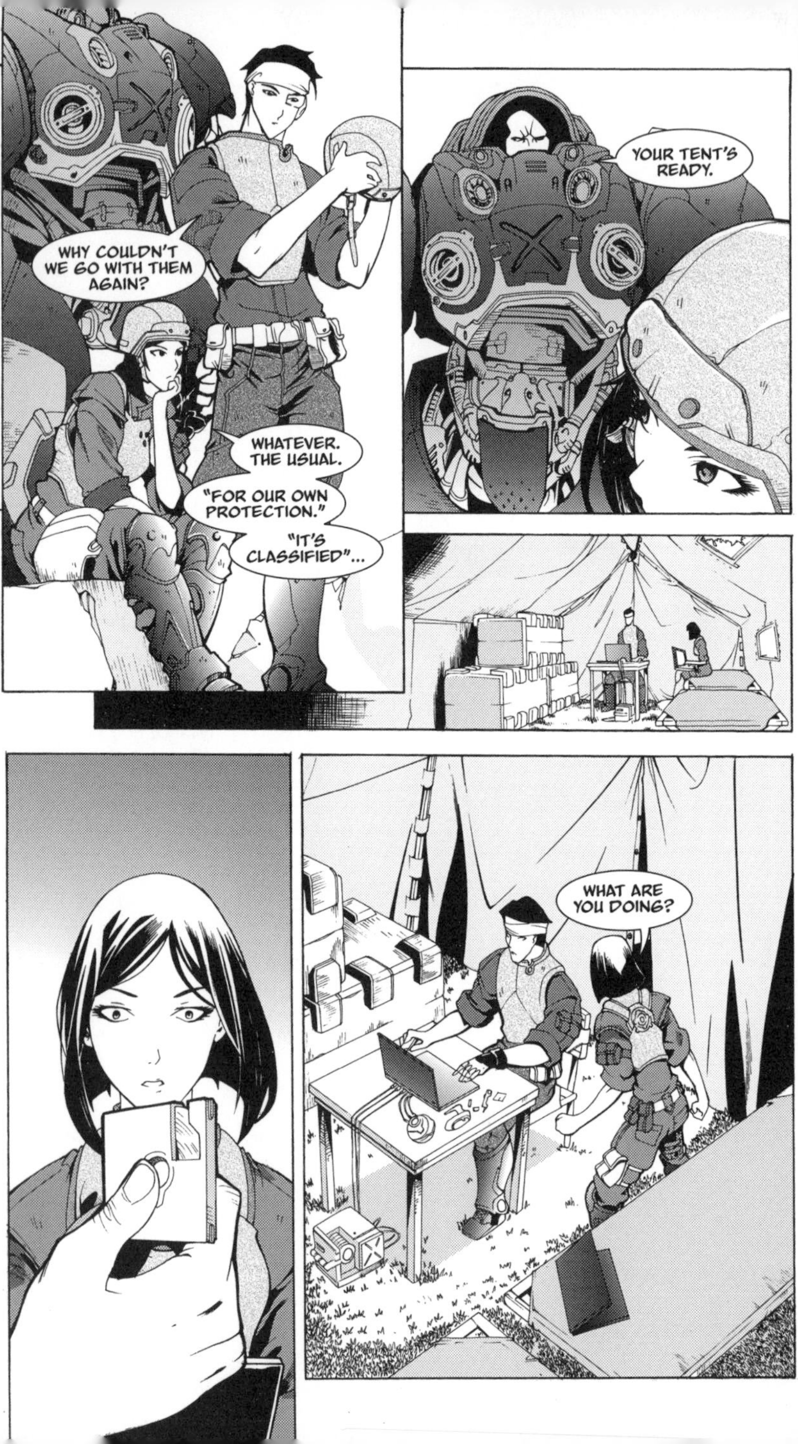
WHY COULDN'T WE GO WITH THEM AGAIN?
WHATEVER. THE USUAL.
"FOR OUR OWN PROTECTION."
"IT'S CLASSIFIED"...
YOUR TENT'S READY.
WHAT ARE YOU DOING?

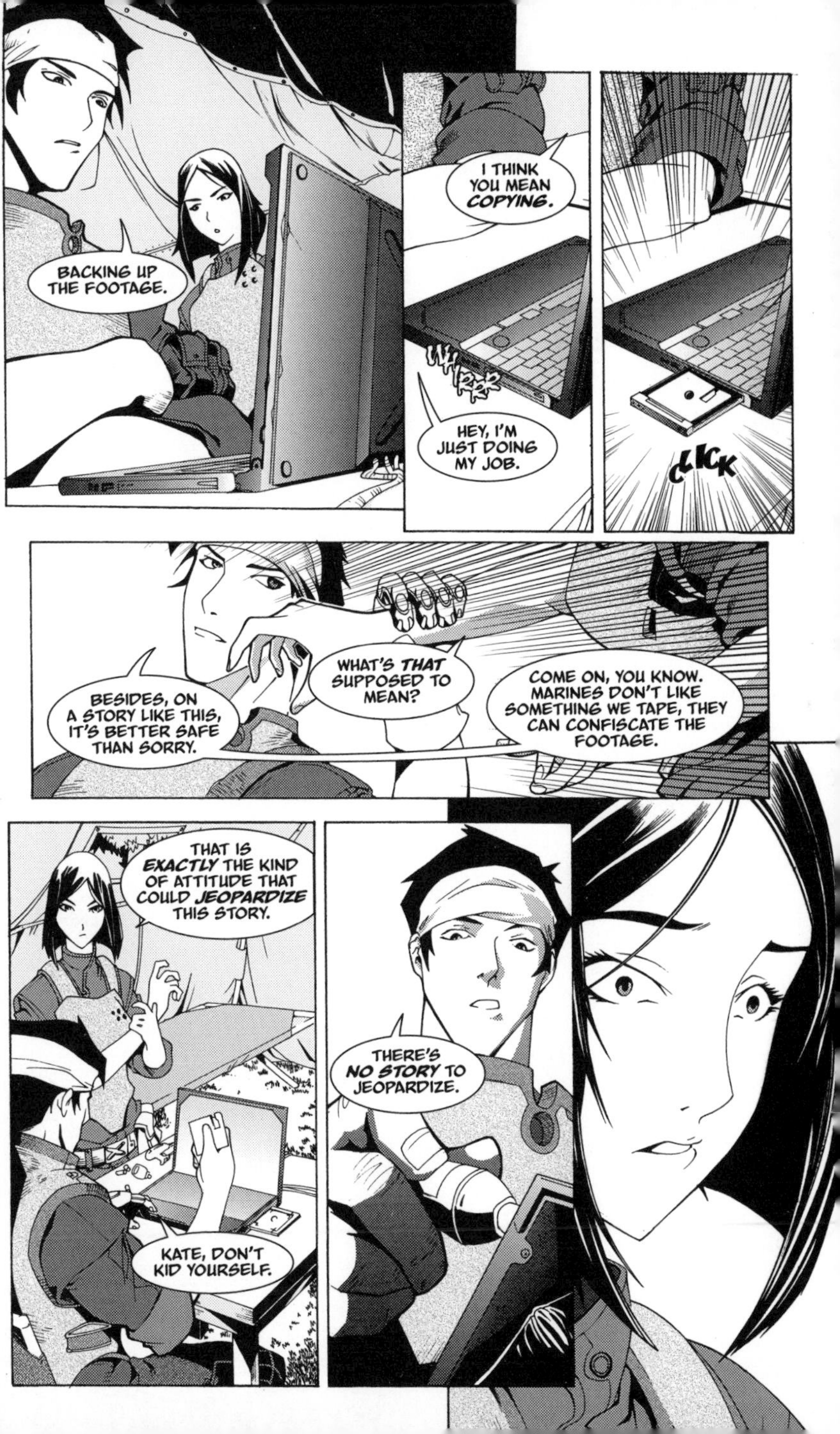
BACKING UP THE FOOTAGE.
I THINK YOU MEAN *COPYING*.
HEY, I'M JUST DOING MY JOB.
CLICK
BESIDES, ON A STORY LIKE THIS, IT'S BETTER SAFE THAN SORRY.
WHAT'S *THAT* SUPPOSED TO MEAN?
COME ON, YOU KNOW. MARINES DON'T LIKE SOMETHING WE TAPE, THEY CAN CONFISCATE THE FOOTAGE.
THAT IS *EXACTLY* THE KIND OF ATTITUDE THAT COULD *JEOPARDIZE* THIS STORY.
KATE, DON'T KID YOURSELF.
THERE'S *NO STORY* TO JEOPARDIZE.

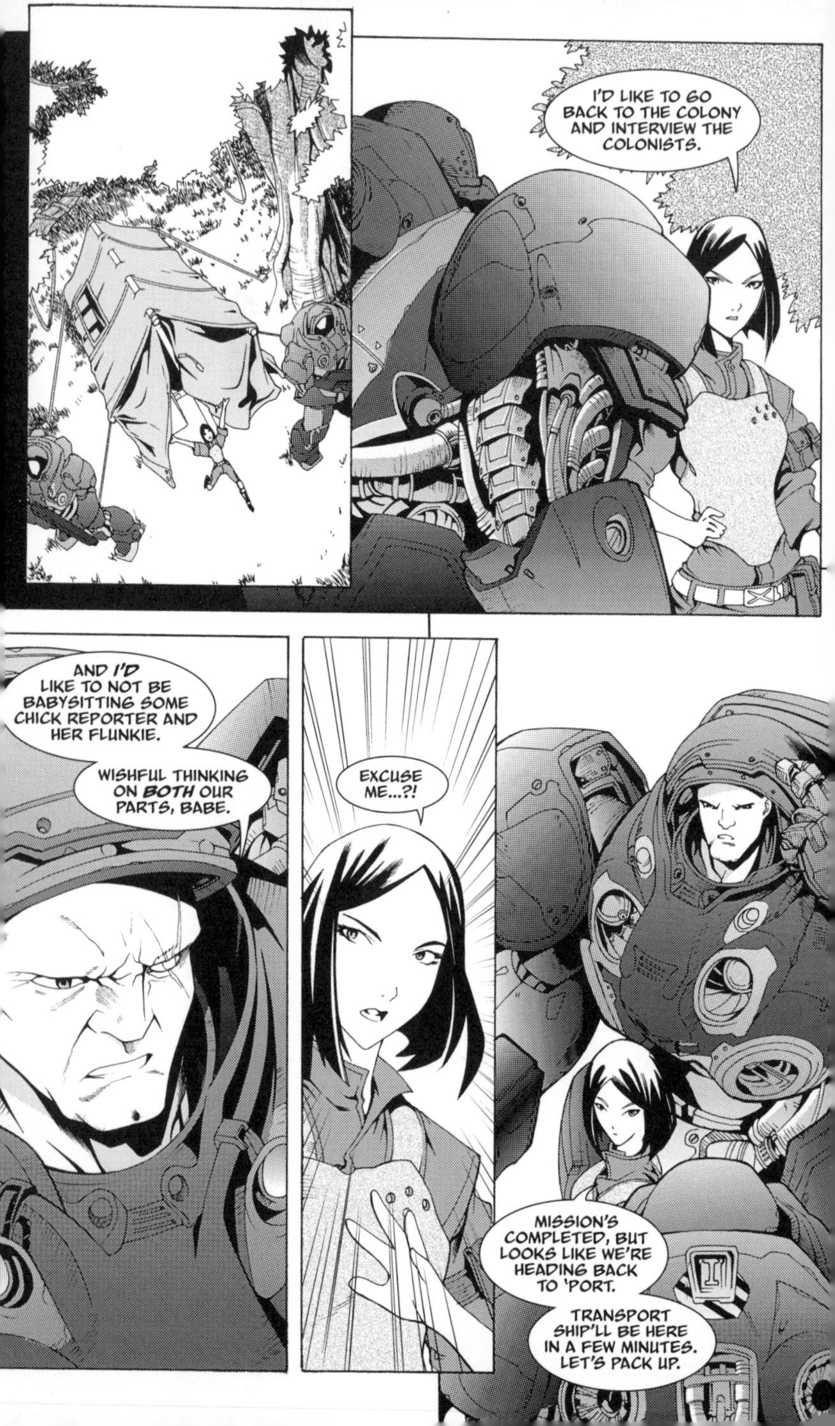
I'D LIKE TO GO BACK TO THE COLONY AND INTERVIEW THE COLONISTS.
AND I'D LIKE TO NOT BE BABYSITTING SOME CHICK REPORTER AND HER FLUNKIE.
WISHFUL THINKING ON BOTH OUR PARTS, BABE.
EXCUSE ME...?!
MISSION'S COMPLETED, BUT LOOKS LIKE WE'RE HEADING BACK TO 'PORT.
TRANSPORT SHIP'LL BE HERE IN A FEW MINUTES. LET'S PACK UP.

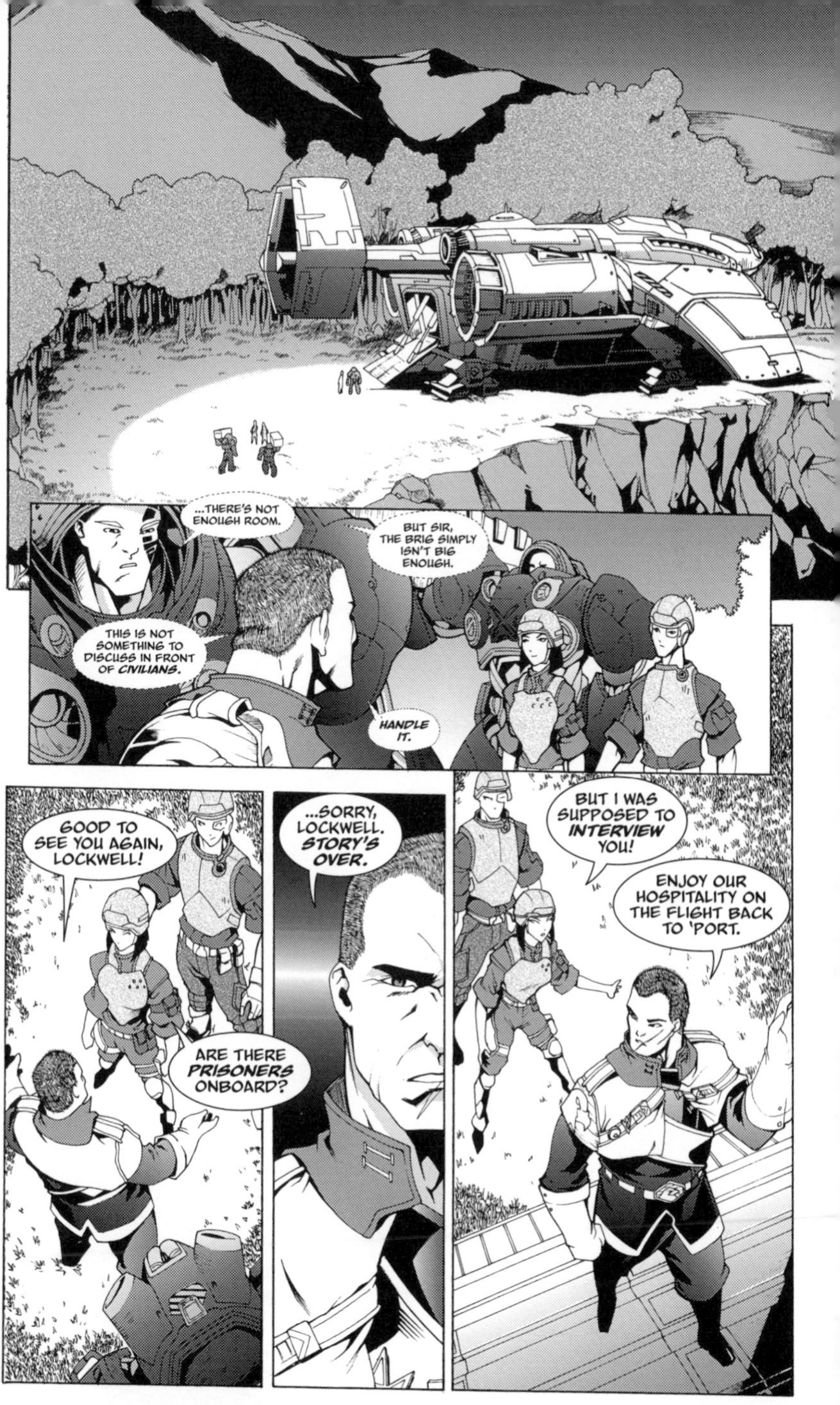

...THERE'S NOT ENOUGH ROOM.
BUT SIR, THE BRIG SIMPLY ISN'T BIG ENOUGH.
THIS IS NOT SOMETHING TO DISCUSS IN FRONT OF CIVILIANS.
HANDLE IT.
GOOD TO SEE YOU AGAIN, LOCKWELL!
ARE THERE PRISONERS ONBOARD?
...SORRY, LOCKWELL. STORY'S OVER.
BUT I WAS SUPPOSED TO INTERVIEW YOU!
ENJOY OUR HOSPITALITY ON THE FLIGHT BACK TO 'PORT.

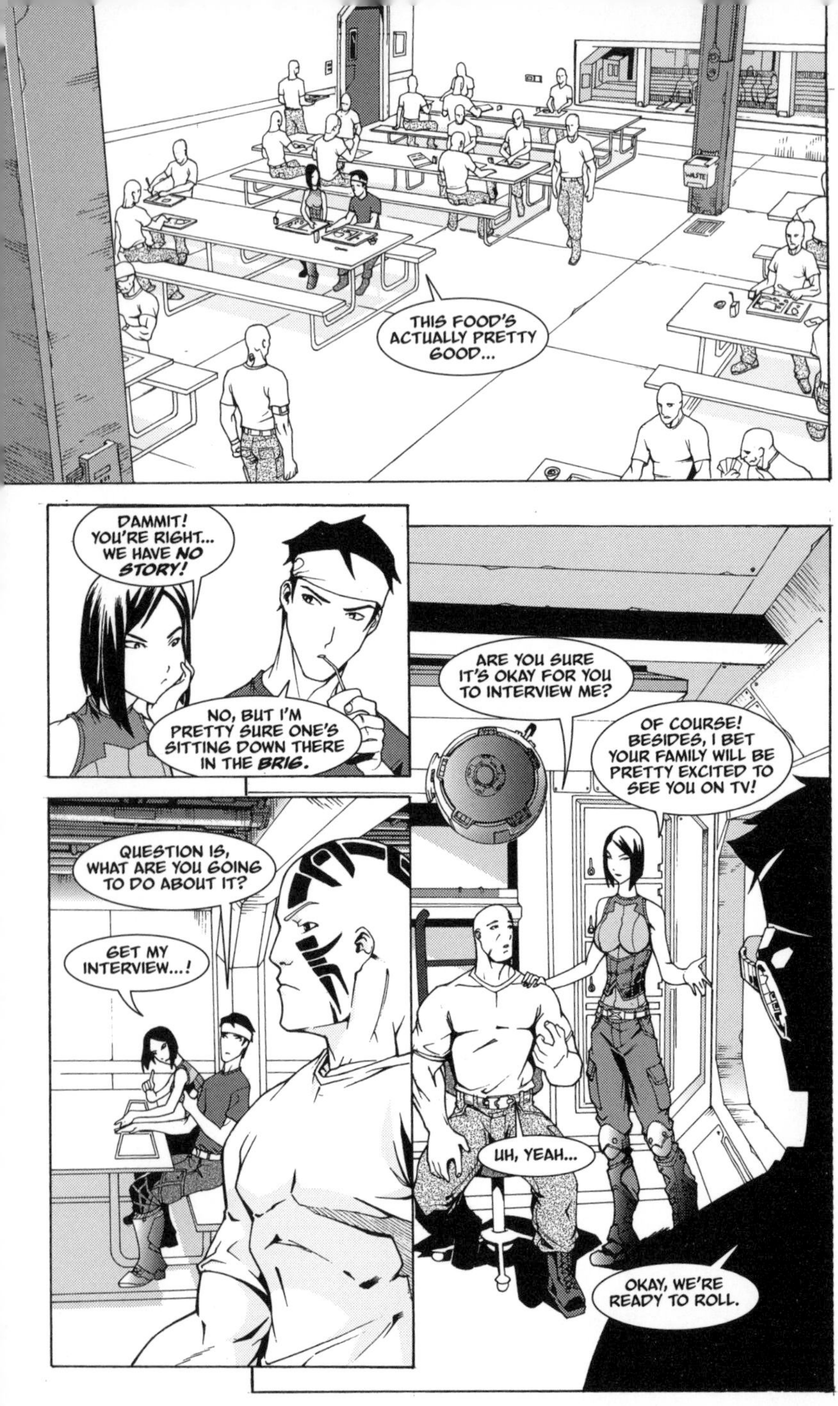
THIS FOOD'S ACTUALLY PRETTY GOOD...
DAMMIT! YOU'RE RIGHT... WE HAVE NO STORY!
NO, BUT I'M PRETTY SURE ONE'S SITTING DOWN THERE IN THE BRIG.
QUESTION IS, WHAT ARE YOU GOING TO DO ABOUT IT?
GET MY INTERVIEW...!
ARE YOU SURE IT'S OKAY FOR YOU TO INTERVIEW ME?
OF COURSE! BESIDES, I BET YOUR FAMILY WILL BE PRETTY EXCITED TO SEE YOU ON TV!
UH, YEAH...
OKAY, WE'RE READY TO ROLL.

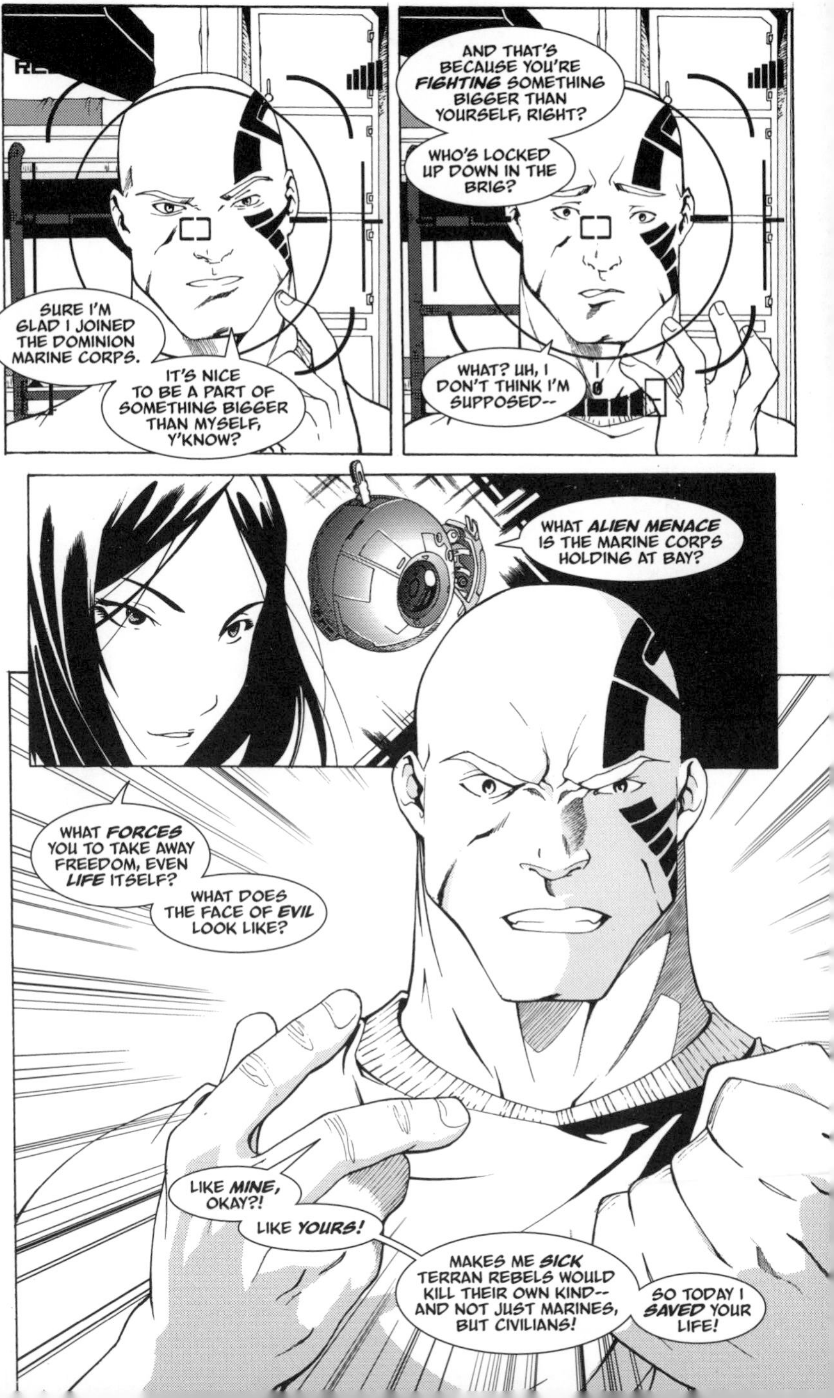
SURE I'M GLAD I JOINED THE DOMINION MARINE CORPS.
IT'S NICE TO BE A PART OF SOMETHING BIGGER THAN MYSELF, Y'KNOW?
AND THAT'S BECAUSE YOU'RE *FIGHTING* SOMETHING BIGGER THAN YOURSELF, RIGHT?
WHO'S LOCKED UP DOWN IN THE BRIG?
WHAT? UH, I DON'T THINK I'M SUPPOSED--
WHAT *ALIEN MENACE* IS THE MARINE CORPS HOLDING AT BAY?
WHAT *FORCES* YOU TO TAKE AWAY FREEDOM, EVEN *LIFE* ITSELF?
WHAT DOES THE FACE OF *EVIL* LOOK LIKE?
LIKE *MINE*, OKAY?!
LIKE *YOURS!*
MAKES ME *SICK* TERRAN REBELS WOULD KILL THEIR OWN KIND-- AND NOT JUST MARINES, BUT CIVILIANS!
SO TODAY I *SAVED* YOUR LIFE!

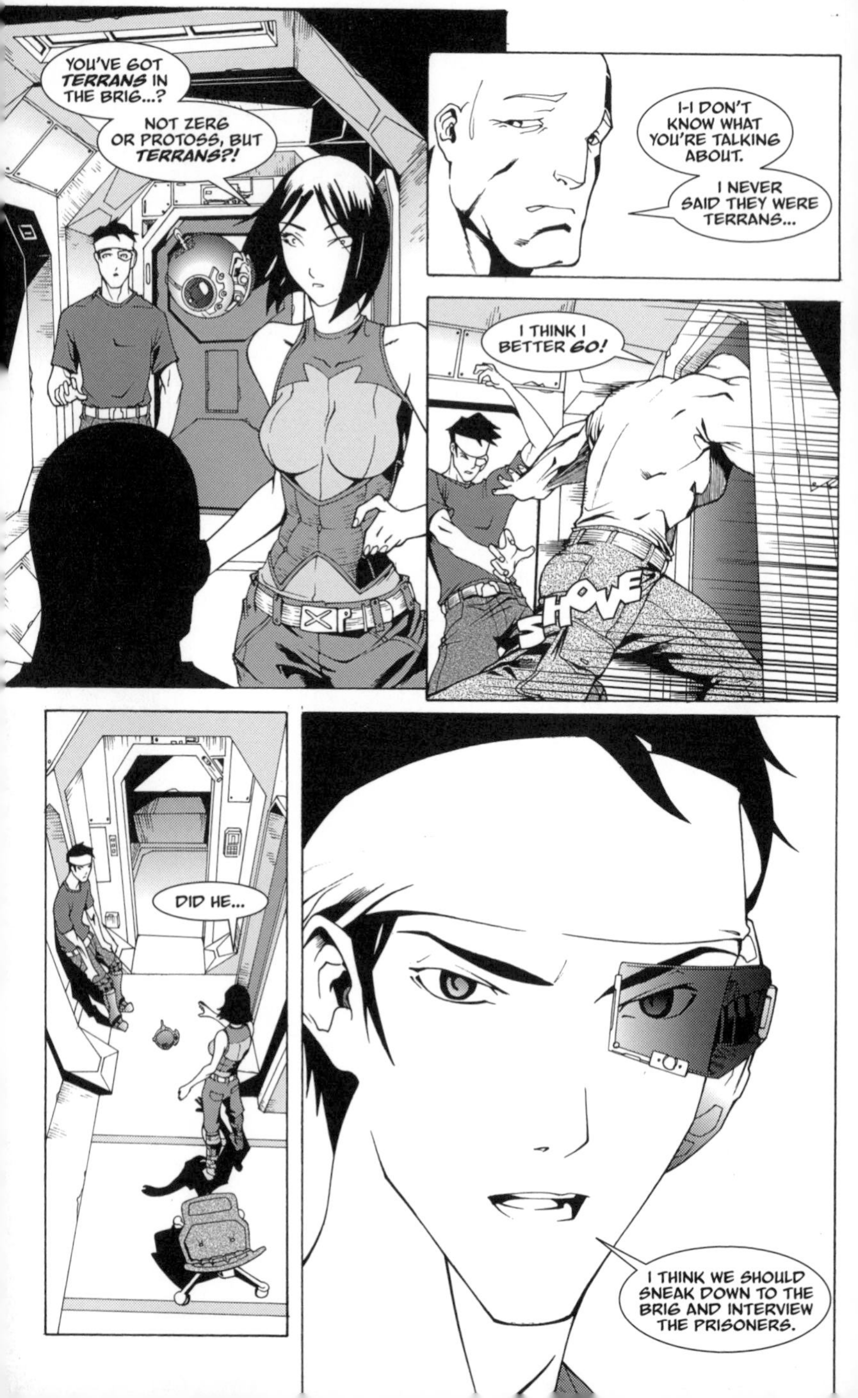
YOU'VE GOT TERRANS IN THE BRIG...?
NOT ZERG OR PROTOSS, BUT TERRANS?!
I-I DON'T KNOW WHAT YOU'RE TALKING ABOUT.
I NEVER SAID THEY WERE TERRANS...
I THINK I BETTER GO!
SHOVE
DID HE...
I THINK WE SHOULD SNEAK DOWN TO THE BRIG AND INTERVIEW THE PRISONERS.

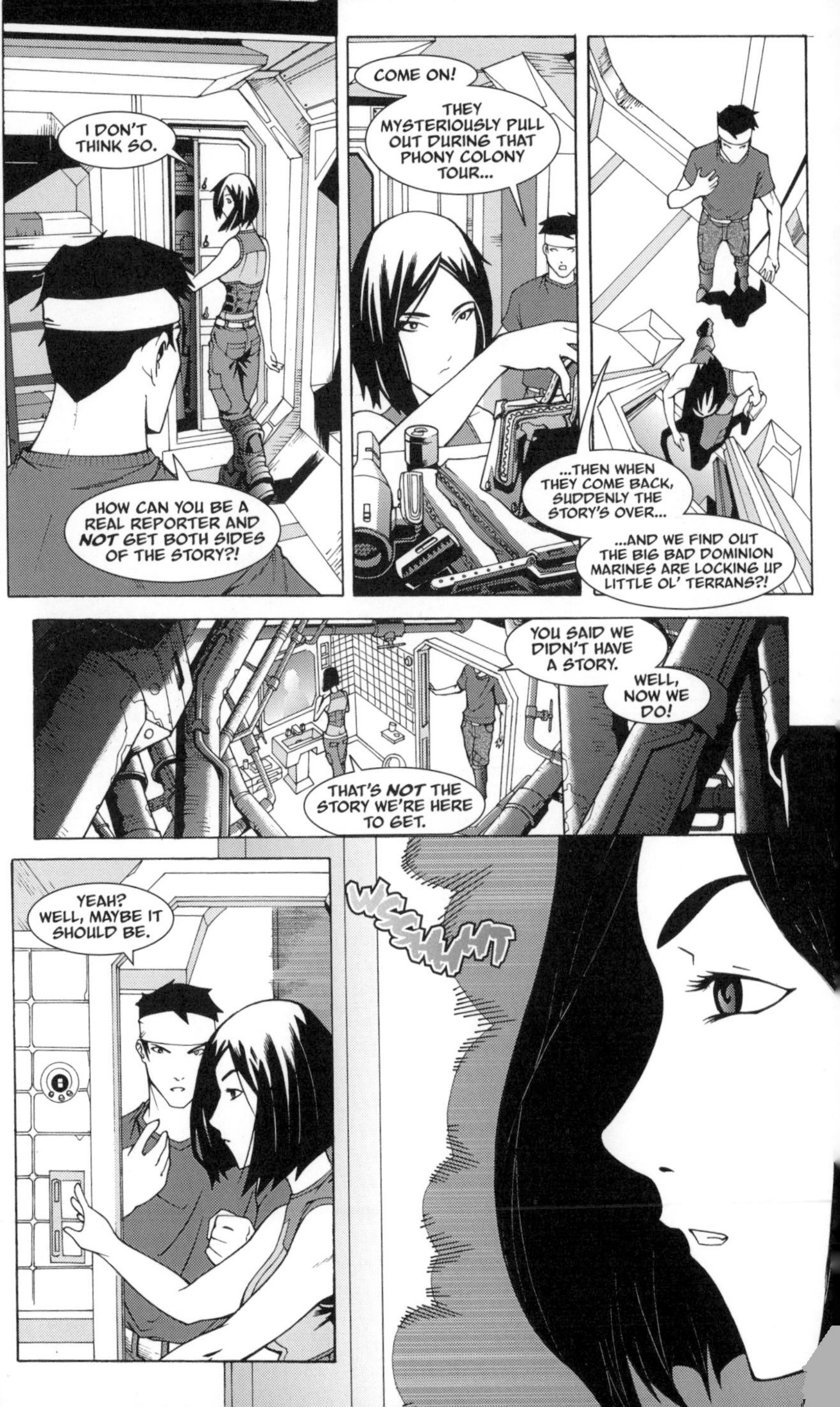

I DON'T THINK SO.
HOW CAN YOU BE A REAL REPORTER AND *NOT* GET BOTH SIDES OF THE STORY?!
COME ON!
THEY MYSTERIOUSLY PULL OUT DURING THAT PHONY COLONY TOUR...
...THEN WHEN THEY COME BACK, SUDDENLY THE STORY'S OVER...
...AND WE FIND OUT THE BIG BAD DOMINION MARINES ARE LOCKING UP LITTLE OL' TERRANS?!
YOU SAID WE DIDN'T HAVE A STORY.
WELL, NOW WE DO!
THAT'S *NOT* THE STORY WE'RE HERE TO GET.
YEAH? WELL, MAYBE IT SHOULD BE.
WSSHHHT

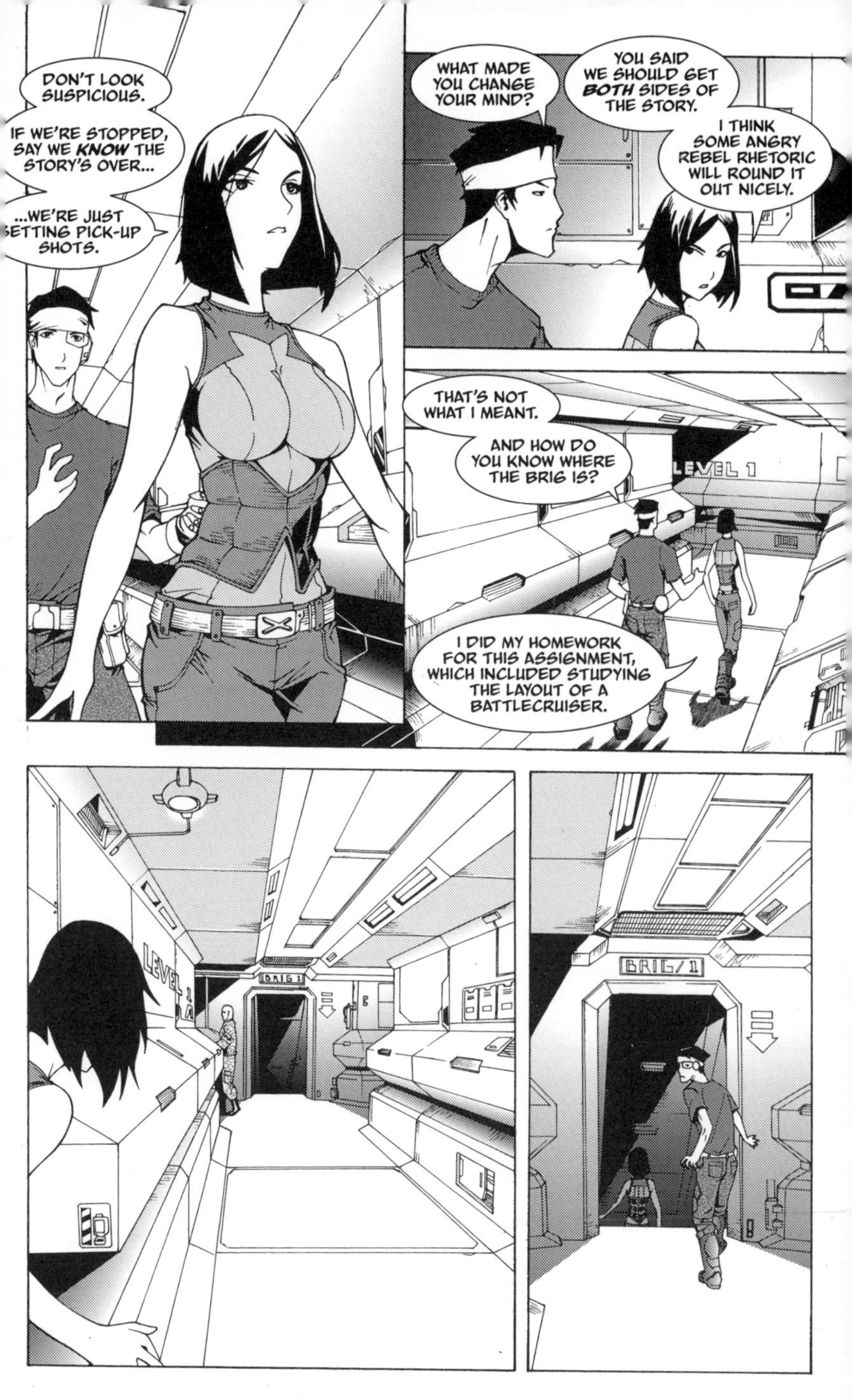
DON'T LOOK SUSPICIOUS.
IF WE'RE STOPPED, SAY WE KNOW THE STORY'S OVER...
...WE'RE JUST GETTING PICK-UP SHOTS.
WHAT MADE YOU CHANGE YOUR MIND?
YOU SAID WE SHOULD GET BOTH SIDES OF THE STORY.
I THINK SOME ANGRY REBEL RHETORIC WILL ROUND IT OUT NICELY.
THAT'S NOT WHAT I MEANT.
AND HOW DO YOU KNOW WHERE THE BRIG IS?
LEVEL 1
I DID MY HOMEWORK FOR THIS ASSIGNMENT, WHICH INCLUDED STUDYING THE LAYOUT OF A BATTLECRUISER.
LEVEL 1
BRIG 1
BRIG/1

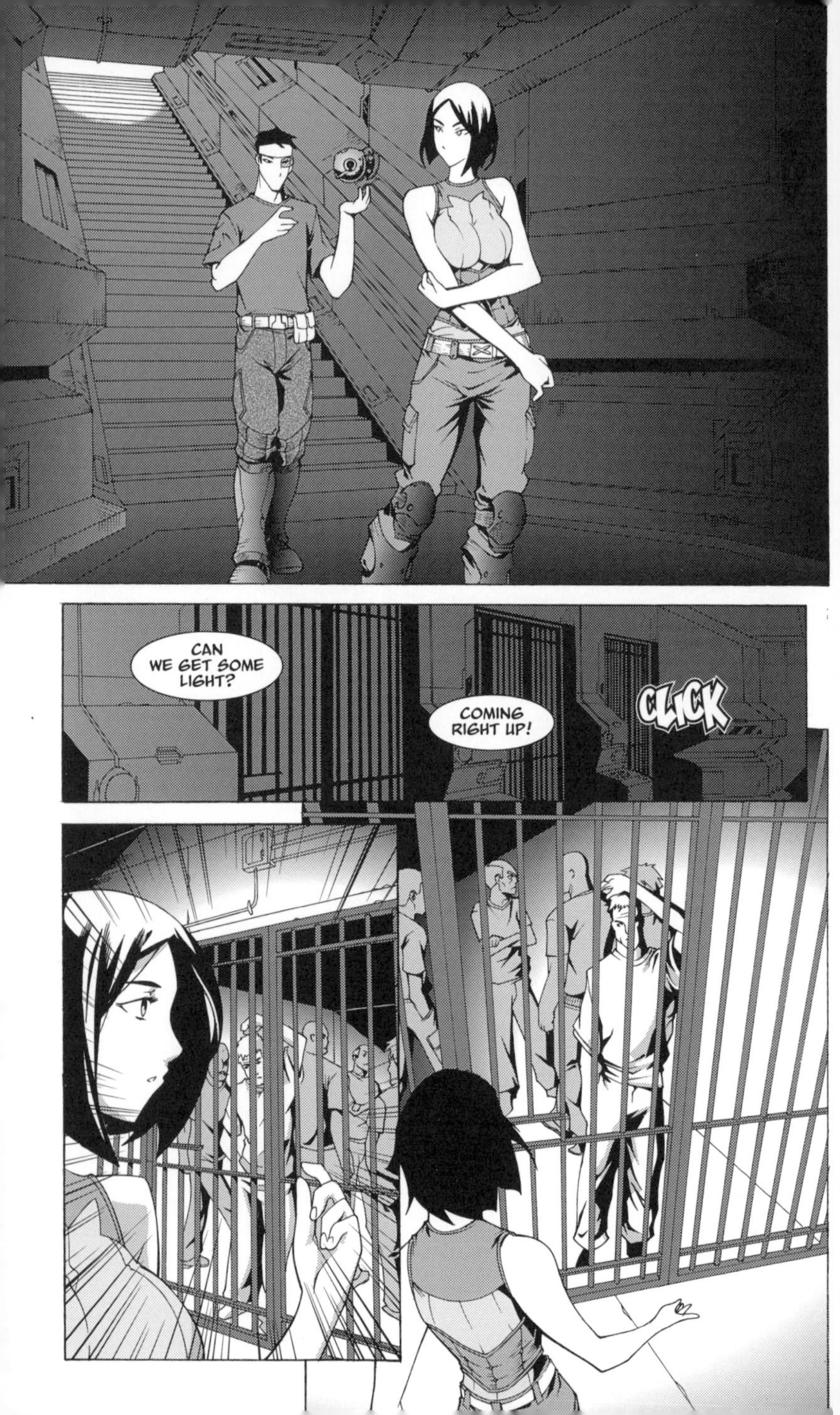
CAN WE GET SOME LIGHT?
COMING RIGHT UP!
CLICK

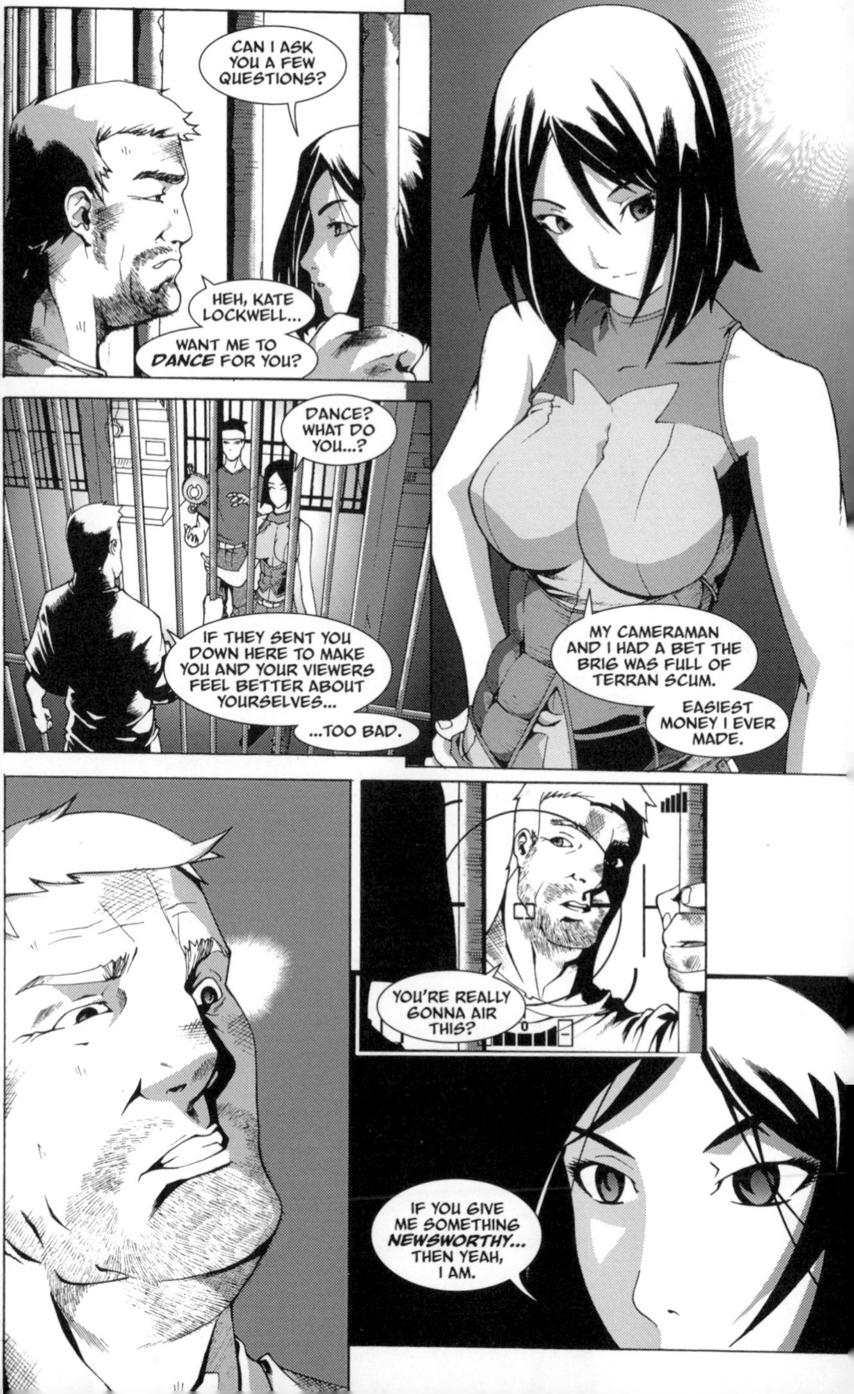
CAN I ASK YOU A FEW QUESTIONS?
HEH, KATE LOCKWELL...
WANT ME TO *DANCE* FOR YOU?
DANCE? WHAT DO YOU...?
IF THEY SENT YOU DOWN HERE TO MAKE YOU AND YOUR VIEWERS FEEL BETTER ABOUT YOURSELVES...
...TOO BAD.
MY CAMERAMAN AND I HAD A BET THE BRIG WAS FULL OF TERRAN SCUM.
EASIEST MONEY I EVER MADE.
YOU'RE REALLY GONNA AIR THIS?
IF YOU GIVE ME SOMETHING *NEWSWORTHY*... THEN YEAH, I AM.

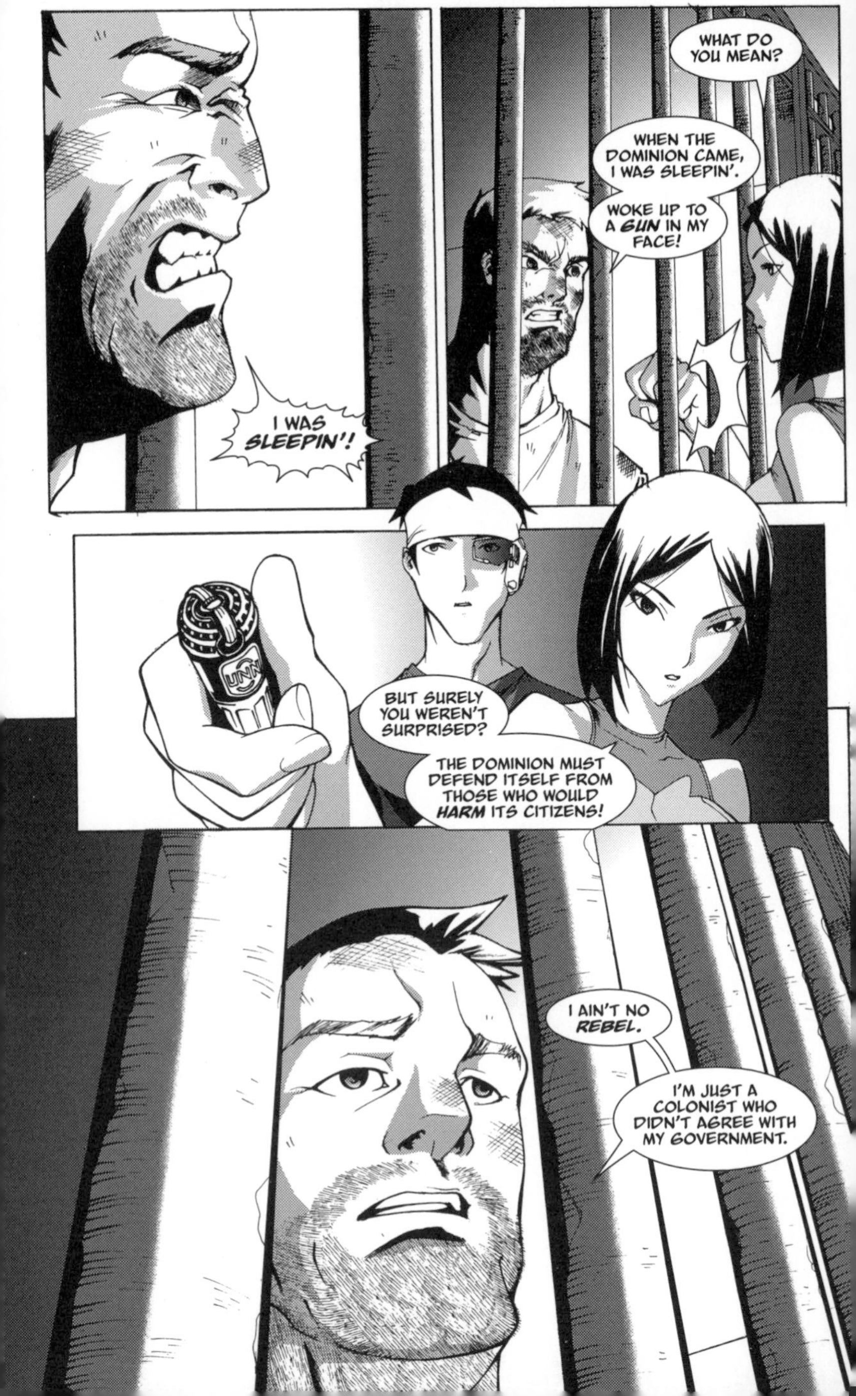
I WAS SLEEPIN'!
WHAT DO YOU MEAN?
WHEN THE DOMINION CAME, I WAS SLEEPIN'.
WOKE UP TO A GUN IN MY FACE!
UNN
BUT SURELY YOU WEREN'T SURPRISED?
THE DOMINION MUST DEFEND ITSELF FROM THOSE WHO WOULD HARM ITS CITIZENS!
I AIN'T NO REBEL.
I'M JUST A COLONIST WHO DIDN'T AGREE WITH MY GOVERNMENT.

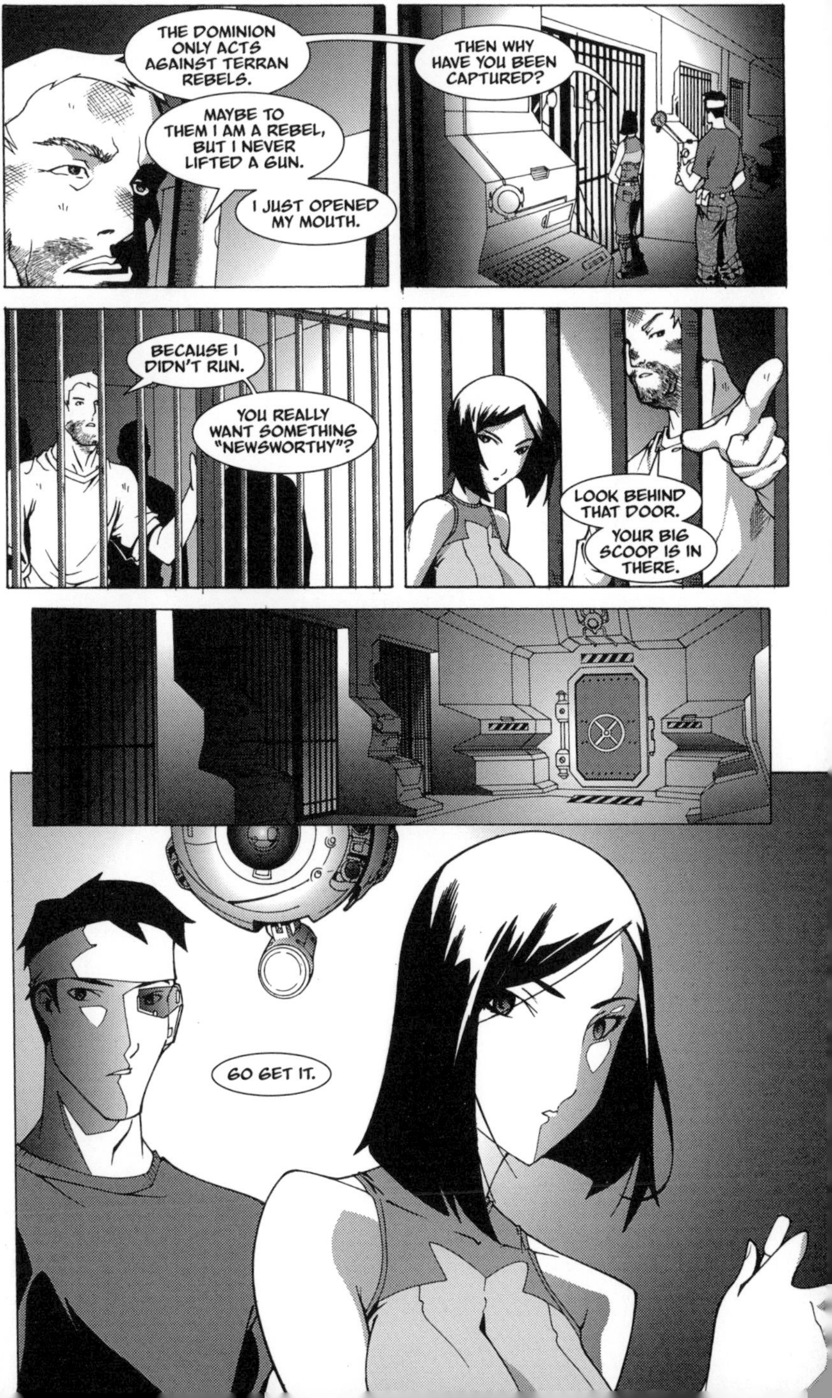

THE DOMINION ONLY ACTS AGAINST TERRAN REBELS.
THEN WHY HAVE YOU BEEN CAPTURED?
MAYBE TO THEM I AM A REBEL, BUT I NEVER LIFTED A GUN.
I JUST OPENED MY MOUTH.
BECAUSE I DIDN'T RUN.
YOU REALLY WANT SOMETHING "NEWSWORTHY"?
LOOK BEHIND THAT DOOR.
YOUR BIG SCOOP IS IN THERE.
GO GET IT.

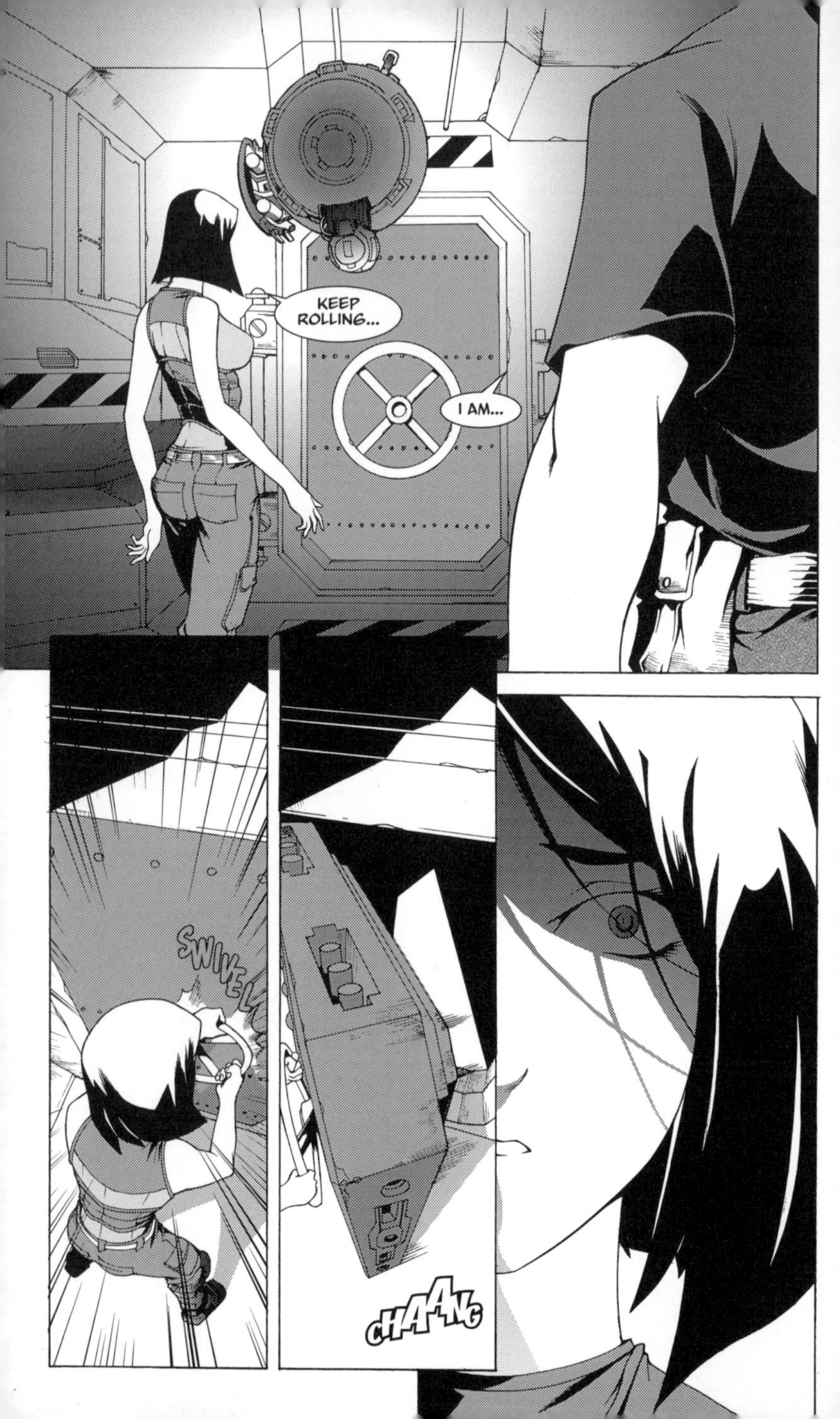
KEEP ROLLING...
I AM...
SWIVEL
CHAAANG

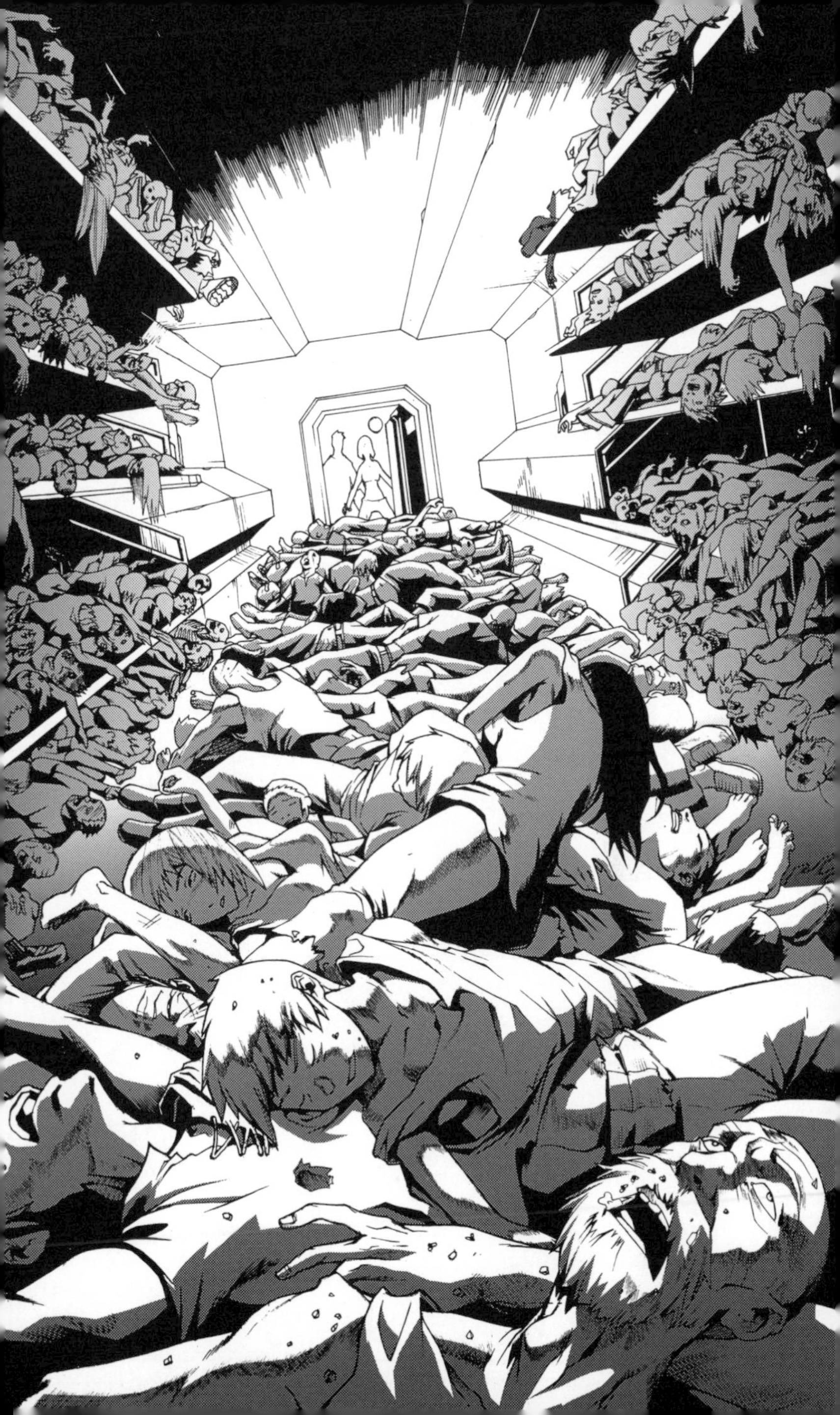

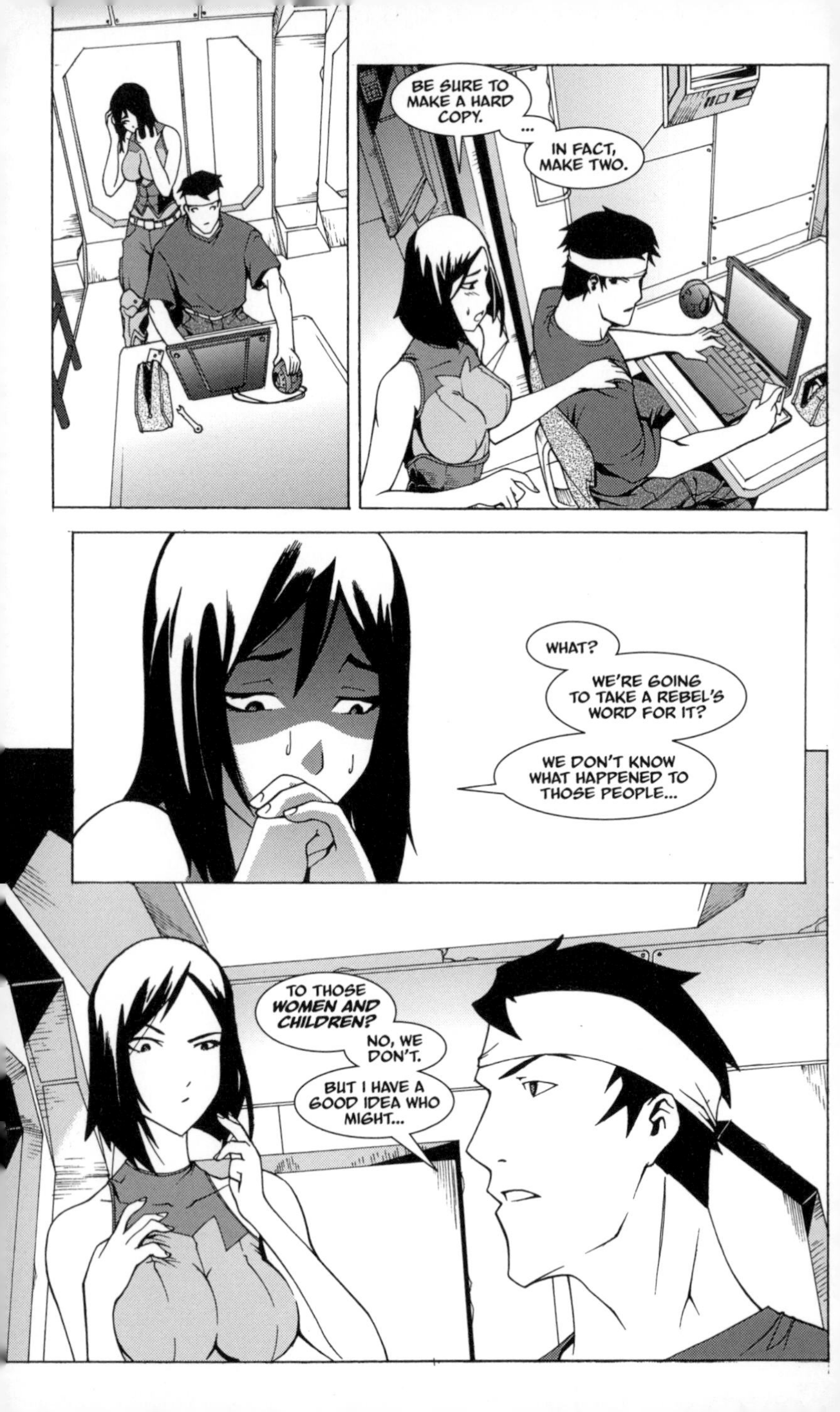
BE SURE TO MAKE A HARD COPY.
...
IN FACT, MAKE TWO.
WHAT?
WE'RE GOING TO TAKE A REBEL'S WORD FOR IT?
WE DON'T KNOW WHAT HAPPENED TO THOSE PEOPLE...
TO THOSE WOMEN AND CHILDREN?
NO, WE DON'T.
BUT I HAVE A GOOD IDEA WHO MIGHT...

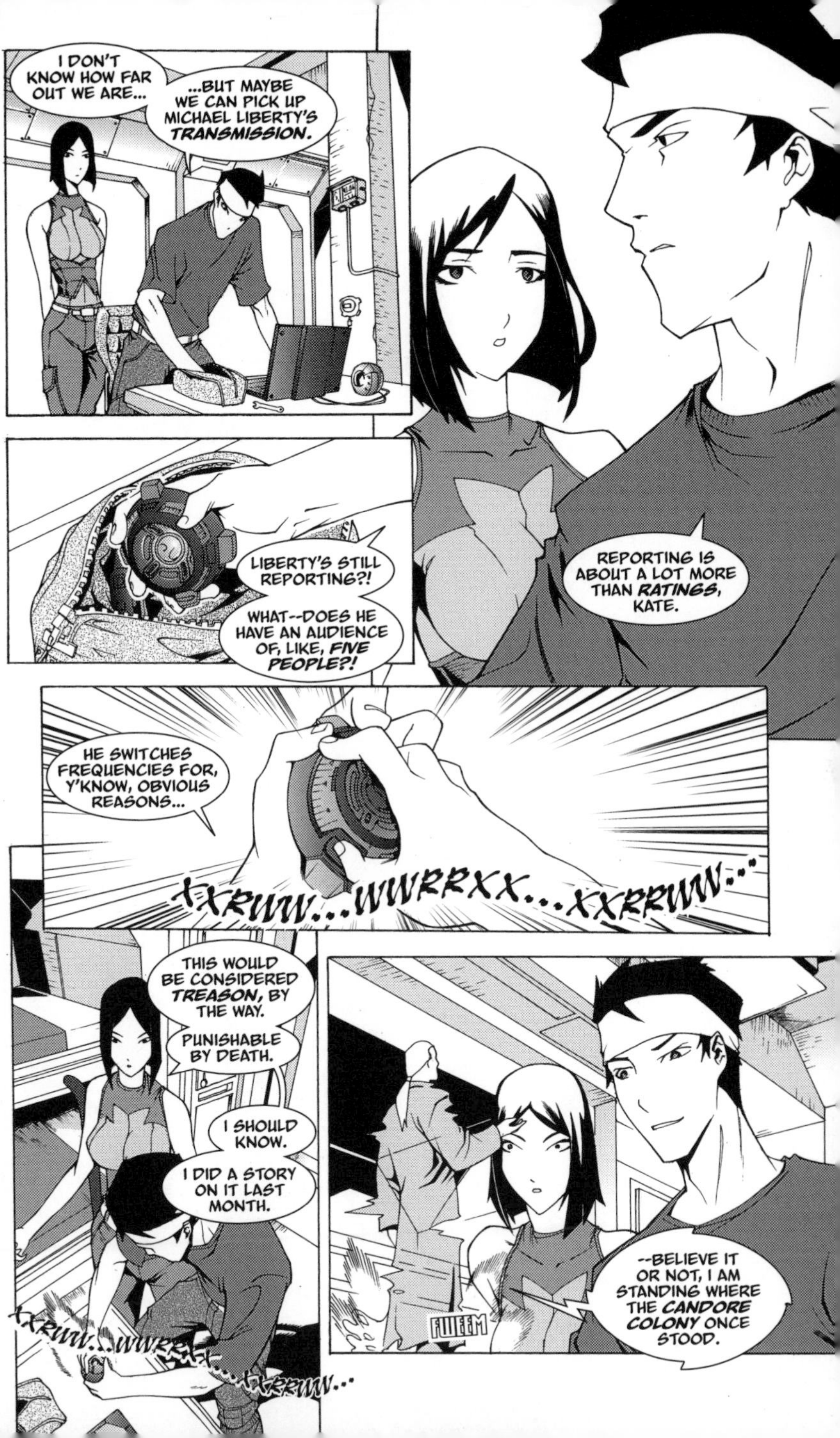

I DON'T KNOW HOW FAR OUT WE ARE...
...BUT MAYBE WE CAN PICK UP MICHAEL LIBERTY'S TRANSMISSION.
REPORTING IS ABOUT A LOT MORE THAN RATINGS, KATE.
LIBERTY'S STILL REPORTING?!
WHAT--DOES HE HAVE AN AUDIENCE OF, LIKE, FIVE PEOPLE?!
HE SWITCHES FREQUENCIES FOR, Y'KNOW, OBVIOUS REASONS...
TXRUWW...WWRRXX...XXRRUWW...
THIS WOULD BE CONSIDERED TREASON, BY THE WAY.
PUNISHABLE BY DEATH.
I SHOULD KNOW.
I DID A STORY ON IT LAST MONTH.
FWEEM
--BELIEVE IT OR NOT, I AM STANDING WHERE THE CANDORE COLONY ONCE STOOD.

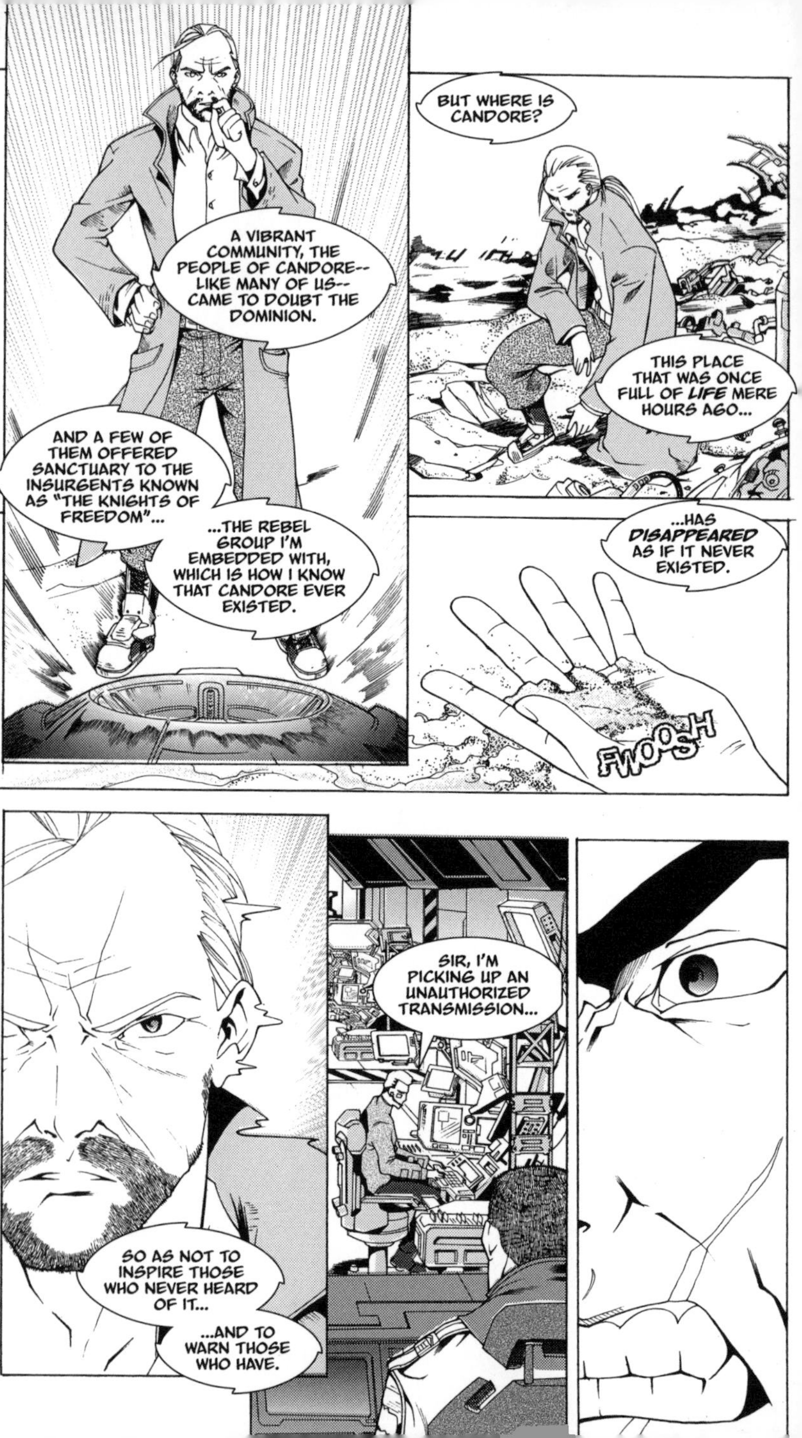
A VIBRANT COMMUNITY, THE PEOPLE OF CANDORE-- LIKE MANY OF US-- CAME TO DOUBT THE DOMINION.
AND A FEW OF THEM OFFERED SANCTUARY TO THE INSURGENTS KNOWN AS "THE KNIGHTS OF FREEDOM"...
...THE REBEL GROUP I'M EMBEDDED WITH, WHICH IS HOW I KNOW THAT CANDORE EVER EXISTED.
BUT WHERE IS CANDORE?
THIS PLACE THAT WAS ONCE FULL OF *LIFE* MERE HOURS AGO...
...HAS ***DISAPPEARED*** AS IF IT NEVER EXISTED.
FWOOSH
SO AS NOT TO INSPIRE THOSE WHO NEVER HEARD OF IT...
...AND TO WARN THOSE WHO HAVE.
SIR, I'M PICKING UP AN UNAUTHORIZED TRANSMISSION...

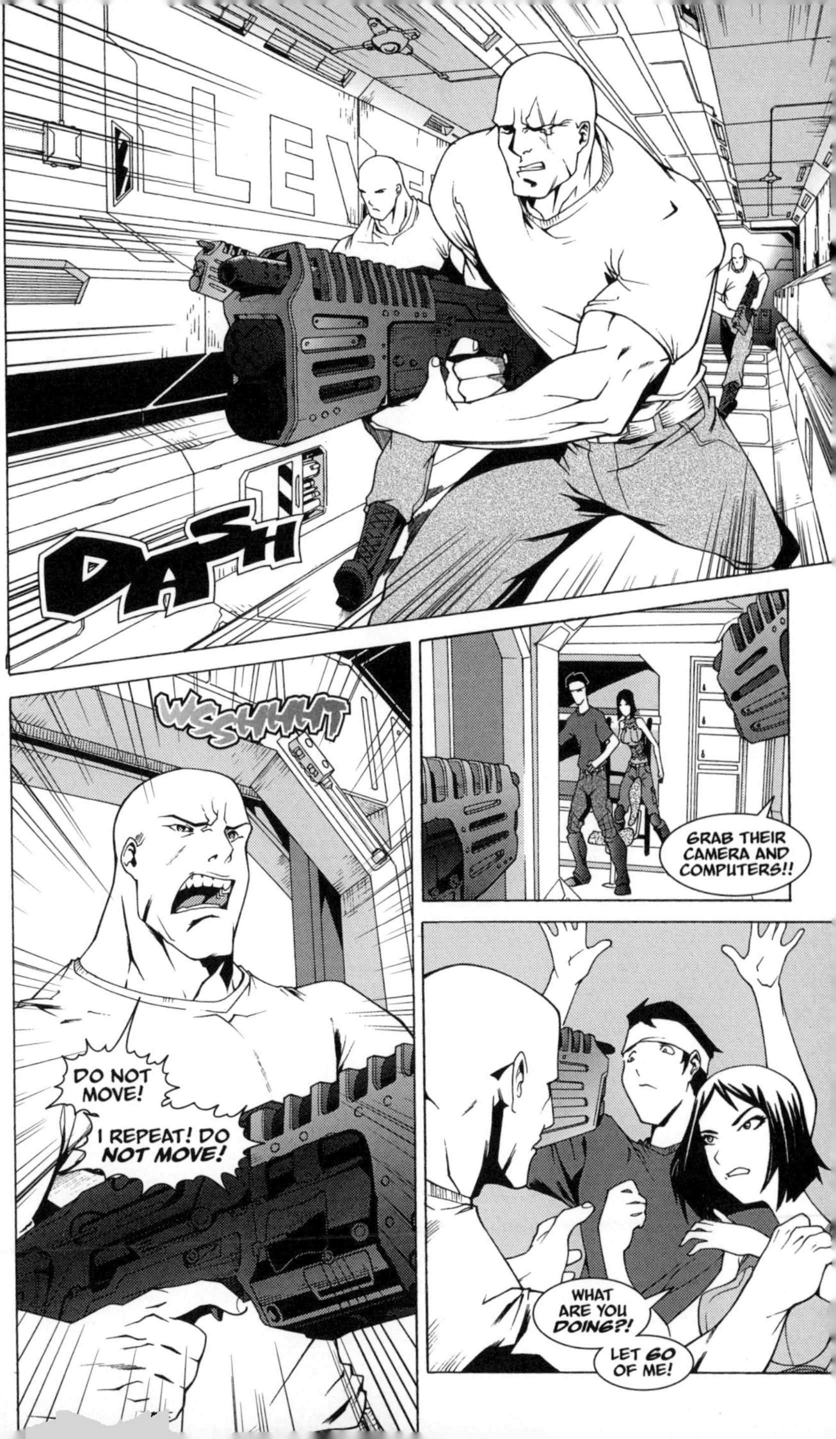
DASH
WSSHHHT
DO NOT MOVE!
I REPEAT! DO NOT MOVE!
GRAB THEIR CAMERA AND COMPUTERS!!
WHAT ARE YOU DOING?!
LET GO OF ME!

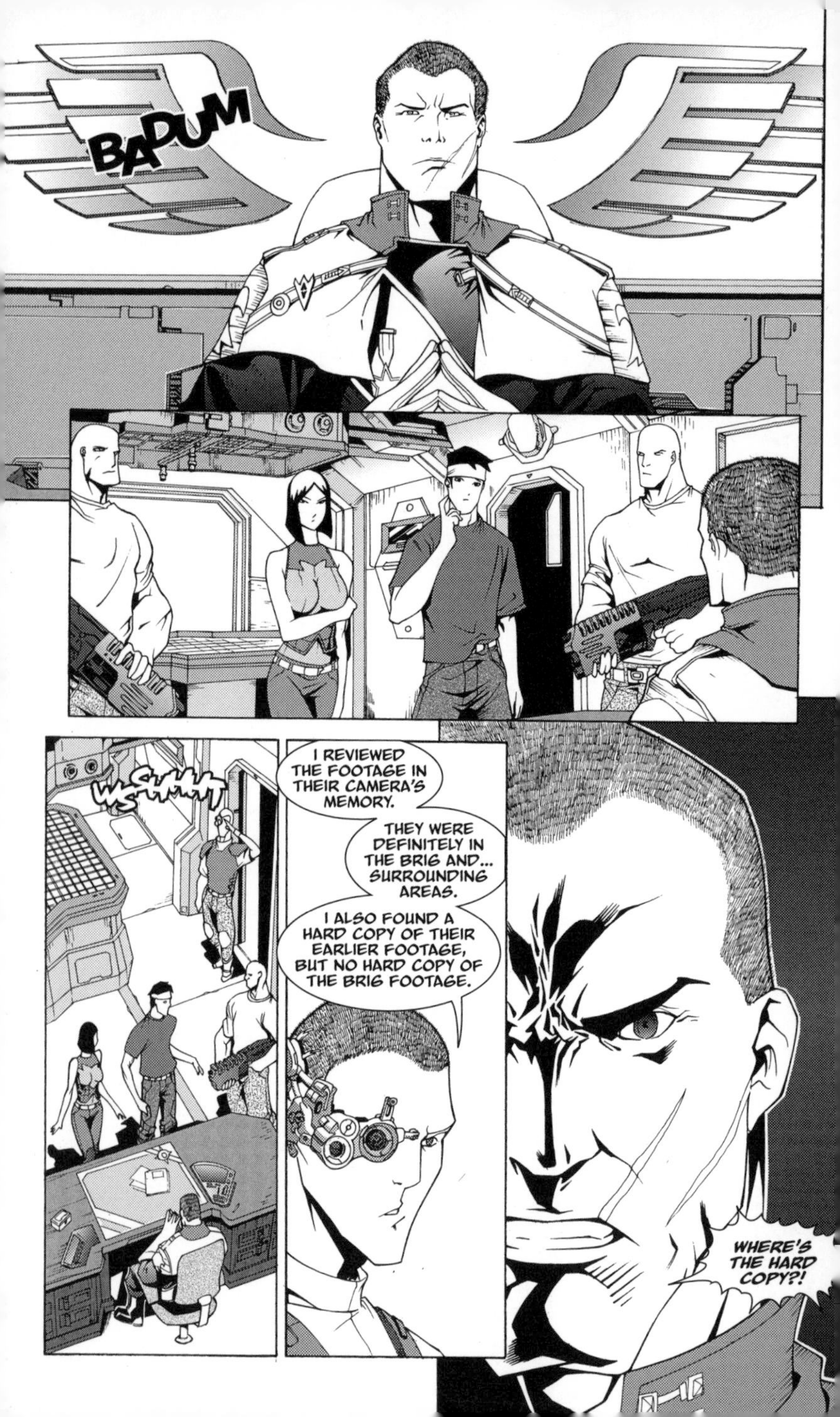
BADUM
WSHHH
I REVIEWED THE FOOTAGE IN THEIR CAMERA'S MEMORY.
THEY WERE DEFINITELY IN THE BRIG AND... SURROUNDING AREAS.
I ALSO FOUND A HARD COPY OF THEIR EARLIER FOOTAGE, BUT NO HARD COPY OF THE BRIG FOOTAGE.
WHERE'S THE HARD COPY?!

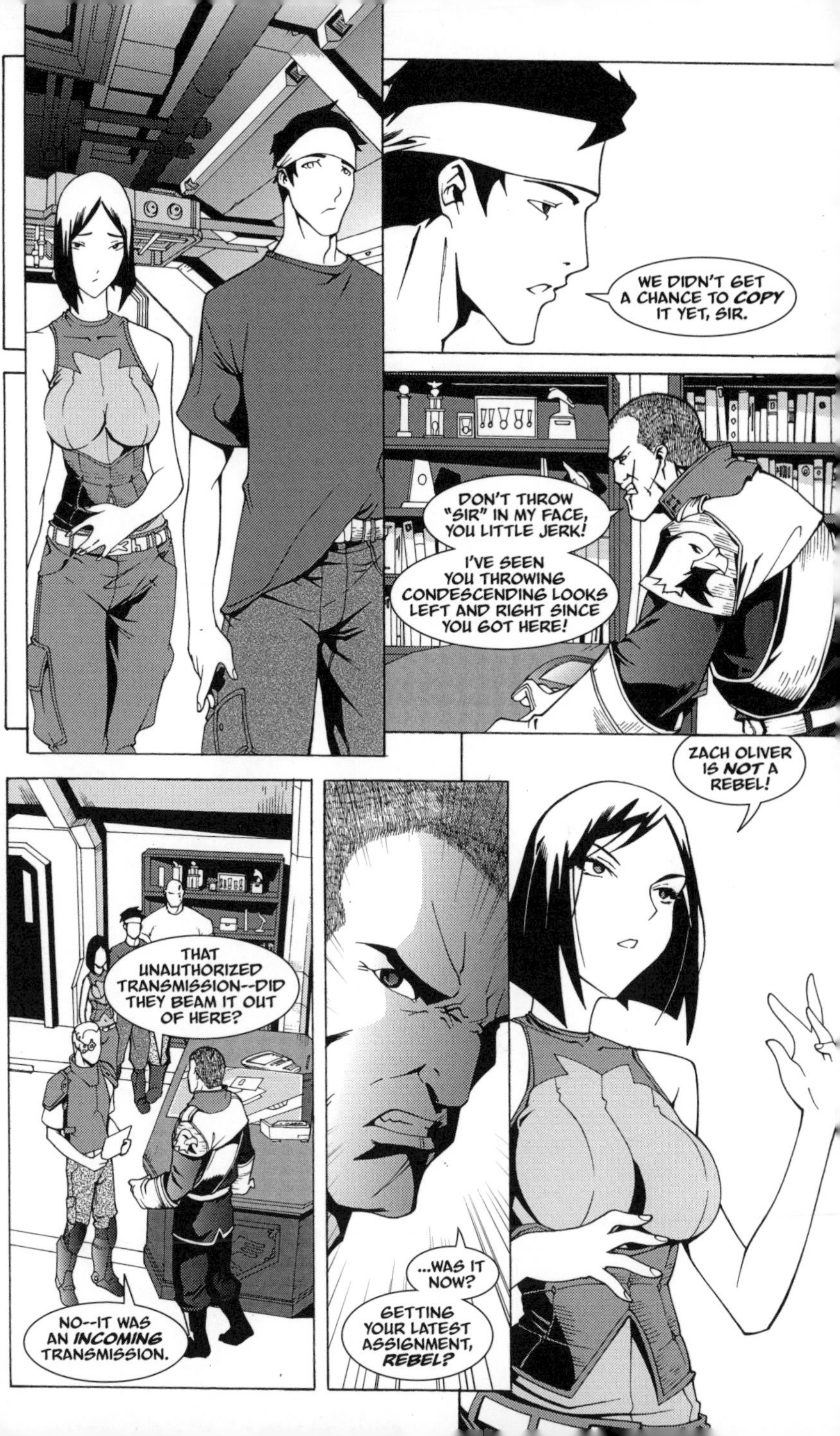
WE DIDN'T GET A CHANCE TO COPY IT YET, SIR.
DON'T THROW "SIR" IN MY FACE, YOU LITTLE JERK!
I'VE SEEN YOU THROWING CONDESCENDING LOOKS LEFT AND RIGHT SINCE YOU GOT HERE!
THAT UNAUTHORIZED TRANSMISSION--DID THEY BEAM IT OUT OF HERE?
NO--IT WAS AN INCOMING TRANSMISSION.
...WAS IT NOW?
GETTING YOUR LATEST ASSIGNMENT, REBEL?
ZACH OLIVER IS NOT A REBEL!

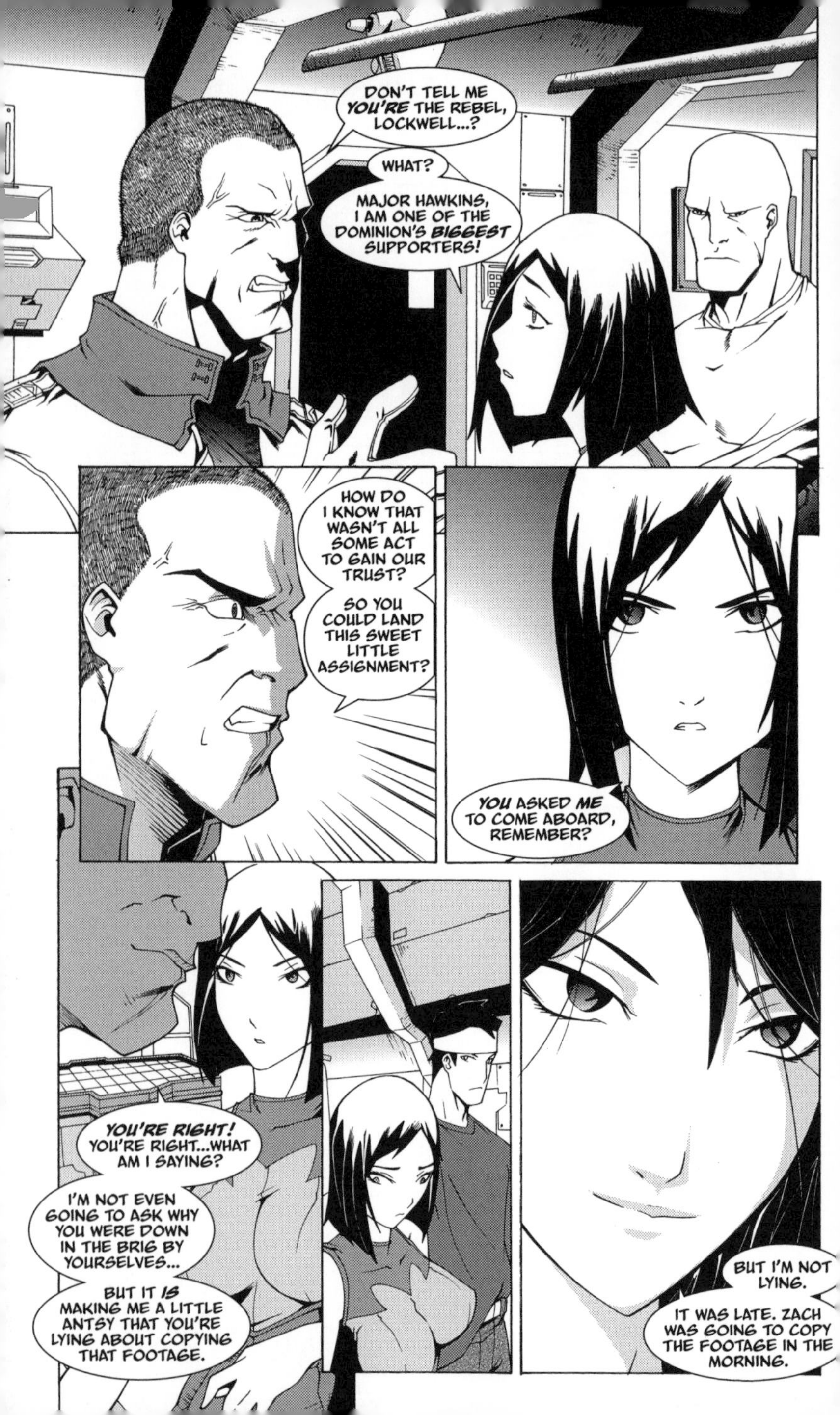
DON'T TELL ME YOU'RE THE REBEL, LOCKWELL...?
WHAT?
MAJOR HAWKINS, I AM ONE OF THE DOMINION'S BIGGEST SUPPORTERS!
HOW DO I KNOW THAT WASN'T ALL SOME ACT TO GAIN OUR TRUST?
SO YOU COULD LAND THIS SWEET LITTLE ASSIGNMENT?
YOU ASKED ME TO COME ABOARD, REMEMBER?
YOU'RE RIGHT! YOU'RE RIGHT...WHAT AM I SAYING?
I'M NOT EVEN GOING TO ASK WHY YOU WERE DOWN IN THE BRIG BY YOURSELVES...
BUT IT IS MAKING ME A LITTLE ANTSY THAT YOU'RE LYING ABOUT COPYING THAT FOOTAGE.
BUT I'M NOT LYING.
IT WAS LATE. ZACH WAS GOING TO COPY THE FOOTAGE IN THE MORNING.

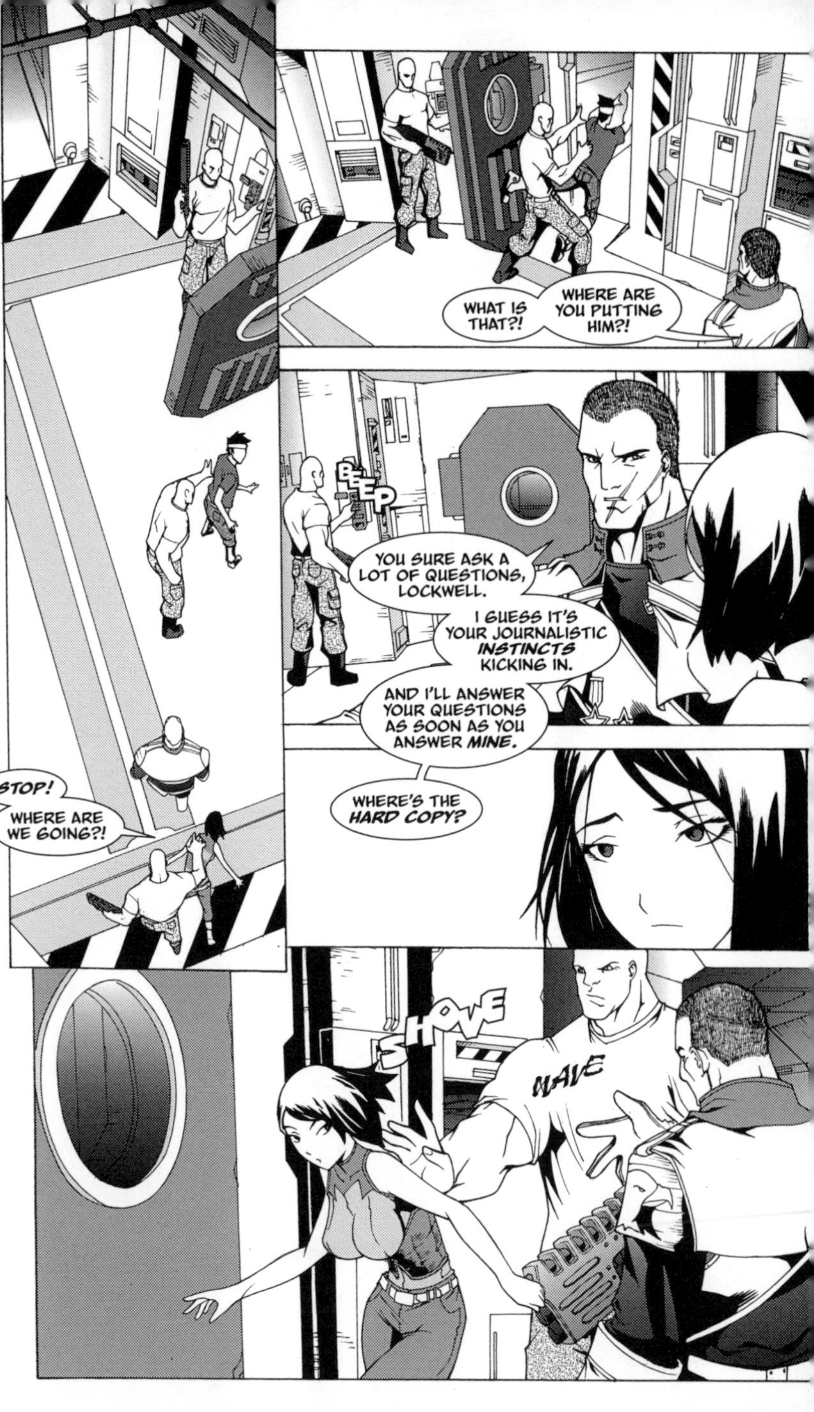
WHAT IS THAT?!
WHERE ARE YOU PUTTING HIM?!
STOP!
WHERE ARE WE GOING?!
BEEP
YOU SURE ASK A LOT OF QUESTIONS, LOCKWELL.
I GUESS IT'S YOUR JOURNALISTIC INSTINCTS KICKING IN.
AND I'LL ANSWER YOUR QUESTIONS AS SOON AS YOU ANSWER MINE.
WHERE'S THE HARD COPY?
SHOVE
WAVE

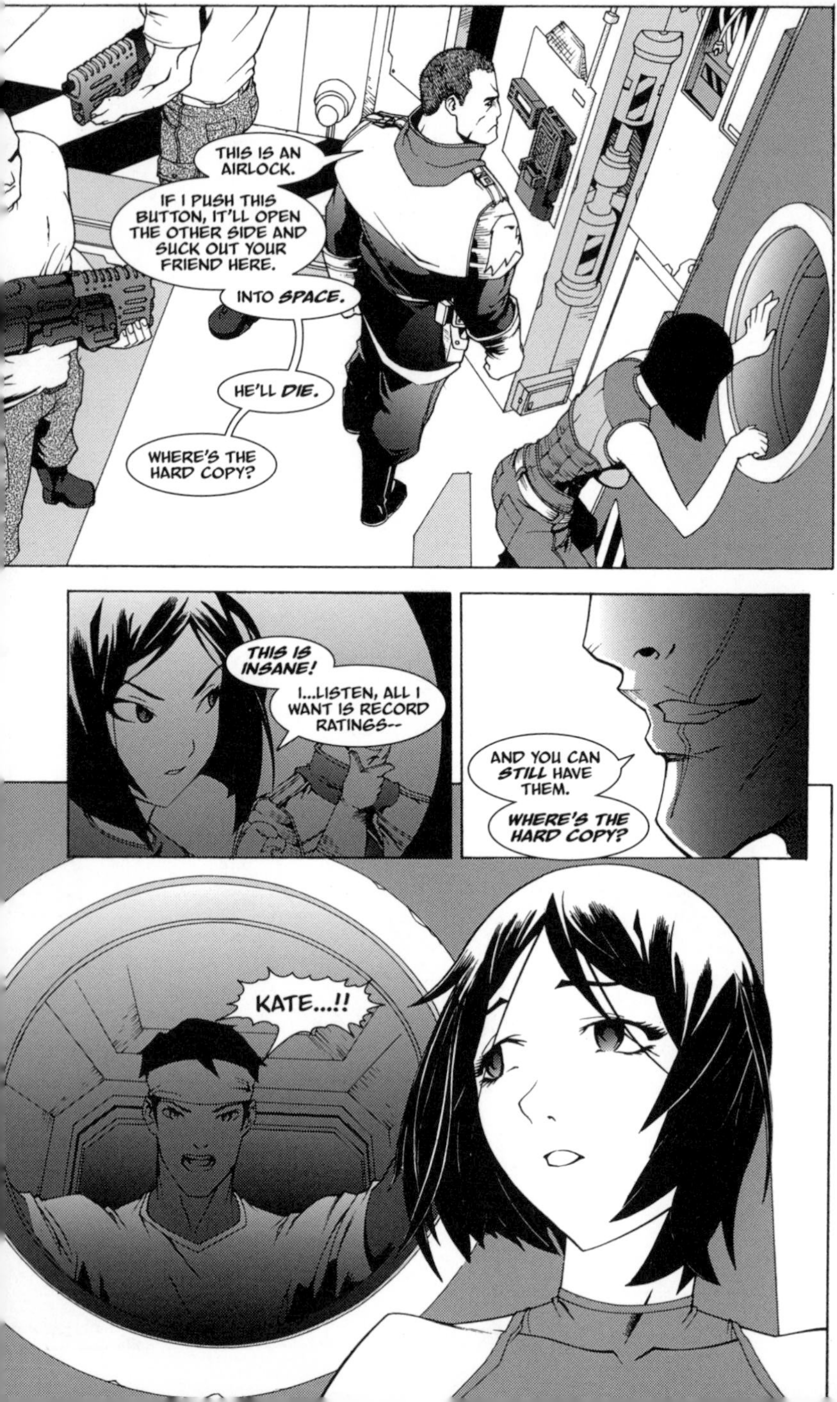
THIS IS AN AIRLOCK.
IF I PUSH THIS BUTTON, IT'LL OPEN THE OTHER SIDE AND SUCK OUT YOUR FRIEND HERE.
INTO *SPACE.*
HE'LL *DIE.*
WHERE'S THE HARD COPY?
THIS IS INSANE!
I...LISTEN, ALL I WANT IS RECORD RATINGS--
AND YOU CAN *STILL* HAVE THEM.
WHERE'S THE HARD COPY?
KATE...!!

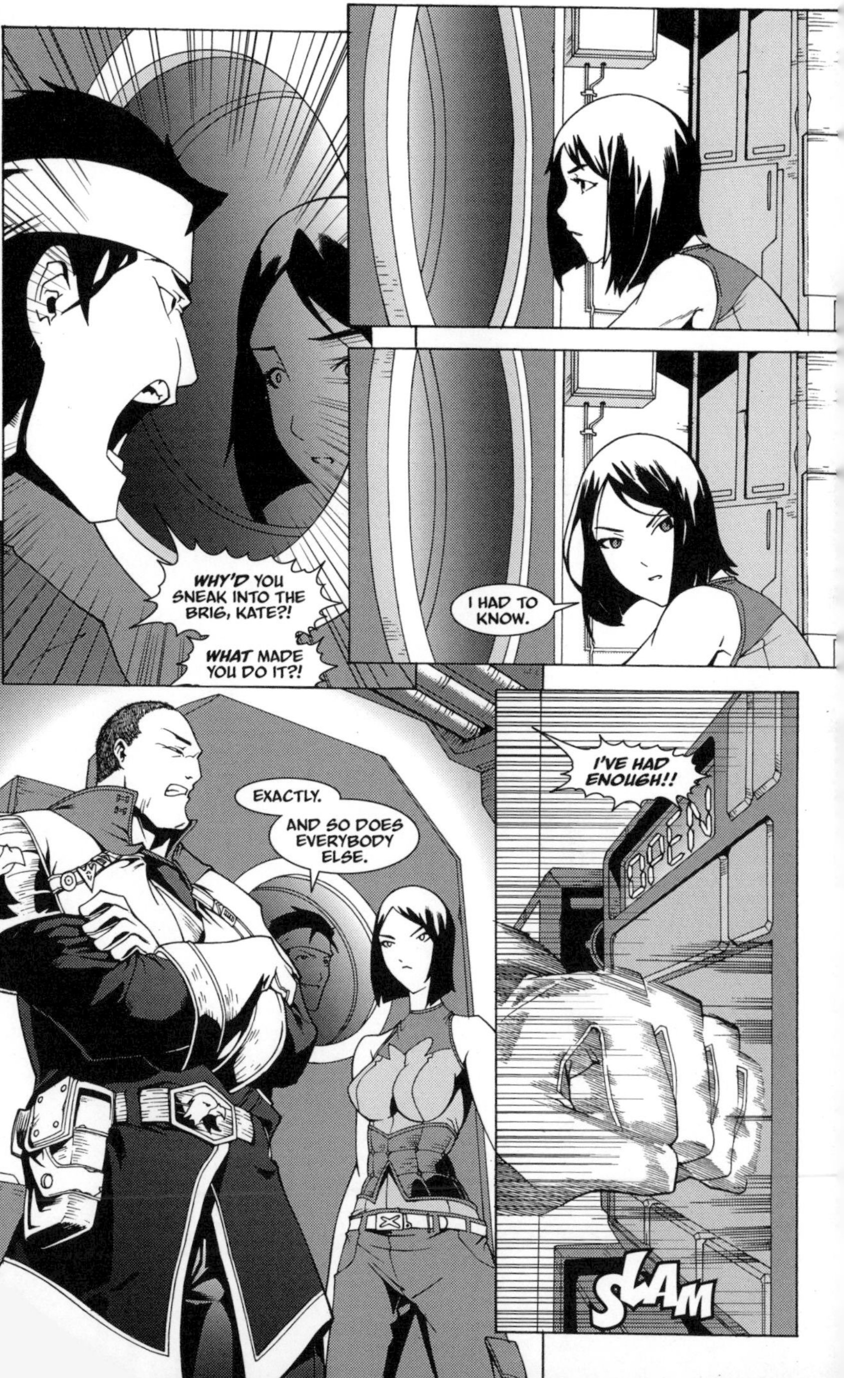
WHY'D YOU SNEAK INTO THE BRIG, KATE?!
WHAT MADE YOU DO IT?!
I HAD TO KNOW.
EXACTLY.
AND SO DOES EVERYBODY ELSE.
I'VE HAD ENOUGH!!
OPEN
SLAM

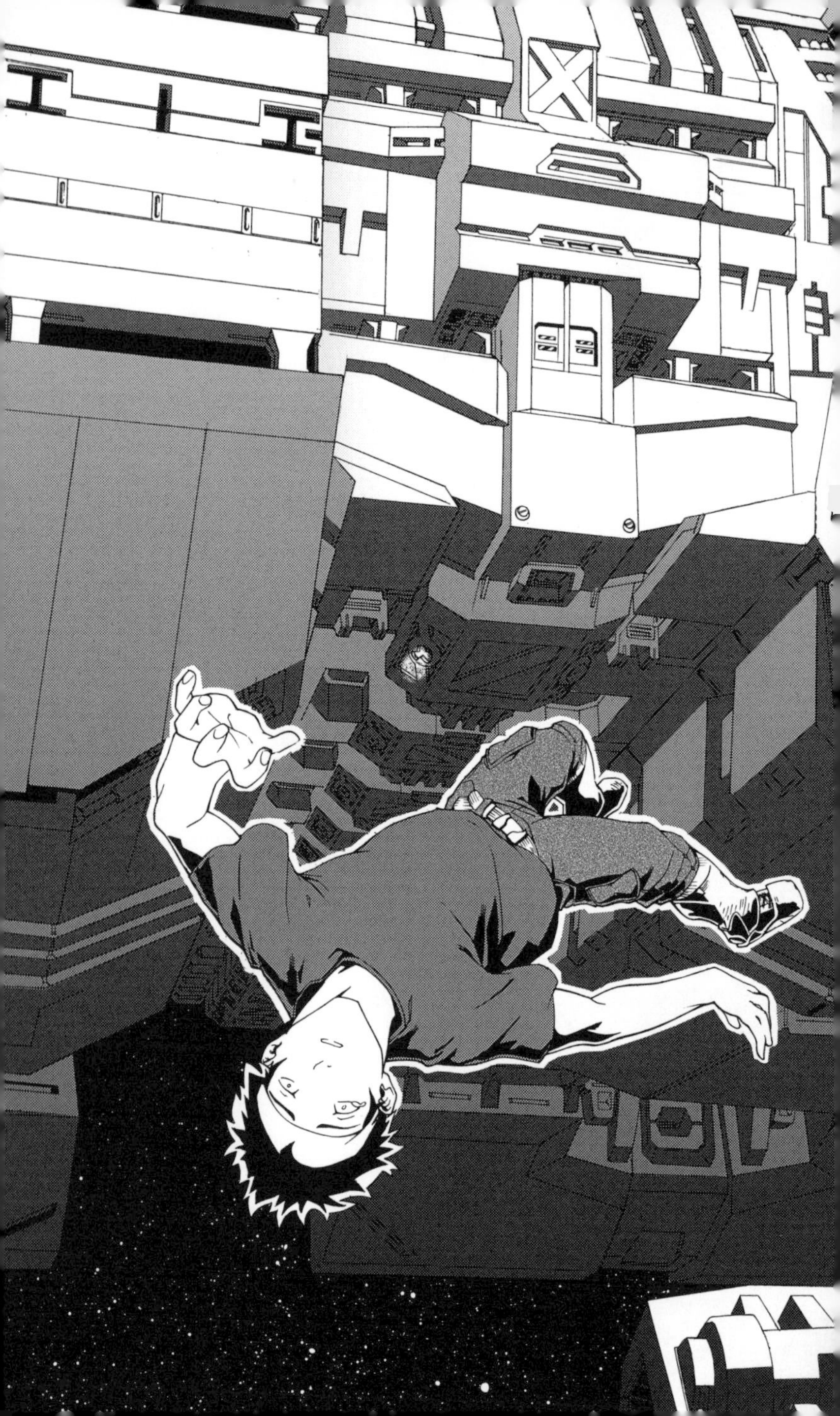

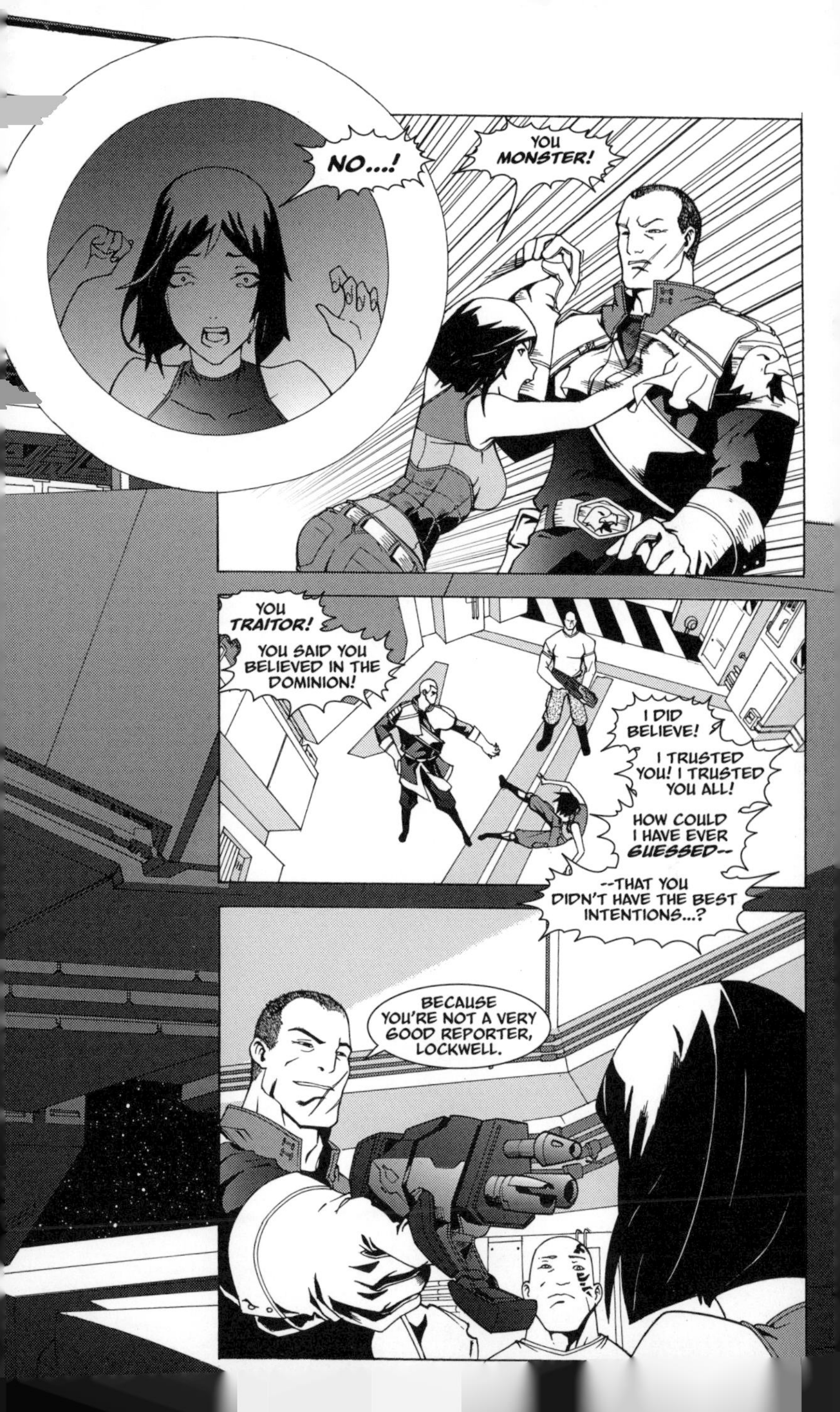
NO...!
YOU MONSTER!
YOU TRAITOR!
YOU SAID YOU BELIEVED IN THE DOMINION!
I DID BELIEVE!
I TRUSTED YOU! I TRUSTED YOU ALL!
HOW COULD I HAVE EVER GUESSED--
--THAT YOU DIDN'T HAVE THE BEST INTENTIONS...?
BECAUSE YOU'RE NOT A VERY GOOD REPORTER, LOCKWELL.

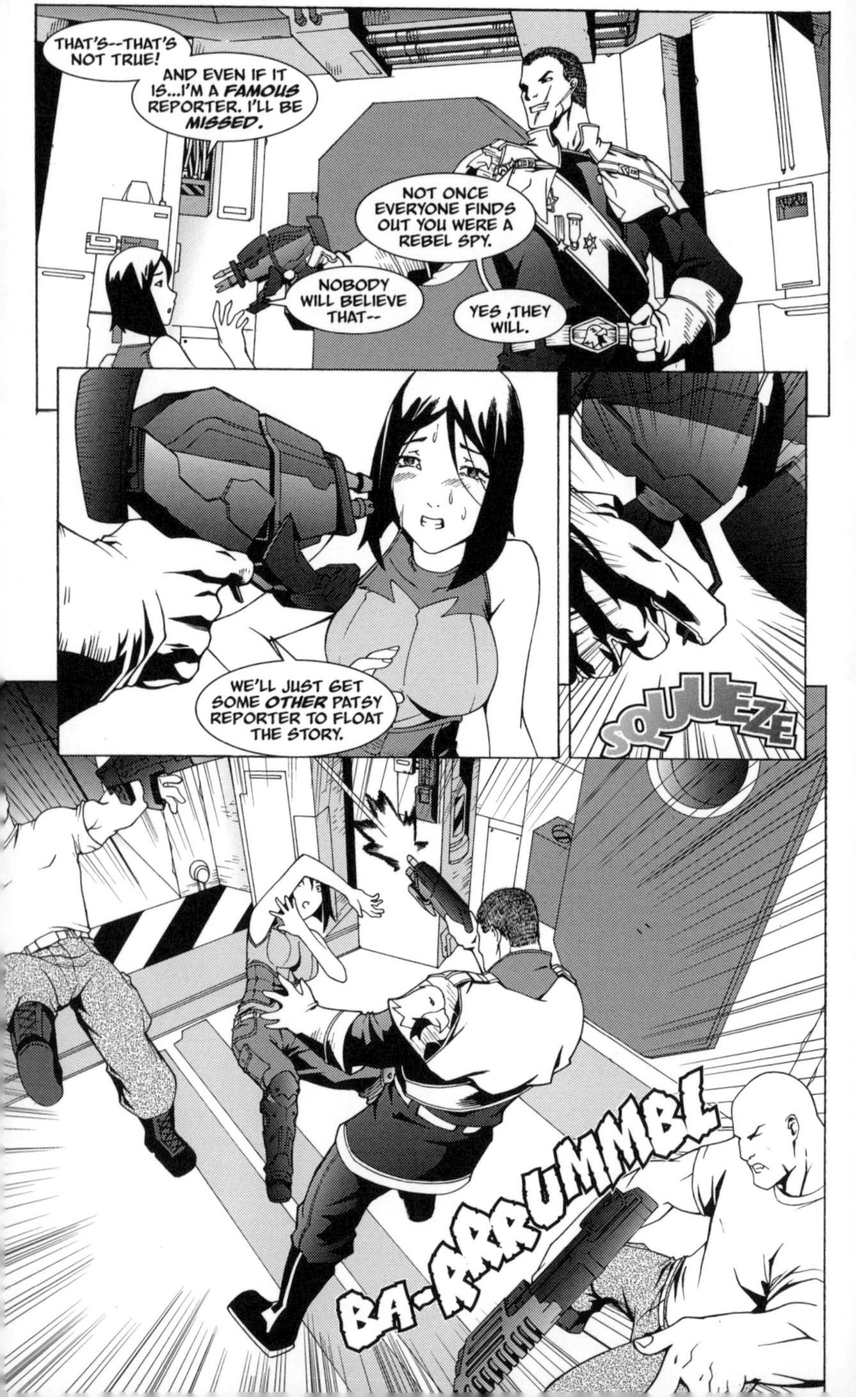
THAT'S--THAT'S NOT TRUE!
AND EVEN IF IT IS...I'M A FAMOUS REPORTER. I'LL BE MISSED.
NOT ONCE EVERYONE FINDS OUT YOU WERE A REBEL SPY.
NOBODY WILL BELIEVE THAT--
YES ,THEY WILL.
WE'LL JUST GET SOME OTHER PATSY REPORTER TO FLOAT THE STORY.
SQUUEZE
BA-ARRUMMBL

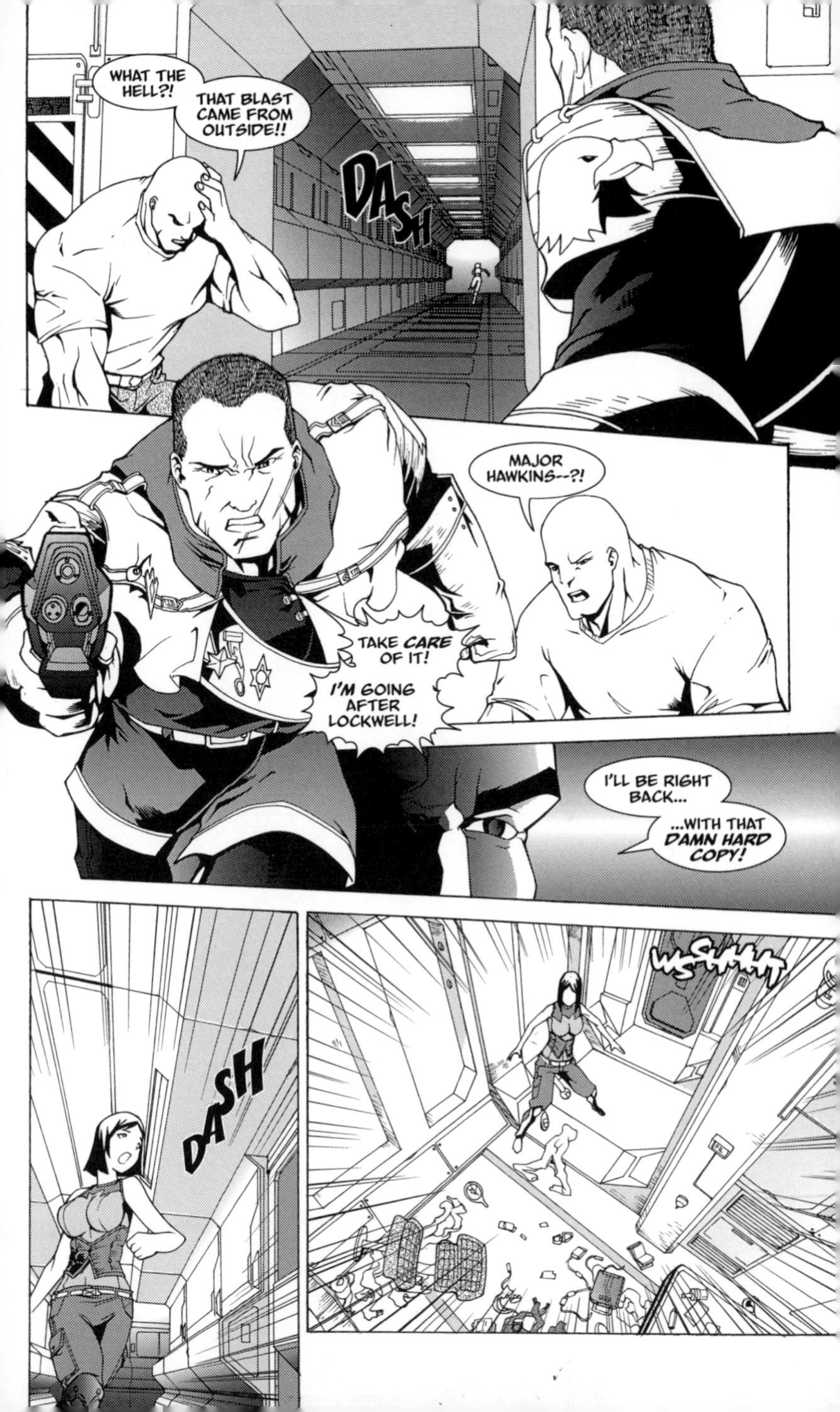
WHAT THE HELL?!
THAT BLAST CAME FROM OUTSIDE!!
DASH
MAJOR HAWKINS--?!
TAKE CARE OF IT!
I'M GOING AFTER LOCKWELL!
I'LL BE RIGHT BACK...
...WITH THAT DAMN HARD COPY!
DASH
WSHHT

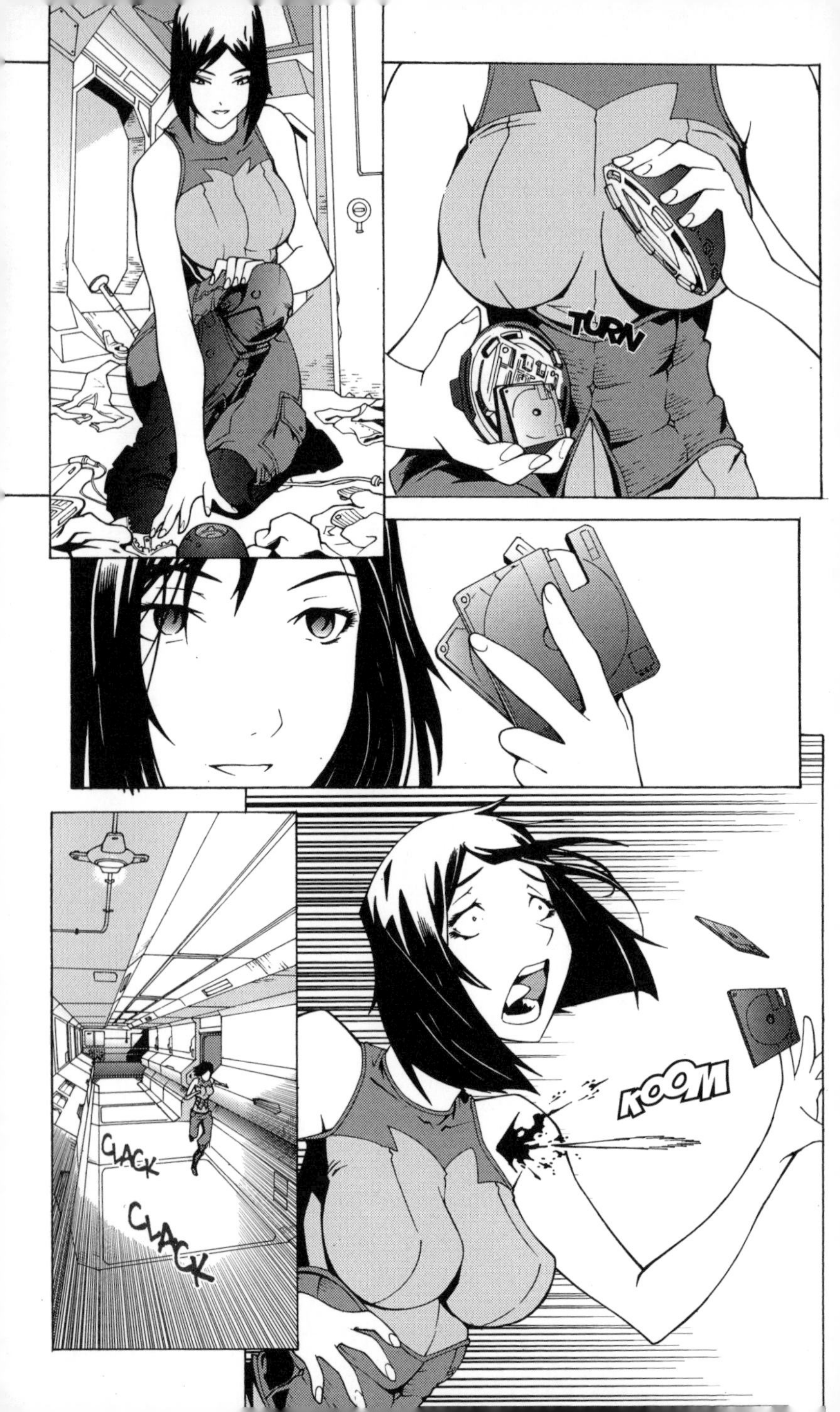
TURN
CLACK
CLACK
KOOM

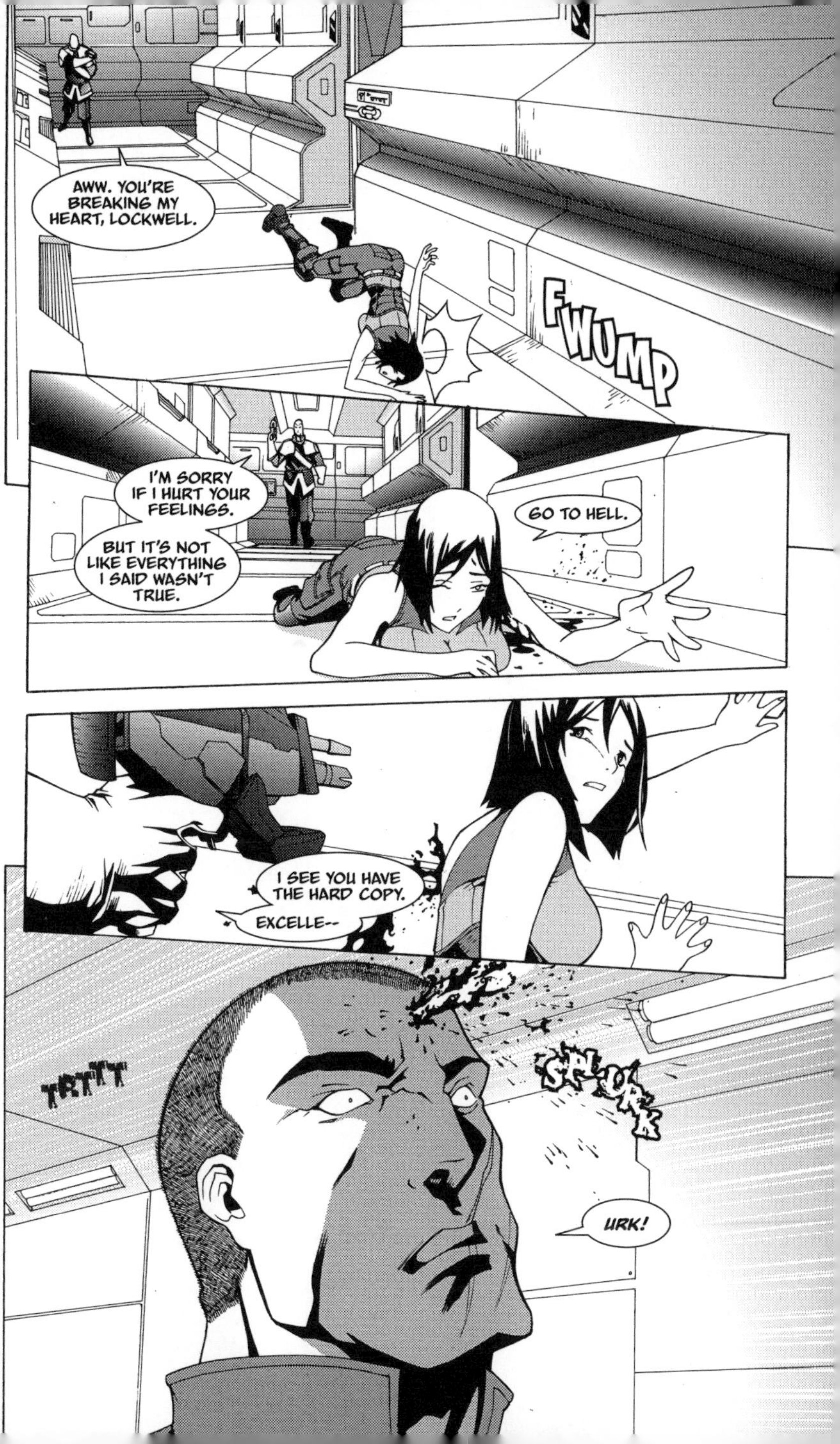
AWW. YOU'RE BREAKING MY HEART, LOCKWELL.
FWUMP
I'M SORRY IF I HURT YOUR FEELINGS.
BUT IT'S NOT LIKE EVERYTHING I SAID WASN'T TRUE.
GO TO HELL.
I SEE YOU HAVE THE HARD COPY.
EXCELLE--
TRTTT
SPLORK
URK!

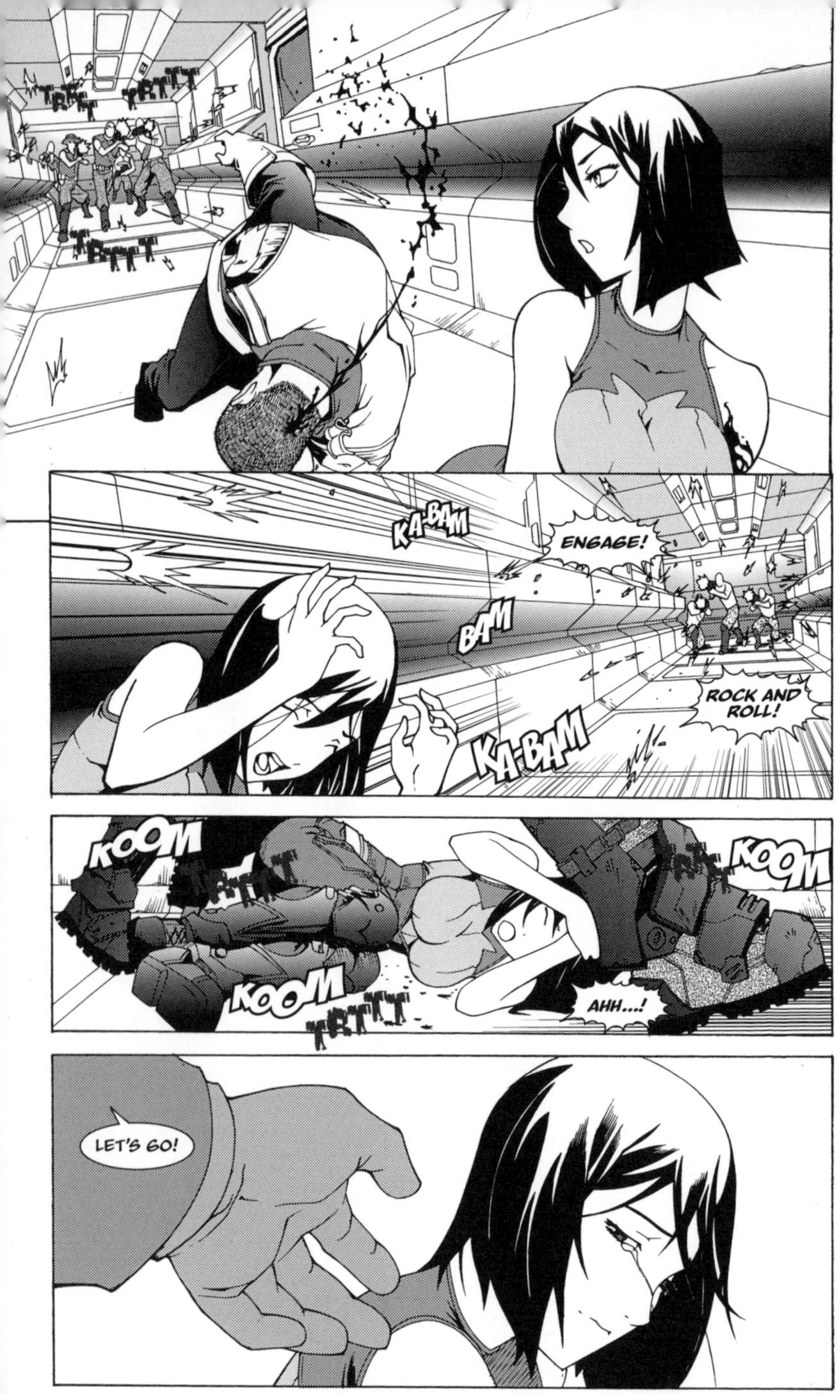
TRRT
TRRTT
TRTTT
KA-BAM
ENGAGE!
BAM
ROCK AND ROLL!
KA-BAM
KOOM
TRTTT
KOOM
KOOM
TRTTT
AHH...!
LET'S GO!

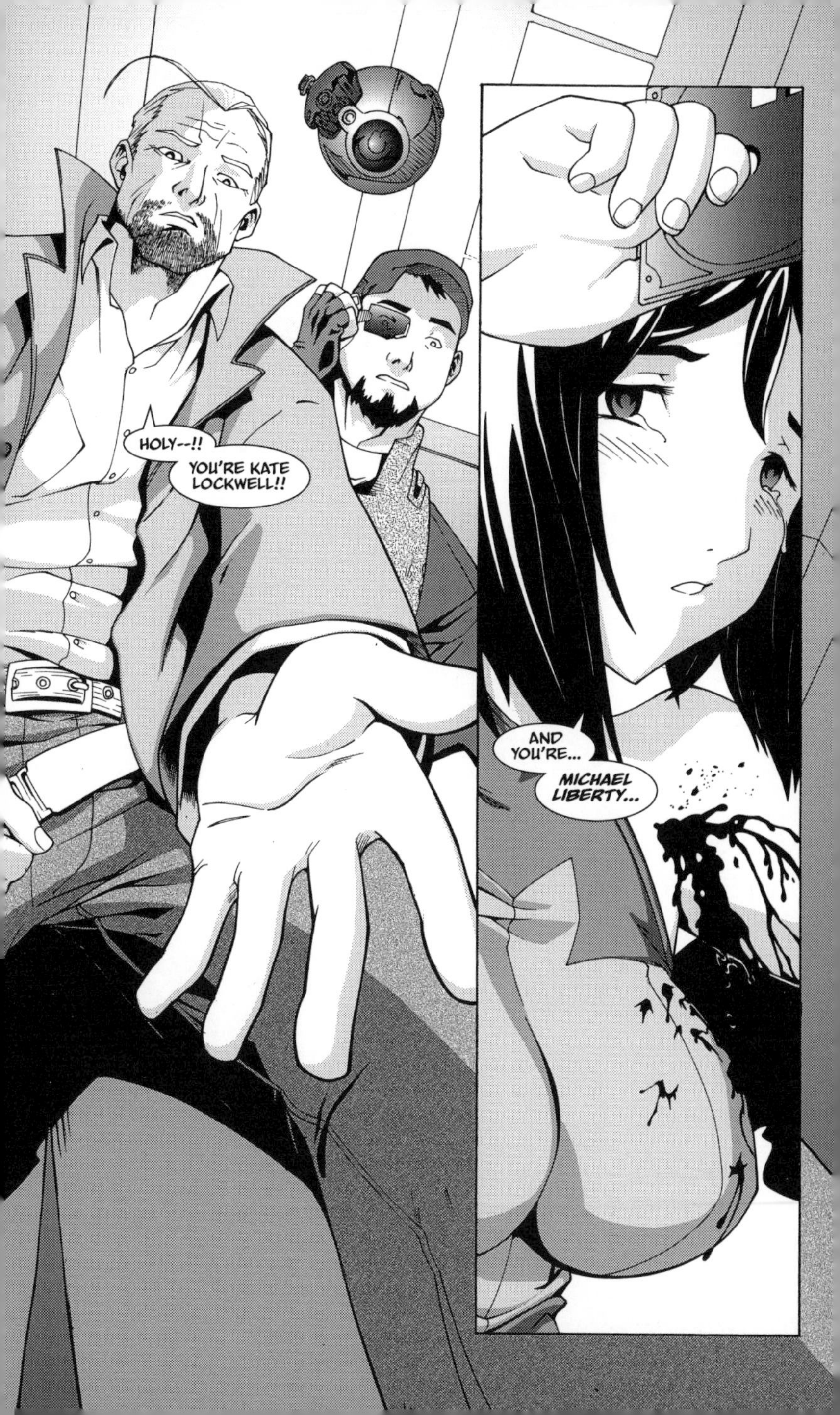
HOLY--!!
YOU'RE KATE LOCKWELL!!
AND YOU'RE... MICHAEL LIBERTY...

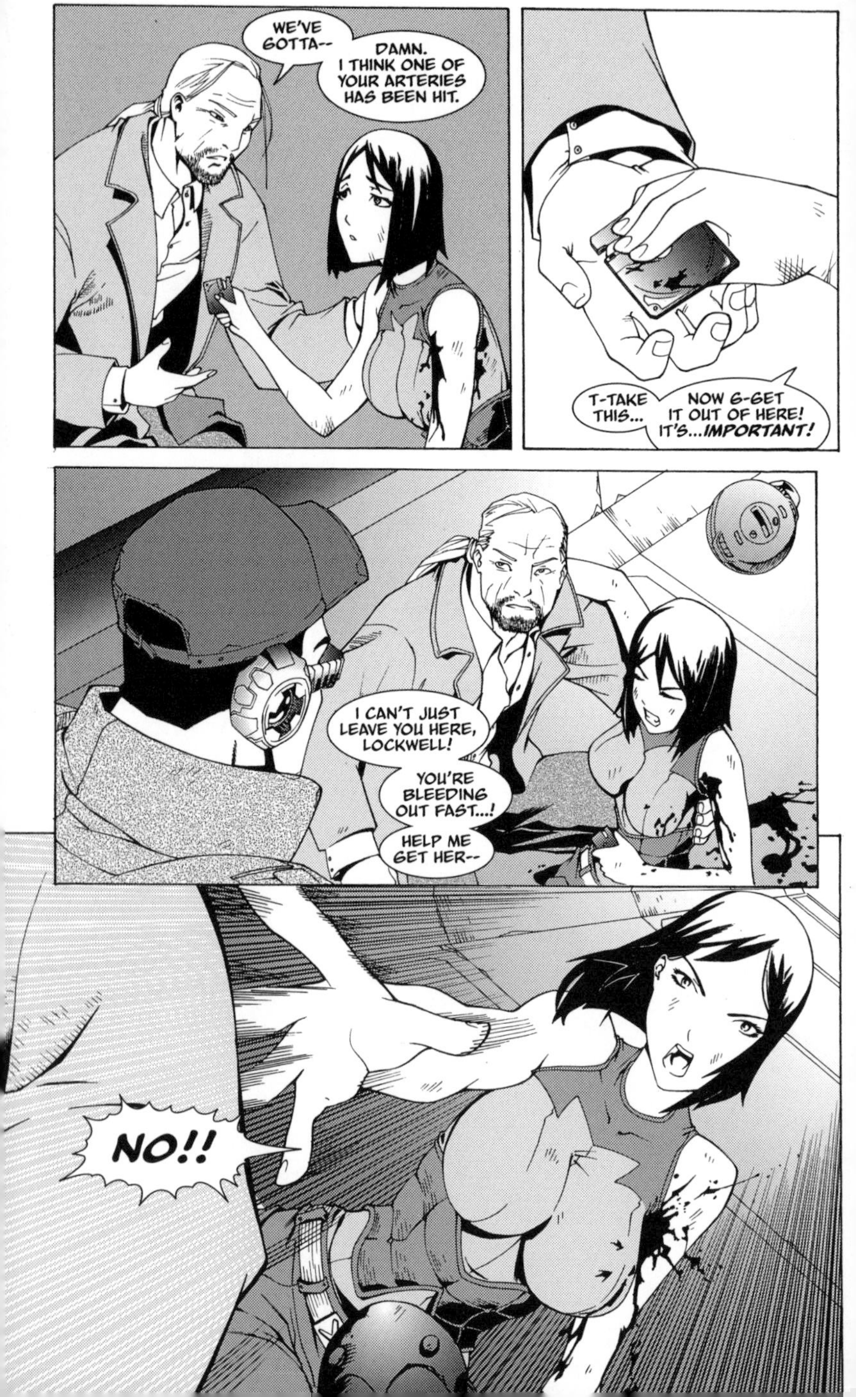
WE'VE GOTTA--
DAMN. I THINK ONE OF YOUR ARTERIES HAS BEEN HIT.
T-TAKE THIS...
NOW G-GET IT OUT OF HERE! IT'S...IMPORTANT!
I CAN'T JUST LEAVE YOU HERE, LOCKWELL!
YOU'RE BLEEDING OUT FAST...!
HELP ME GET HER--
NO!!

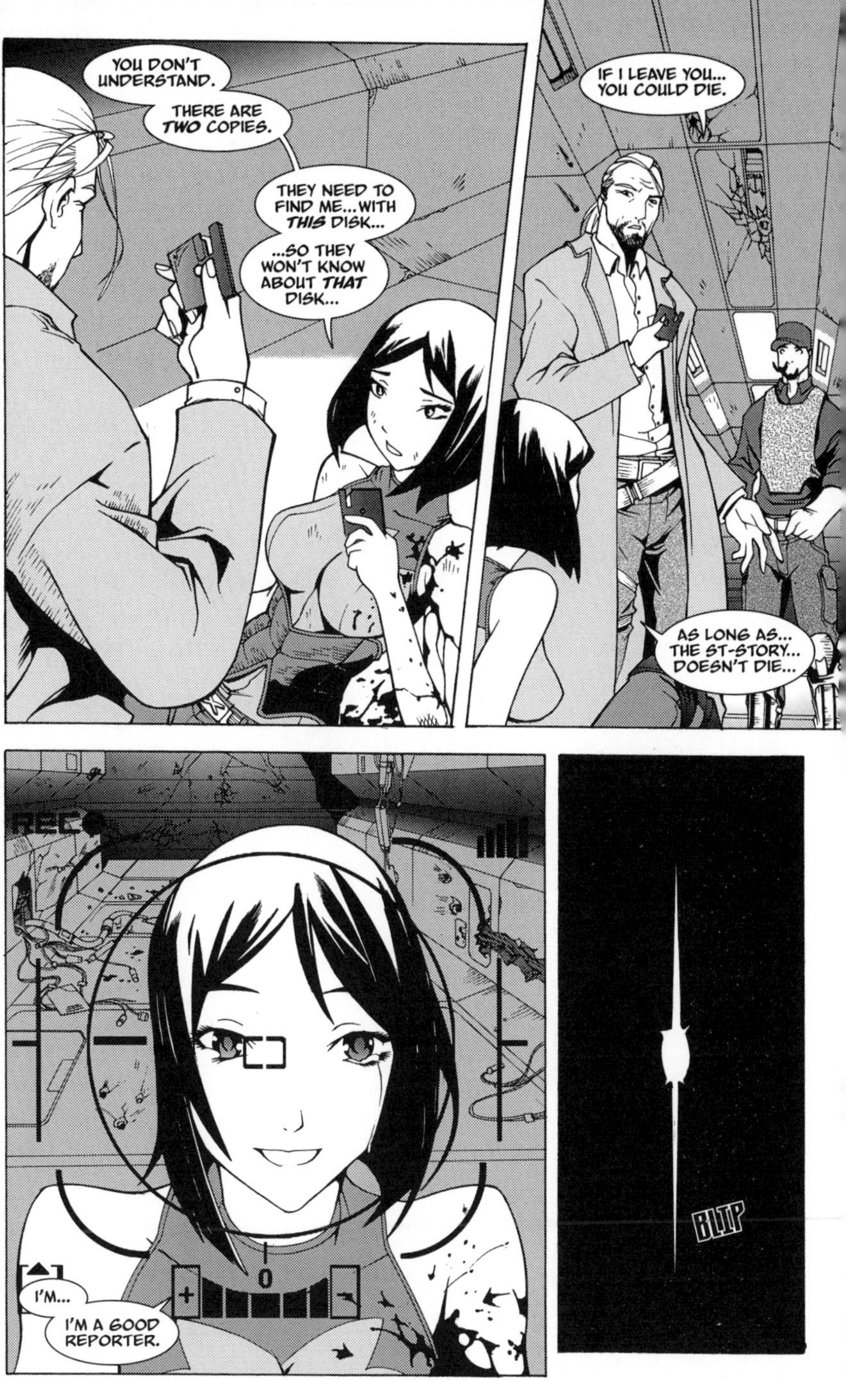
YOU DON'T UNDERSTAND.
THERE ARE *TWO* COPIES.
THEY NEED TO FIND ME...WITH *THIS* DISK...
...SO THEY WON'T KNOW ABOUT *THAT* DISK...
IF I LEAVE YOU... YOU COULD DIE.
AS LONG AS... THE ST-STORY... DOESN'T DIE...
REC
I'M...
I'M A GOOD REPORTER.
BLIP

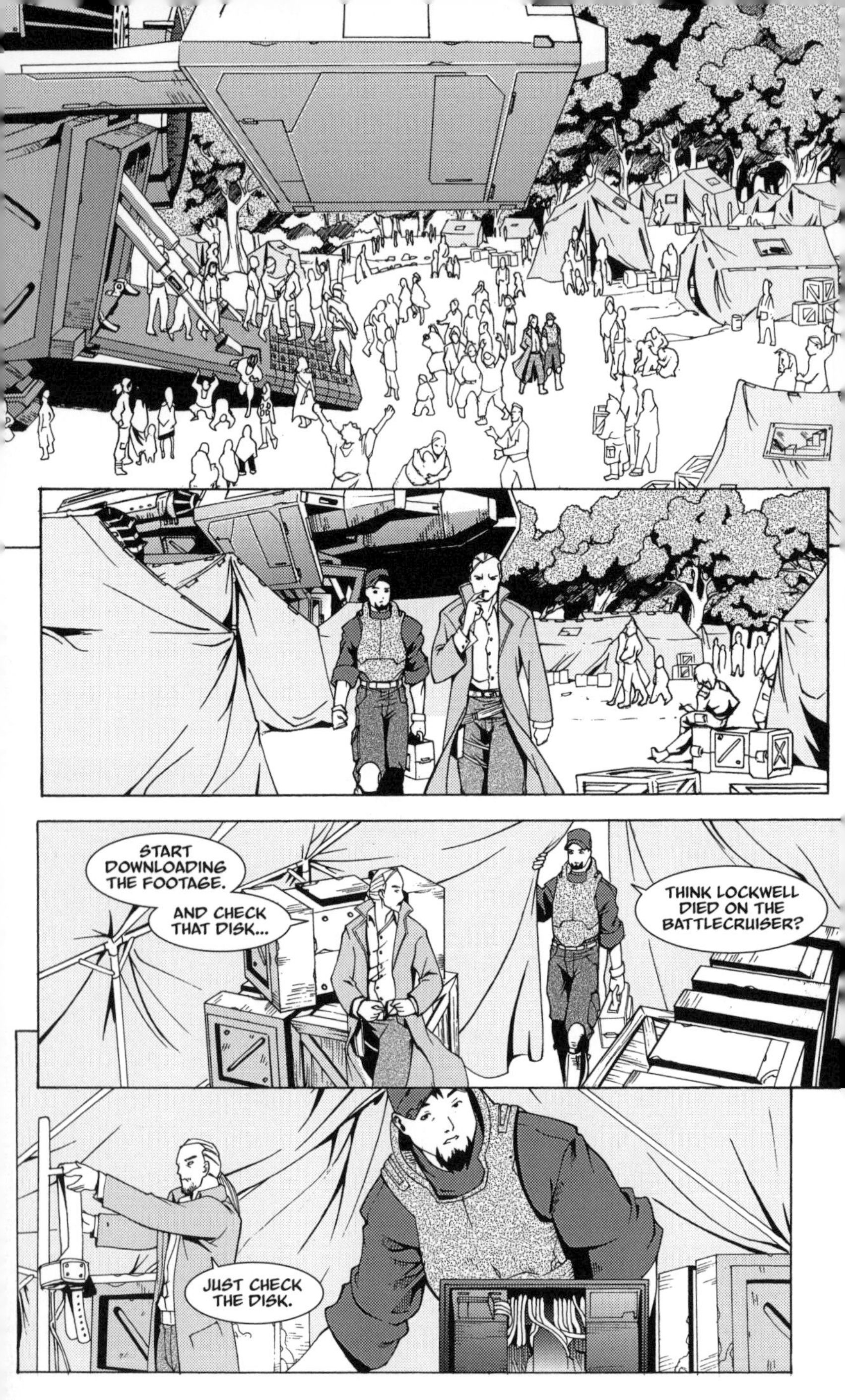
START DOWNLOADING THE FOOTAGE.
AND CHECK THAT DISK...
THINK LOCKWELL DIED ON THE BATTLECRUISER?
JUST CHECK THE DISK.

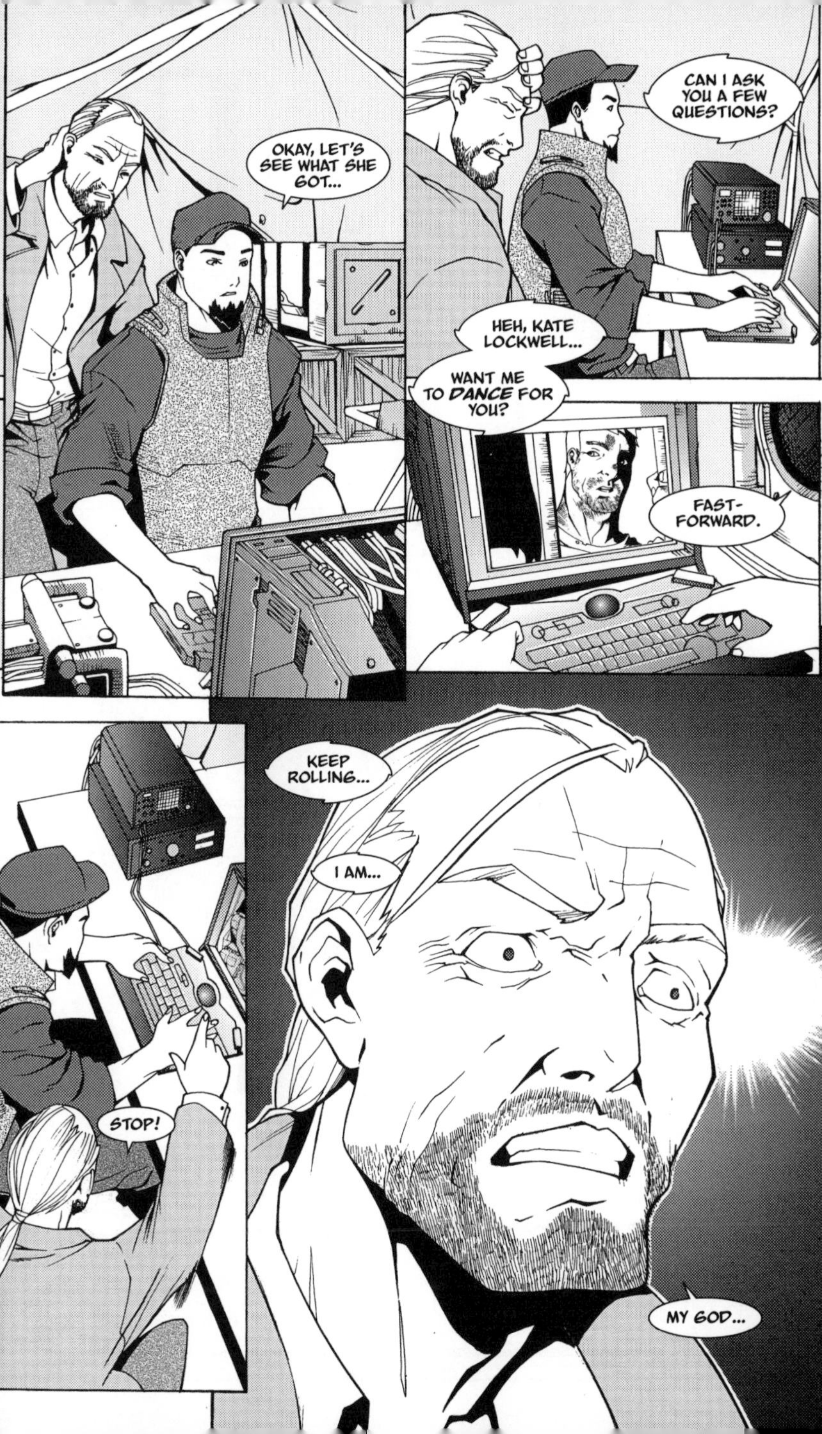

OKAY, LET'S SEE WHAT SHE GOT...
CAN I ASK YOU A FEW QUESTIONS?
HEH, KATE LOCKWELL...
WANT ME TO *DANCE* FOR YOU?
FAST-FORWARD.
KEEP ROLLING...
I AM...
STOP!
MY GOD...

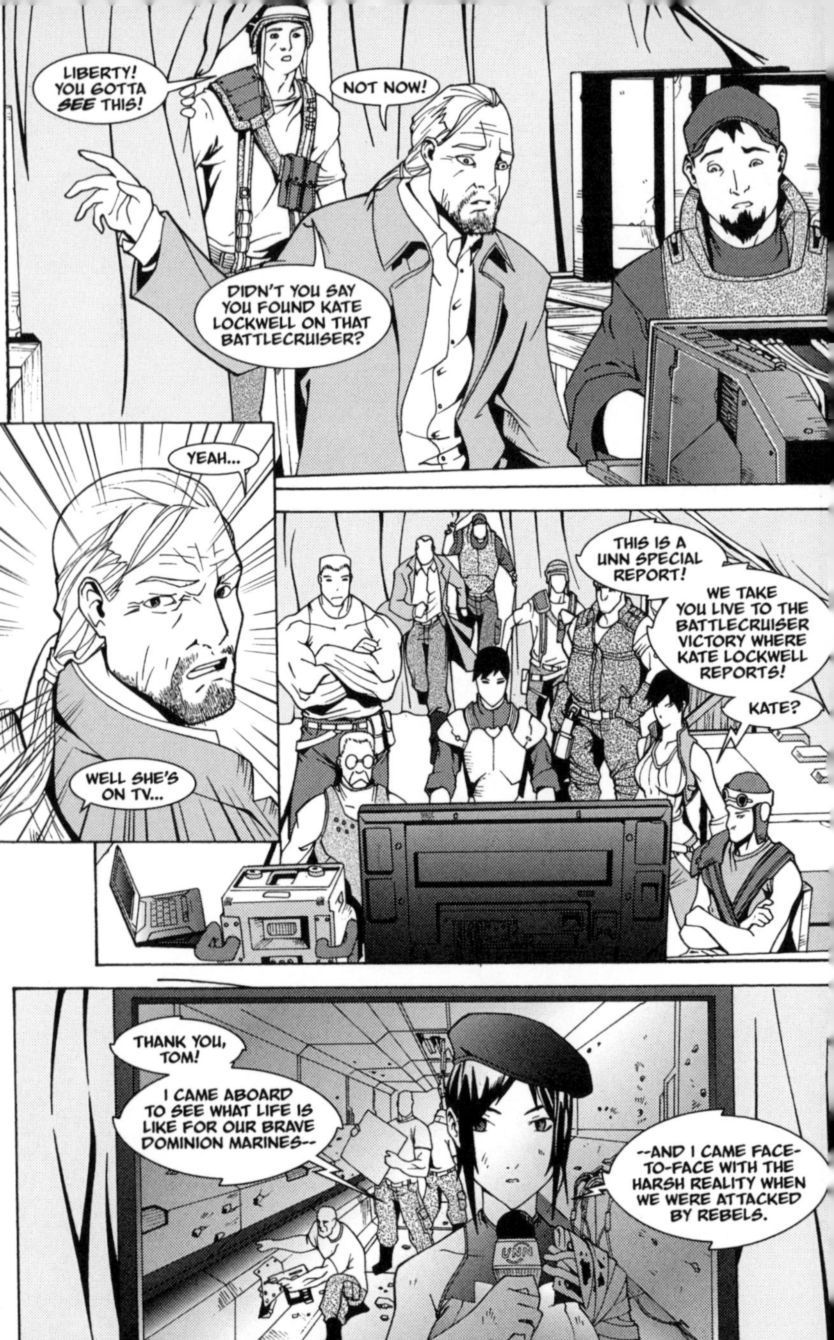
LIBERTY! YOU GOTTA SEE THIS!
NOT NOW!
DIDN'T YOU SAY YOU FOUND KATE LOCKWELL ON THAT BATTLECRUISER?
YEAH...
WELL SHE'S ON TV...
THIS IS A UNN SPECIAL REPORT!
WE TAKE YOU LIVE TO THE BATTLECRUISER VICTORY WHERE KATE LOCKWELL REPORTS!
KATE?
THANK YOU, TOM!
I CAME ABOARD TO SEE WHAT LIFE IS LIKE FOR OUR BRAVE DOMINION MARINES--
--AND I CAME FACE-TO-FACE WITH THE HARSH REALITY WHEN WE WERE ATTACKED BY REBELS.
UNN

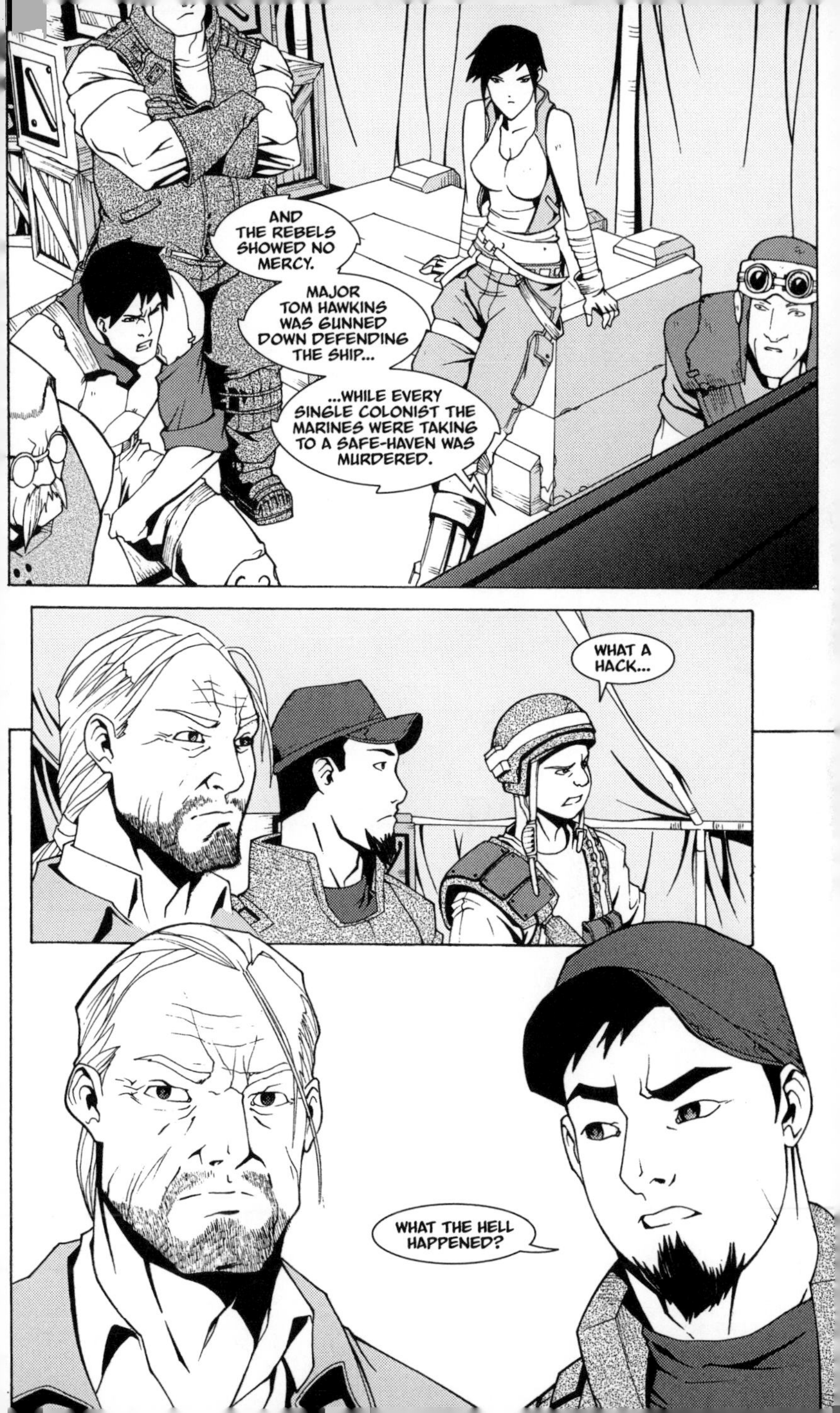
AND THE REBELS SHOWED NO MERCY.
MAJOR TOM HAWKINS WAS GUNNED DOWN DEFENDING THE SHIP...
...WHILE EVERY SINGLE COLONIST THE MARINES WERE TAKING TO A SAFE-HAVEN WAS MURDERED.
WHAT A HACK...
WHAT THE HELL HAPPENED?

STARCRAFT

FRONTLINE
VOLUME 2

A GHOST STORY

Written by Kieron Gillen

Art by Hector Sevilla

Letterer: Michael Paolilli

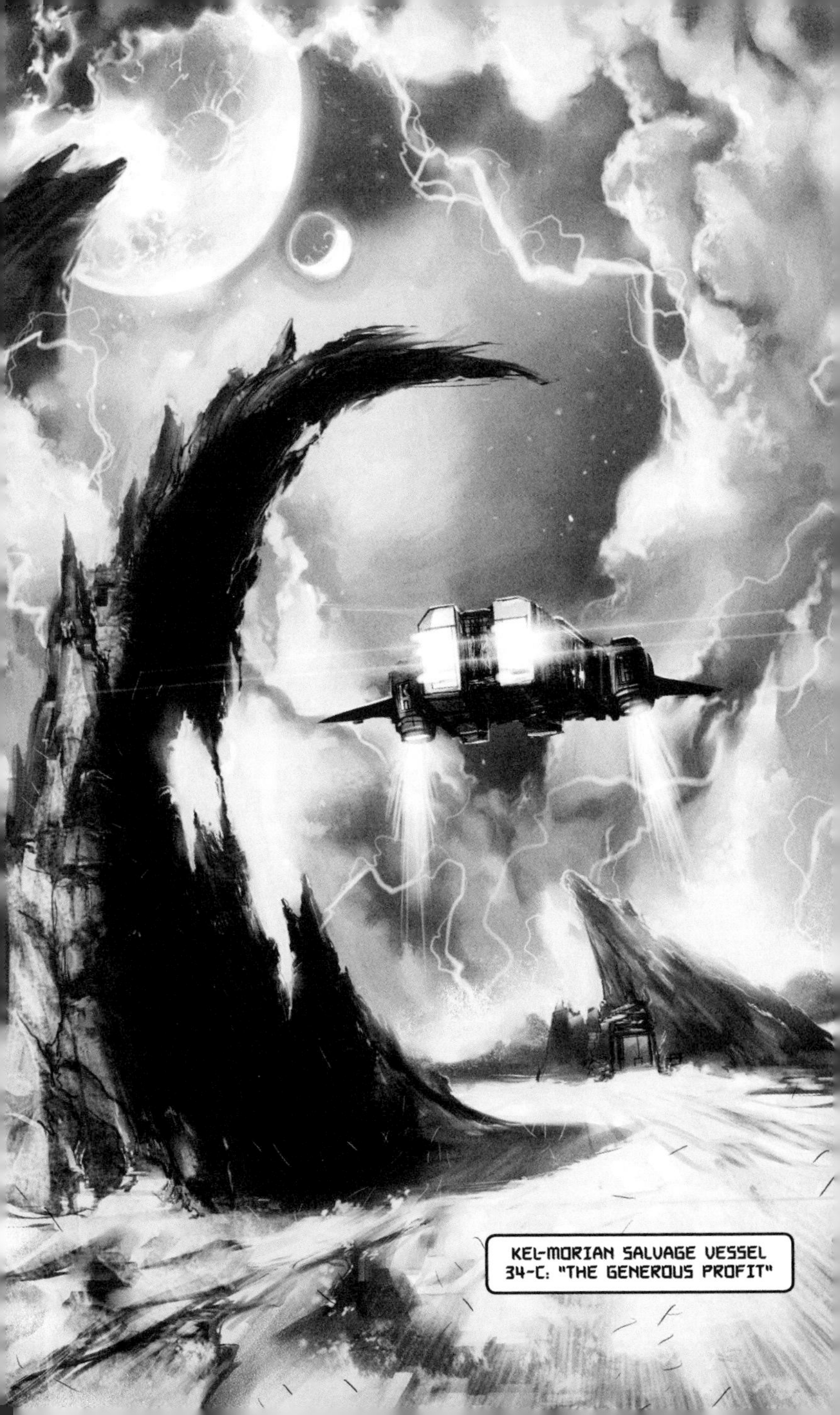
KEL-MORIAN SALVAGE VESSEL 34-C: "THE GENEROUS PROFIT"

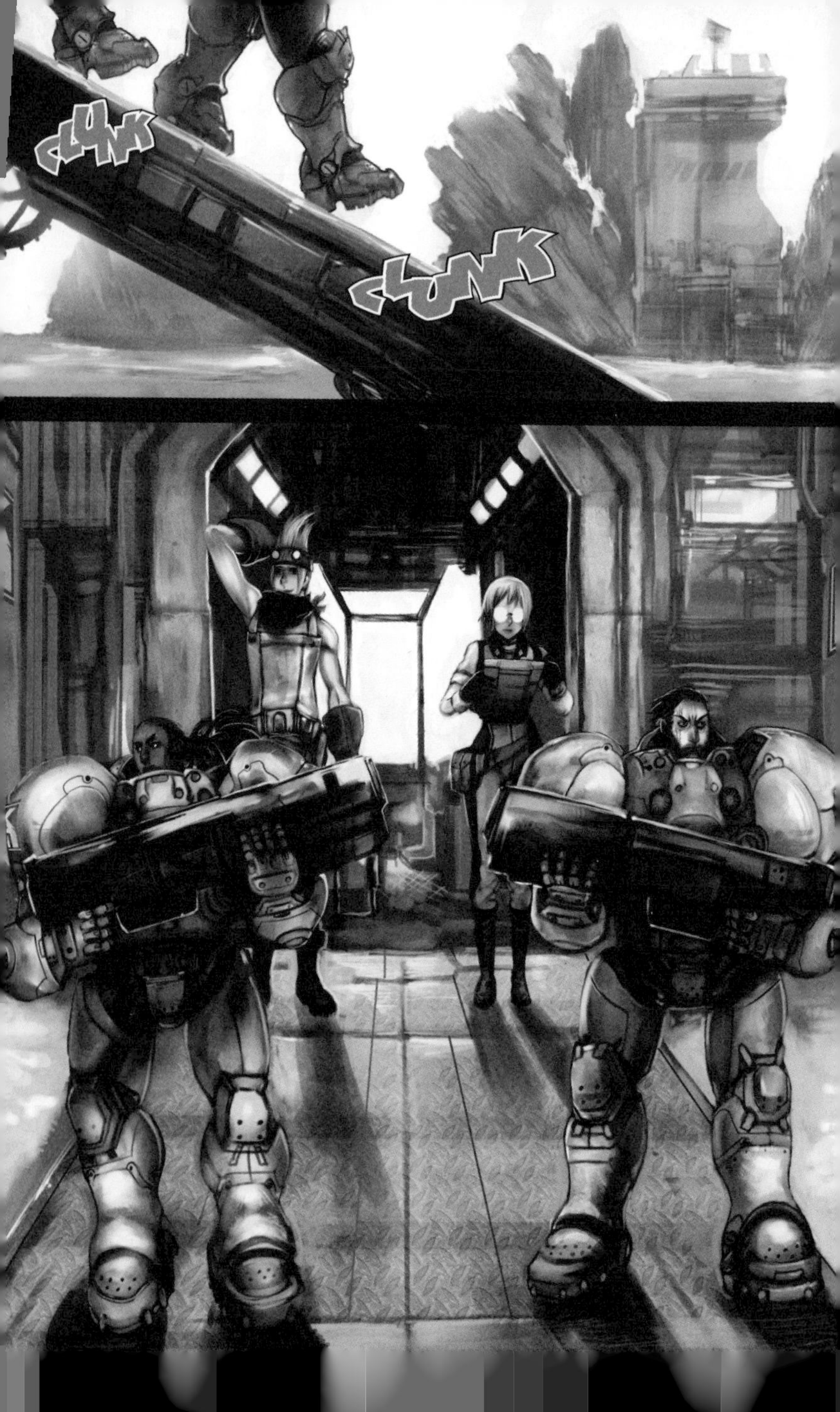
CLUNK
CLUNK

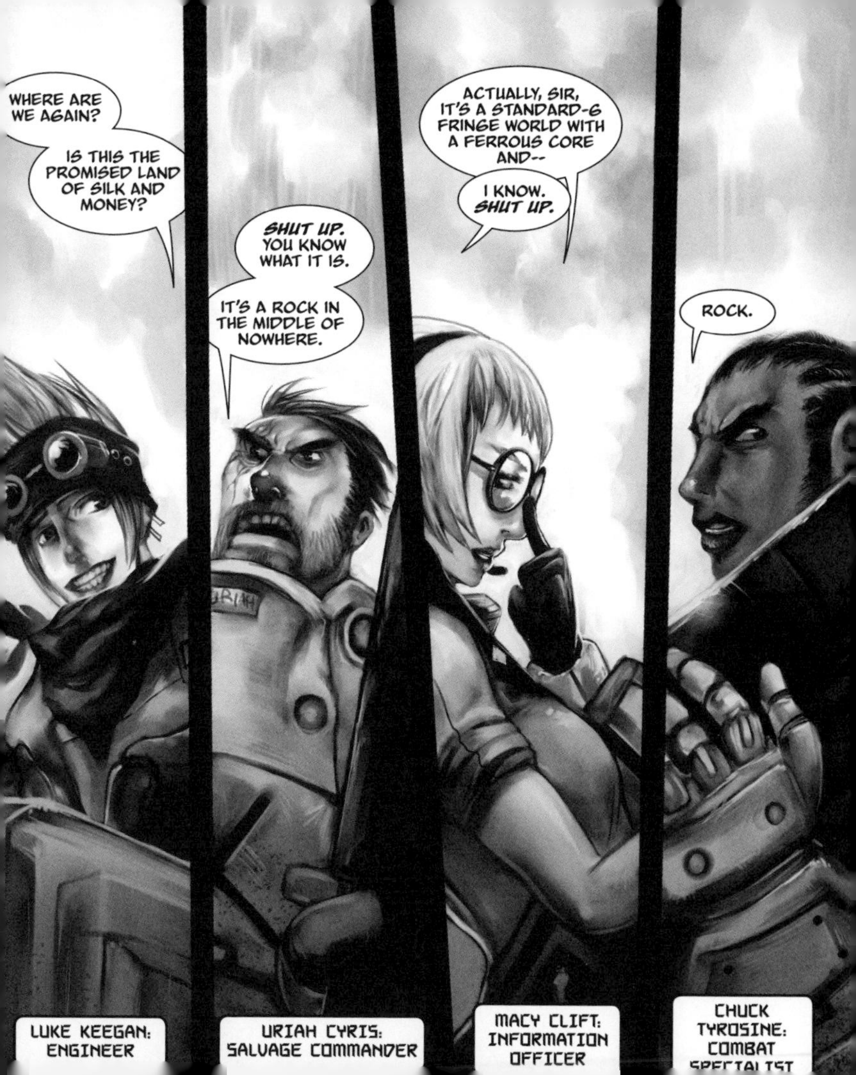
WHERE ARE WE AGAIN?
IS THIS THE PROMISED LAND OF SILK AND MONEY?
SHUT UP. YOU KNOW WHAT IT IS.
IT'S A ROCK IN THE MIDDLE OF NOWHERE.
ACTUALLY, SIR, IT'S A STANDARD-6 FRINGE WORLD WITH A FERROUS CORE AND--
I KNOW. SHUT UP.
ROCK.
LUKE KEEGAN: ENGINEER
URIAH CYRIS: SALVAGE COMMANDER
MACY CLIFT: INFORMATION OFFICER
CHUCK TYROSINE: COMBAT

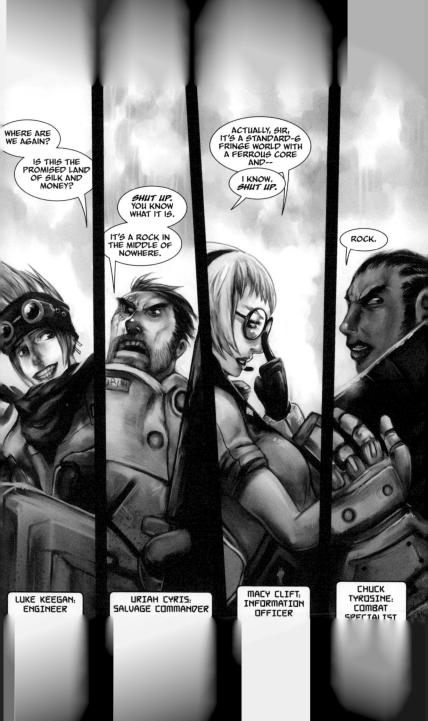

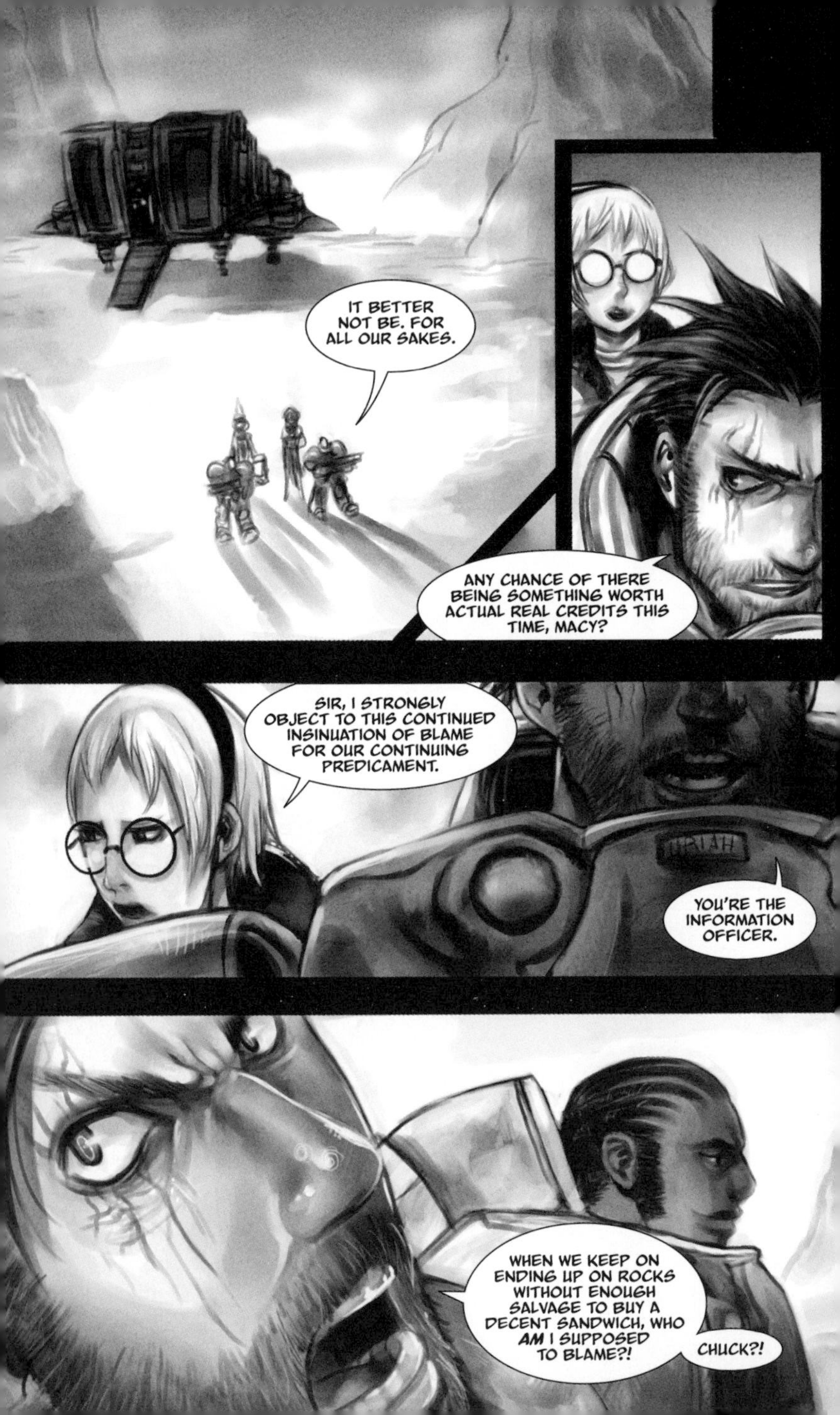

IT BETTER NOT BE. FOR ALL OUR SAKES.
ANY CHANCE OF THERE BEING SOMETHING WORTH ACTUAL REAL CREDITS THIS TIME, MACY?
SIR, I STRONGLY OBJECT TO THIS CONTINUED INSINUATION OF BLAME FOR OUR CONTINUING PREDICAMENT.
URIAH
YOU'RE THE INFORMATION OFFICER.
WHEN WE KEEP ON ENDING UP ON ROCKS WITHOUT ENOUGH SALVAGE TO BUY A DECENT SANDWICH, WHO *AM* I SUPPOSED TO BLAME?!
CHUCK?!

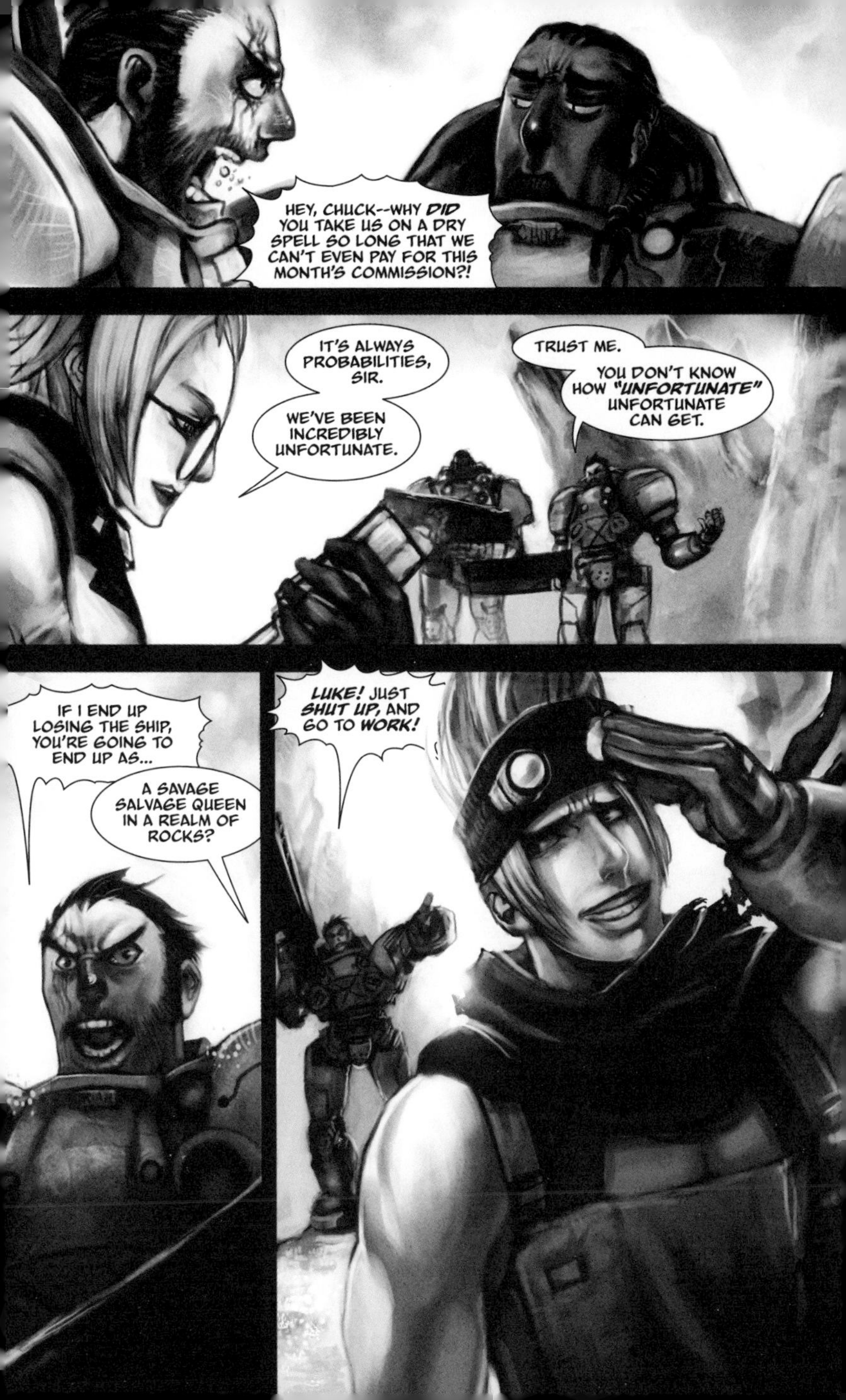
HEY, CHUCK--WHY *DID* YOU TAKE US ON A DRY SPELL SO LONG THAT WE CAN'T EVEN PAY FOR THIS MONTH'S COMMISSION?!
IT'S ALWAYS PROBABILITIES, SIR.
WE'VE BEEN INCREDIBLY UNFORTUNATE.
TRUST ME.
YOU DON'T KNOW HOW *"UNFORTUNATE"* UNFORTUNATE CAN GET.
IF I END UP LOSING THE SHIP, YOU'RE GOING TO END UP AS...
A SAVAGE SALVAGE QUEEN IN A REALM OF ROCKS?
LUKE! JUST *SHUT UP,* AND GO TO *WORK!*

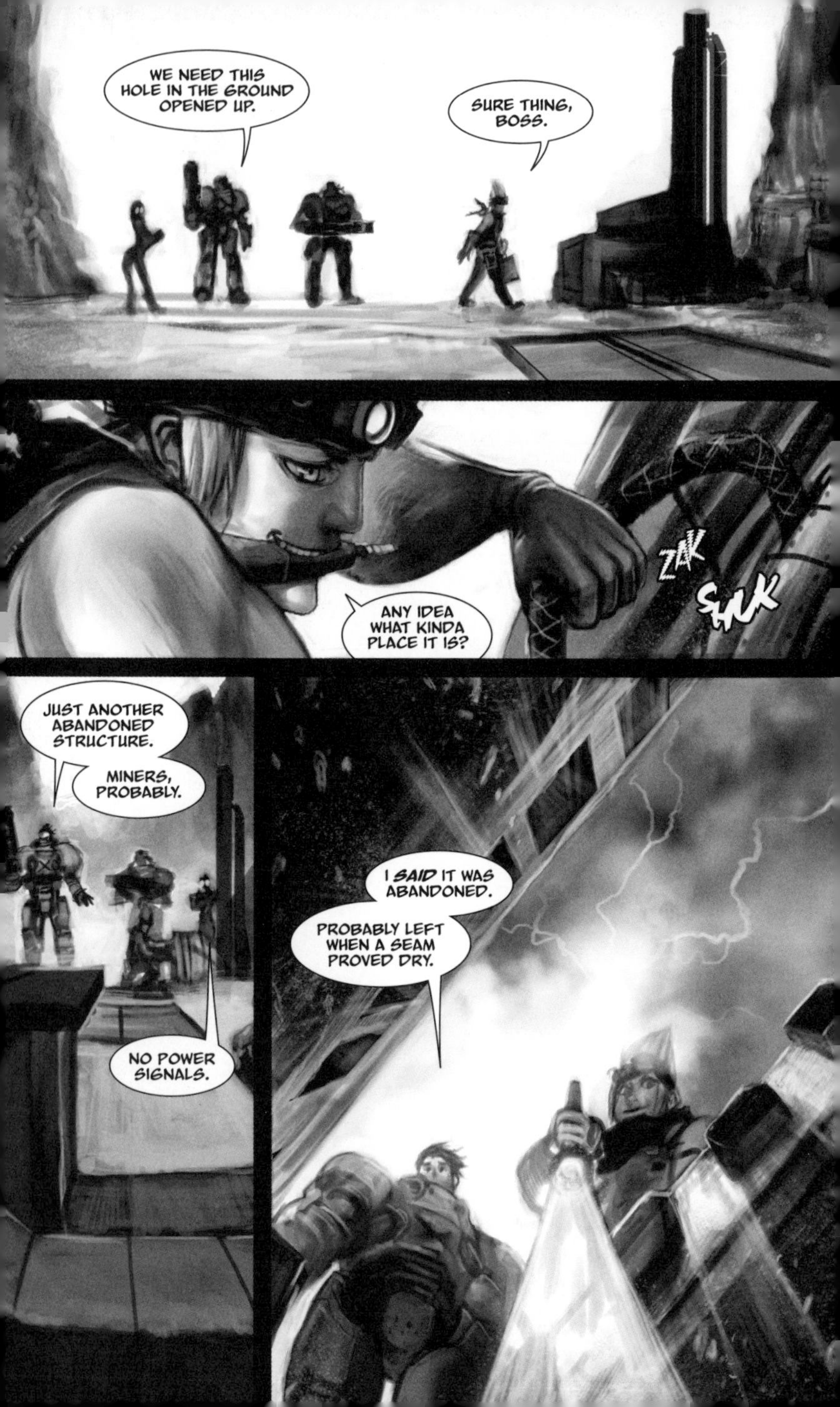
WE NEED THIS HOLE IN THE GROUND OPENED UP.
SURE THING, BOSS.
ANY IDEA WHAT KINDA PLACE IT IS?
JUST ANOTHER ABANDONED STRUCTURE.
MINERS, PROBABLY.
NO POWER SIGNALS.
I *SAID* IT WAS ABANDONED.
PROBABLY LEFT WHEN A SEAM PROVED DRY.

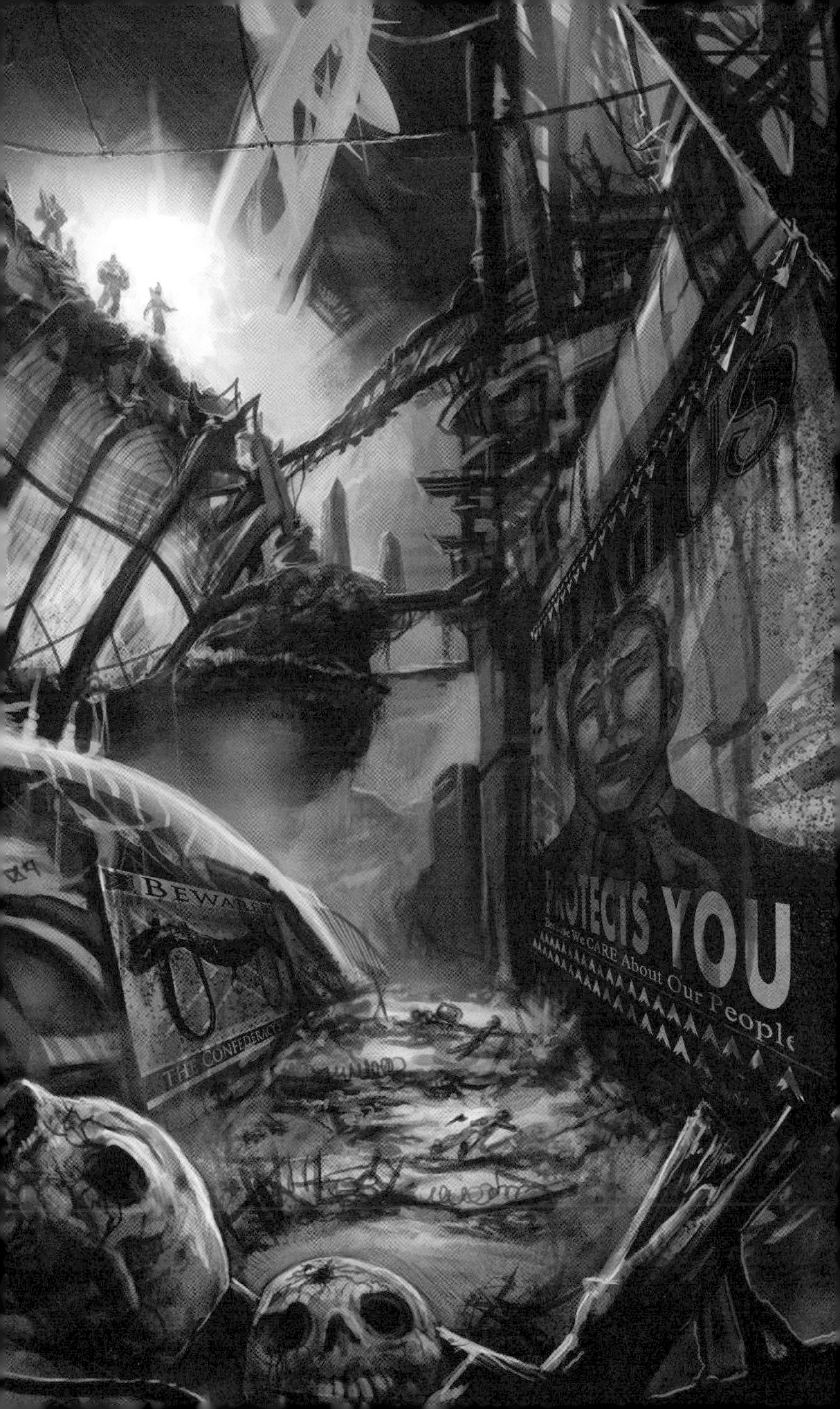

BEWARE
THE CONFEDERACY'S
PROTECTS YOU
WeCARE About Our People

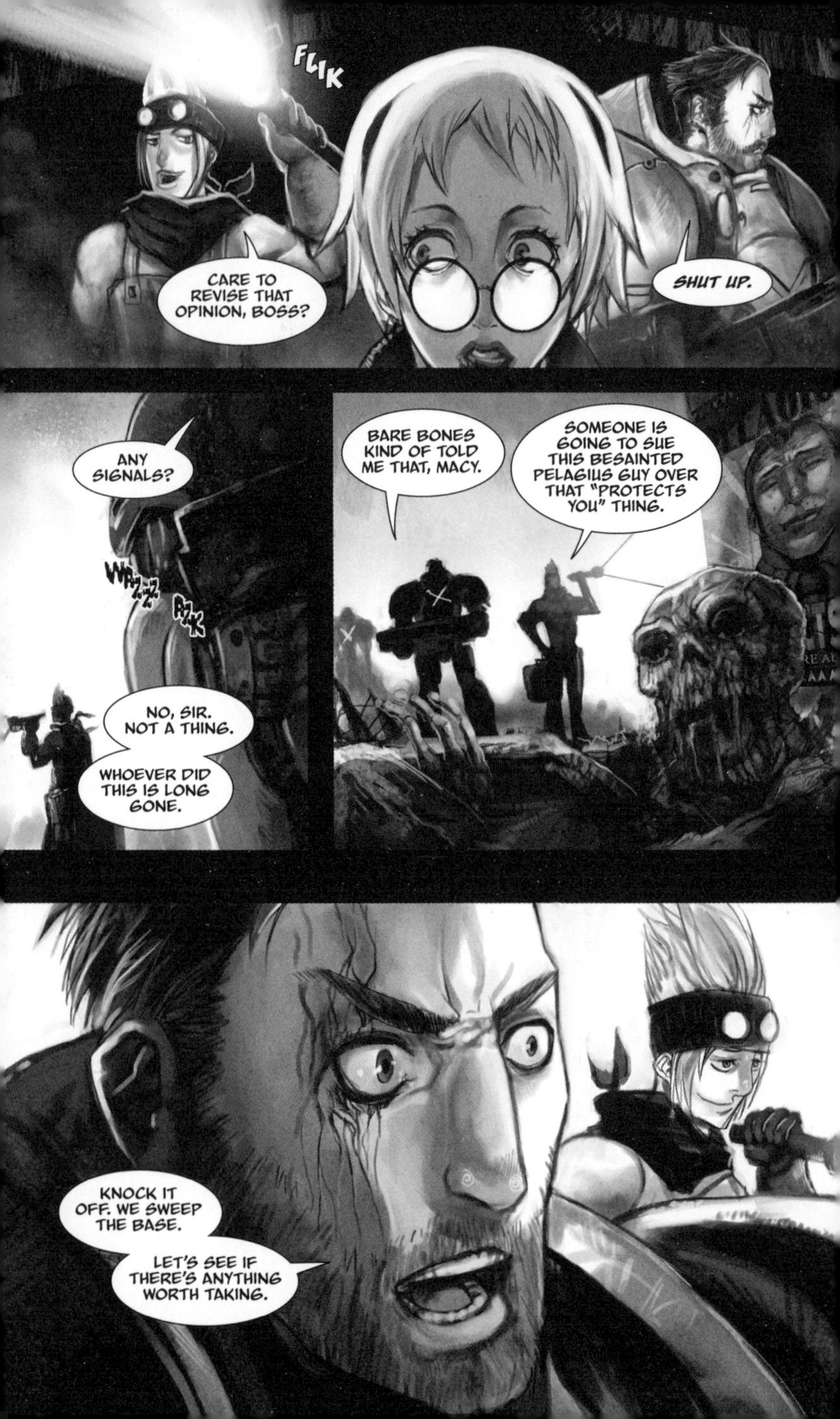

FLIK
CARE TO REVISE THAT OPINION, BOSS?
SHUT UP.
ANY SIGNALS?
NO, SIR. NOT A THING.
WHOEVER DID THIS IS LONG GONE.
BARE BONES KIND OF TOLD ME THAT, MACY.
SOMEONE IS GOING TO SUE THIS BESAINTED PELAGIUS GUY OVER THAT "PROTECTS YOU" THING.
KNOCK IT OFF. WE SWEEP THE BASE.
LET'S SEE IF THERE'S ANYTHING WORTH TAKING.

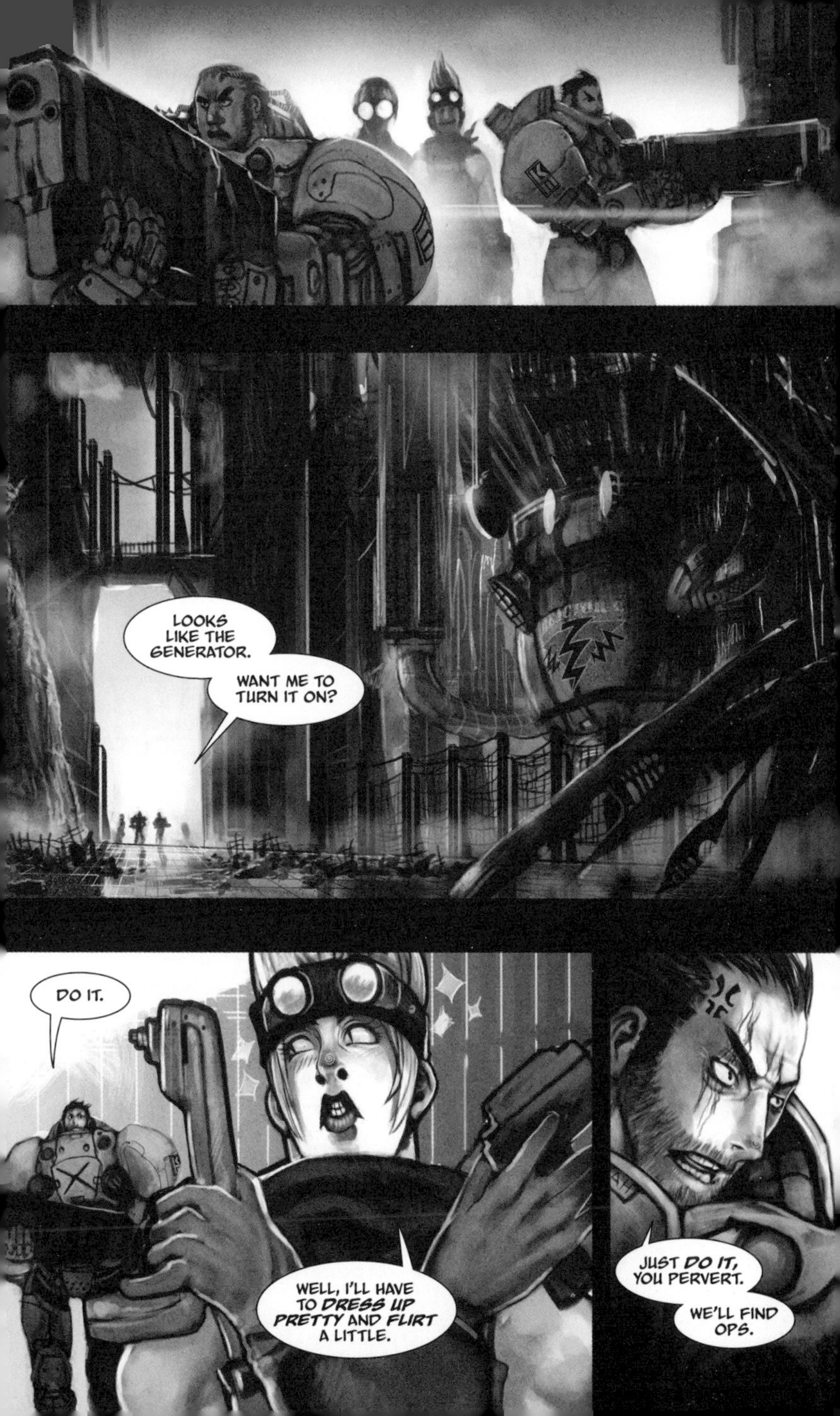
LOOKS LIKE THE GENERATOR.
WANT ME TO TURN IT ON?
DO IT.
WELL, I'LL HAVE TO *DRESS UP PRETTY* AND *FLIRT* A LITTLE.
JUST *DO IT*, YOU PERVERT.
WE'LL FIND OPS.

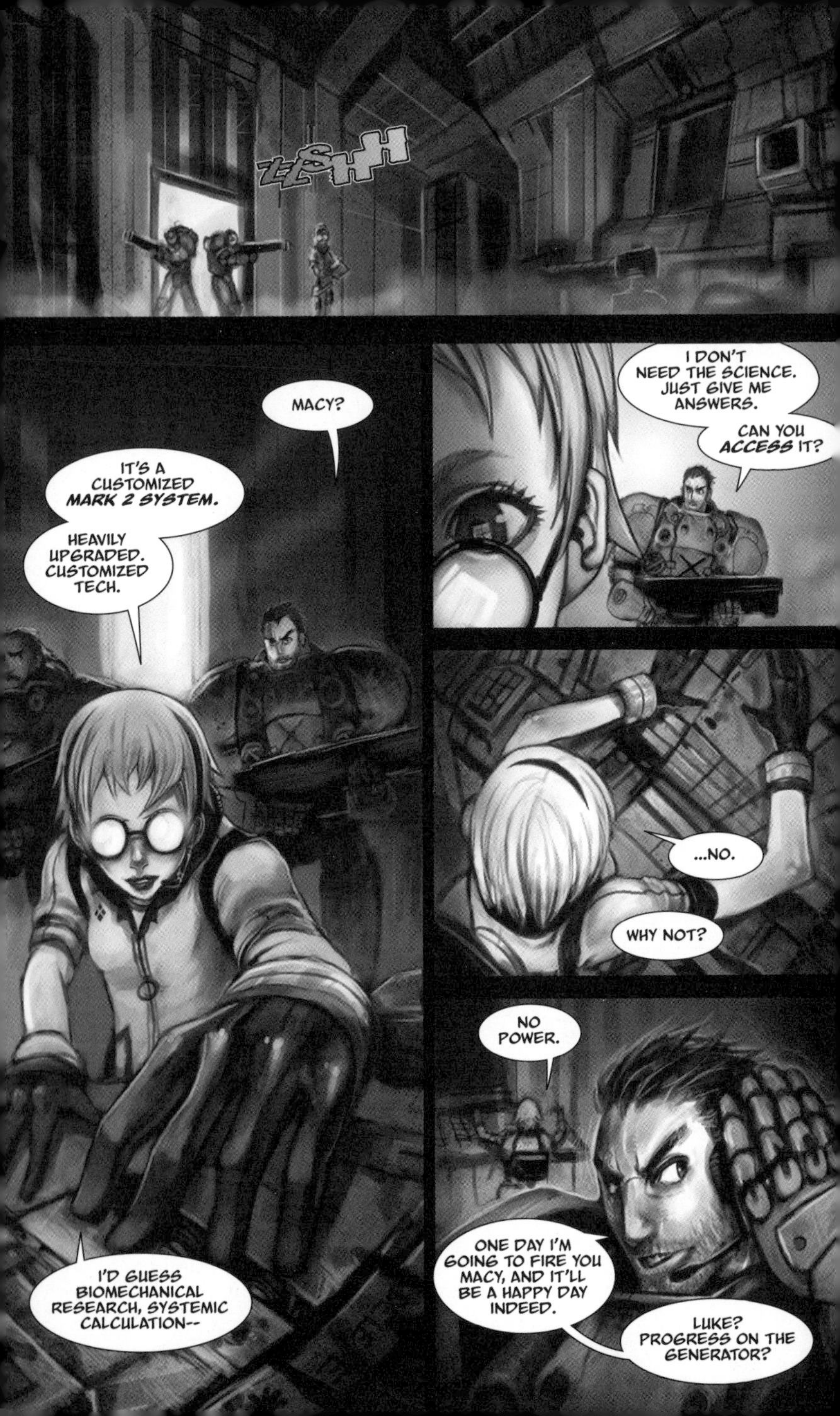
ZZSHH
MACY?
IT'S A CUSTOMIZED MARK 2 SYSTEM.
HEAVILY UPGRADED. CUSTOMIZED TECH.
I'D GUESS BIOMECHANICAL RESEARCH, SYSTEMIC CALCULATION--
I DON'T NEED THE SCIENCE. JUST GIVE ME ANSWERS.
CAN YOU ACCESS IT?
...NO.
WHY NOT?
NO POWER.
ONE DAY I'M GOING TO FIRE YOU MACY, AND IT'LL BE A HAPPY DAY INDEED.
LUKE? PROGRESS ON THE GENERATOR?

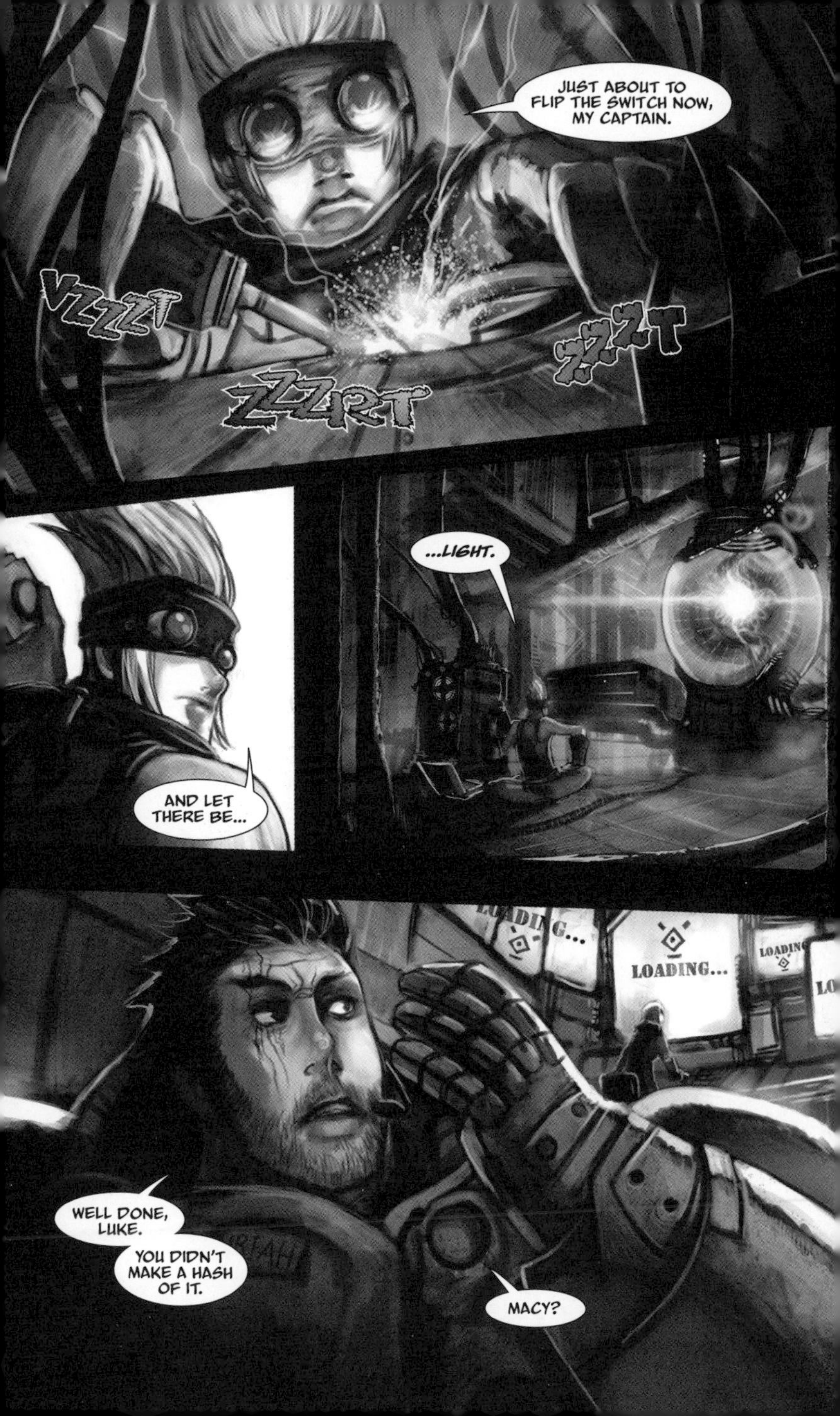
JUST ABOUT TO FLIP THE SWITCH NOW, MY CAPTAIN.
VZZZT
ZZZRT
ZZZT
AND LET THERE BE...
...LIGHT.
LOADING...
LOADING...
WELL DONE, LUKE.
YOU DIDN'T MAKE A HASH OF IT.
MACY?

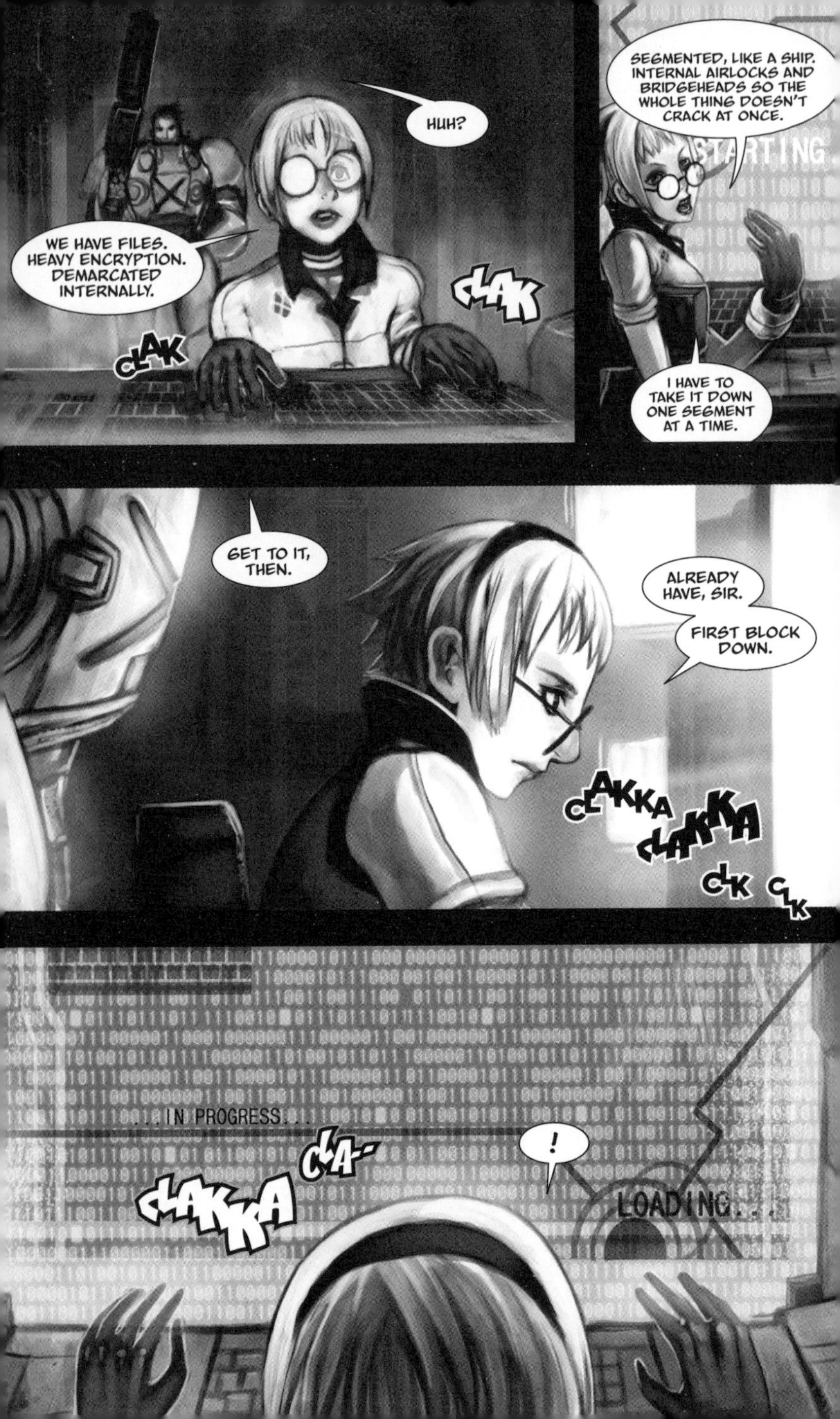
HUH?
WE HAVE FILES. HEAVY ENCRYPTION. DEMARCATED INTERNALLY.
CLAK
CLAK
SEGMENTED, LIKE A SHIP. INTERNAL AIRLOCKS AND BRIDGEHEADS SO THE WHOLE THING DOESN'T CRACK AT ONCE.
STARTING
I HAVE TO TAKE IT DOWN ONE SEGMENT AT A TIME.
GET TO IT, THEN.
ALREADY HAVE, SIR.
FIRST BLOCK DOWN.
CLAKKA CLAKKA
CLK CLK
...IN PROGRESS...
CLAKKA CLA-
!
LOADING...

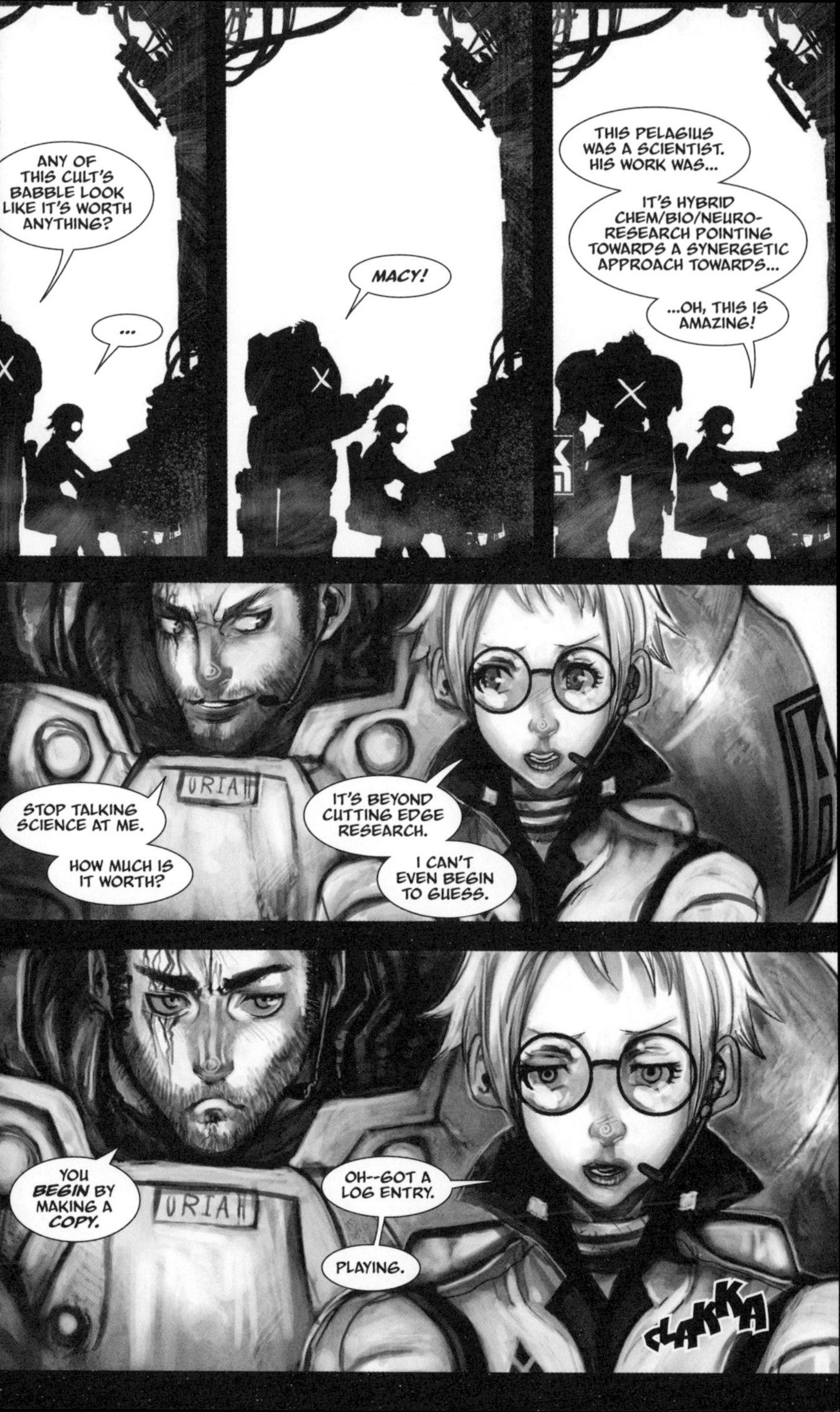
ANY OF THIS CULT'S BABBLE LOOK LIKE IT'S WORTH ANYTHING?
...
MACY!
THIS PELAGIUS WAS A SCIENTIST. HIS WORK WAS...
IT'S HYBRID CHEM/BIO/NEURO-RESEARCH POINTING TOWARDS A SYNERGETIC APPROACH TOWARDS...
...OH, THIS IS AMAZING!
URIAH
STOP TALKING SCIENCE AT ME.
HOW MUCH IS IT WORTH?
IT'S BEYOND CUTTING EDGE RESEARCH.
I CAN'T EVEN BEGIN TO GUESS.
URIAH
YOU *BEGIN* BY MAKING A *COPY*.
OH--GOT A LOG ENTRY.
PLAYING.
CLAKKA

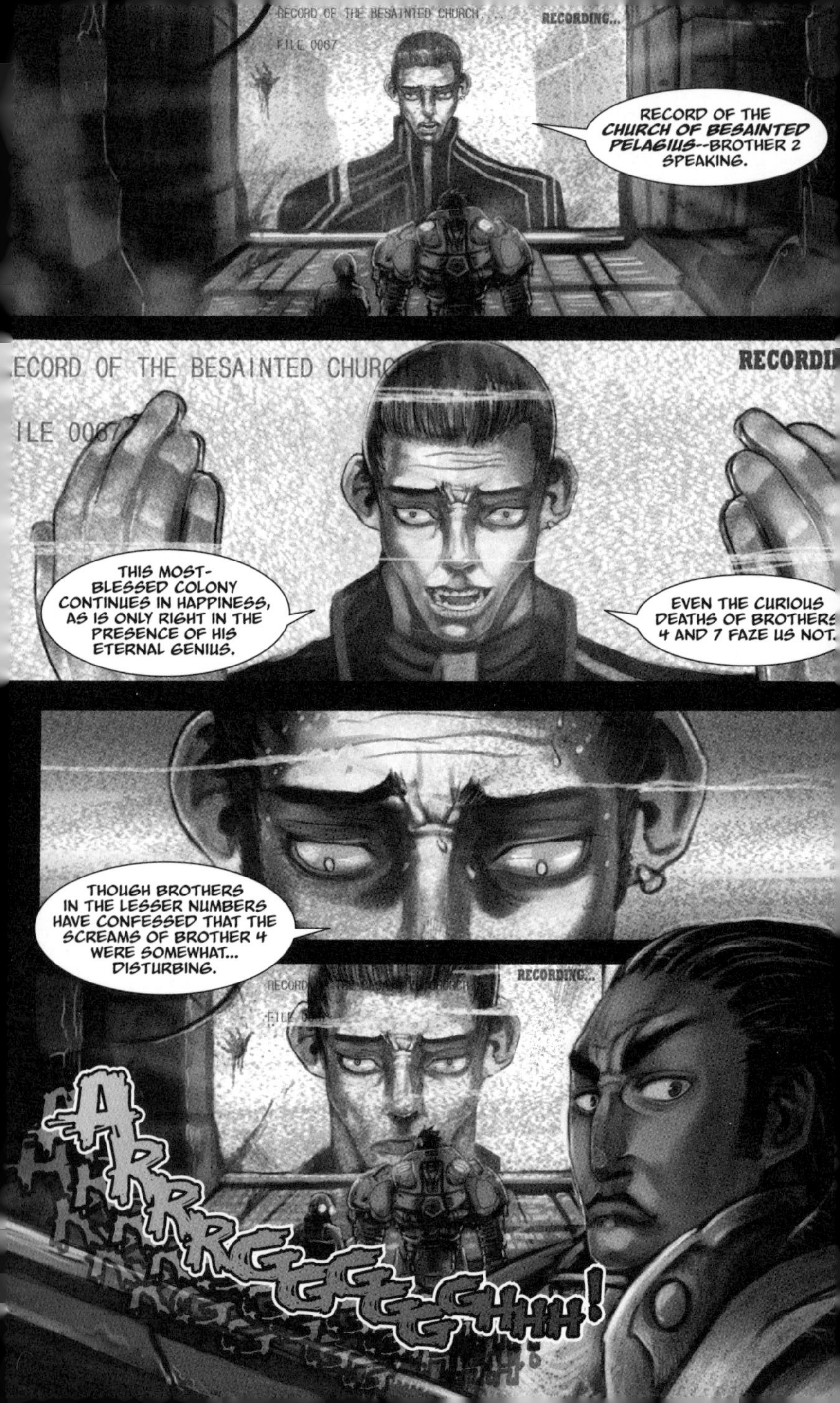
RECORD OF THE BESAINTED CHURCH...
RECORDING...
FILE 0067
RECORD OF THE *CHURCH OF BESAINTED PELAGIUS*--BROTHER 2 SPEAKING.
ECORD OF THE BESAINTED CHUR
RECORDI
ILE 006
THIS MOST-BLESSED COLONY CONTINUES IN HAPPINESS, AS IS ONLY RIGHT IN THE PRESENCE OF HIS ETERNAL GENIUS.
EVEN THE CURIOUS DEATHS OF BROTHERS 4 AND 7 FAZE US NOT.
THOUGH BROTHERS IN THE LESSER NUMBERS HAVE CONFESSED THAT THE SCREAMS OF BROTHER 4 WERE SOMEWHAT... DISTURBING.
RECORDING...
ARRRGGGGHHHH!

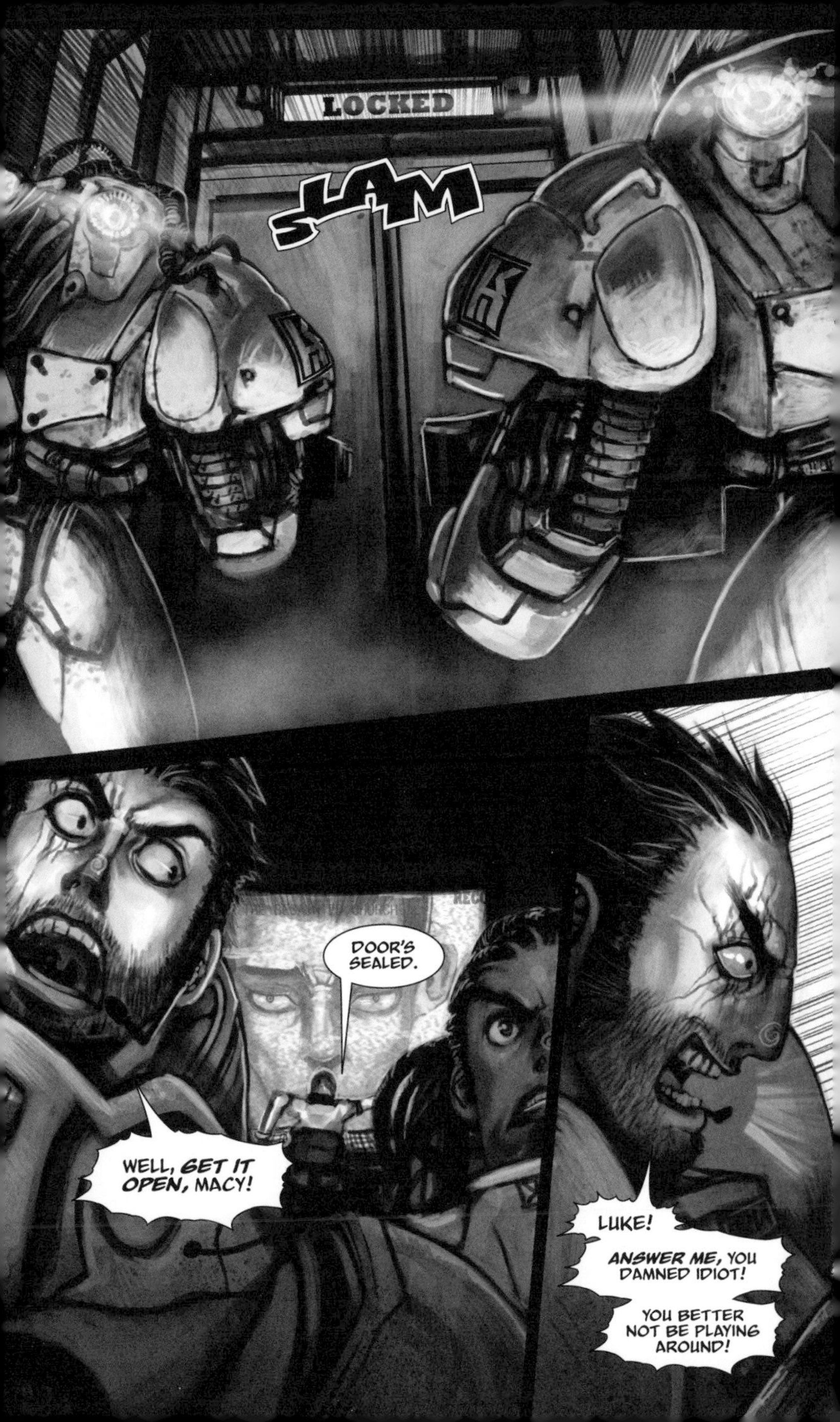
LOCKED
SLAM
DOOR'S SEALED.
WELL, GET IT OPEN, MACY!
LUKE!
ANSWER ME, YOU DAMNED IDIOT!
YOU BETTER NOT BE PLAYING AROUND!

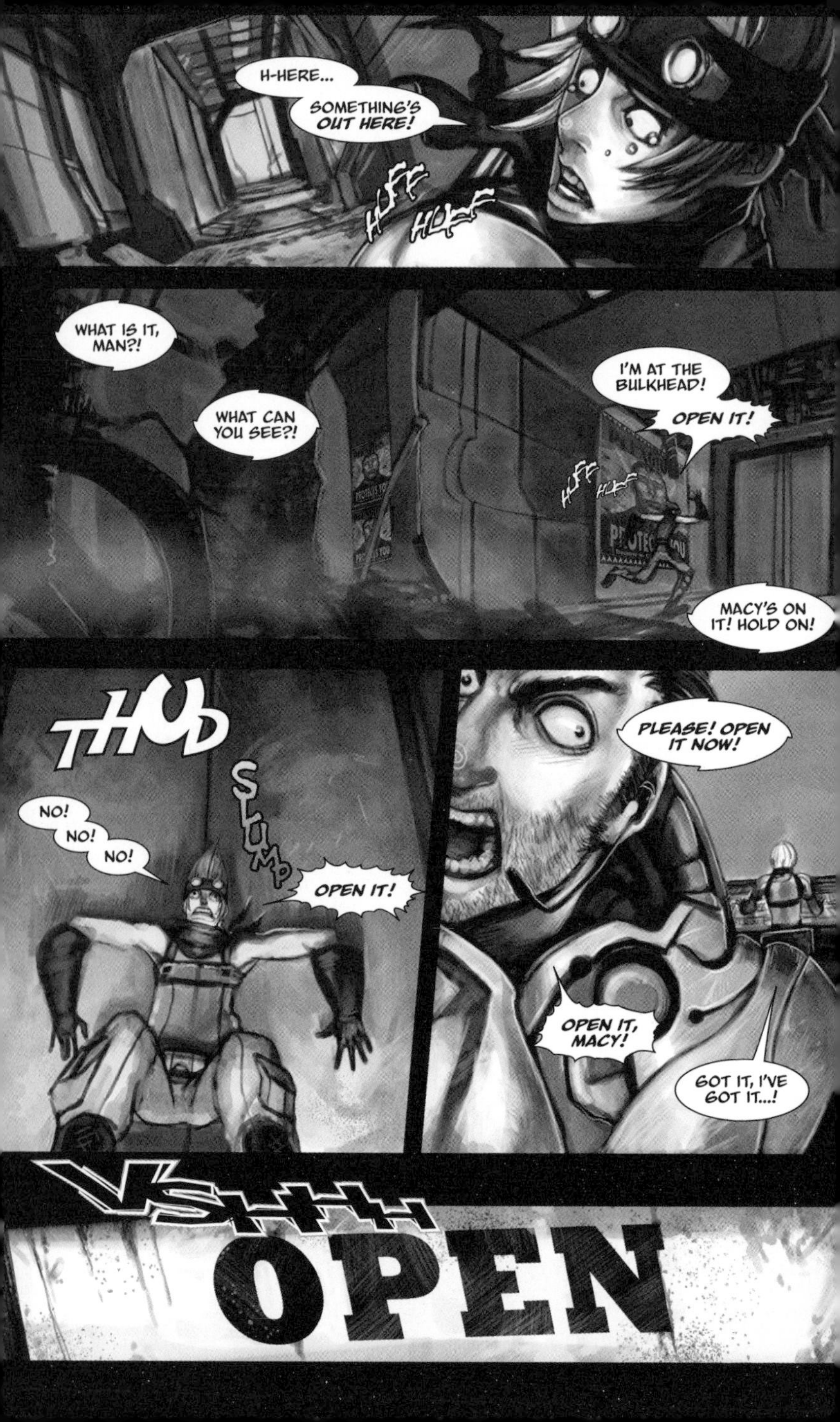

H-HERE...
SOMETHING'S OUT HERE!
HUFF
HUFF
WHAT IS IT, MAN?!
WHAT CAN YOU SEE?!
I'M AT THE BULKHEAD!
OPEN IT!
HUFF
HUFF
MACY'S ON IT! HOLD ON!
THUD
SLUMP
NO!
NO!
NO!
OPEN IT!
PLEASE! OPEN IT NOW!
OPEN IT, MACY!
GOT IT, I'VE GOT IT...!
VSHHH
OPEN

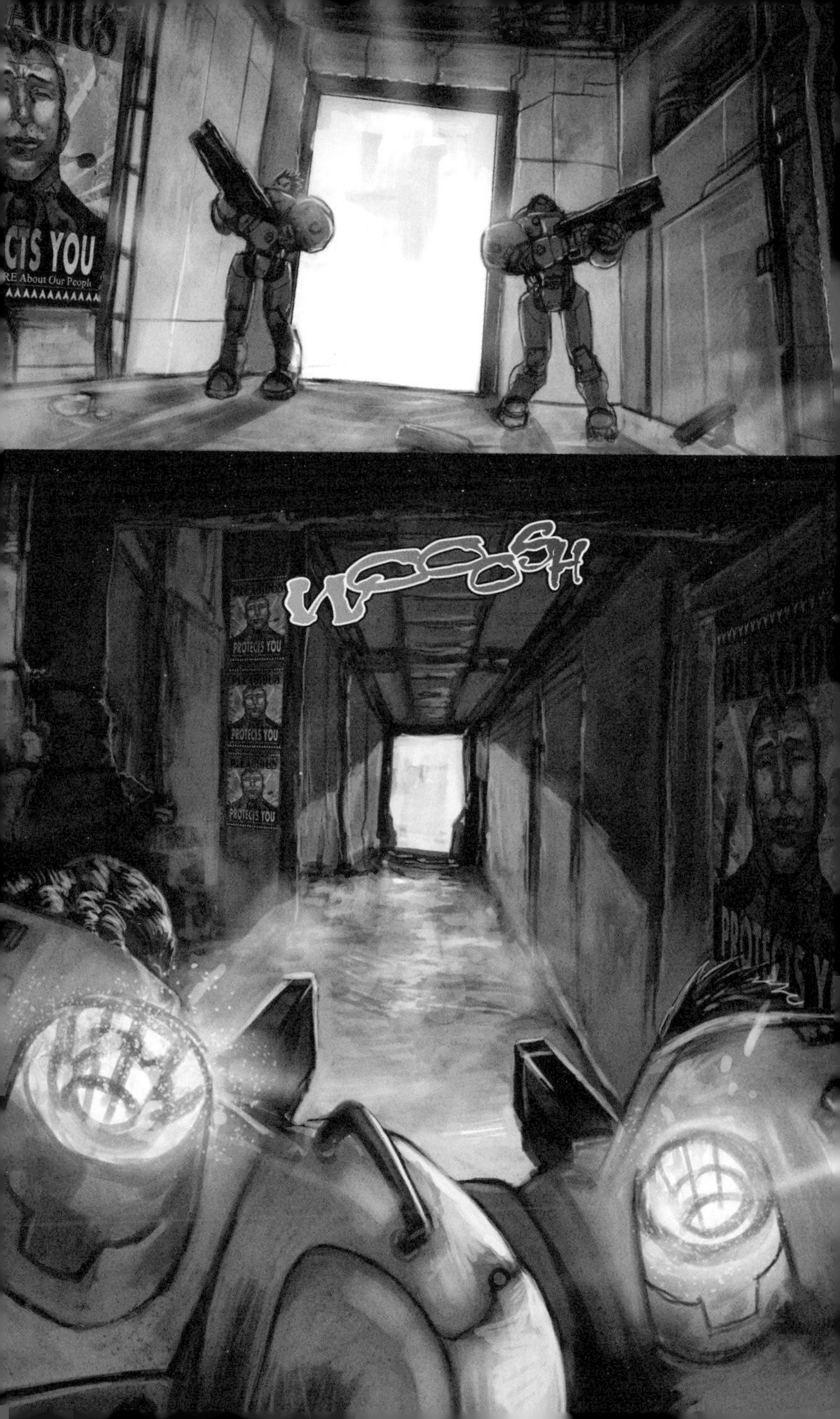
WOOOSH

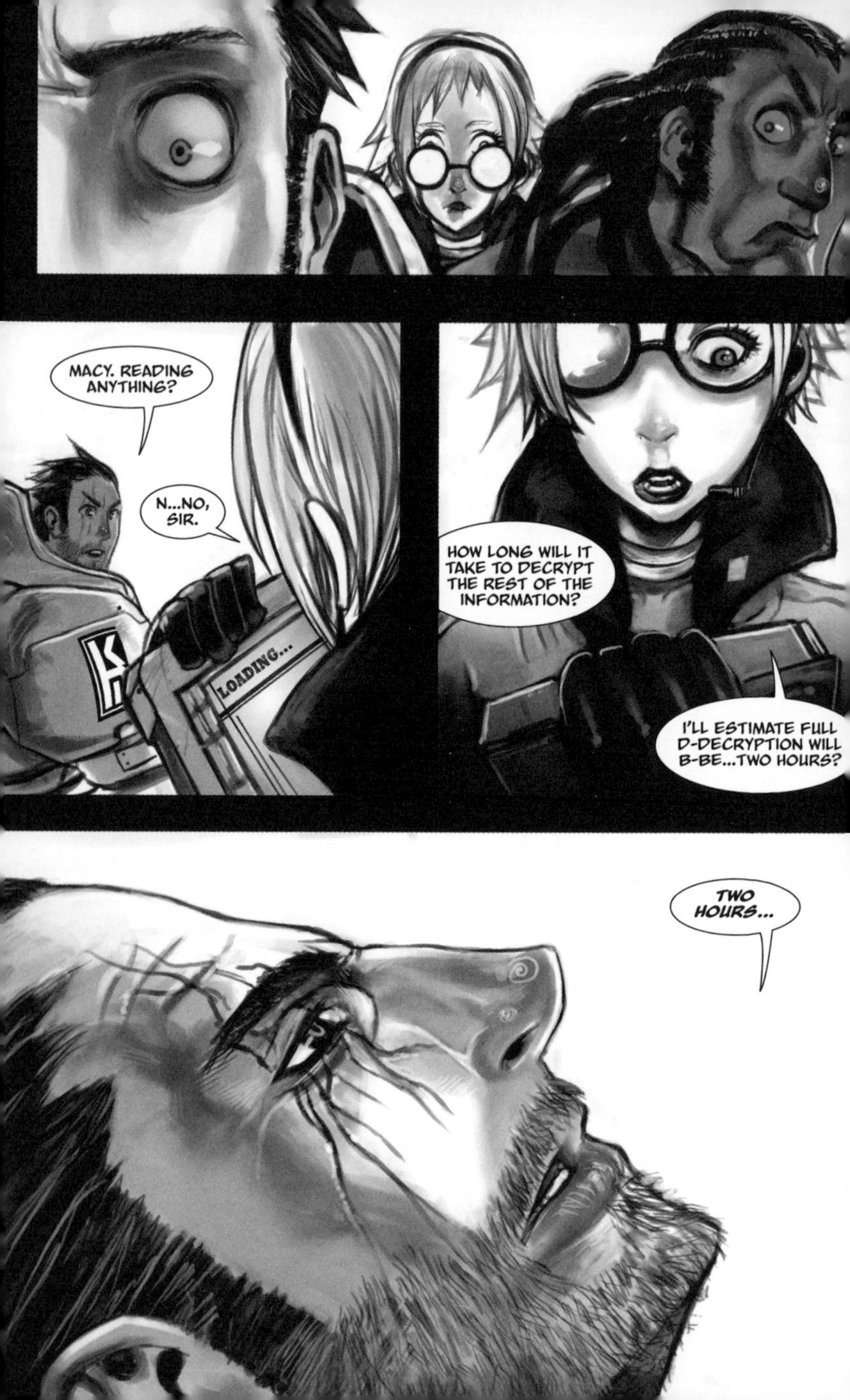
MACY. READING ANYTHING?
N...NO, SIR.
LOADING...
HOW LONG WILL IT TAKE TO DECRYPT THE REST OF THE INFORMATION?
I'LL ESTIMATE FULL D-DECRYPTION WILL B-BE...TWO HOURS?
TWO HOURS...

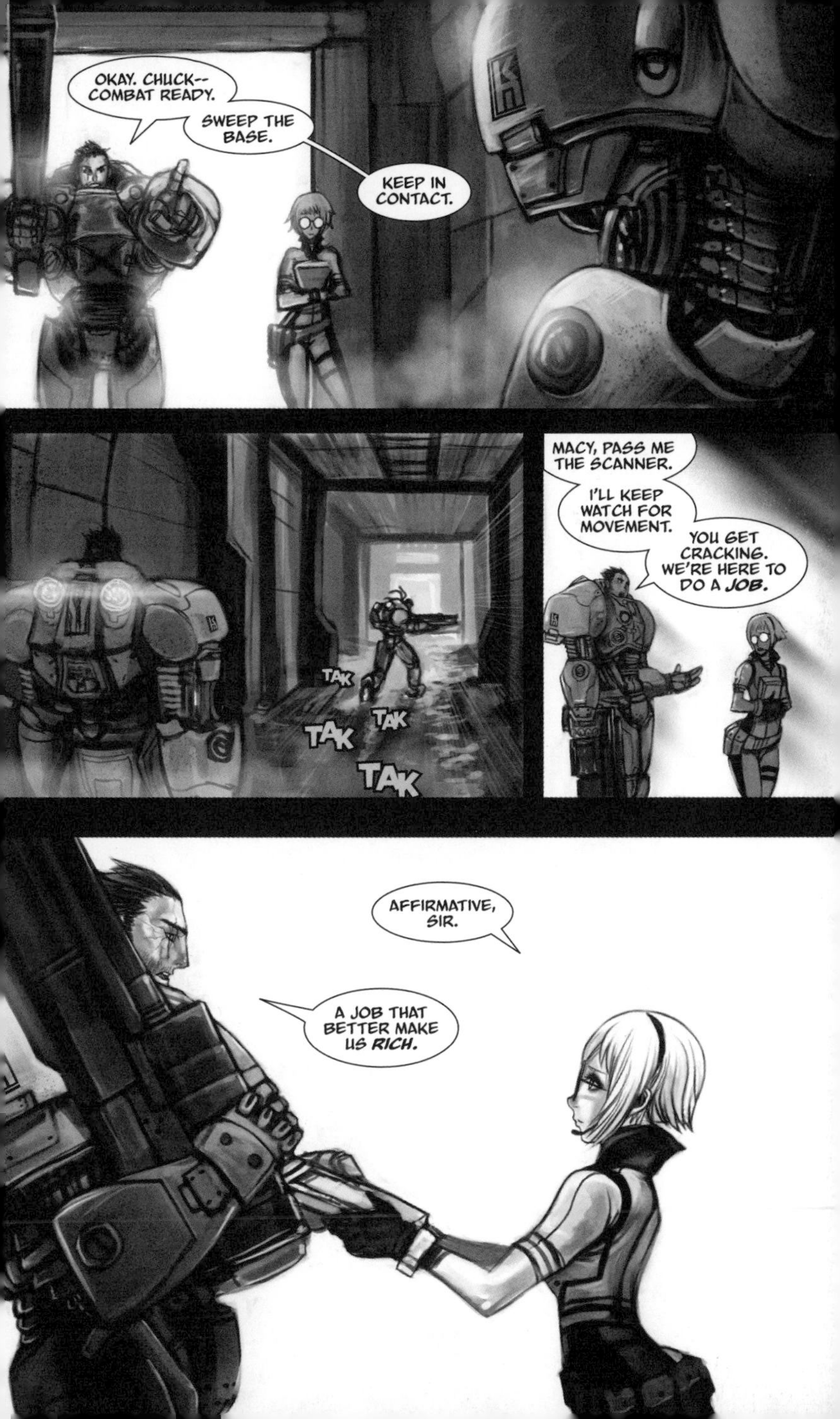
OKAY. CHUCK-- COMBAT READY.
SWEEP THE BASE.
KEEP IN CONTACT.
TAK
TAK
TAK
TAK
MACY, PASS ME THE SCANNER.
I'LL KEEP WATCH FOR MOVEMENT.
YOU GET CRACKING. WE'RE HERE TO DO A *JOB*.
AFFIRMATIVE, SIR.
A JOB THAT BETTER MAKE US *RICH*.

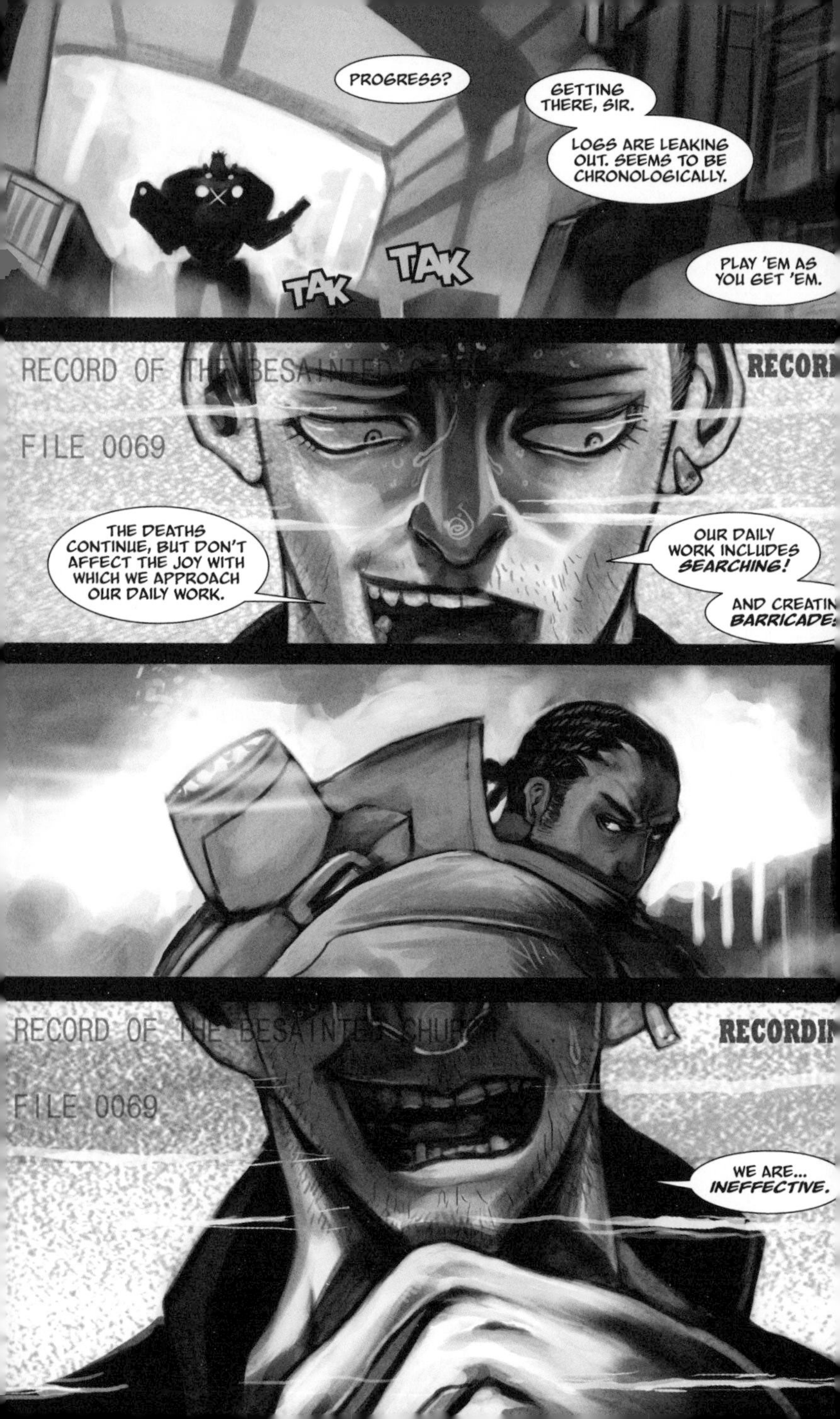
PROGRESS?
GETTING THERE, SIR.
LOGS ARE LEAKING OUT. SEEMS TO BE CHRONOLOGICALLY.
TAK
TAK
PLAY 'EM AS YOU GET 'EM.
RECORD OF THE BESAINTED CHURCH
FILE 0069
THE DEATHS CONTINUE, BUT DON'T AFFECT THE JOY WITH WHICH WE APPROACH OUR DAILY WORK.
OUR DAILY WORK INCLUDES SEARCHING!
AND CREATIN BARRICADE
RECORD OF THE BESAINTED CHURCH
RECORDIN
FILE 0069
WE ARE... INEFFECTIVE.

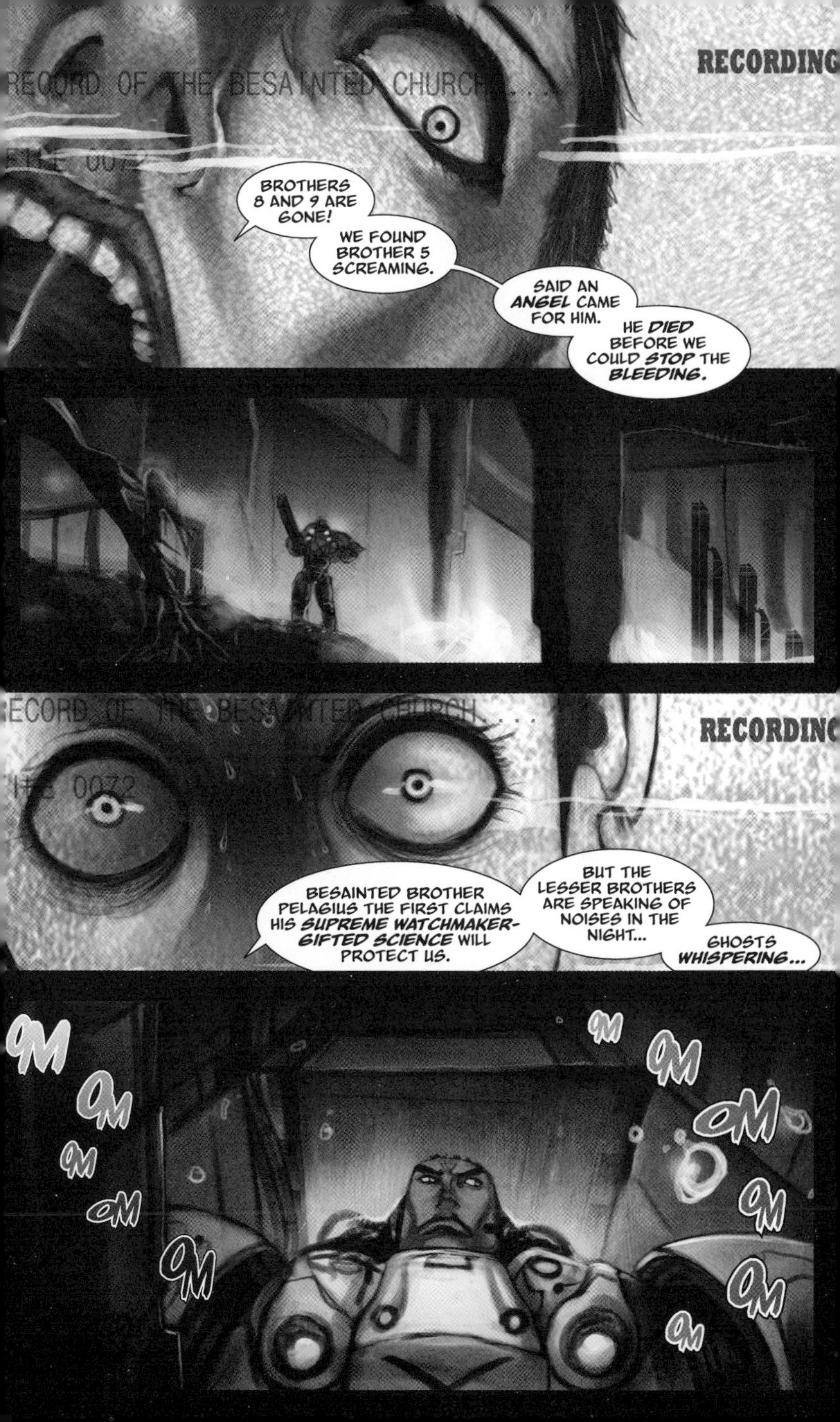

RECORDING
ECORD OF THE BESAINTED CHURCH...
BROTHERS 8 AND 9 ARE GONE!
WE FOUND BROTHER 5 SCREAMING.
SAID AN ANGEL CAME FOR HIM.
HE DIED BEFORE WE COULD STOP THE BLEEDING.
RECORDING
BESAINTED BROTHER PELAGIUS THE FIRST CLAIMS HIS SUPREME WATCHMAKER-GIFTED SCIENCE WILL PROTECT US.
BUT THE LESSER BROTHERS ARE SPEAKING OF NOISES IN THE NIGHT...
GHOSTS WHISPERING...
OM OM OM OM OM
OM OM OM OM OM OM OM

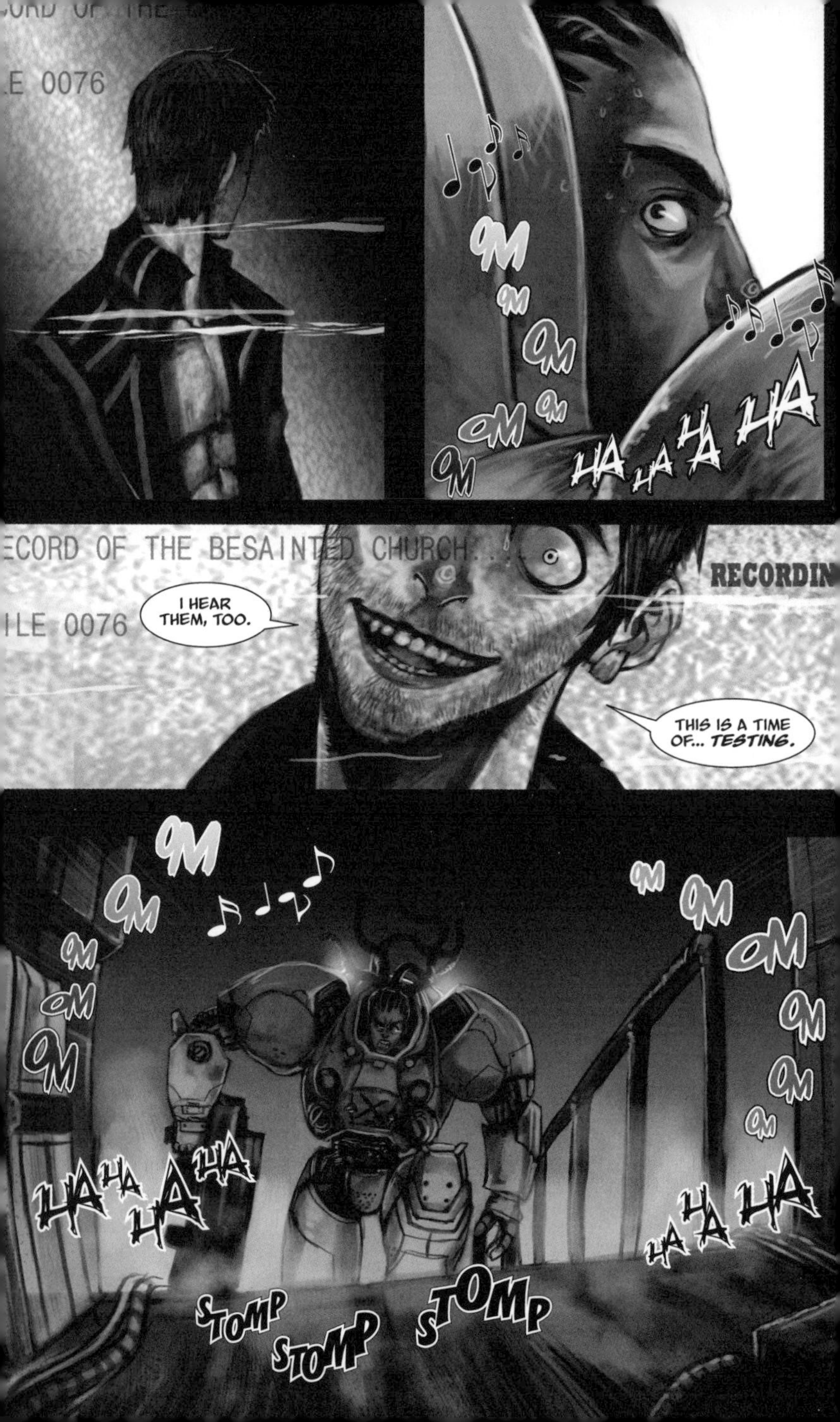

E 0076
OM
OM
OM
OM
OM
OM
HA HA HA HA
ECORD OF THE BESAINTED CHURCH...
RECORDIN
ILE 0076
I HEAR THEM, TOO.
THIS IS A TIME OF... TESTING.
OM
OM
OM
OM
OM
HA HA HA HA
OM
OM
OM
OM
OM
OM
HA HA HA HA
STOMP
STOMP
STOMP

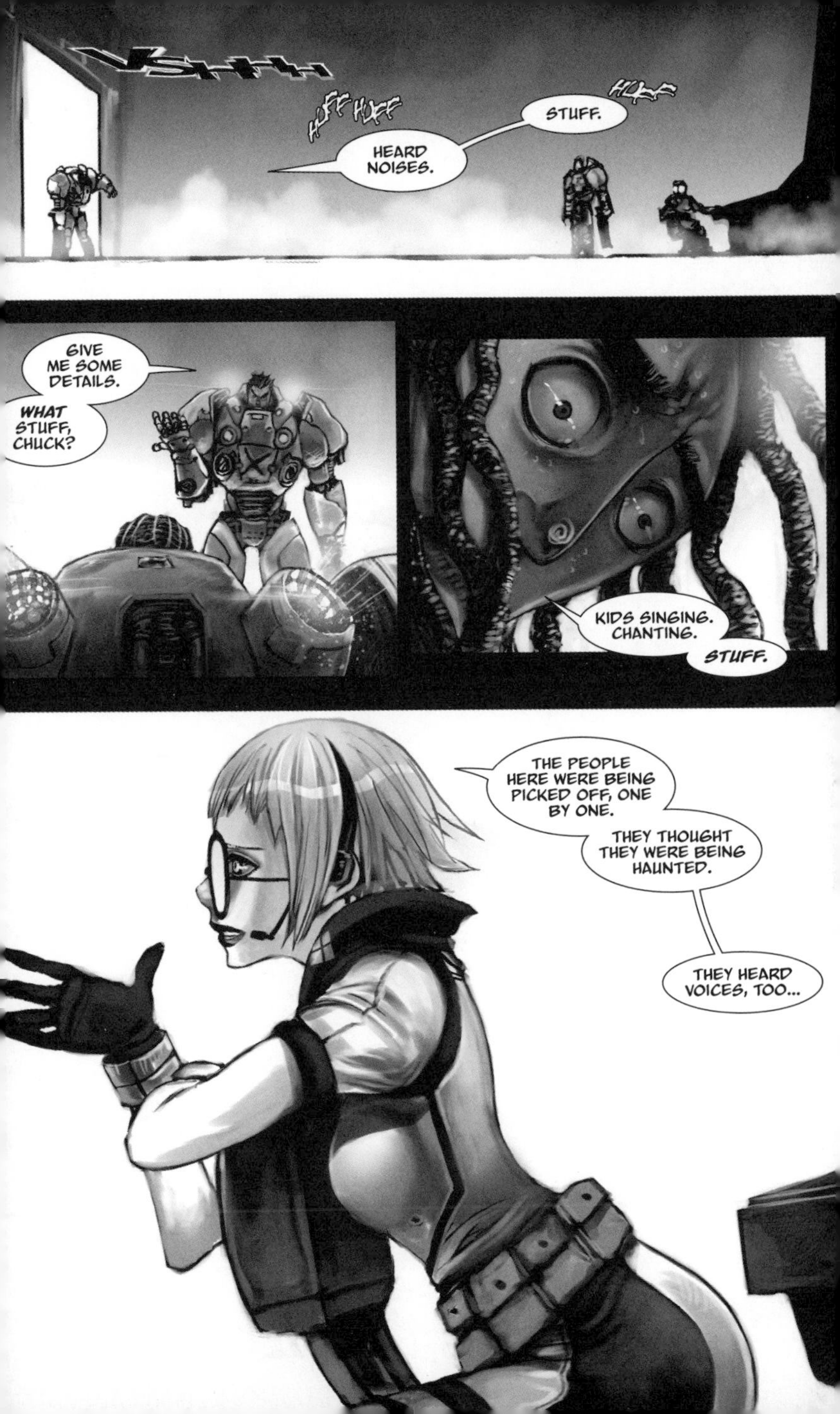
HUFF HUFF
HEARD NOISES.
HUFF
STUFF.
GIVE ME SOME DETAILS.
WHAT STUFF, CHUCK?
KIDS SINGING. CHANTING.
STUFF.
THE PEOPLE HERE WERE BEING PICKED OFF, ONE BY ONE.
THEY THOUGHT THEY WERE BEING HAUNTED.
THEY HEARD VOICES, TOO...

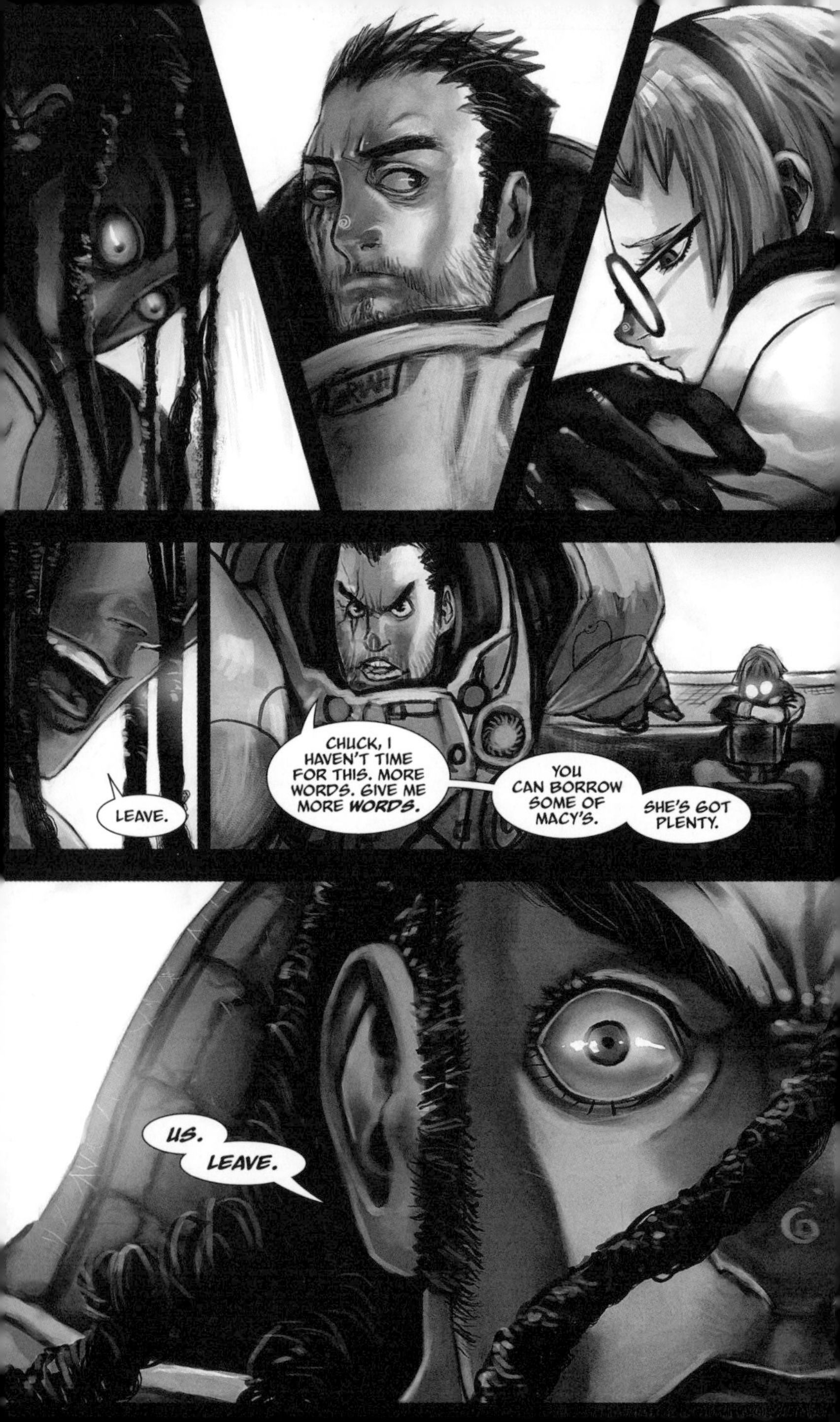
LEAVE.
CHUCK, I HAVEN'T TIME FOR THIS. MORE WORDS. GIVE ME MORE *WORDS.*
YOU CAN BORROW SOME OF MACY'S.
SHE'S GOT PLENTY.
US.
LEAVE.

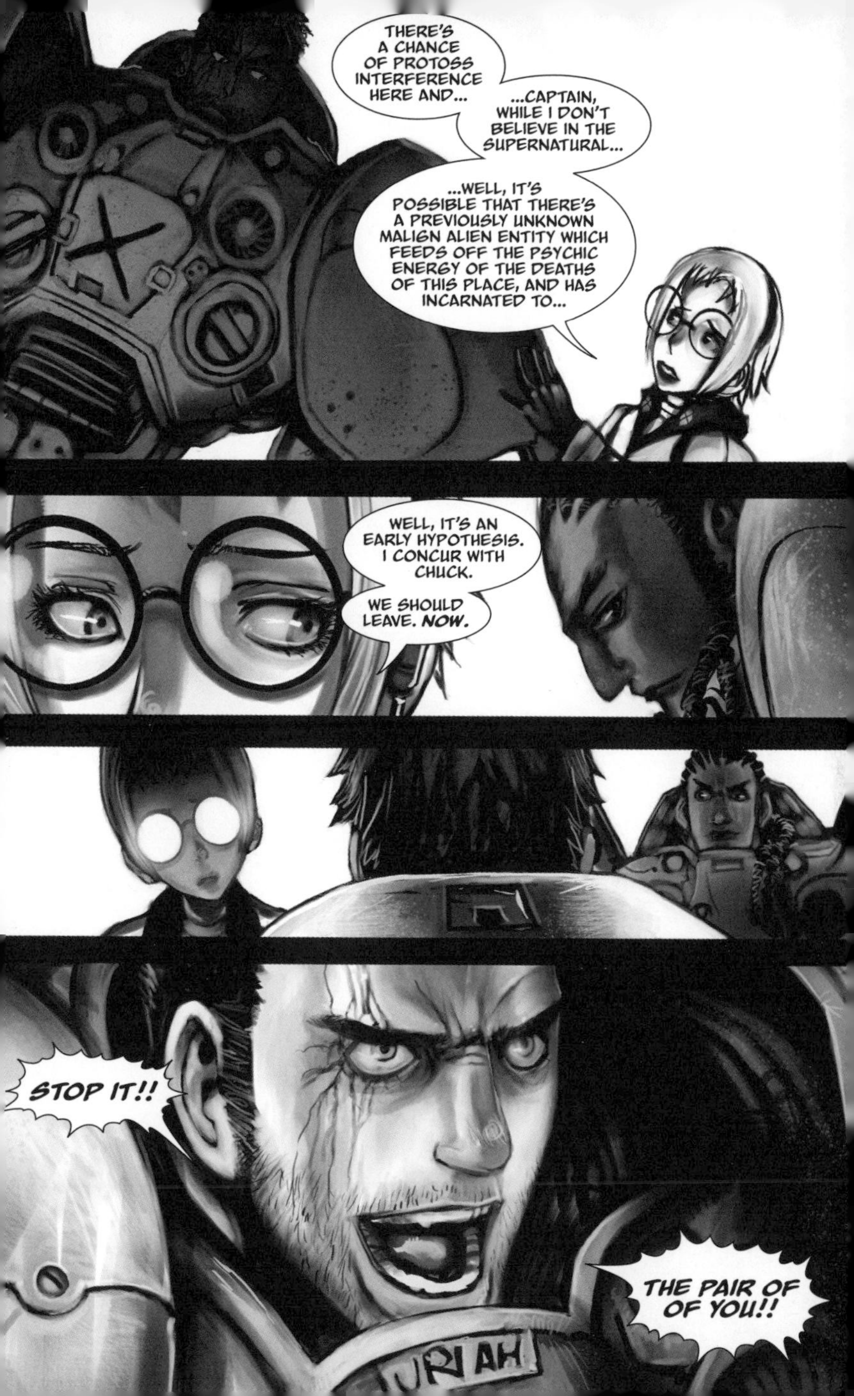
THERE'S A CHANCE OF PROTOSS INTERFERENCE HERE AND...
...CAPTAIN, WHILE I DON'T BELIEVE IN THE SUPERNATURAL...
...WELL, IT'S POSSIBLE THAT THERE'S A PREVIOUSLY UNKNOWN MALIGN ALIEN ENTITY WHICH FEEDS OFF THE PSYCHIC ENERGY OF THE DEATHS OF THIS PLACE, AND HAS INCARNATED TO...
WELL, IT'S AN EARLY HYPOTHESIS. I CONCUR WITH CHUCK.
WE SHOULD LEAVE. NOW.
STOP IT!!
THE PAIR OF OF YOU!!
URIAH

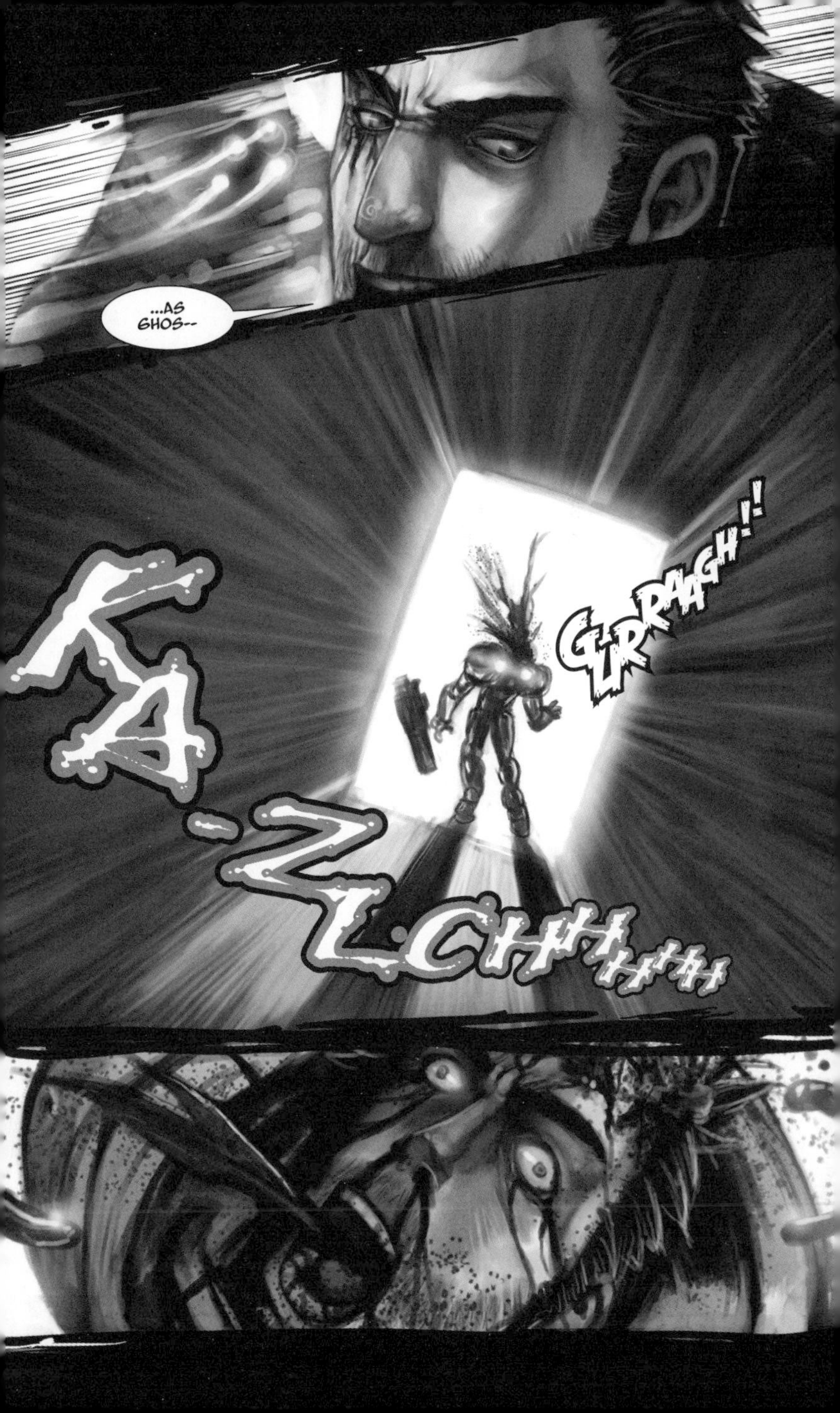
...AS GHOS--
KA-ZZLCHHHHHH
GURRAAGH!!

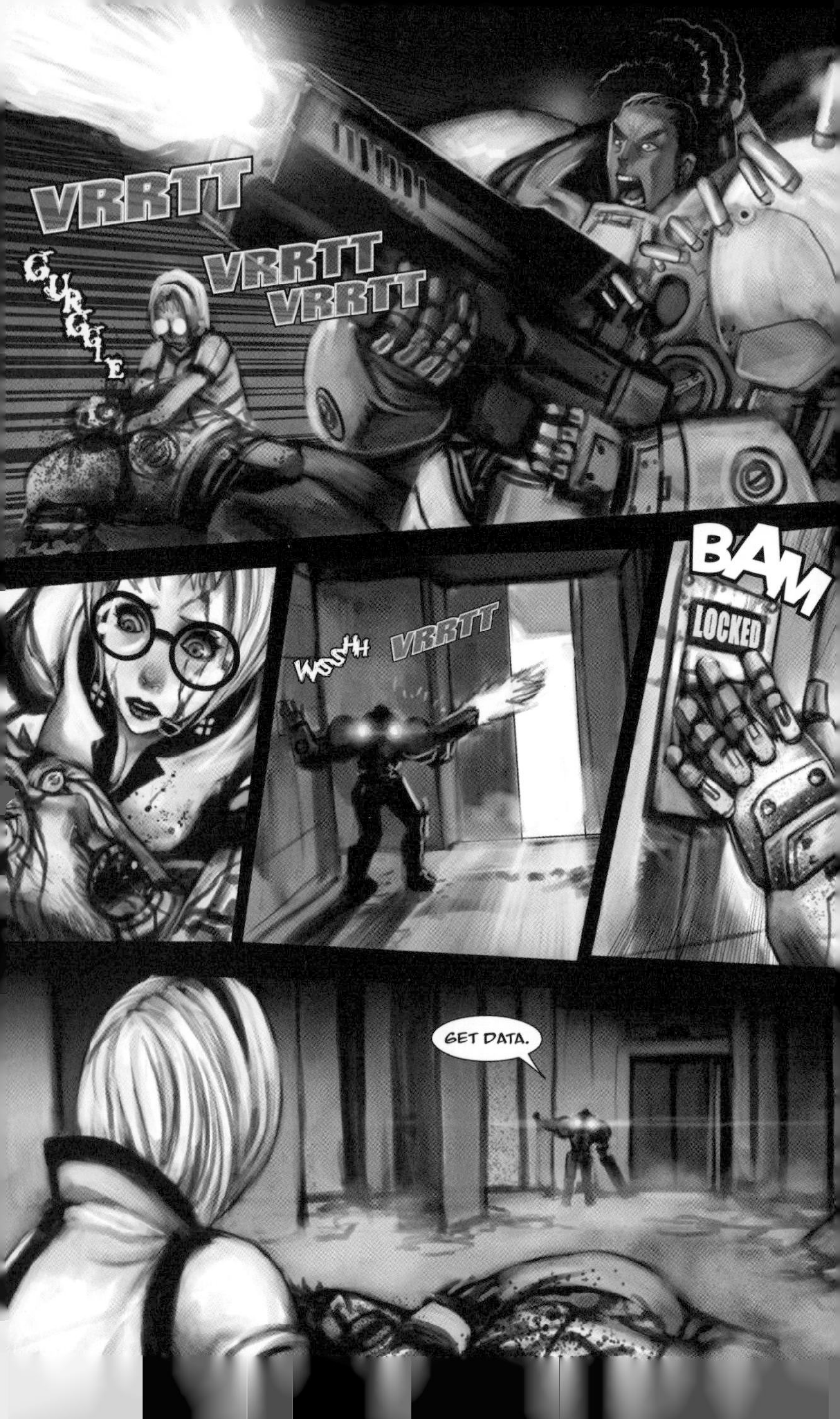
VRRTT
GURGGLE
VRRTT
VRRTT
BAM
LOCKED
WOOSHH
VRRTT
GET DATA.

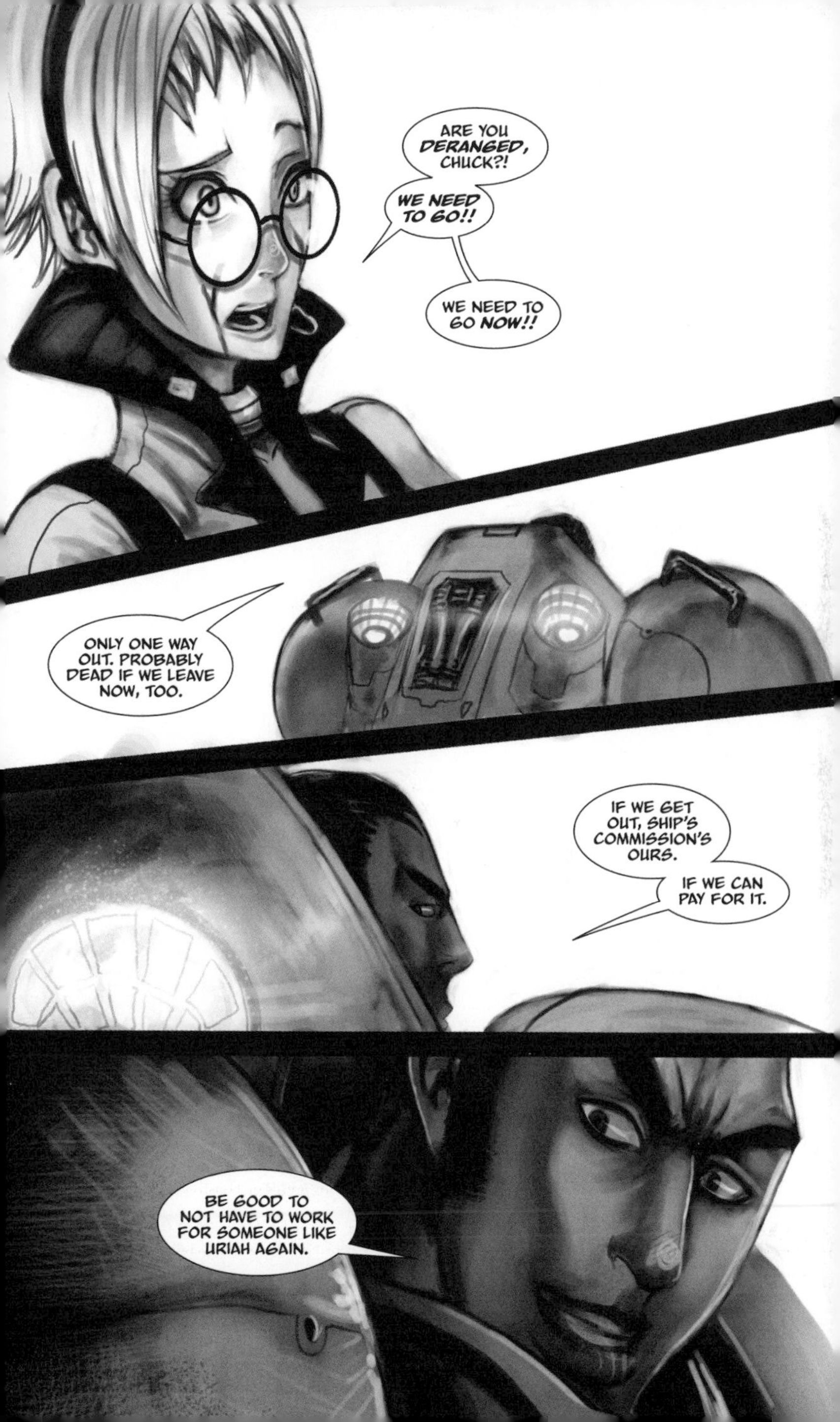
ARE YOU DERANGED, CHUCK?!
WE NEED TO GO!!
WE NEED TO GO NOW!!
ONLY ONE WAY OUT. PROBABLY DEAD IF WE LEAVE NOW, TOO.
IF WE GET OUT, SHIP'S COMMISSION'S OURS.
IF WE CAN PAY FOR IT.
BE GOOD TO NOT HAVE TO WORK FOR SOMEONE LIKE URIAH AGAIN.

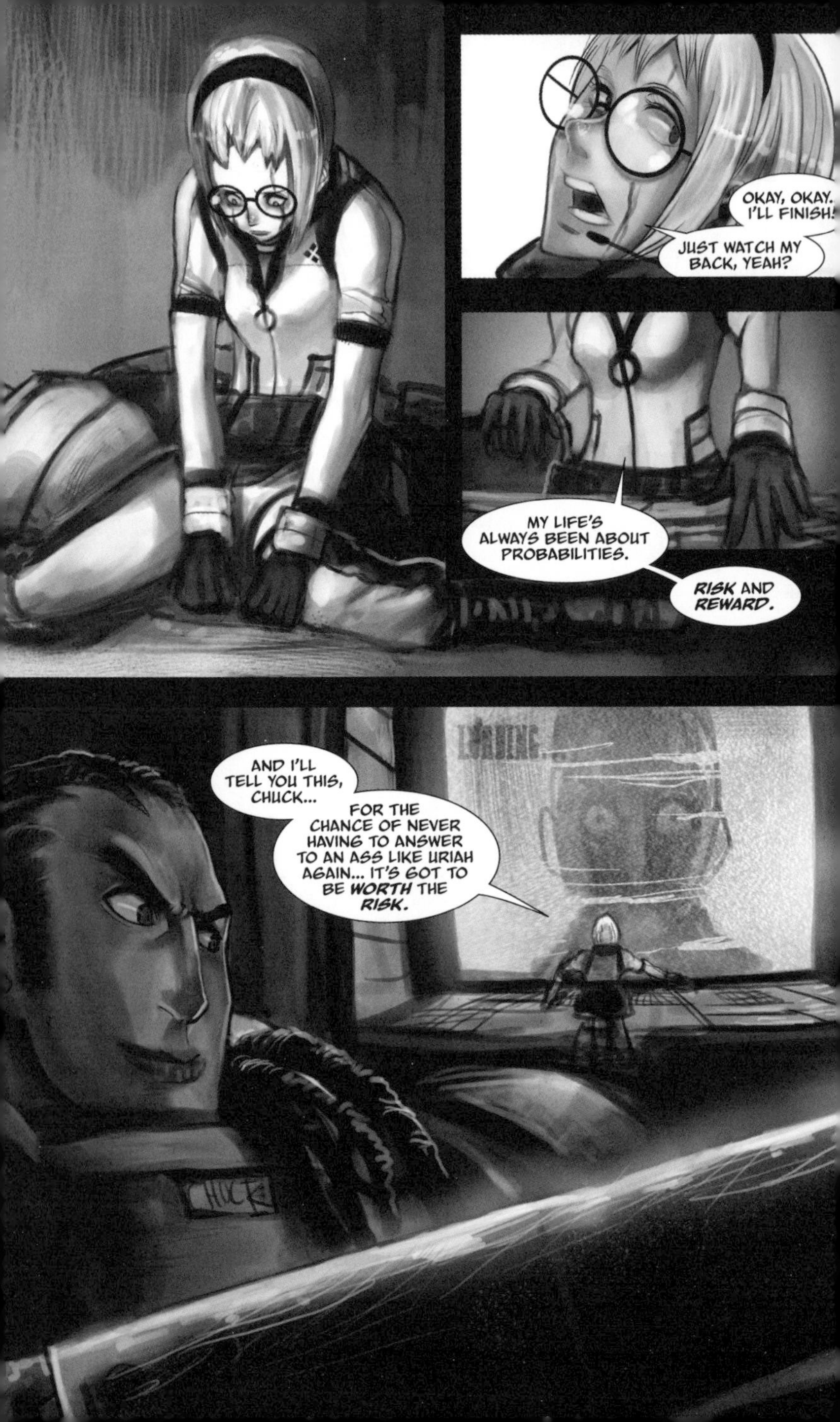
OKAY, OKAY... I'LL FINISH!
JUST WATCH MY BACK, YEAH?
MY LIFE'S ALWAYS BEEN ABOUT PROBABILITIES.
RISK AND REWARD.
AND I'LL TELL YOU THIS, CHUCK...
FOR THE CHANCE OF NEVER HAVING TO ANSWER TO AN ASS LIKE URIAH AGAIN... IT'S GOT TO BE WORTH THE RISK.

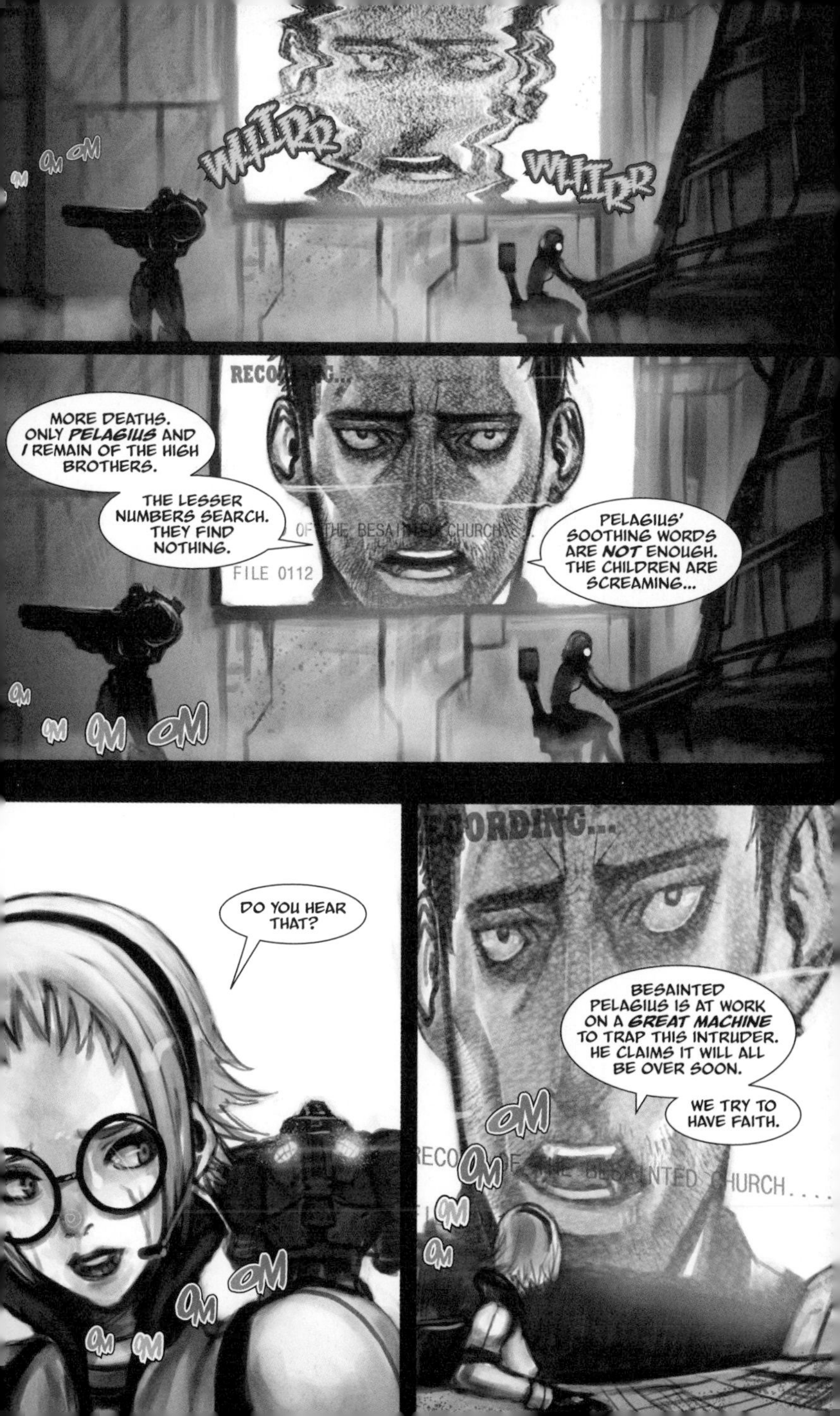
WHIRR
WHIRR
OM OM OM
MORE DEATHS. ONLY *PELAGIUS* AND I REMAIN OF THE HIGH BROTHERS.
THE LESSER NUMBERS SEARCH. THEY FIND NOTHING.
FILE 0112
PELAGIUS' SOOTHING WORDS ARE **NOT** ENOUGH. THE CHILDREN ARE SCREAMING...
OM OM OM OM
DO YOU HEAR THAT?
BESAINTED PELAGIUS IS AT WORK ON A ***GREAT MACHINE*** TO TRAP THIS INTRUDER. HE CLAIMS IT WILL ALL BE OVER SOON.
WE TRY TO HAVE FAITH.
OM OM OM OM
OM OM OM OM

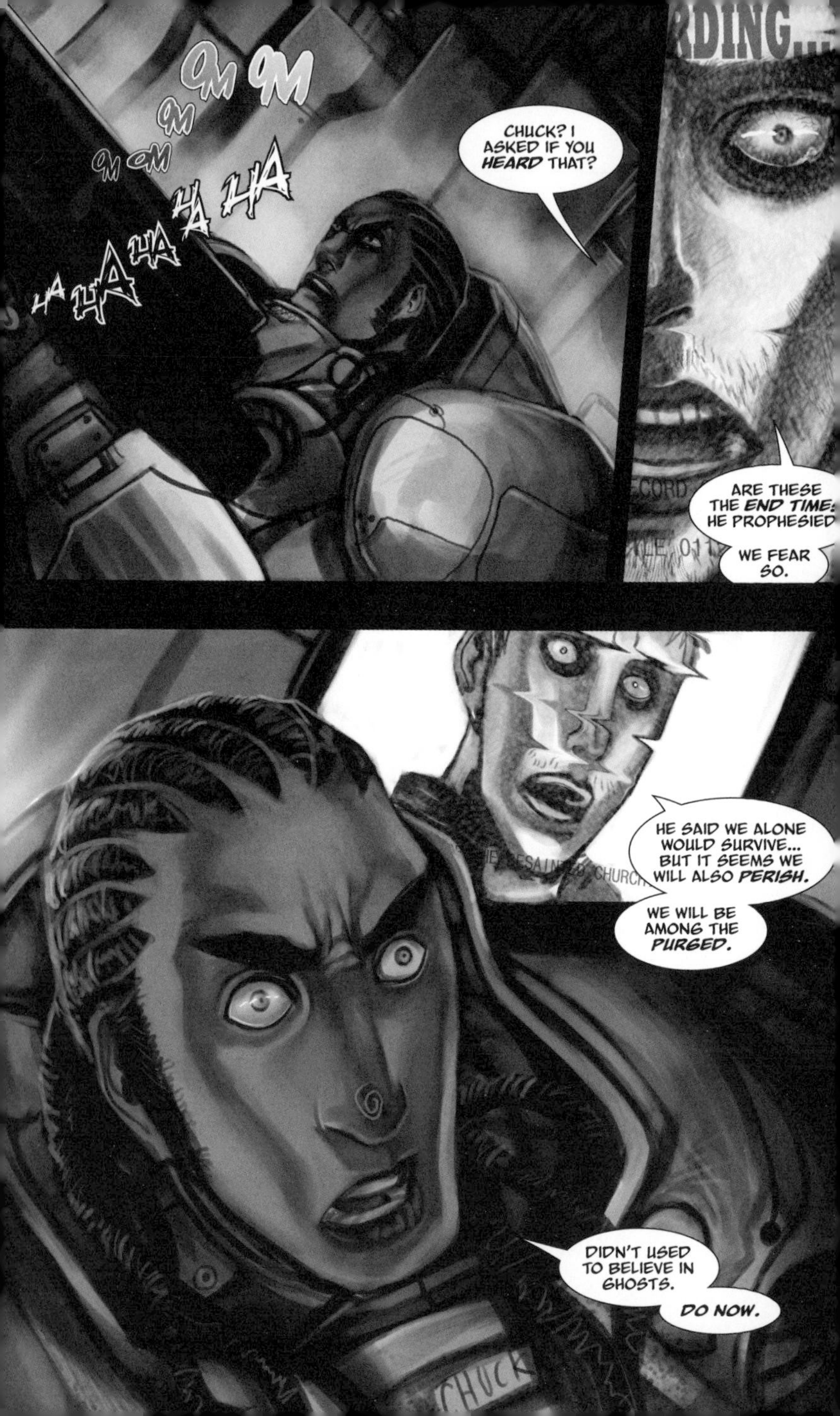
RDING...
OM OM OM
OM OM
HA HA HA HA HA HA
CHUCK? I ASKED IF YOU HEARD THAT?
ARE THESE THE END TIMES HE PROPHESIED
WE FEAR SO.
HE SAID WE ALONE WOULD SURVIVE... BUT IT SEEMS WE WILL ALSO PERISH.
WE WILL BE AMONG THE PURGED.
DIDN'T USED TO BELIEVE IN GHOSTS.
DO NOW.
CHUCK

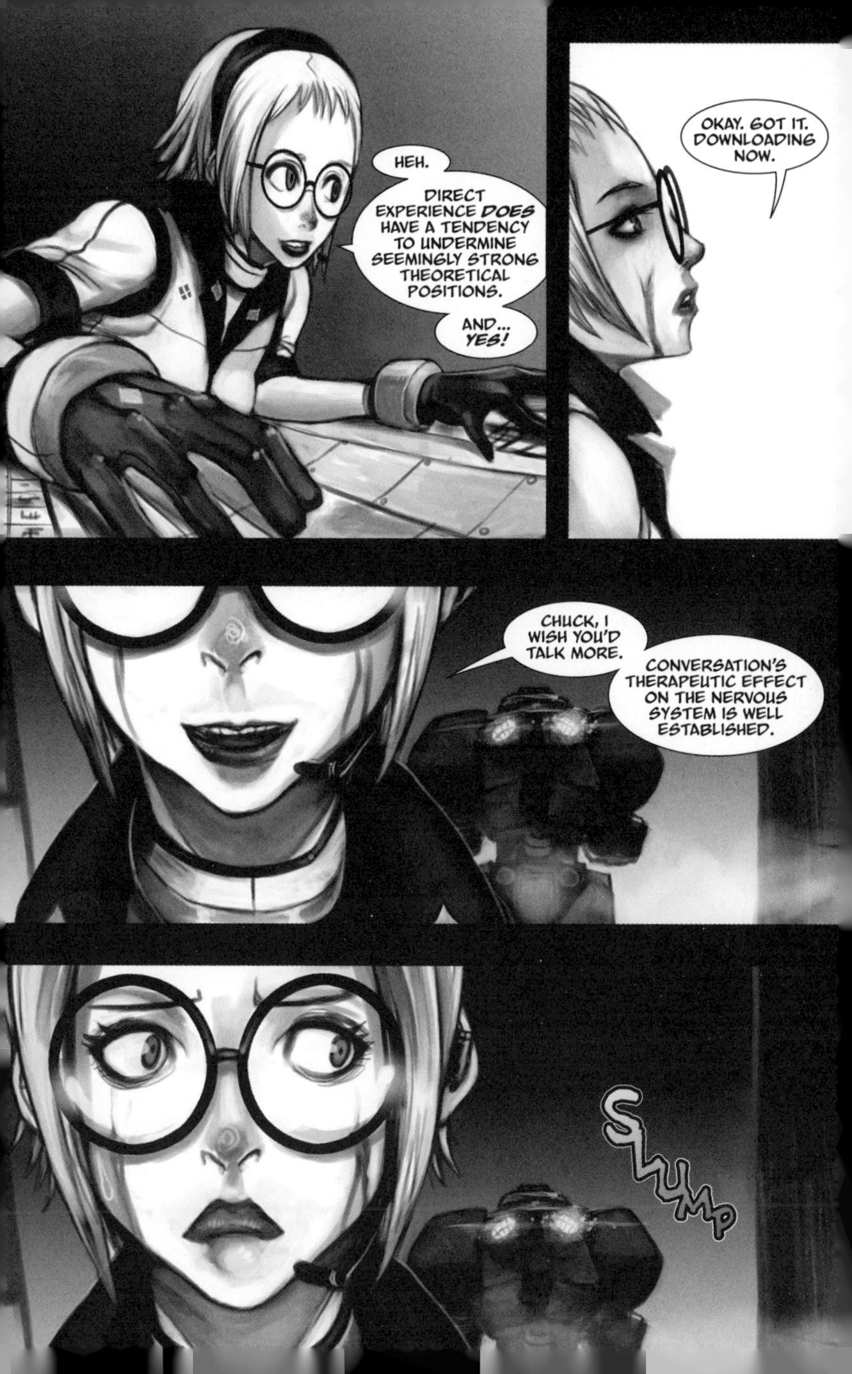
HEH.
DIRECT EXPERIENCE *DOES* HAVE A TENDENCY TO UNDERMINE SEEMINGLY STRONG THEORETICAL POSITIONS.
AND... *YES!*
OKAY. GOT IT. DOWNLOADING NOW.
CHUCK, I WISH YOU'D TALK MORE.
CONVERSATION'S THERAPEUTIC EFFECT ON THE NERVOUS SYSTEM IS WELL ESTABLISHED.
SLUMP

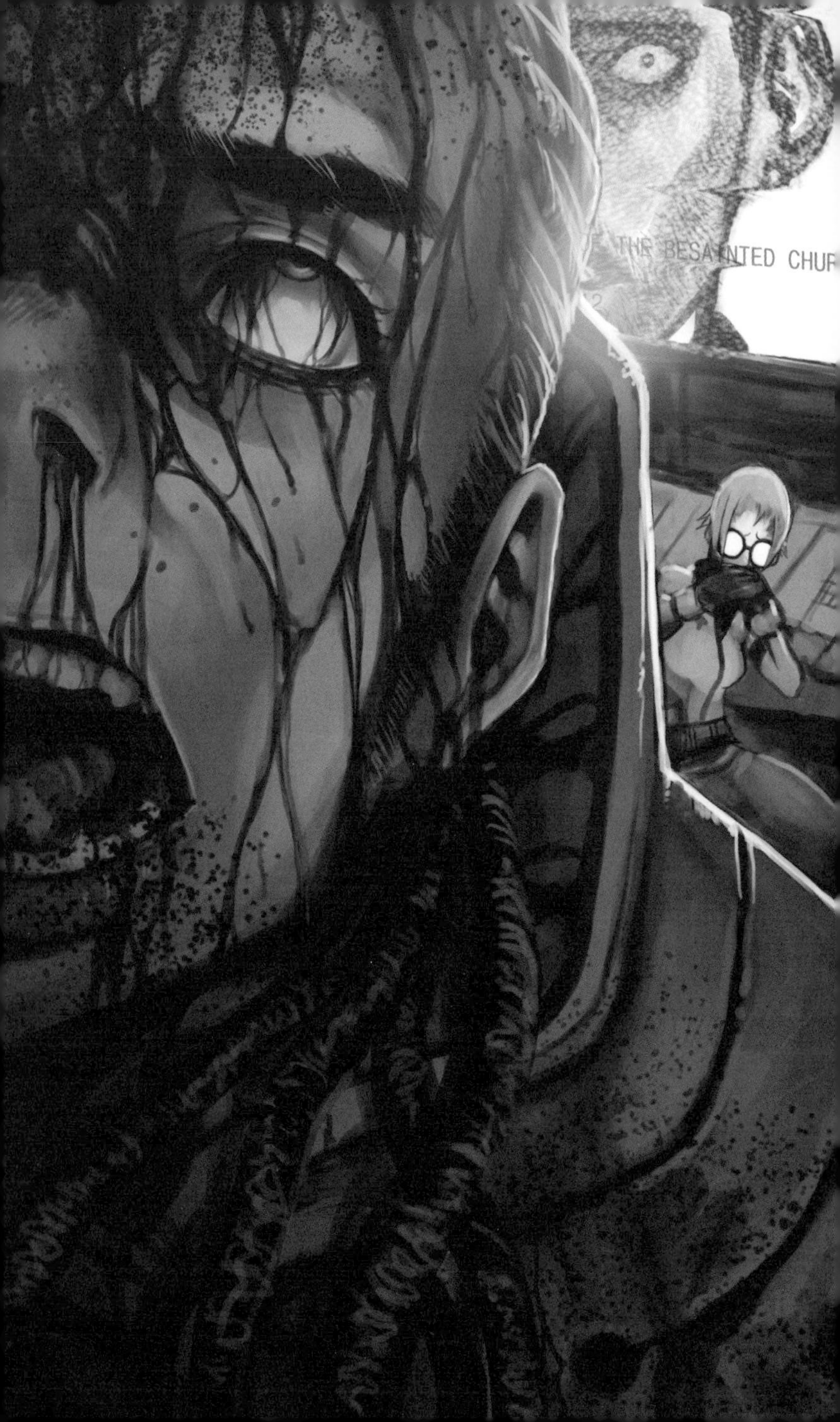
THE BESAINTED CHUR

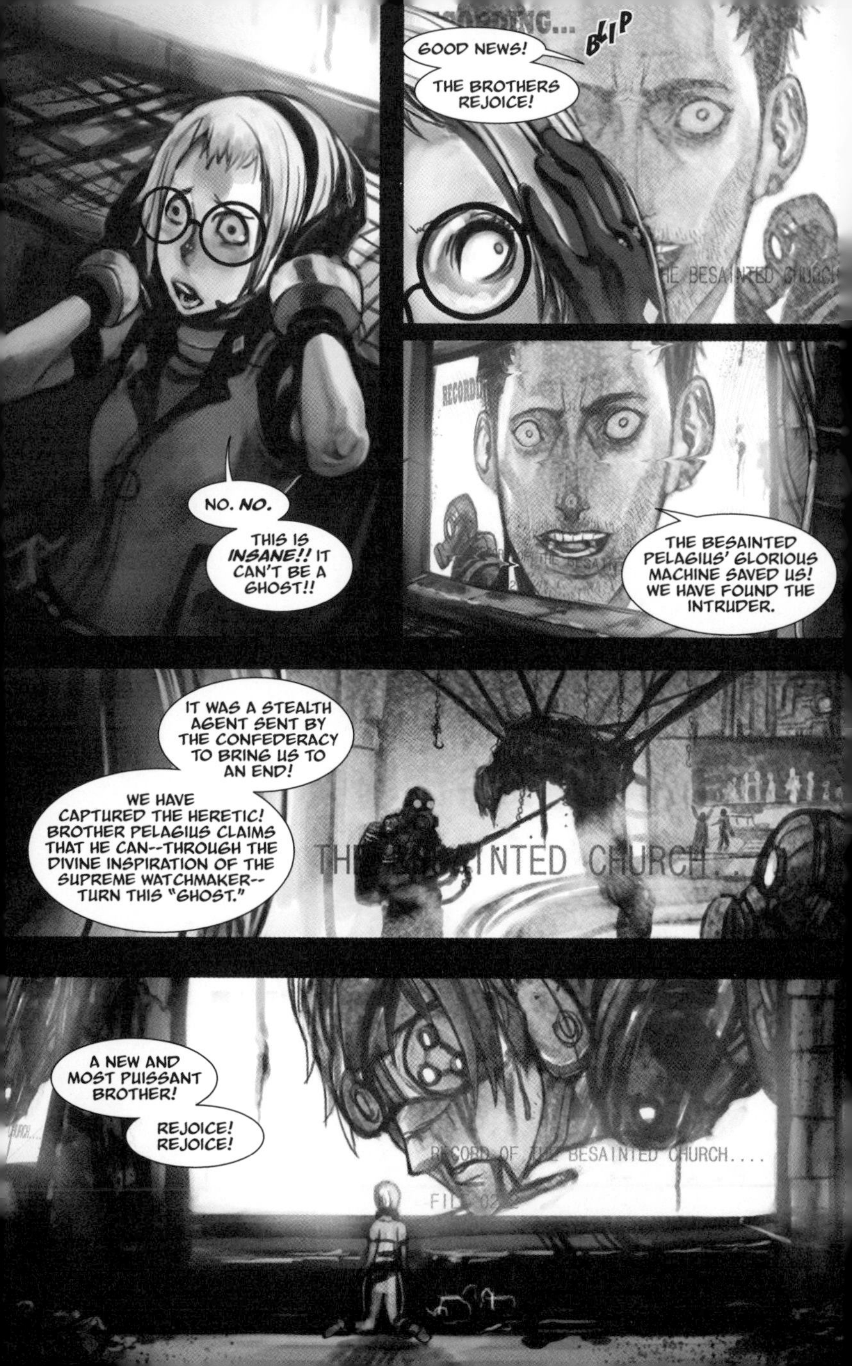
RECORDING... BLIP
GOOD NEWS!
THE BROTHERS REJOICE!
THE BESAINTED CHURCH
NO. *NO.*
THIS IS *INSANE!!* IT CAN'T BE A GHOST!!
THE BESAINTED PELAGIUS' GLORIOUS MACHINE SAVED US! WE HAVE FOUND THE INTRUDER.
IT WAS A STEALTH AGENT SENT BY THE CONFEDERACY TO BRING US TO AN END!
WE HAVE CAPTURED THE HERETIC! BROTHER PELAGIUS CLAIMS THAT HE CAN--THROUGH THE DIVINE INSPIRATION OF THE SUPREME WATCHMAKER--TURN THIS "GHOST."
A NEW AND MOST PUISSANT BROTHER!
REJOICE! REJOICE!

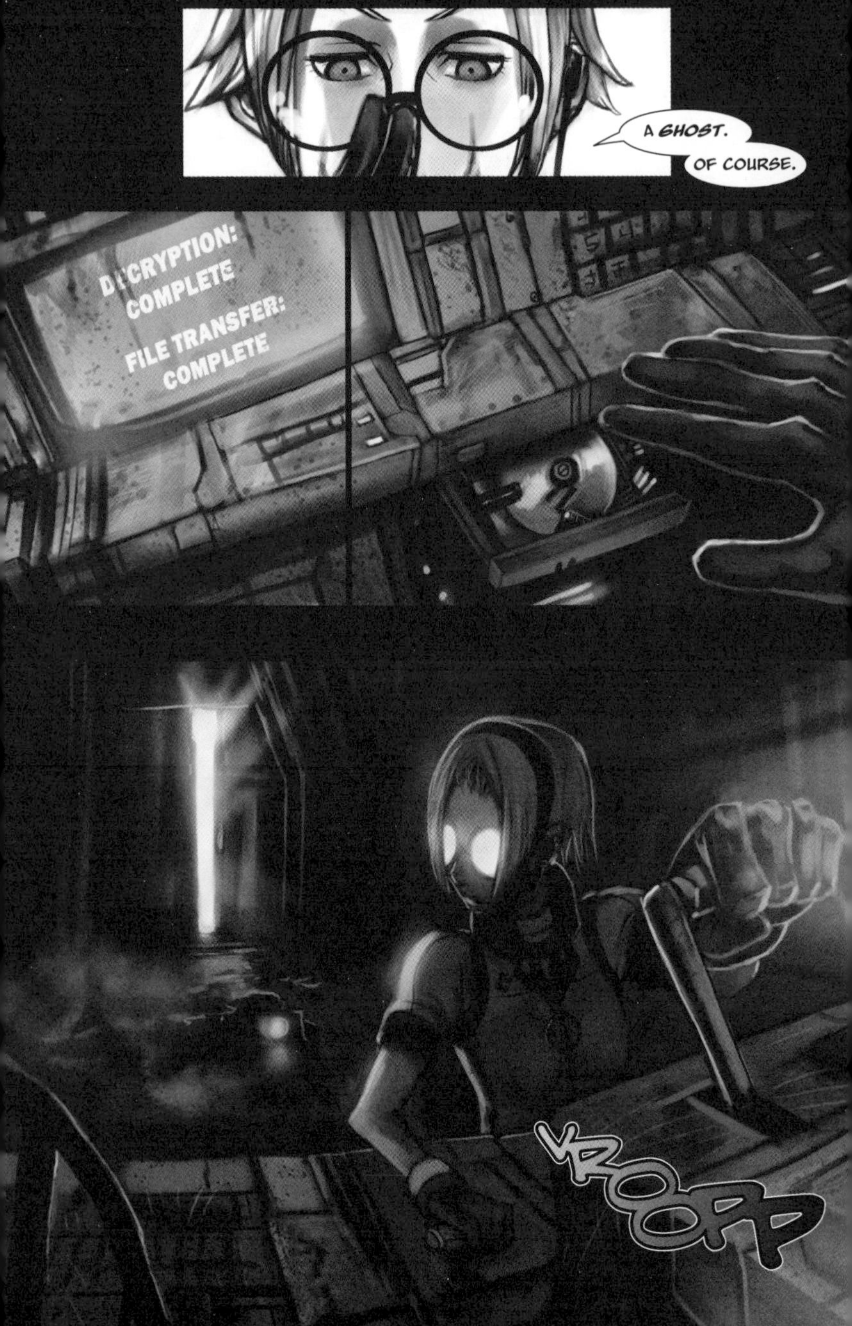
A GHOST.
OF COURSE.
DECRYPTION: COMPLETE
FILE TRANSFER: COMPLETE
VROOP

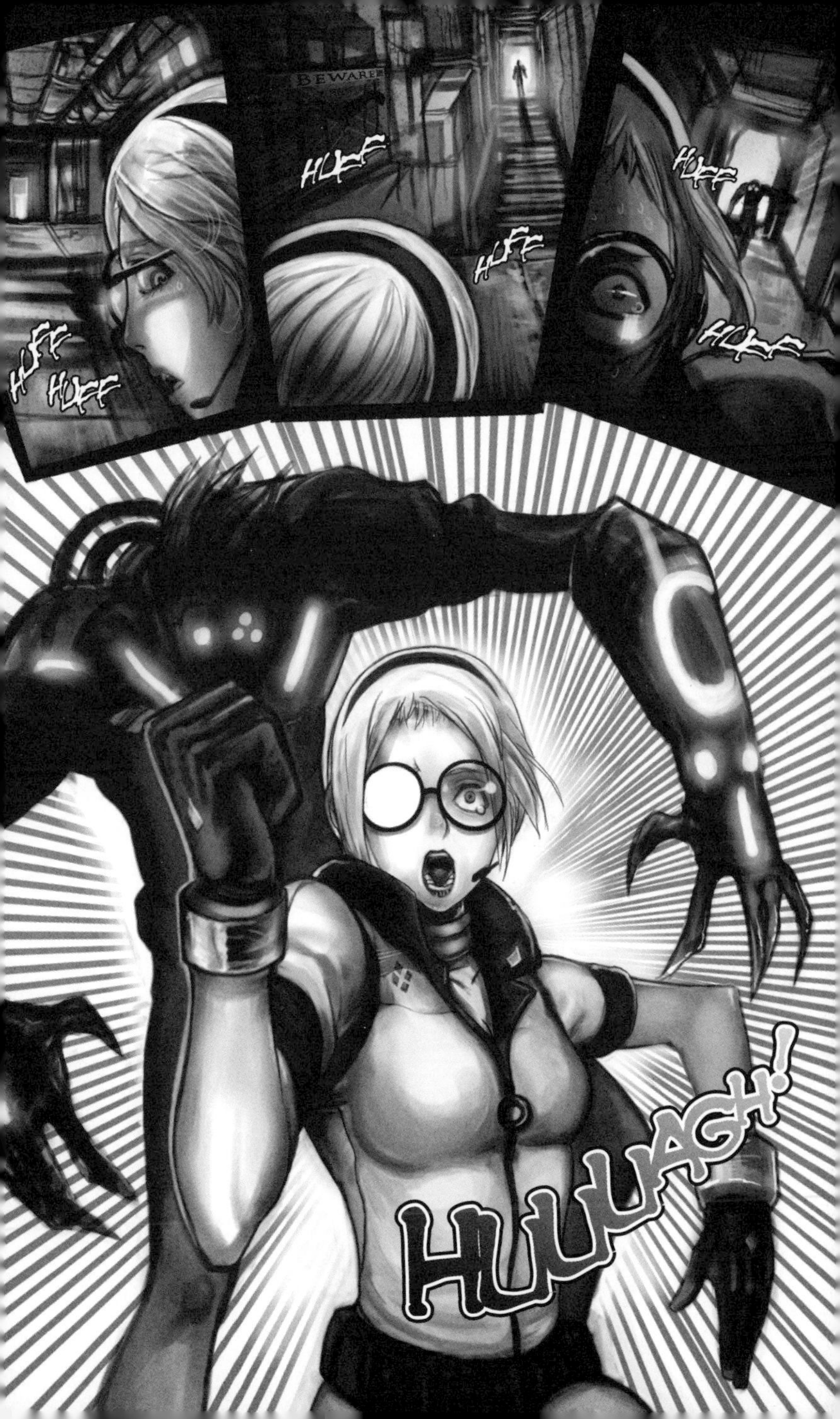

HUFF
HUFF
BEWARE
HUFF
HUFF
HUFF
HUFF
HUFF
HUUUAGH!

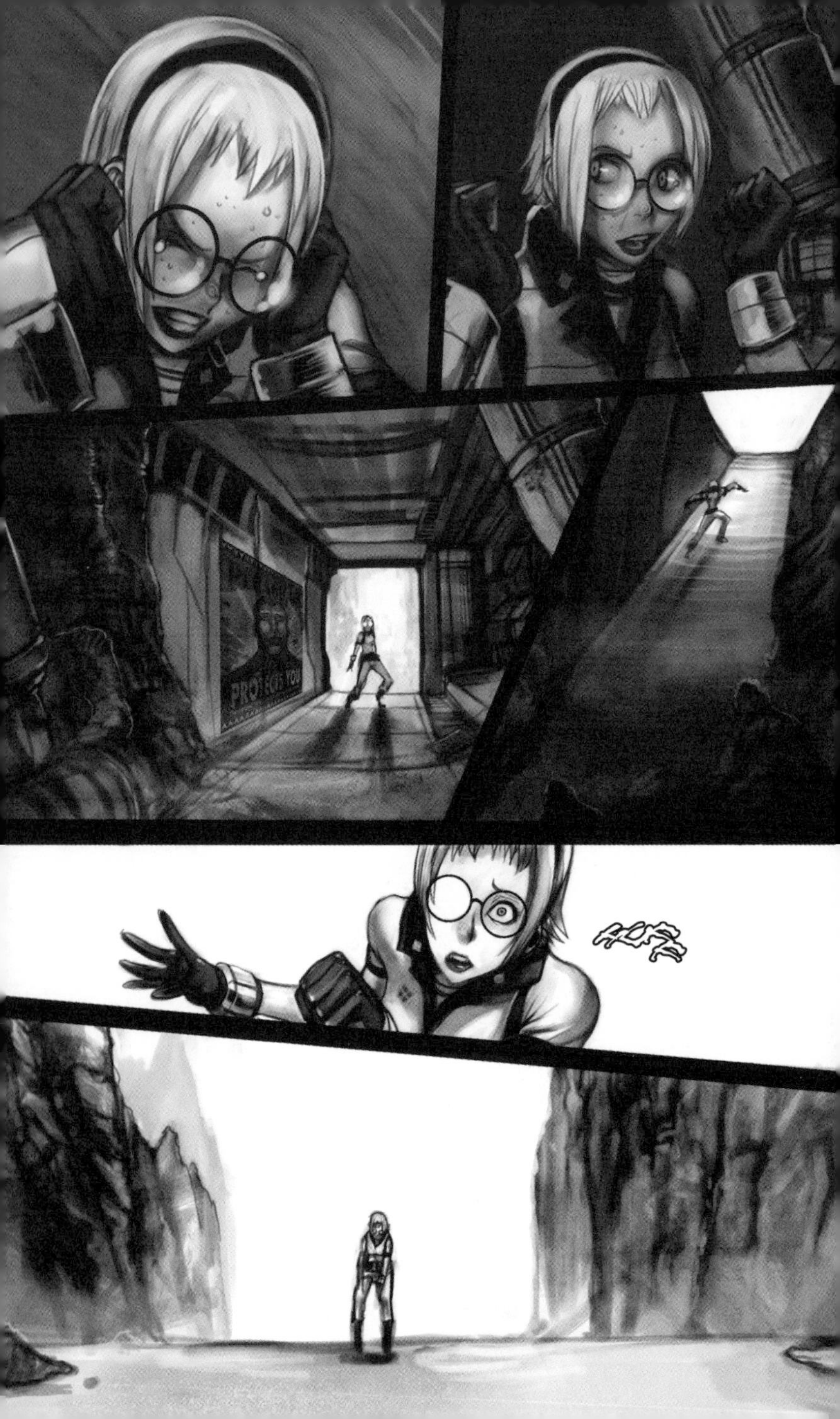
PROTECT YOU
HUFF

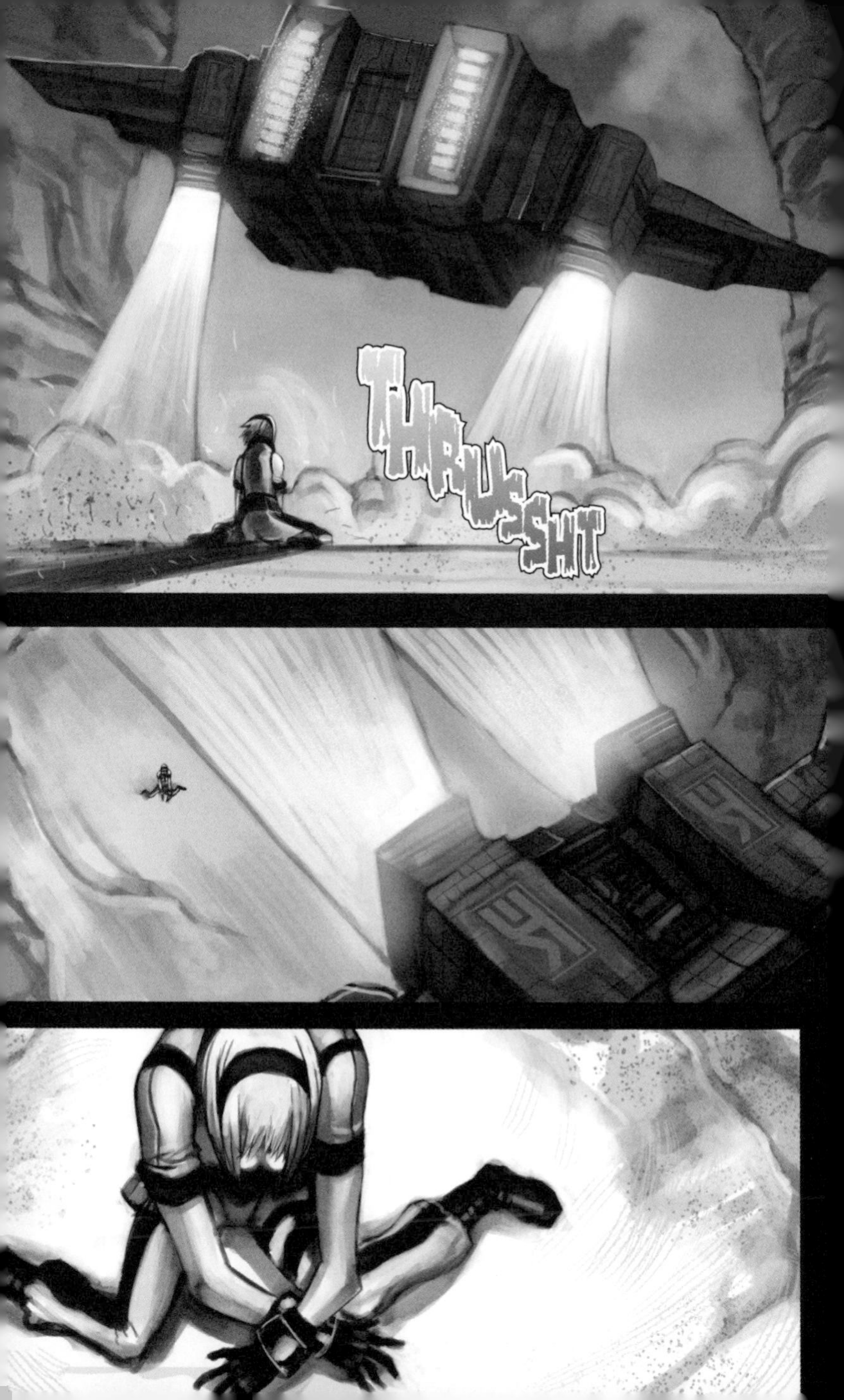
THRUSSHT

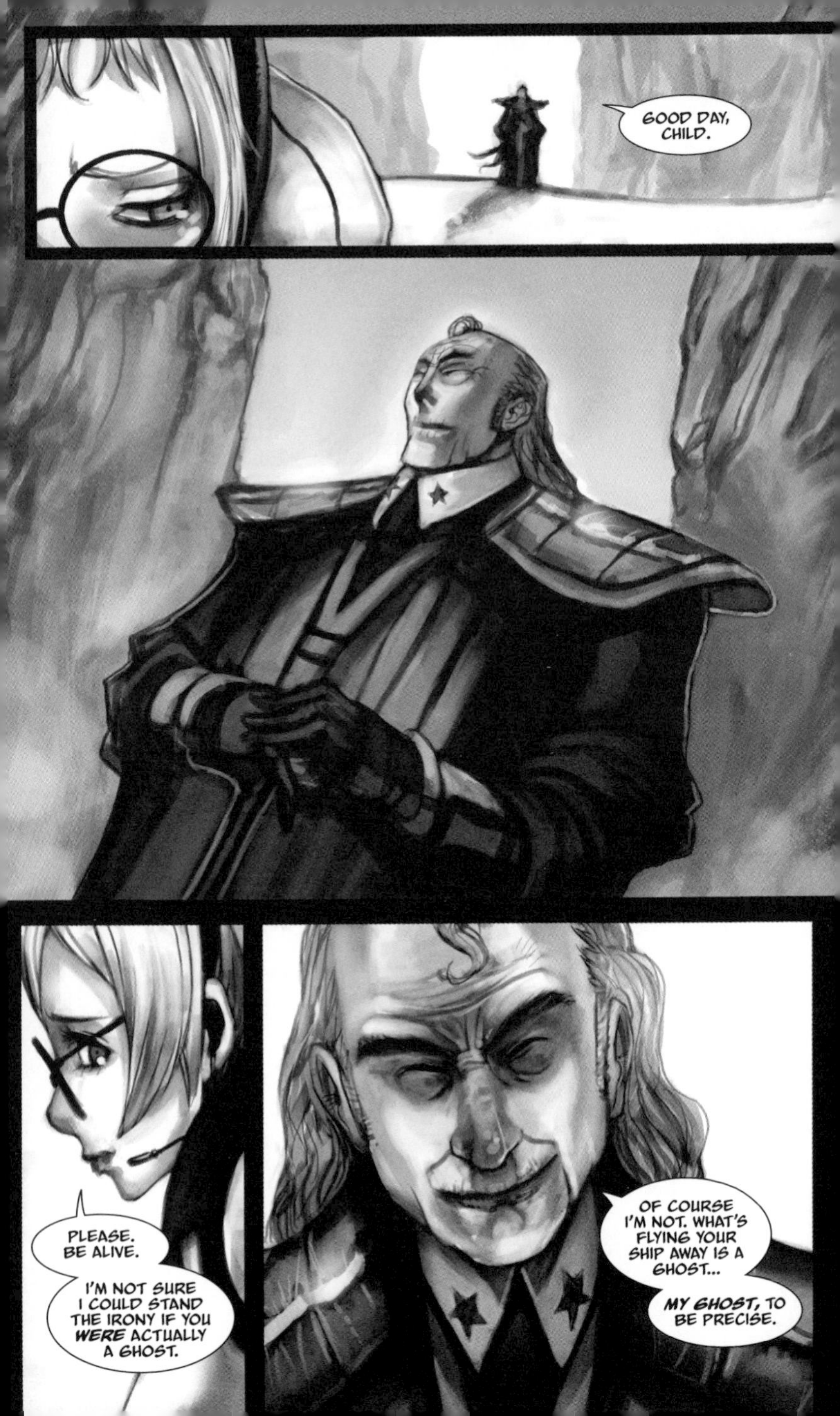
GOOD DAY, CHILD.
PLEASE. BE ALIVE.
I'M NOT SURE I COULD STAND THE IRONY IF YOU *WERE* ACTUALLY A GHOST.
OF COURSE I'M NOT. WHAT'S FLYING YOUR SHIP AWAY IS A GHOST...
MY GHOST, TO BE PRECISE.

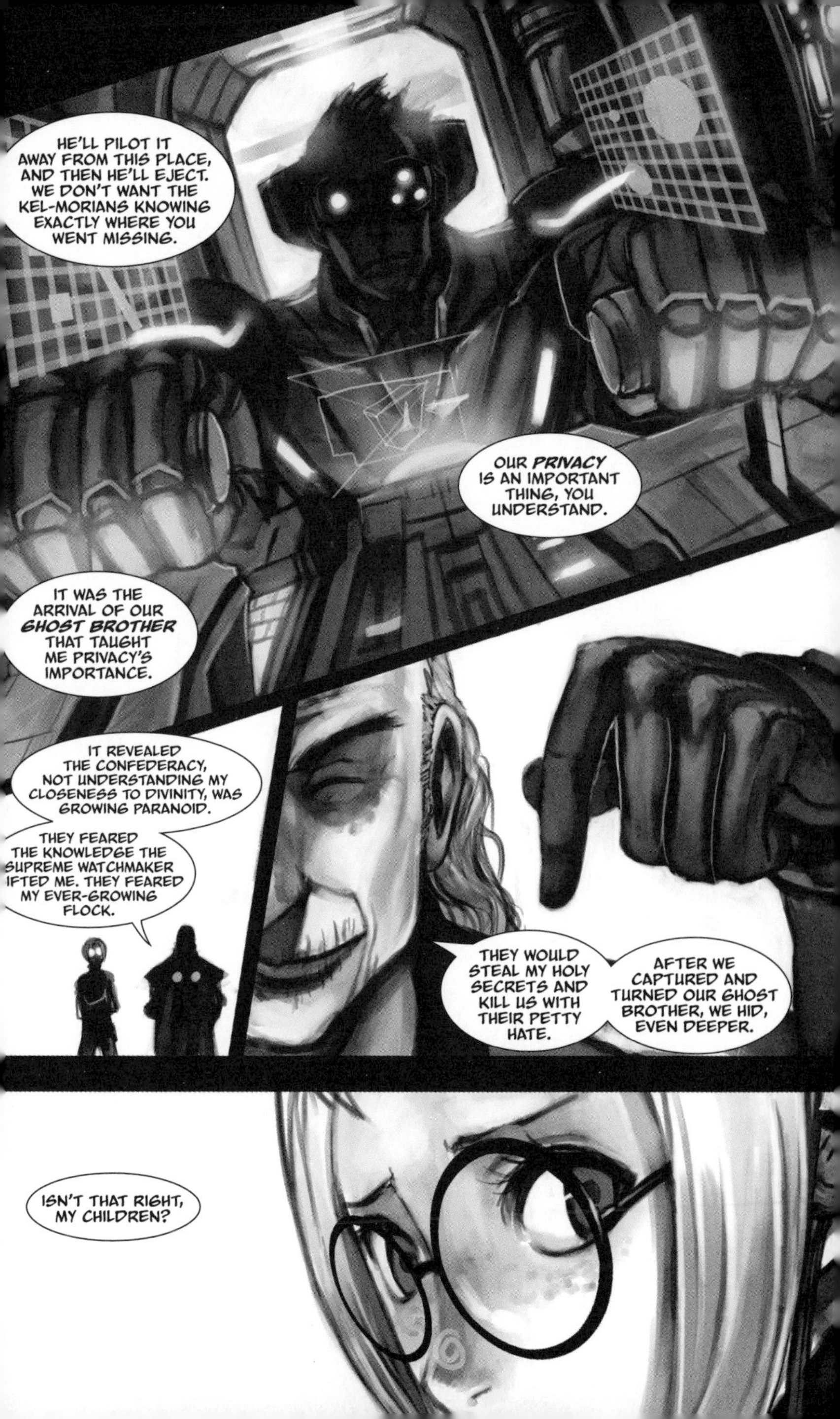
HE'LL PILOT IT AWAY FROM THIS PLACE, AND THEN HE'LL EJECT. WE DON'T WANT THE KEL-MORIANS KNOWING EXACTLY WHERE YOU WENT MISSING.
OUR *PRIVACY* IS AN IMPORTANT THING, YOU UNDERSTAND.
IT WAS THE ARRIVAL OF OUR *GHOST BROTHER* THAT TAUGHT ME PRIVACY'S IMPORTANCE.
IT REVEALED THE CONFEDERACY, NOT UNDERSTANDING MY CLOSENESS TO DIVINITY, WAS GROWING PARANOID.
THEY FEARED THE KNOWLEDGE THE SUPREME WATCHMAKER IFTED ME. THEY FEARED MY EVER-GROWING FLOCK.
THEY WOULD STEAL MY HOLY SECRETS AND KILL US WITH THEIR PETTY HATE.
AFTER WE CAPTURED AND TURNED OUR GHOST BROTHER, WE HID, EVEN DEEPER.
ISN'T THAT RIGHT, MY CHILDREN?

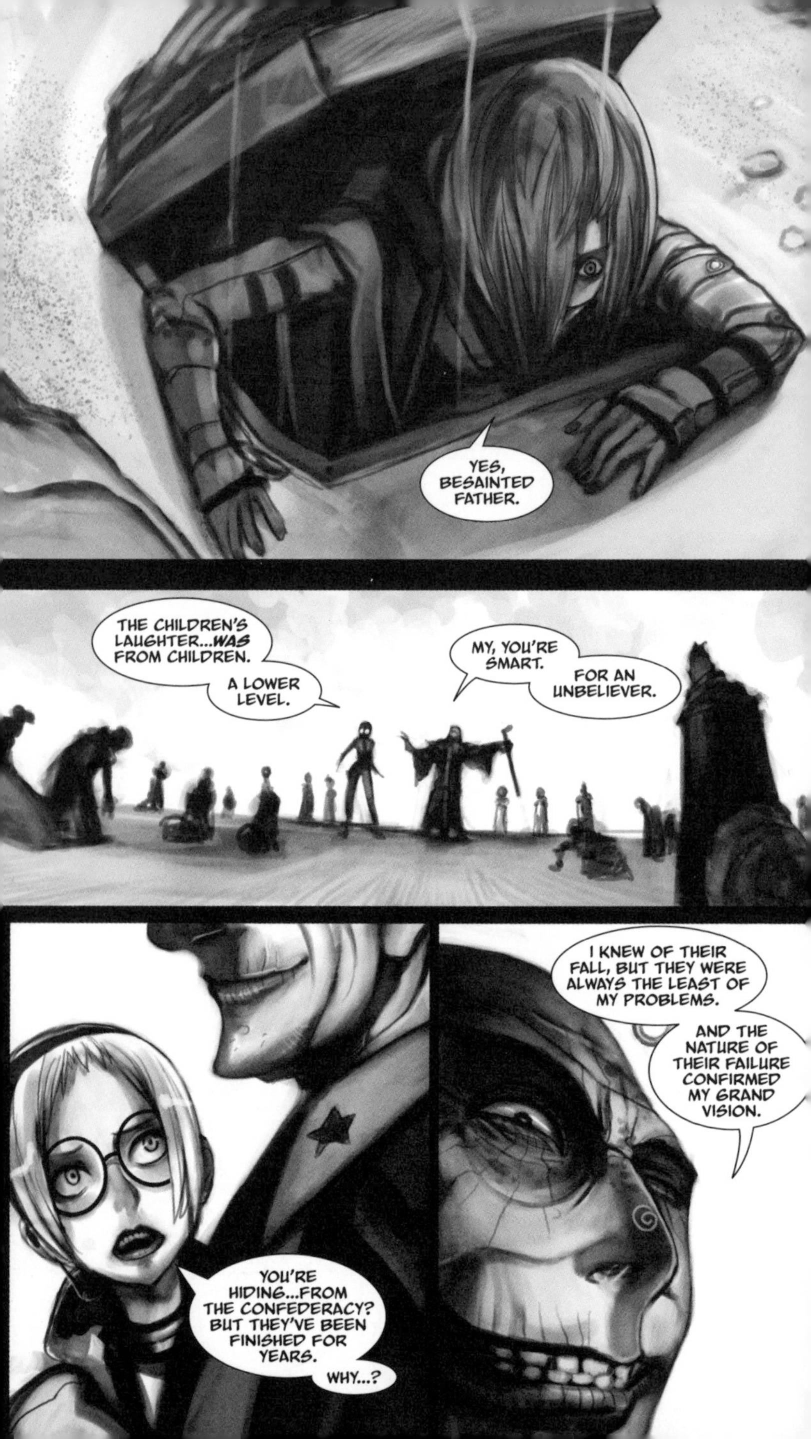
YES, BESAINTED FATHER.
THE CHILDREN'S LAUGHTER...*WAS* FROM CHILDREN.
A LOWER LEVEL.
MY, YOU'RE SMART.
FOR AN UNBELIEVER.
YOU'RE HIDING...FROM THE CONFEDERACY? BUT THEY'VE BEEN FINISHED FOR YEARS.
WHY...?
I KNEW OF THEIR FALL, BUT THEY WERE ALWAYS THE LEAST OF MY PROBLEMS.
AND THE NATURE OF THEIR FAILURE CONFIRMED MY GRAND VISION.

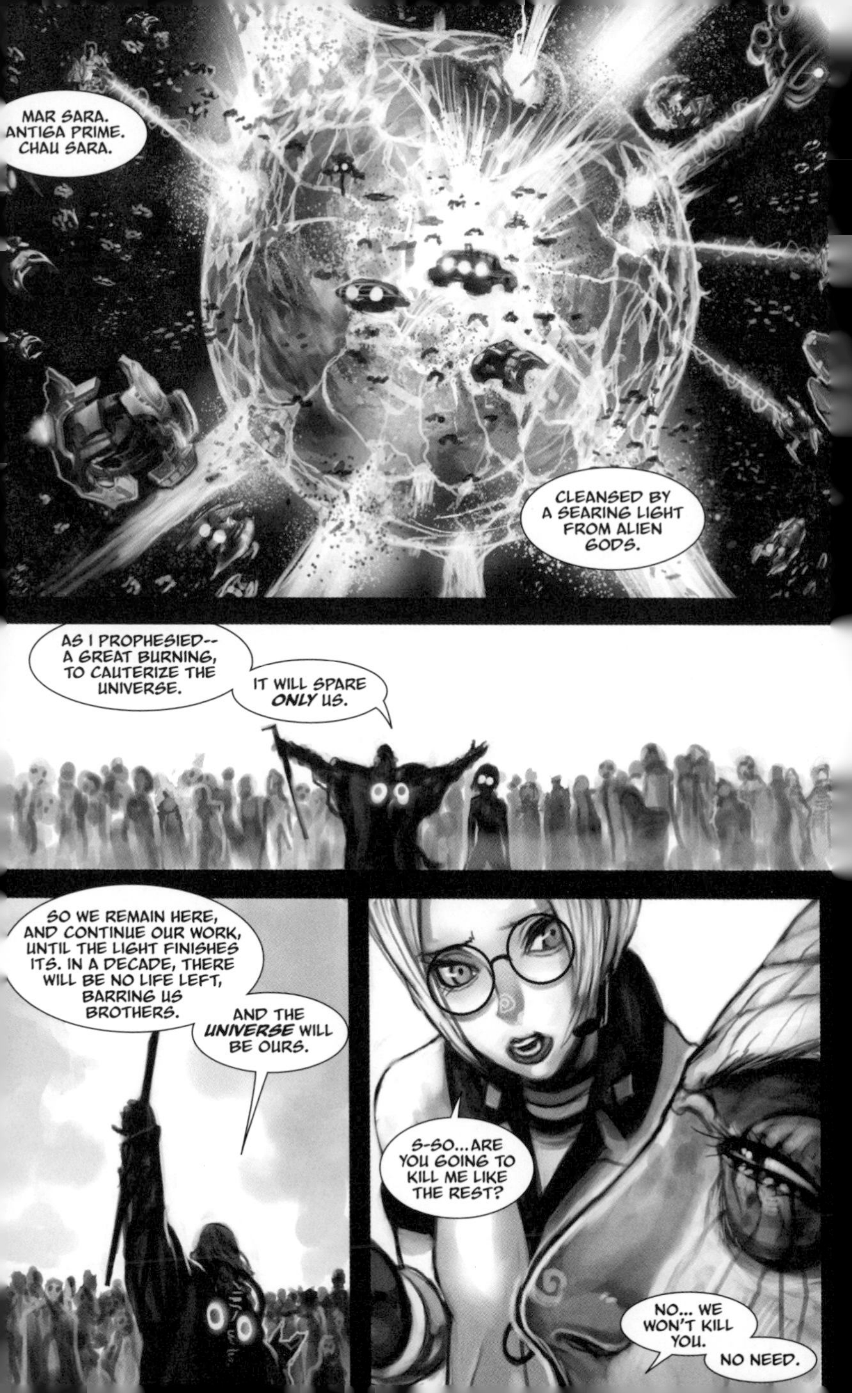
MAR SARA. ANTIGA PRIME. CHAU SARA.
CLEANSED BY A SEARING LIGHT FROM ALIEN GODS.
AS I PROPHESIED-- A GREAT BURNING, TO CAUTERIZE THE UNIVERSE.
IT WILL SPARE *ONLY* US.
SO WE REMAIN HERE, AND CONTINUE OUR WORK, UNTIL THE LIGHT FINISHES ITS. IN A DECADE, THERE WILL BE NO LIFE LEFT, BARRING US BROTHERS.
AND THE *UNIVERSE* WILL BE OURS.
S-SO...ARE YOU GOING TO KILL ME LIKE THE REST?
NO... WE WON'T KILL YOU.
NO NEED.

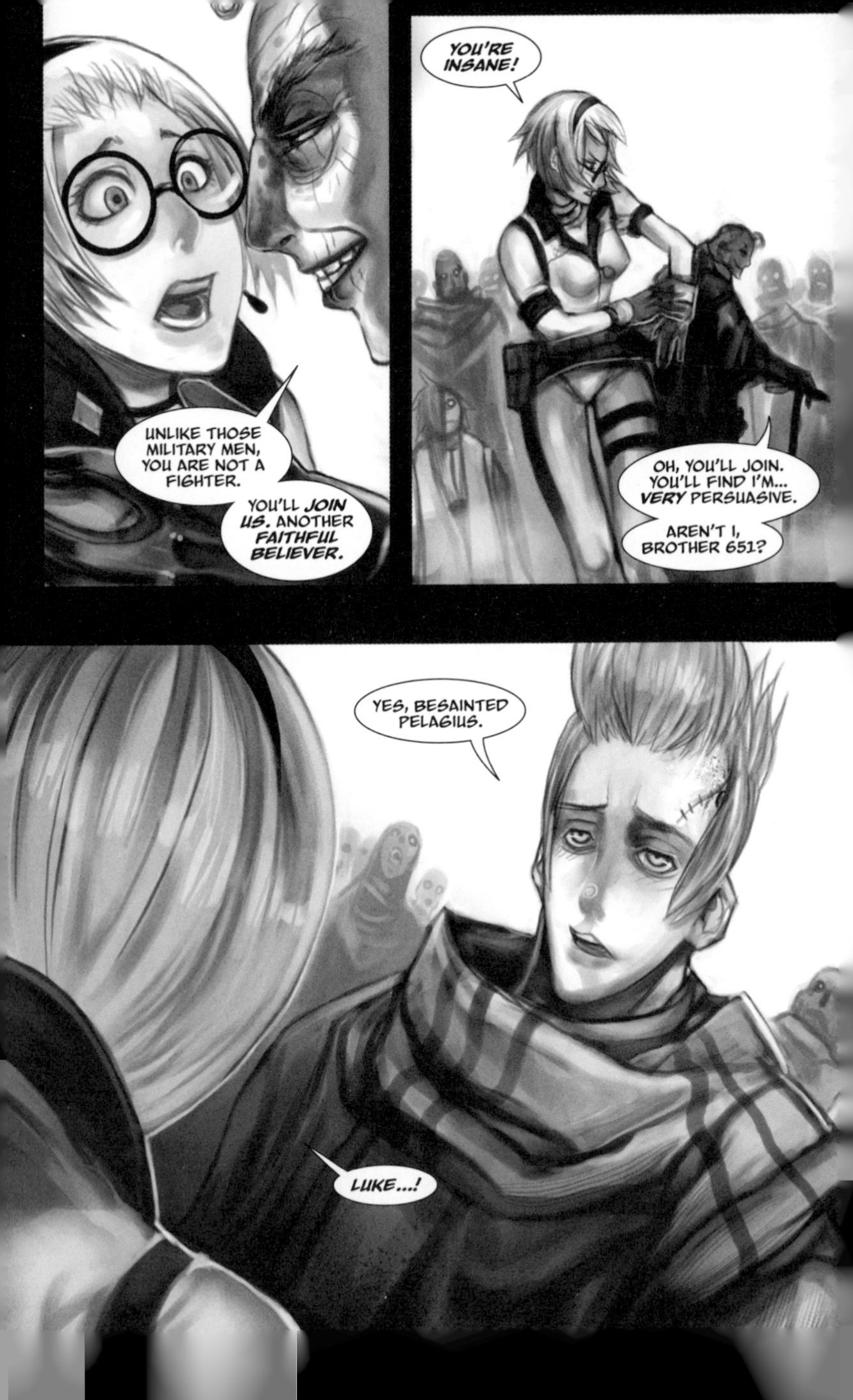
UNLIKE THOSE MILITARY MEN, YOU ARE NOT A FIGHTER.
YOU'LL *JOIN US.* ANOTHER *FAITHFUL BELIEVER.*
YOU'RE INSANE!
OH, YOU'LL JOIN. YOU'LL FIND I'M... *VERY* PERSUASIVE.
AREN'T I, BROTHER 651?
YES, BESAINTED PELAGIUS.
LUKE...!

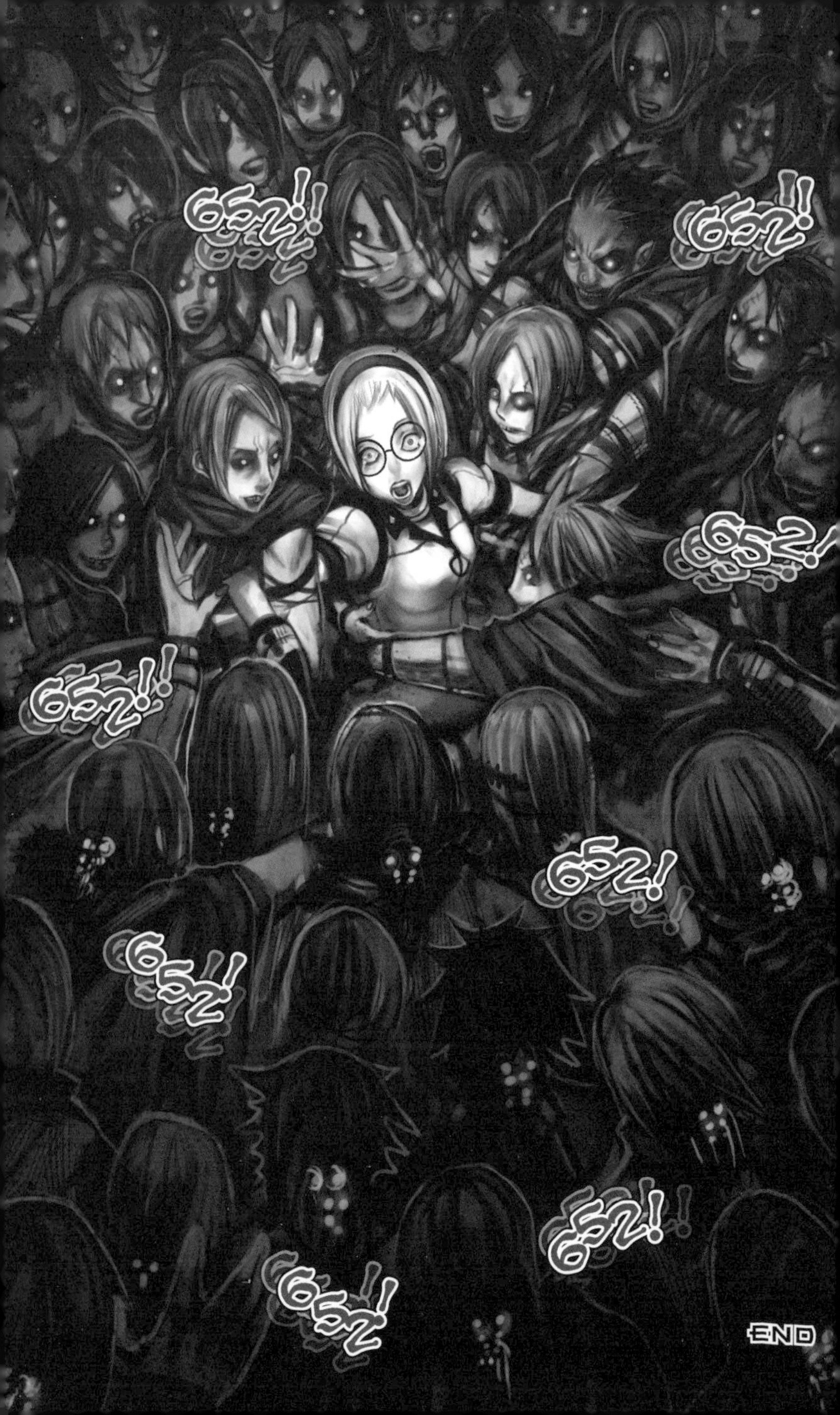
END